Pattern
of
Shadows

Pattern
of
Shadows

Judith Barrow

HONNO MODERN FICTION

Published by Honno
'Ailsa Craig', Heol y Cawl, Dinas Powys, South Glamorgan,
Wales, CF64 4AH.

1 2 3 4 5 6 7 8 9 10

A catalogue record for this book is available from the British
Library.

Published with the financial support of the Welsh Books Council.

ISBN 978-1-906784-05-8

Cover photographs: © Getty Images
Cover design: Jenks Design
Text design: Graham Preston
Printed in Wales by Gomer Press

For David

Acknowledgments

I would like to express my gratitude to all those who helped with the writing of *Pattern of Shadows*.

Thanks to the staff of the Oldham Local Studies and Archives for their unstinting help with my research. For their patience with my many questions and requests. Thanks to Caroline Oakley and Helena Earnshaw of Honno for their individual expertise, and their time, in setting me off on this journey of publication. This book wouldn't have been possible without them.

Special thanks to my penfriends, who have encouraged and supported my efforts through the years and without whom this book would never have been completed, Sharon Tregenza, Jane Scott and Kath Levell; exacting critics, fantastic friends.

Lastly, my thanks to David for his love and the time he gives me to ignore the 'domestic trivia' and write.

PROLOGUE

February 1945

Frank Shuttleworth knows this will be his only chance to kill Peter Schormann.

The guard company has been in position, along the full length of the long narrow road leading up to the camp, hours before the February light reluctantly started the day. Now, as dawn arrives thinly, the prisoners stand in lines of five, the thick rolls of barbed wire on each side hemming them in. In the floodlights the frost sparkles like sugar on the tarmac, emphasising the dark backdrop of the North Country moors.

A white haze of breath rises over the men. The coughs, the mutterings echo in the stillness as they wait.

In the sentry box, behind the fence and ten foot above them, Frank also waits, his eyes moving across each line of prisoners until finally he gives up, unable to make out their faces in the distance, and stands up straight, glaring down at those closest to him.

He watches the sergeant stroll back and forth along the road, checking that the guards are in place and ready for the command to start the roll call which will take all day. When it comes, the four thousand men move forward in compressed shuffling. On the opposite side of the road, at one of the allocated places where the prisoners are counted, one of Frank's mates, a corporal like himself, gives him the thumbs up but Frank ignores him, concentrating only on looking for his one special enemy amongst the slow-moving mass of men.

Five yards past Frank's post the prisoners straggle into single file, stepping through the west gate of the compound to be double-checked by a sergeant of the provost staff with his clipboard; one tick for each man. Every few minutes the procession halts to allow the crush of men inside the compound to disperse.

'Get a fucking move on.' Frank grits his teeth, his lips a thin line.

As though they hear him, the guards chivvy the men and they sullenly move away to lean against the gritty stone walls of the Granville, the old cotton mill, now their prison. Some, sucking on cigarettes, complain loudly about the tedious tallying, and huddle deeper into their greatcoats, others stare with blank eyes towards the distant hills in obstinate rejection of their surroundings.

Squinting into the light of the pale low sun, Frank leans over his Bren gun and moves it slowly along the lines. Even though he knows Schormann was the doctor on duty in the camp hospital he can't rely on him to be wearing his white coat. As *Lagerführer* of the prisoners Schormann could just as well be in officer uniform.

The Germans still waiting in the lines portray a self-conscious indifference to the proceedings. They realise that today's well-organised registration replaces the daily tally on each of the four floors of the converted mill that they have constantly rendered useless by their rebellious refusal to stand still. Now, marking time at each hold up, they bellow out a rendition of *Heil Deutschland*, swaying in synchronization, and when they inch forward, they stamp their feet, their boots thudding on the tarmac. One or two give insolent Nazi salutes as they pass each British guard, ignored by some, given vicious jabs with rifles by others.

Streets away a cluster of old men, sitting on the bench outside The Crown, chatting and smoking, idle their time until it opens. They hear the echoes of the singing and fall silent, remembering their own war.

The ice melts into wetness. Grey clouds roll overhead, covering the weak sunlight. Beyond the barbed wire on the opposite side of the road to the Granville, the bare branches of the tall sycamores drip water into the wide ditches dug years ago by the first prisoners of the camp. Beyond them the allotments are still deserted. Despite the cold, a hint of steam hovers over the dense crowd of men. Sporadic attempts to revive the singing fade into weariness; the Germans are tired and hungry. The acrid smell of cigarettes that has been wafting up towards Frank disappears. Few of the prisoners have any tobacco left and for the first time he senses anger from them and, despite his own discomfort, he grins.

But this new enforced tallying is an extra burden for all and there is suppressed rage on both sides as the day drags on. Any attempt to move out of allocated lines is thwarted as the guards shove them back, prodding the jaded men with their rifles when they defiantly attempt to sit down during the long delays. Harsh shouts cut across truculent grumbles. Swearing, hidden within the captives' language, accompanies arms raised with a shaken fist or crude gestures.

Occasionally a prisoner is allowed out of line to stand by the barbed wire and, to the cheers of his mates, piss as high as he can towards the compound fence in the hope that the urine, vaporizing in the cold, will drench the guard standing by him.

Hours later they are still shambling forward, a resigned calmness settling over them as they wait to get back into camp. In the dwindling light of dusk Frank strains to examine each passing face.

The outlines of the old mill merge with the murky night sky, shadowy figures move behind dimly lit rows of rectangular windows on each level, resigned to lying on their bunks in the knowledge that there will be no food until the count is complete.

It begins to rain. Frank's eyes ache. He realises he's allowed his mind to wander. His body is tense, his right knee, now permanently stiffened, throbs. Shifting his stance, he pushes his arms down by his side, desperately wanting to raise them above his head and stretch. But he can see the bloody Staff Sergeant, eyes narrowed, watching from the ground, waiting for a chance to bollock him. Tightening and relaxing the muscles in his thighs, he clenches his buttocks together, takes his weight onto his good leg and shifts his feet, now leaden in the cold. A yawn is creeping up his chest. Glancing down again and seeing the Staff Sergeant with his back to him, he allows himself the luxury of a jaw-cracking inhalation.

Dusk is swept away in an instant by floodlights; a curtain of sparkling drizzle hangs over the men. At the same time one prisoner breaks rank and runs. Yelling angrily, the man charges along the pavement towards one of the gunners and Frank, looking down the sight, swerves the Bren gun to follow him. He hears the soldier shout a warning, then another.

'Just shoot the bugger.' Frank's breath comes in short shallow gasps.

The prisoners turn to watch the progress of their comrade, a strange silence amongst them. Then, leaning forward, Frank sees Schormann. His scalp prickles. Schormann's is the only face turned upwards, his eyes just two dark holes in his pale gleaming skin. It seems to Frank, even from this distance, that he is looking at him with loathing: the feeling is mutual. Frank bends low over the Bren, narrows his eyes in concentration and holds his breath. His finger tightens on the trigger at the same time as the soldier on the ground fires.

Chapter 1

March 1944

The rain trickled out of the downspout and rattled onto the tin roof of the coal shed outside Jean's house.

'I'll have to go. I'm dying for a pee. See you later.' Mary gave her friend a hug and ran across the street, clutching her cape at her throat. 'I'll call for you at seven o'clock.' She hurried along the alleyway at the back of the terraced houses anxious to get to the lavvy before it was too late. Behind the blank gates on either side there was the usual racket of radios, children screaming and the high-pitched exasperation of mothers.

She heard the shouting inside her own house as soon as she stopped at the gate of number twenty-seven. The catch was broken and the wooden panels grated on the stone flags as she pushed them open. Closing the gate with her backside, she jiggled around, struggling with her knickers inside the door of the little brick building before sitting on the lavatory with a sigh of relief. Partly closing the door with an outstretched foot, Mary listened to the voices. It was her Dad and Patrick arguing. Again. God, she was sick of them.

She tried not to listen. Some days she felt as though she couldn't take any more and this was definitely one of them; it had been a difficult shift with a batch of Italian patients newly arrived at the camp. Mary listed them in her head: two men with pneumonia, six with a variety of injuries and wounds. She stopped, closing her eyes, when she came to the one that had distressed her most, a young German lad, barely nineteen, so badly burned she was sure he would die before she arrived back on duty in the morning, his cries echoed in her head.

All day: '*Mutti, Mutti.*'

In the end she'd leant over him, thanking God for the smattering of phrases she'd picked up from Sergeant Strauss. The interpreter seemed to enjoy sharing his language with her and Mary liked him. So what if he was the enemy? It meant that as she held the young soldier's hand she'd been able to comfort him. '*Ich bin hier, sohn, Ich bin hier.*' He'd quietened then.

Of course Doctor Müller had disapproved. She'd known he would.

'He is a fighting man, Sister Howarth, not a baby.'

'He's a dying boy, Doctor Müller.'

She'd walked away before she lost her temper and even thinking about it now still made her seethe.

*

6

'I think Matron wastes her breath with all her lectures on fraternization,' she'd said to Jean on their way home. She dipped her head against the rain and shifted her gas mask to the other shoulder. Fitting end to the day, she thought, feeling the cold wetness seeping through her cape. 'With men like Müller, I could go off the whole male species.'

Her friend laughed. 'He'll be gone soon.'

'Well, I won't be sorry. Arrogant pig! He showed his true colours when the Commandant caught him passing notes to that patient last month.'

'I think we should separate the Nazis from the rest of the patients.'

'And me.' Mary grimaced. 'What happened to him, that Nazi, by the way? One shift he was in the first bed and the next he was gone, and he wasn't fit enough to be discharged.'

'Dunno, sent off to Canada same as Müller will be, I suppose,' Jean said. 'Well away from being able to cause any trouble.'

They huddled closer and quickened their steps.

'You'd think they'd have stopped transporting them by now,' Mary said. 'You don't hear much about threats of invasion on the news any more.'

'We'll be the last to find out what's happening. Bloody hell!' Jean clamped a hand on her cap against the sudden gust of wind. 'We're just supposed to patch them up enough to get them back into camp.' She leaned towards Mary. 'My head's dizzy sometimes with the way they ship them in and out. I swear I nearly gave the patient in bed three an enema for his appendix op. before I realised he was a different bloke.'

Despite herself, Mary giggled. 'You didn't?'

Jean grinned. 'No but it made you laugh, didn't it?'

'Don't, I'm dying for the lavvy.'

And by the time they'd reached the end of the Jean's street, Mary was in such a hurry she didn't even feel the usual twinge of irritation when she saw Jean's mother peering at them from behind the net curtain on the landing window.

Now she shifted her body slightly and tilted her neck, resting her head on the lime-washed wall. God she was tired. A sudden cold draught snaked its way round the door flapping at the squares of newspaper fastened by string to a nail on the wall. She tore the first one off and narrowed her eyes to read the print in the fading light.

Road Deaths in Britain for '43 almost total 6,000. And underneath: **More Than Half Occurring During the Blackout**.

'Well, what do they expect?' She'd had a few close calls herself, both going in on night shifts and coming home first thing in the winter mornings. It sometimes seemed the darkness was smothering her. Yet even that was better than the nights of the last two months. The constant air raids over Manchester, which ripped buildings apart and destroyed streets, also embraced the towns and villages around the city. And the indiscriminate pattern of smouldering fires, which lit up the start of the days and silhouetted the silent figures searching through the rubble, were becoming a familiar sight in Ashford.

Mary heard the rain quickening to a steady beat.

She used the piece of paper and pulled up her knickers.

The rubber soles of her shoes slipped on the greasy green flags around the grid, sunken into the middle of the yard, as she moved quietly towards the house. She leant against the doorframe, listening to the shouting inside. Her gas mask brushed against the tin bath hanging on a large nail on the wall, moving it slightly against the brickwork and dislodging heavy drops of rain that ran down in tearful streaks.

Peeping in at the kitchen window, Mary saw her mother sitting in her usual place, on the rocking chair by the range. Standing next to her was a man Mary didn't recognise. Casually leaning against the wall and resting one arm along the iron mantelpiece, he contradicted his apparent nonchalance by chewing on the nails of his other hand. Their faces were pale and blank through the net curtain. Neither was speaking, seemingly ignoring the shouting behind them.

'What now?' Mary could see and hear the two men in the hall beyond the kitchen. She put her thumb on the spoon-shaped latch, gently pressed it down and slipped into the room.

She saw Patrick loom over her father and square up to him as the older man flung a fist, punching his chest.

'Waste of bloody space.'

Patrick caught hold of her father's arm, forcing it down to his side. 'Don't bloody try that again.' He jutted his face forward. 'I didn't ask to go down the bloody mines. Fucking Ernest Bevin!'

'You do what you're told in a war; you don't 'ave any bloody choice.'

'I wanted to go in the army. I signed up for the army. I didn't want to go down the damn mines.'

'I didn't want to go in the trenches but I'd no choice and look at the state of me now, coughin' my bastard lungs up.'

'Yeah, and I'll finish up in the same way stuck down that hellhole. So if I do have to go, I want paying a proper bloody wage. So get off my bleedin' back. If we want to strike, we will.'

'I've told you, man, it's unofficial. You'll get nowhere.'

'We will, if we stick together.'

'An' in the meantime I'm supposed to keep you?'

'You'll get your money when we get ours. Now piss off and leave me alone.'

'Don't bloody talk to me like that. Is this what I fought for?' Mary saw her father's face was blood red. 'So me own son can swear at me? A man who can 'ardly get 'is breath on account of being gassed?'

He took a long drag at his Woodbine and gulped, narrowing his eyes. The smoke was let out in an explosive cough of air, snot and spit as he leant one palm flat against the pattern of pink cabbage roses that lined the walls in the hallway. Wreathed in blue haze of cigarette smoke, he bent forward in a long choking session, shoulders rounded and neck, scrawny as a tortoise, sticking out of his collarless white shirt. His scalp, purple and pitted with old scars, showed through the few grey strands. Mary watched him; no one went near him. They knew better; all the family had had a backhander at one time or another for going to his aid.

'Mam?'

Her mother glanced up at her in weary resignation. Mary pushed back her hood and took off her cape. Reaching up, she draped it over the end of the clothes rack that dangled from the ceiling and went through to the scullery to wash her hands in the deep stone sink. Turning off the tap, she held on to it for a moment, head drooped, before going back into the kitchen. Pulling the damp white cap of her head, she dropped it on the table and waited, looking from her mother to the stranger. No explanation for his presence was offered so she went over to the stairs, ignoring the debacle in the hall. Hesitating, she held back the velvet curtain that covered the doorframe and glanced at the young man. He was watching her. She nodded at him. In turn, he slightly inclined his head, his eyes still fixed on hers, and she registered their colour, dark grey. She was aware of the glint of amusement in them, though the rest of his face was serious. Then he slowly raised one eyebrow in insolent familiarity. Ignoring him, Mary turned to her mother and gestured with her head, silently offering an escape. 'Upstairs?'

Flapping a hand at her, Winifred shook her head.

Giving the warring two a last glare, Mary let the curtain fall behind her. At the top of the stairs she paused, leaning on the banister, as she heard her father's clogs scrape across the lino in the kitchen. If he started on her mother she'd go back down. Then she heard him hawk a globule of phlegm into the fire and her mouth moved in disgust as she pictured the green flecks of spit sizzling on the fender. She listened for a couple of minutes before crossing the landing to the bedroom she shared with her sister.

Then, her hand on the door, she paused again as she heard Patrick shouting from the front parlour. She could picture him, pacing the floor, smacking one fist into the palm of the other, a habit he'd copied from her father.

'I wanted to fight,' he was shouting. 'I wanted to get at the Jerries. Bloody Bevin, Bloody Bevin Boys. Bollocks to being a Bevin boy.'

Mary knew how mortified he felt; some of the men down the mine were conscientious objectors and Patrick let everybody know he resented the possibility that he could be mistaken for one of them or that anyone would think he was a coward. Mary knew how bitterly he hated what his older brother stood for. She heard him shout again, 'I'm not bloody Tom.'

No, you're not, she thought.

Ellen held both legs straight out in front of her, twisting them so she could inspect her calves. Clothes were scattered on the floor and over the double bed the sisters shared.

'Hell's bells, have you listened to them two at it again.' Eyes half-closed against the smoke of her cigarette she looked up at Mary. 'I scarpered up here as fast as I could when Patrick gave his big announcement. Pity really. His friend's a bit of all right, isn't he?'

'Patrick's friend? Is that who he is?' Mary was careful to sound indifferent. She always thought that if her brother was anything to go by, good-looking men were always too cocky.

'Yeah, apparently. He's a guard at the camp,' Ellen said. 'God, Mary, haven't you even noticed him? You're hopeless!'

'I've better things to do at work than ogle the guards. You do enough flirting for the both of us.'

'You do realise you'll be left on the shelf if you don't watch out?' Carefully pulling her dressing gown to one side, Ellen examined her knees. She dipped a cloth into the brown liquid in the pudding basin balanced on her lap and dabbed it on her leg. Indifferent to Mary's comment

12

she said, 'They were going at it hammer and tongs when I got in from work. You'd think this was the first time Dad had heard of the strike. Everyone knows it's been brewing since the beginning of the year. It's been in all the papers. He's just been waiting to have a go at Patrick.'

Mary tried to straighten the unmade sheets on the bed.

'Here, Mary, watch it. I'm waiting for this lot to dry.' Ellen lowered her legs. 'I pinched some of Mam's new gravy browning. It's thicker than the other stuff. What do you think?'

'I think you could have tidied up a bit in here; it's a pigsty.' Mary walked over to the window and adjusted the blackout curtains, pulling the reluctant material along the plastic-covered wire. 'And am I the only one who cares what happens to this family?'

'Oh don't be such a bloody martyr.'

Mary turned and folding her arms, stared at her sister.

'What's up with you, then?' Ellen said.

'That lot downstairs, of course.'

'Good God, I would have thought you'd be used to it by now. Be like me, ignore them.' Ellen's tone was light. Mary knew she had little patience with Patrick. Even though he was two years older than her Ellen always maintained he acted like a spoiled brat. 'There's nothing you can do anyway.' She lifted her legs out in front of her again. 'Well?'

'Doesn't it ever bother you? All that Mam has to put up with?'

Ellen frowned and peered closer at her knees. 'I've missed a bit there.' She shrugged. 'Like I said, there's nothing either of us can do about it.'

'You could. You could talk to Dad. He lets you get

away with anything, he always has.'

'Don't be daft.' Ellen blew a plume of smoke upwards.

'I'm not. You know you can't do wrong as far as he's concerned.'

'Not jealous by any chance, are you?'

'Don't be stupid.'

'Look, I'm saying nothing. He's just as likely to turn on me as you.'

That wasn't true. Mary watched Ellen admiring her legs. What was it about her that got everybody running around for her, never demanding anything from her? Especially Dad. From the minute Ellen was born nobody else got a look in with their father. It wasn't that she didn't love her sister, but when they were growing up Mary had soon grasped that Bill's infatuation with Ellen was as blatant as his lack of interest in her. She hadn't cared. She'd told herself she had Tom and once she realised how indifferent the girl was to her father she'd almost felt sorry for him. Almost.

'Come on Ellen, you know you could make things easier for Mam.'

'If you want to have a row with him, go ahead,' Ellen said. 'Just don't get me involved. Anyway I'm off to the Palais tonight. You never know, I might meet someone … anyone … who'll take me away from this bloody miserable house.'

What about me? Mary thought again. Who's going to take me away from this bloody miserable house? 'You be careful, our Ellen.'

'I'm just having a good time while I can.'

When didn't she? She'd been allowed to do what she wanted all her life. All the family had spoiled her …

except for Patrick, Mary corrected herself, he only looked out for himself. She could hear him still shouting.

Ellen patted the tip of her finger on her thigh to test if the colouring had dried. 'Can I borrow some of your perfume, that lily of the valley one?'

'It's in with my undies.'

Ellen stood up, crushed what was left of the cigarette in the saucer on top of the tallboy and opened a drawer. She dabbed the perfume behind her ears and at her throat and put the bottle back. Choosing a blue dress with a small white Peter Pan collar she took it off the hanger. 'It wouldn't do you any harm, to have a bit of fun sometimes.' Her voice became peevish.

'What's up with you tonight?' Mary sat on the edge of the bed and unclipped the suspenders from her dark regulation stockings.

Ellen wouldn't return her gaze. Waiting for her to say something, it struck Mary how thin her sister had become. Her underskirt, made from a small piece of parachute that Winifred had miraculously produced, moulded every rib and revealed the sharpness of her hips. 'Are you okay? You've lost loads of weight. Are you eating properly?' she said. 'I only ever seem to see you with a cigarette in your mouth these days.'

'Stop fussing, you're off duty now.' Ellen stepped into the dress and pulled it up carefully over her legs. 'And never mind me; you should get out more.'

'If you must know, I'm meeting Jean tonight. We're going to see Clarke Gable and Vivien Leigh in a film at the Roxy.'

'What an exciting life you have.' Ellen pushed her arms through the short sleeves of the dress and turned one way then the other to see herself in the wardrobe mirror. 'You do know, don't you, that Jean's only your friend so she can get closer to Patrick? She's been sweet on him for ages.'

'Don't be nasty.'

'Sorry.' Ellen sat down heavily next to her. 'I don't know what's wrong with me these days. I'm not sleeping properly. And the bloody air raids. I never know whether to go to the shelter in Skirm or chance it under the stairs, putting up with those two –' she dipped her head towards the floor '– needling one another. And I keep wondering when it'll be our house, our street that gets it.'

There was a long silence. Downstairs their father started ranting again. Oh God, Mary thought, no more. She stopped unrolling her stocking and covered her sister's fingers with her own.

'It frightens me too, Ellen. It's hard not to worry but you'll make yourself ill. We just have to get on with our jobs.'

'That's just it. Whatever else is happening, you're satisfied with what you do. Ever since we were little you've wanted to be a nurse,' Ellen said.

'You were always a good little patient.' Mary smiled.

Ellen pushed her lower lip out. 'While me, I can't wait to get out of that bloody factory every day.' She pleated the material of her dress between her thumb and forefinger. 'Honestly, it's driving me mad in there. It's so boring, sitting at the same bench, day after day, making the same part day after day and listening to the same nattering, day after bloody day. You should hear them, Mary.' She smoothed out the creases and buttoned the bodice of the dress with her free hand. 'They only talk about rationing, clothes coupons, their kids' ailments and the latest letter from their husbands. I'm eighteen, I've nothing in common with any of them; there's no one under thirty and they're all married. And they're so bloody cheerful. It only takes one and before you know it they're all singing along to the bloody BBC. Bloody unbelievable!' Stopping for breath she stood up, tugged at the skirt of her dress and pulled the narrow belt tightly around her waist. She saw Mary trying not to smile. 'It's not funny.' She was indignant, yet couldn't resist grinning. 'If I was with Edna and the others on the next floor it wouldn't be so bad, but there … *Music While You Work*. I ask you.'

Mary laughed, quickly covering her mouth so she wouldn't be heard downstairs and, before long, Ellen joined in. She flopped back down on the bed and tucked her head into her sister's neck. Arms around each other's waist, they giggled.

'You are daft. Why don't you ask for a transfer? They're so short of workers they won't care which section you're on as long as you're there.' Mary squeezed her. 'Ask for a transfer. Tomorrow,' she added firmly. 'Here.' She lifted her pillow and picked up a small purse. 'Put a bit of this on.' She handed Ellen a small metal tube. 'Not too much, mind, that's got to last.'

Ellen carefully applied the red lipstick. 'How's that?'

'Lovely. Now, get out there and knock 'em dead. You look gorgeous.' Ellen stood up and Mary looked without envy at her sister. She *was* beautiful: blonde hair waved to her shoulders, eyes a startling blue and a wide full-lipped mouth. She gave her a small push on the backside. 'Go on, shoo! I'll see you later and mind what I said. Be careful.'

Ellen gave her a quick peck on the cheek and, pulling at the padded shoulders of her dress, she took the shoes that

17

her sister handed to her. 'Thanks, our Mary, I will.'

'Don't forget your gas mask.'

'I won't.' Ellen left the bedroom, jumping down the stairs two at a time. Mary heard her shout to their mother. Then the back door crashed shut.

Mary unbuttoned the bodice of her uniform and massaged the back of her aching neck; sometimes she felt ninety-two not twenty-two. She studied herself in the wardrobe mirror. She wasn't too bad, similar features to her sister, though not as striking, she conceded. So why had she never had a proper boyfriend? She knew the answer without really thinking about it; she'd been too busy studying, too tied up with her job. Fighting her father's determination to push her into one of the factories, Mary had known she must succeed. And she had.

Anyway, between those two downstairs and Müller, she was better staying clear of men. The face of Patrick's friend came into her mind. Mary put a hand to her cheek, feeling the sudden heat in her face. She leaned forward and pulled out the Kirby grips, letting her hair hang so she was enclosed in the dark curtain.

An envelope fell out of her pocket: Tom's letter. She picked it up and, flicking her hair back, started to open it then stopped, uncertain whether she wanted to read it.

She felt the familiar guilt. Tom had looked after her since she was a baby. Running her fingers along the back of the envelope she smiled, remembering the battered old pink pram he took her around in. The other boys had laughed at him but he didn't care. She must have been five when the carriage eventually collapsed and she'd cried, so he'd taken the wheels off and made a go-cart for her and Patrick.

But the last four years in and out of prison had changed him. He was pessimistic, more cynical these days and it made Mary sad; she hated what it had done to him. She put the letter to one side. She needed ten minutes of peace and quiet.

She heard her father's heavy tread on the stairs and, closing the door, she flicked the light switch. Except for the dim glow from the landing filtering underneath the door, the room was in darkness. A few moments later the bed in her parents' room gently groaned a protest and, almost immediately, the familiar crackling snores sounded through the wall.

Mary unhooked her dressing gown off the nail on the door and, putting it on, flopped onto her own bed. The wire springs twanged loudly and she froze, but there was no break in the noisy rhythmic breathing. Relieved, she tucked up her feet and wrapped her dressing gown round them. She could do without one of his rants at her. Grabbing the hem of one of the blackout curtains she tugged it back. The window, like all the others in the street, was criss-crossed with sticky tape, giving the terraced houses a strangely wounded appearance. The rain had stopped and the wind had carried the clouds away on its back. Through the smeared glass the stars were bright pinholes in the black sky over the town.

Perhaps Ellen was right, making the best of things, having a good time while she could. Maybe she should do the same. Mary chewed on the inside of her cheek, thinking about Patrick's friend again, seeing the half-mocking, half-inviting grin. She dragged the eiderdown over her and snuggled down. Cocooned in the feather warmth, the drowsiness made her body heavy. She curled her arm around her pillow and drew it closer, tucking it under her neck.

Chapter 2

Mary woke with a start and focussed on the clock on the bedside table; she'd slept for over an hour. Kneeling up, she closed the curtains. Her skin prickled as she walked on the cold lino to switch on the light and she jumped back onto the rag rug at the side of the bed.

She dressed quickly in a woollen jumper and thick trousers, the warmest clothes she had. The March wind would be sure to find its way into the Roxy and there was no heating in the draughty old building. Holding her shoes, scarf and hat, she opened the door and paused, listening to her father's laboured breathing. Then, avoiding the top creaky tread, she crept downstairs.

In the kitchen, her mother was raking dead ashes from under the grate.

'Dad's flat out up there now, Mam. I'm off. Are you all right?' Her mother didn't look up. 'Where's Patrick?' Mary said.

'He's in his room as well. His friend's left. Mortified I am. Quarrelling like that in front of strangers. And the language. I'm ashamed, Mary, really I am.'

'Don't worry about it. He looked the sort to have heard it all before.' Mary waited, studying her mother's stooping figure. It was almost as though she hadn't really seen her for a long time. The woman who had always been so strong, standing before her family, protecting them from her father's rages had now shrunk, become fragile. 'I'll be back by ten.' She paused. 'Shall I stop in?' Even as she asked, she regretted the impulse.

'Get on with you. I need a bit of peace after that little lot tonight.'

Winifred pushed the poker into the coal bucket between the range and the fireplace and straightened up. Smiling, she produced a thin paperback book from behind the back of the mantelpiece clock. 'With your Dad out of the way I can have a good read, without him moaning that I'm wasting time and finding things for me to do. And I've got that bottle of stout he brought me last night.'

Putting on her coat, Mary kissed the older woman's cheek, smelling the blend of carbolic soap, lavender and beer. She gave her mother a hug. 'Build that fire up, Mam. There's plenty of that slack our Patrick brought home last week.'

'Yes, well, I think that'll be the last for a while so we'd better be careful.' Winifred dragged her grey shawl from the back of her chair.' If there's only me in here, this'll do for now.'

Mary knew there would be no arguing with her. Instead she said, 'I had a letter off Tom this morning. If you're still up when I get home we can read it together.'

Her mother's shoulders stiffened but she spoke softly. 'That would be lovely, our Mary, I'll look forward to it.'

Mary closed the back door and peeped in at her mother. She saw her shudder from the cold flow of air that had streamed in from the night and knew she would be thinking of Tom in his cell in the prison, wondering if he was warm enough; it was a question she often voiced. Mary watched as her mother covered her head with the shawl, leaned closer to the glow of the embers in the grate and opened her book.

The broken wood scraped on the flags as Mary pulled the gate behind her. The alleyway was quiet and dark. Mary trod carefully on the cobbles. Counting the number of yard gates, she felt her way to the end of the crumbling brick wall until it finished. Turning on to Shaw Road, and feeling for the continuation of the last terraced house, her outstretched hands touched a solid softness. Mary jumped and gave a small scream. 'Who's that?'

'Sorry, didn't mean to scare you. It's Frank, Patrick's mate.' A red point of light glowed briefly in the blackness, lit up the man's face. 'We met earlier.' The pungent smell of cigarette smoke drifted towards her.

'What are you're doing here?'

'Waiting for you.'

'What?' she said. 'Why?' She stood still, remembering the mocking glint in his eyes.

'Thought I'd ask you out.'

Mary could tell he was smiling. She'd been right … conceited individual. 'Well, you wasted your time.' She drew herself up. 'Now if you don't mind …'

'Sorry,' he said for the second time.

Mary hesitated. He sounded almost genuine. 'If you're a pal of Patrick, how come I've never seen you before?'

'We only met a couple of months ago in The Crown.' He took a long drag on his cigarette.

'Oh.' She stared in his direction for a moment, there didn't seem to be anything else to say. 'Well, I have to go. Goodnight.' Mary turned away and crossed the road. She wished there was a bit more light. She wasn't normally nervous but there again, neither was she used to strange men waiting on street corners for her.

Frank flicked his cigarette into the gutter and followed. 'I'll walk with you a bit, make sure you get where you're going. Okay?' He raised his voice.

'No need.'

'Honest, no bother. You do know I'm one of the civvy guards at the Granville?'

'No, I didn't know. Why should I?' Mary wasn't about to tell him that she already knew. 'I haven't seen you there.' At least that was the truth.

'I came just before Christmas, transferred from a camp down south.' He caught up with her. 'I'm usually in one of the towers at the front and I've seen you go past to the hospital. Sometimes see you coming down Shaw Road with Patrick before he turns off for the mines. I thought he was your boyfriend at first.' When Mary stayed silent he said, 'So now you know I'm a respectable bloke how about coming for a drink with me? They serve a good ale in The Crown. Can I tempt you?'

'No thanks, I'm meeting a friend.'

'Boyfriend?'

'None of your business.'

'I'll walk with you then.'

'There's no need.'

'Well, looks as if we're going the same way anyhow.'

Mary didn't answer.

'Look, I am sorry, honest. Scaring you like that,' he said, 'stupid thing to do.'

He might mean the apology but she still didn't like the idea that he'd been watching her coming and going from work. She sniffed.

'Sorry,' he said again.

'I just don't like the idea of anyone spying on me.'

'It's not spying,' he protested, 'just admiring a pretty girl.'

'Oh, please.' She quickened her pace but then became aware he was limping. 'Are you all right?'

'Nothing I can't handle.' His breathing was laboured. 'Did my knee in ... I was invalided out of the Army.'

'Oh.' Mary felt obliged to slow down but when they passed The Crown at the top of Newroyd Street and he didn't leave her, she said, 'Aren't you going to the pub?'

'Later.'

They walked in awkward silence, Mary wondered where he was going. When he next took out his packet of cigarettes, he offered one to her.

'No thanks,' she said, 'not something I ever fancied.' She watched him as he stopped to strike the match. When he glanced up at her and caught her looking at him, he smiled. Not the mocking smirk, she thought, just a nice straightforward smile. She smiled back. 'Look, I'll have to hurry,' she said, 'my friend will think I've left her in the lurch.'

'Ah, *her*,' Frank said, 'so I'm not muscling in on another bloke's territory?'

Mary didn't know what to say. She had never learned how to flirt and she had no intention on starting now with a friend of her brother's, especially one who appeared to be so confident. She walked on.

At the cinema there were no queues lined up on either side of the open doors of the large red brick building. Before the war the elaborate frontage with its swags of concrete flowers and the Corinthian columns would have been lit up by the lights through the mullioned windows and its name, The Roxy, emblazoned from the roof.

Nowadays the building was in darkness and seemed to crouch down on the pavement, only faint light showing from the pay box in the foyer. Mary stood under the glass canopy that acted as a shelter for the patrons of the cinema and looked anxiously around. She could hear the opening bars of the introduction of the Pathé News. 'She's gone in without me, I bet.' She could imagine Jean waiting in the queue getting more and more cross; she hated being late for anything. It began to rain again. 'I'll have to try to find her.' She ran up the steps.

A plump woman was closing the doors. 'You're late, love. The main film's just starting,' she said and bustled to the back of the ticket office, reappearing at the counter behind the glass. 'Just the one, is it?' She looked enquiringly behind Mary who glanced over her shoulder. Frank was standing at her shoulder.

'What are you doing? You can't come in with me.'

'It's a free country. Now I'm here I might as well stay. I've nothing better to do tonight, thanks to your brother.' He reached round her and paid. 'One and sixpence, all right?'

Mary could picture Jean's face. 'Well, you can't sit with us,' she said, realising too late how childish she sounded.

Picking up her ticket she ran towards the swing doors that led to the stalls. Frank followed and the woman slammed the shutters and, locking the back door of the small booth, ran after them. She stood in their way, panting. 'Tickets please.' She jutted out her lower lip and blew away a strand of hair that had escaped the large bun on top of her head. 'Hurry up,' she said, waggling her hand, 'we'll miss it.'

Mary thrust the pink piece of paper at the woman,

hopping from one foot to the other as she waited for her half to be given back. Then she plunged through the door into the darkness.

The light from the large screen flickered over the rows of seating and some of the audience glanced over their shoulders in annoyance at the pair's hasty flurried entrance. One of them was Jean. Mary shuffled her way sideways along the row whispering apologies until she reached the seat next to her friend. She pulled it down, sitting quickly before it could spring back into position.

'What happened to you?'

'Sorry Jean, problems at home.'

'I thought you weren't coming, I had to come in on my own and you know I hate doing that.' Jean pursed her lips and looked past Mary. 'Who's that?' she hissed. Frank was leaning forward and pulling off his coat. 'Who've you brought with you?'

'I haven't … he's a mate of Patrick's. He was at the house when I got home. I tried to get rid of …'

'Well, thanks a lot,' Jean interrupted, 'thanks a lot. You didn't tell me I was going to be a gooseberry. Now, if you don't mind I'd like to watch the film.' She tightened her lips and leaned away from Mary.

Mary glared at Frank. She turned back to her friend. 'Sorry, Jean.'

'I said I'm watching the film.'

For a moment Mary considered walking out. She was so sick of people's moods and tempers. She seethed with frustration for a while but gradually, shoulder to shoulder in the darkness, she became increasingly aware of the warmth of Frank's body and the masculine mix of cigarettes, Brylcreem and shaving soap.

After a while he moved closer and whispered, 'Enjoying it?' She felt him touching her hand, which was rested on the smooth velvet covering of the armrest. Before she could stop him he'd threaded his fingers over hers. Mary disentangled herself and shifted away from him. 'Do you mind?'

He relaxed into his seat with a low laugh. Mary sucked on the inside of her lip to suppress her smile.

Just at the moment when Clarke Gable looked into Vivien Leigh's eyes, the familiar noise of the air raid siren drowned out the background music. To the groans of the audience the film stopped, dim lights lit the ornate decorations on either side of the screen and the manager of the cinema appeared on the stage. 'Usual thing, ladies and gentlemen. The police advise only those who live within a five minute walk of their homes to leave. The show will go on for those who choose to remain.'

Jean bent down hurriedly to pick up her handbag while struggling into her coat.

'What are you doing Jean? You'll never get home in time.'

'I will if I run,' Mary's friend replied tartly. 'Anyway, I've had enough. You've made an idiot of me tonight.'

'No I haven't,' Mary said, 'don't be silly.'

'I'll thank you not to call me silly.' She stood up and paused for a moment as she buttoned her coat, staring pointedly at Mary. Instantly there were calls from the people behind telling her to move.

'I'll come with you,' Mary said.

'Please don't bother.' Jean shoved past their knees and joined those jostling along the row to get to the centre aisle.

Mary blew out a hard breath and stood up.

'Why don't you stay?' Frank said.

'Look, I have to go with her. You stay, if you're that bothered.'

'Don't be daft. I'm only here because of you.'

Mary caught up with Jean as they pushed their way through the swing doors. 'It seems a good film though, doesn't it?' Why was she trying to placate her? She spoke loudly, glowering at Frank. 'We'll try again tomorrow, on our own.' Jean didn't reply. Head down, she pushed her way through the crowd.

'Load of rubbish, if you ask me.' Frank was now following them out of the building.

'Nobody did.' Mary knew she could be on the receiving end of one of Jean's moods over the next few days.

'There's time for a pint,' Frank said cheerfully.

'You two do what you want,' Jean said. 'I've had enough, more than enough, and I'm going home. I'll see you tomorrow, in work.'

'Jean, wait!'

'No!' She hurried away.

'God, I pity the bloke what finishes up with that one.' Frank said.

Mary ignored him. Buttoning her coat she ran after Jean. Frank was right behind her.

'Off the street!' The warden loomed out of the darkness. 'Now!'

'OK, OK,' Frank shouted, 'we're going.' He caught hold of Mary's sleeve. 'You're not going to make it to your house,' he said, 'and they won't let us back in the flicks.'

Mary hesitated. There was no sign of Jean. 'I should see if she's all right.'

'If we catch up with her, we'll get her to come with us but we have to get a move on,' he urged. 'Look, we could make it to The Crown in two minutes. They use the cellars as a shelter. And happen we could get a drink.' He took hold of Mary's hand. 'Come on, I dare you.'

'I don't know …' Mary couldn't remember the last time she'd acted impulsively. Had she ever? Her life seemed to have been mapped out for her for years.

'Yes?' Frank tugged on her hand. His strong fingers engulfed hers.

She felt a tremor of excitement. 'Oh, what the heck.'

They turned and ran, at first awkwardly, and then in step.

Chapter 3

Mary heard a faint drone in the distance. The searchlights over Grass Mount cut through the sky, lighting up the barrage balloon that hung over Bradlow, the next town.

They arrived at The Crown out of breath. Stan Green, the landlord, poked his head around the large red door, running his palm over the strands of greasy grey hair swept carefully across his head from one ear to the other. 'Hurry up, you're nearly too late, I were just closing up. Siren went a good ten minutes since. Warden'll be after me. Come on, come on, get in.'

He reached an arm around the back of Frank and pushed him into the pub, slamming the door into its frame. 'Come on, come on, I 'aven't got all night,' he grumbled. But he grinned at them and took the opportunity to pat Mary on the backside as they stooped to go through the low cellar doorway. 'Ow's yer Dad, Mary? 'Aven't seen him today.'

'He's at home, Mr Green. I think his chest's bothering him a bit.'

They clattered down the steps into the gloom of the long narrow cellar filled with about a dozen people cramped together in the thick fug of cigarette smoke. Two gas lamps, fastened to the wall on opposite sides of the room, shed greenish pools of light. Small wooden crates, stacked three deep in a corner farthest away from the steps, were joined together by the weft and weave of thick dusty cobwebs. A few large barrels were lined up around the ramp directly under the bolted trap door in the ceiling that opened up to the street above. As Mary and Frank shoved past them, the barrels bounced against each other with a soft hollow clunk. Except for a nod of the head or a quick smile aimed in their direction their presence was ignored. Holding onto her elbow, Frank guided her towards a space between five men perched on bar stools, playing cards on the top of an upturned crate, a stubby candle flickering in the middle, and an old woman squatted on a pile of sacks, crooning into a glass of Guinness. Mary stood, uncertain whether to sit on the flagged floor or the dirty crates.

Frank unbuttoned his coat and threw it down. 'We'll be OK here.' He brushed flakes of whitewash from her hair and she breathed in, savouring the male smell of his skin.

Nearby the elderly landlord and his wife were having a hissed argument, ignored by the young woman sitting nearby who was resting against a stack of boxes filled with empty bottles. Mary recognised their daughter; she was Ellen's age but already had two children. She watched as the girl heaved a sleeping little boy further onto her shoulder and began to breast-feed the baby hidden by the shawl she'd draped across herself.

Mary glanced at Frank but he seemed oblivious to the little family in front of him. 'So much for getting a drink, it looks as if we're too late.' he said.

'You are that, lad,' Stan Green called. 'Too busy getting down 'ere to pull any more jars.'

'I wouldn't drink anyway,' Mary said, dragging her arms out of her coat and leaving it across her shoulders. 'I've got work in the morning. I'm on earlies … with Jean.' She frowned. 'I hope she got home all right.'

'She will have.' Frank sat down and pulled his left leg towards him so that his foot, flat on the floor, balanced him, while his right leg was stuck stiffly out in front of him. 'I should have been on shift tonight. Still, can't do anything about that. We might as well make the best of things.' He shifted and groaned.

Mary remembered his obvious discomfort when they were running earlier. 'Does it hurt?' She saw the muscles around his jaw knot under his skin. 'Sorry, if you don't like talking about it…'

He shrugged. 'No problem, it was just the running set it off. Normally it doesn't much bother me except when I stand too much. Which is a bit of a bugger, seeing the job I'm in.' The humour didn't reach his eyes but she could understand that, she'd seen the same kind of reaction in many of the patients she'd treated, the self-mocking, the false jokes. When he spoke again, he said, 'Right, which of us is going first?'

'What?'

'Life story – yours or mine?'

Mary stiffened. 'I'd rather not.'

31

'Well, we could be here a long time, so we'll have to talk about something. Go on.' He nudged her. 'Don't be shy.'

'It's not that, there's just not a lot to tell,' Mary said. They sat in silence. She realised he wouldn't be put off. She sighed. 'Oh all right then, I'm a nurse, I've always wanted to be a nurse. I qualified at Bradlow General and I love what I do but I'm in a hospital I wouldn't be in if it wasn't for this awful war. Don't get me wrong,' she hastened to add, 'I chose to work at the camp when it opened in 'forty-one. I don't think there are many that have a hospital attached to them like ours, in fact I only know of two others and there are Q.A.s there, not civilian nurses, so I was lucky.' She repeated the words that Tom had said to her when she told him she was going to the Granville, 'Patients are patients whoever they are,' a phrase that had helped her whenever questioned about her job over the years. 'I'm just there to do the work I love: nursing.' She didn't notice the way Frank's mouth was pulled in at the corners. 'It's near home and, within a year of my being there a Sister's post became vacant. I applied and got it.' She lifted her shoulders. 'That's it really.' She wasn't prepared to tell him about all the rows she'd had from her father over her decision to work at the camp or about the fact that he ignored her if she mentioned the hospital, though she knew he was glad enough of the extra money her promotion had brought into the house.

'That's not what I meant.' Frank shook his head. 'I want you to tell me about you. Have you got a chap? What do you like doing when you're not working? Have you got a chap? Your hopes, your dreams? Or...' He held out his hand, palm upwards and laughed. 'Have you got a chap?' He hadn't spoken quietly but no one appeared to be interested in them. Still, she didn't answer. 'All right,' he conceded, 'let's talk about something else. How about families? Tell me about your family. Patrick's told me a bit.' She glanced at him. 'Just pub chat, you know. He said you have a sister?'

'Yes. Ellen.'

'What does she think about all this?' He waved his hand around. She could hear the crump of bombs in the distance.

'She's too busy chasing the boys and finding ways to look beautiful,' she said. 'No, actually, that's not fair. She works in the munitions factory, even though she hates it. She always swore she was going on the stage, she's a good singer and dancer. But the war's put paid to that idea for now, it seems. She's lovely. We get on well. That's all, really.'

They'd all been involved in the usual school plays and the pageants and procession that the Church had organised, even Tom, although he always managed to keep in the background. But only Ellen had really enjoyed it. Mary remembered watching her practice her lines, her movements, even her smile, in the mirror so that as a child she wasn't sure if Ellen was genuinely happy or, as Mary often remarked, just, 'arranging her face for a performance.' Mind, she had to admit Ellen was good; she was, as their mother often said, 'light as a feather on her feet and with the voice of an angel.' She'd been taken on by the Apollo Theatre in Bradlow when she was not quite fourteen. True, it was only in the chorus but, as Bill had boasted one night after he'd warded off what he called 'the door johnnies' and escorted her home, the producer had told him she was destined for great things. Ellen had been unbearable for weeks. Mary could smile about it now but at the time she could have cheerfully throttled her sister.

She realised Frank was still speaking. 'Sorry, what?' she said.

'I asked if she was good.'

'Oh, yes. Yes she was, but the theatre where she was closed down in 'forty-two and she had to get a job.' She didn't add that Bill had refused to let Ellen go to London to be in a show there. 'Look, let's talk about something else, all right?'

'OK.'

The noise outside faded away and conversation between the groups resumed. Mary struggled to think of a subject. Eventually she said, 'Tell me about you, how you finished up in Ashford.'

He pinched his earlobe between thumb and forefinger. 'The army helped me to get into the security side of the MOD and the pay's OK. The Granville's a cushy number, if I'm honest, and at least I get the satisfaction of seeing some of them bastard Krauts locked up, so I can't complain.'

For a moment Mary thought about the young German soldier in the hospital and wondered if he was still suffering. 'It must have been a bad injury for you to be out of the army so young. I have a friend who still works at Bradlow General and she says they're patching them up and sending them back to France as soon as possible these days.'

'Yes, well, they couldn't bloody patch me up enough at the time to make me useful to them, so they got rid.'

'I'm sorry, I didn't mean …'

'No, take no notice. It's a bit of a touchy subject. I wanted to carry on, but all they offered in the regiment was a desk job and that wasn't me, so here I am. I brought my mother up here with me. She'd been living on her own, just outside Rhyl in North Wales, so she's glad of the company, and I can keep an eye on her. Anyhow,' he said with a smile, 'I'm fine now and if it hadn't happened, I wouldn't have met you, now, would I?' He put his other hand to his chest and said, in a theatrical voice, 'The love of my life.'

Mary couldn't tell if he was making fun of her or not. Staring down at the floor, she felt her face flush. 'Don't talk daft.'

Neither spoke for a few minutes. They listened to the increased noise of engines above them. She felt his right leg beginning to tremble slightly and making an impatient clicking noise through his teeth, he pushed down hard on his bad knee until the shaking stopped.

'This place reminds me of France,' he said.

'What?'

'I said this place –' he held out his hands and spread his fingers '– reminds me of somewhere I was in France.'

'Oh.' She waited. 'Is that where … where you were hurt?' God, what a stupid thing to ask. What was wrong with her? She couldn't remember feeling this awkward since her first date. Her one and only proper date, she corrected herself; studying and work had prevented what her father called 'shenanigans'. She turned her head away, knowing her cheeks were scarlet. 'I'm sorry,' she said

'It's OK.' Frank took a packet of Woodbines out of his jacket pocket, tugged the flap open and pulled out a half-smoked cigarette. Striking a match, he cupped his hands around the flame and lit it. Loudly inhaling he tipped his head back and blew a spiral of smoke towards the ceiling. 'It was an old lace factory on the border of France and Belgium near a place called Lille.' He slapped his hand on the gritty flags next to him. 'We slept on the stone floor there the whole winter of '39. It was in the middle of a bloody swamp. For some daft reason they had us laying miles of barbed wire setting up defence posts. We never did work out why.'

There was a burst of laughter from one corner of the cellar. Two young women were looking in Frank's direction and whispering. One raised a hand and waved at him. He grinned at them and nodded. 'Two of the regulars here,' he explained. 'Pair of tarts.'

The fleeting annoyance she'd felt towards the girls subsided. She'd always envied the ones who went so casually into public houses, but if Frank's opinion was typical of what men truly thought perhaps the war hadn't changed people's values that much after all. She took in a quick breath; she should try talking to Ellen again. Maybe she and her friends weren't as 'modern' as they thought.

Frank was speaking again. 'First two months it never stopped raining. Then the cold weather set in.' He jerked his chin upwards. 'It was bloody freezing. We had two blankets each, two sodding blankets. We were supposed to wash in a mobile bath unit but nobody wanted to take their clothes off so we stayed mucky,' he snorted, 'and stinking … not that we cared.' The two vertical lines etched between his eyebrows deepened.

'In the January we were moved to a place called Arras. That's where a flu bug hit us. The "blitz flu" they called it. I didn't get it but I lost two mates to it.' He stopped and taking a deep drag on the cigarette, rested the back of his head on the wall.

Mary drew her legs towards her chest and held on to her knees. She felt the quivering of the outstretched limb again, against her buttock, aware this time that he disregarded the movement. The cigarette, held inwards towards his palm between his fingers and thumb, was close to his flesh but he seemed indifferent to the heat of the burning tobacco. His teeth, the front two slightly overlapping, were clamped on his lower lip. Then he shrugged and gave a short laugh. 'Do you know what the worst bit was? The boredom … the waiting … the not knowing what the hell we were doing there. We were all fired up to kill the bloody Jerries and we never saw a bloody one. Not then anyway.' He sneered. 'Saw too many of the bastards later.' Suddenly he swore and dropped the burning stub onto the floor. As he crushed it underfoot he flapped his hand, embarrassed. The landlord laughed but his wife called out, 'You OK, lad?'

'Yeah.' Frank turned to Mary. 'Now look what you've done, getting me to rabbit on.' He said in a wry tone, 'You should have shut me up.'

'It was interesting.' The trivial words hung in the air. Embarrassed she said, 'I mean …'

Frank rolled his shoulders. 'Don't worry about it. Nothing you can say, really.' His voice trailed away. Suddenly he said, 'Patrick's angry about being in the mines, isn't he? He told me how he tried to join up, how he drew the short straw. He should realise how lucky he is. It looks like it's no picnic out there now. I bet your mother is relieved he's not in the thick of it, being her only son, like.'

37

So Patrick hadn't told him about Tom. Typical. But in a way she was glad her younger brother wouldn't have told his friend what her older brother was really like. Both Patrick and her father had seen Tom's stance as an insult to them. Bill had despised the sight of his stepson for years. Tom revealing his loathing for war, five years ago, gave him the perfect excuse to totally reject him. And Patrick was so terrified that anyone would think he felt the same never had a good word to say about Tom. 'He's not her only son. I have another brother,' Mary now said and then stopped; she wasn't ready to tell him about Tom. She straightened her legs and leant on the wall. The cold stone dug into her back.

Frank waited for her to start talking again but she didn't. He wasn't bothered; he liked a girl who kept quiet sometimes. He looked over at the two women again. One of them winked. Bloody brass. He turned towards Mary. He could smell the faint floral perfume on her skin and feel the tiny movements against his side as Mary breathed and he felt himself stir. He closed his eyes. He knew she would be worth waiting for. He'd known it the first time he'd watched her pass through the barrier at the camp back in January. In contrast to that short dumpy girl she was always with and all the other stupid, giggling nurses, she held herself aloof from all the easy banter between them and the guards. Frank liked a girl who had self-respect.

The room was filled with muted sounds until, amid groans from the others, one of the men playing cards laughed loudly and thumped on top of the barrel. With one sweep of his arm he gathered the pile of pennies towards him. There was a general shuffling and scraping as the bar stools were shifted and the men stood up. One of them stretched his arms out to the side of him and yawned irritably, raising his flat cap above his head between his thumb and forefinger and rubbing his scalp with the heel of his hand. 'Bloody sick of all this hanging about night after night,' he declared.

There was a general murmur of agreement.

'Well, Jim, nothing we can do about it.' The landlord sat up, his head cocked to one side. 'Shurrup a minute, I can hear something.' They listened. Someone was banging on the pub's front door. Then, from above them, on the trap door, there was a loud thumping and a male voice shouted urgently, 'Hello, is there anyone down there? Landlord? We need to use your shelter.'

Sighing, Stan struggled to his feet and, with the side of his boot, pushed the tin box he had been sitting on towards his wife.

'Here, look after this, Betty, and watch it, I've counted it all.'

'Cheeky bugger,' she said.

They listened to him cross the floor of the bar and pull back the heavy rasp of the bolts on the door, suddenly aware of the louder drone of aeroplanes.

'They seem pretty close tonight,' one woman whispered and was instantly hushed. Everyone waited, glad of a diversion to the boredom, curious to see who would come down the steps.

A young couple clattered down, followed by Stan, shaking his head in disapproval. 'Mary?' he called to her, indicating the girl with his thumb.

'Oh my God,' she whispered, 'Ellen.' Her instinctive reaction to protect her sister was swamped by mortification. The man, a GI, was supporting her, his arm around her waist. She lolled against him, giggling softly. The American removed his cap and confidently greeted his silent audience. 'Sorry folks. We've been dancing in Bradlow and I was walking my girl here home when the sirens went. I don't know these parts too well, so a warden pointed us in the right direction. Anyway, we'll just sit down over there, out of everybody's way.' As he guided Ellen, he glanced over his shoulder. 'Thanks again, landlord. I'm sure grateful to you.'

Stan grunted. The man called Jim spoke loudly, 'You should be bloody ashamed of yourself, flashing your cash and getting the lass in that state. Bloody ashamed.' There were murmurs of agreement.

The landlord's wife folded her arms under her sagging bosom. 'Disgraceful,' she said through pursed lips.

Unconcerned, the American half-carried Ellen towards the far end of the room to where the dusty crates were stacked. She stumbled over the two young women and shrieked with laughter. 'Whoops, mind out.'

They pushed her away angrily.

'Just watch it, stupid cow.'

'Clear off.'

Ellen lurched sideways and grabbed a barrel. It tilted, the contents sloshing and the two girls yelled in alarm.

The soldier reached out and steadied it. 'Come on, honey, let's get you sitting down.' She fell against the wall and slid down on to the floor.

'Just settle down, now,' Stan said. He gave Mary another glance; he obviously thought she should do something about Ellen. When she didn't, he shrugged and raised his voice. 'They seem to have hit Manchester badly, again. It'll be a rotten morning for that lot.'

Mary stared at her sister, anger vying with shame. She saw the soldier stroke her sister's face with a forefinger, lifting her chin so he could kiss her whilst his other hand came slowly to rest over Ellen's breast. 'Ellen!' Shocked into action, Mary now launched herself across the cellar. 'You dirty beggar, that's my sister.' The American lifted an arm above his head as Mary lashed out at him. 'She's eighteen, not old enough to drink and look at her. Get your hands off her.'

'Bloody Yanks!' Frank, using the wall for support, struggled to his feet, but Stan was there first.

'Now, now, Mary, enough of that.' He held on to her arm. 'I said enough, lass.'

'It's OK, Mr Green.' Mary shook him off. 'I'll see to her.'

Ellen opened her eyes. 'Mary, what are you doing here?' She squinted upwards. 'Al?' Between them Mary and Frank dragged the protesting girl to her feet. Everyone watched, enjoying the drama. 'Get off me, Mary, give over.' She glowered at Frank, 'Take your hands off me. Al?'

The soldier shrugged, holding out his hands in defeat. 'Sorry, babe.'

The noise woke up the old woman and she broke wind. There were groans all around and one of the men who had been playing cards shouted at her, 'Oi, behave Martha, the air's bad enough in here without your help.' Frank manoeuvred past her and they sat down next to the publican.

'I'm so sorry,' Mary said, mortified. 'Mam'll go spare when she sees her.'

'As long as she knows she didn't get like that here, love,' the woman said. 'We don't want any trouble. It's hard enough making a living out of the business these days without the bobbies coming down on us.'

Mary glared over at the American, who tipped his cap over his eyes, folded his arms and slouched against the wall.

Frank touched her arm. 'I'll help you to get her home.'

She nodded. Ellen's snores prevented more conversation. Eventually, one arm around her sister, Mary also fell asleep. When the all clear siren howled it was turned midnight.

They stumbled out of the cellar into the darkness supporting Ellen between them. 'I'll see you two home before I go to work,' Frank said. 'They'll understand why I'm late with that lot going on tonight.'

'Thanks, I'd appreciate that.'

The roads were quiet, blackly damp from the earlier rain. Musky smoke wafted through the air. They heard the rattle of bells and, in the distance, a dull orange glow contrasted against the dark clouds that had reappeared. A dog barked, a frantic yapping that culminated in a howl. Soon its call was picked up by another and another until the night was filled with canine distress.

'Listen to those dogs,' Mary said, glad to break the awkward silence between them. She stopped, the weight of her sister dragging on her arm.

'Here, give her to me.'

'I could murder her. I bet you wish you'd just gone for a pint on your own.'

42

'Don't worry about it.'

Mary relinquished the sagging figure as Frank bent down and scooped Ellen up into his arms.

'Can you manage?'

'Course.'

The noise from the dogs rose into a crescendo. 'Poor things,' Mary said.

'Like dogs?' Frank's words were clipped with the pain in his knee.

'Yes, we've never had one, though. Dad hates them.'

'I had one when I was in France. Skipper, I called him.' Stopping to hitch Ellen closer to his chest, he half-turned towards Mary. 'Little black and white spaniel. Brought him back with me hidden under my blanket on the stretcher. When we landed back in Southampton they took him away. Told me they were going to put him in quarantine but I found out they'd put him down in case he carried rabies. Bastards!'

'That's awful!'

'Aye, well, it was only a dog.' They fell silent as they walked past the large shadow of the church.

Mary pointed across the road. 'There's a short cut just past the cemetery, through Skirm.' They entered the local park, gateless since the early days of the war, and slowly made their way along the paths. The moon, previously hovering behind the skein of clouds, now hazily revealed itself and the stark branches of the trees were etched against the fuzzy disc of pale lemon. Mary gazed upwards. 'Good job the moon wasn't out when the raid was on.'

When they reached the park lake, she could hear the small rowing boats rubbing together as they swayed and the water slapping against the wooden platform where they were tied up. 'Tom, my elder brother, used to take me on the boats all the time when I was a kid,' she said.

Frank looked surprised. 'He's not at home now, though?'

'No.' Mary wavered. She almost told him about Tom, then didn't. She wasn't ashamed of her brother but she didn't know Frank. He seemed kind enough, despite his earlier cockiness; look what he was doing for her now. But still…

'How old is he?'

'Thirty-four, twelve years older than me.'

Frank raised his eyebrows.

'Mam was … Mam was married before.' So? she thought, a white lie, so what?

He pointed to the wooden bench at the side of the path. 'Do you want to sit there for a minute?'

She glanced at Ellen whose head rested against his shoulder. A strand of blonde hair had fallen over her face and Mary tucked it behind her ear.

Ellen flailed a hand in the air and wriggled irritably. 'Stop it.'

Mary sighed. 'No, it'll still be wet from the rain. Anyway, we'd better get her home. Put her down now, Frank, let's see if she can walk.' Although in the shadows, she could still see the strain on his face, the tightness of his lips, and Mary fumed at the situation Ellen had put her in. She spoke sharply, 'Come on you, try walking.' She patted her sister's arm. 'Come on, stand up.'

Pausing twice while Ellen heaved up the result of her night out, they made their way through the park. Mary tried to ignore the occasional stifled sounds of lovemaking in the darkness. When Frank joked, 'God, they must be desperate in this cold,' she felt her face grow hot and didn't answer him and there was no more talk between them until they reached the back alleyway at the top of Greenacre Street.

'I can manage, now,' Mary said. 'I don't know how I would have got her home if you hadn't been there.' The thought entered her mind that under normal circumstances she wouldn't have been in the pub either. She shuddered. Who knows what would have happened to Ellen then. She had a lot to thank Frank for.

'Good job we were, eh?' It was almost as if he'd read her mind.

'I'm very grateful, thanks.' She held out her hand.

He propped Ellen against the wall as though she was a sack of coal, took hold of Mary's fingers and then kissed her on the cheek. 'Sure you can manage her?'

'Yes, sure, thanks again.' She could tell he was watching them as they trod cautiously over the cobbles. At the gate, she glanced backwards. She could just make him out, his shoulders level with the top of the yards walls on either side of him. 'Goodnight.' He didn't reply but raised one hand. Mary shoved the Ellen between the shoulder blades. 'Get in, you.' A small bank of cloud drifted across the face of the moon and the terraced houses on both sides closed in on her.

Mary grabbed hold of the crossbar on the gate and lifted it open. Swinging her sister by the arm towards the lavatory, she said, 'Get in there and have a pee. I'm not coming back out here again with you. And if you think you're going to be sick again, stop in there until you've finished.' She pulled at the door.

'Don't close it, our Mary. I can't see what I'm doing.' Ellen's voice wavered and, for a second, Mary felt sorry for her, but then remembered the humiliation she had put her through.

'Just get a move on, I'm freezing, thanks to you.' She leant against the yard wall, tucking her hands up into the sleeves of her coat and ignoring the snuffling coming out of the small building. Above her, the sky imperceptibly lightened. The yard was half in blackness. Next door's wall cast a long straight shadow and on the divide of the muted light and darkness Mary could see water pooled around the grid, a layer of scum around the edges: the residue of Winifred's washing day. 'Have you done?'

Ellen appeared, holding onto the doorframe. 'I'm sorry, Mary, I don't know what …'

'I don't want to talk about it. Let's get you in the house.'

She heard the click of the latch on the back door. A pale flickering light filtered out onto the flags.

'Is that you, Mary? I'm worried, Ellen isn't home yet.'

'It's all right, Mam, we're both here. Just close the door before the warden sees; he'll be on his rounds now. We'll be in, in a moment.'

When the two girls crossed the yard. Mary held the door open just enough for her sister to get through into the kitchen.

'I've been ironing, I couldn't sleep.' Winifred had her back to them and was standing on the small three-legged stool as she unscrewed the connection of the iron from the flex on the ceiling and re-fitted the light bulb. Holding onto the edge of the table, she stepped down awkwardly on to the floor. 'I was worried when the sirens went and you both were still out. You said you'd be home by ten, Mary.'

'Yes, I know. I'm sorry.' Mary flicked the switch and blinked against the brightness. A thin stream of black smoke rose upwards from the old-fashioned gas mantles above the fireplace. She crossed the kitchen and turned them off. 'You could damage your eyes trying to iron by the light of these things.'

'Well, at least I don't notice the creases.' Winifred turned around as she spoke. 'And Ellen, you've got work in the …' A tired frown trammelled her forehead. 'She's drunk!'

'She is,' Mary said shortly.

Ellen swayed, attempting to take off her coat. Failing, she flopped onto the kitchen chair by the back door and pushing against the heel of one shoe with the toe of the other, she forced it off her foot. All three women stared as it flipped up and then skidded across the kitchen floor.

'How did she get like this? She's eighteen. She's not even old enough to go in a pub.'

'It's a long story, Mam.' Mary hauled Ellen out of the chair and took off her coat, throwing it on top of the pile of ironed clothes on the table before pushing her towards the stairs. Ellen wobbled as she ducked through the curtain. 'Let me get her to bed.'

'Try not to make a noise; Dad's having a bad night. That do with Patrick's upset him more than he'll admit. Anyway I don't want him down here. We'll never hear the last of it if he sees her.' She paused. 'And make sure the throne's on her side, in case she's sick.'

Hanging onto the wooden banister, Mary pushed Ellen up the narrow staircase. 'Watch the last step,' she hissed.

'Mind the creaky one.'

Ellen took an exaggerated long stride to pass the loose tread, avoided it, but collapsed onto the landing with a yelp. Mary clutched at her but, unable to hold on, fell and they lay side by side, breathing heavily. Both froze as their father coughed harshly. They heard his muttered curse, the twang of the springs on his bed as he rolled over and then the rush of urine on the china chamber pot. Ellen giggled.

'Shush.' Mary placed a hand over her sister's mouth and hauled her upright. They tiptoed into their bedroom.

Before long Ellen's laughter had turned to tears. She held on to Mary until the paroxysm had halted. 'I'm sorry, Mary.'

'Come on, it's all over and done with and no bones broken: you're home safe now.'

'I think I love him, you know.'

'Nonsense.' She unbuttoned the girl's dress and pulled it down around her waist, wrinkling her nose at the smell of vomit.

Ellen fell back on the bed, content to be undressed.

Mary tucked the covers around her. 'Now, get some sleep,' she said. 'Work in the morning, remember.'

Ellen groaned and huddled down under the bedclothes.

Mary unhooked her dressing gown, grabbed Tom's letter and crept downstairs.

Winfred was stirring the embers of the fire, coaxing the last heat from the cinders. 'I'm worried about that girl,' she said, 'she's far too flighty.'

'She's young, needs some fun.' Even as she reassured her mother Mary felt a twinge of resentment. Sometimes it seemed they were always making excuses for her sister.

The four years between them might as well be forty for all that their father's illness and the family's poverty had affected Ellen.

Mary pulled on her pyjamas; goosebumps prickled her arms and legs. She unfolded Tom's letter it and held it out to Winifred. 'Do you want to read it now, Mam?'

Winifred's fingers hovered over the sheets of paper. Then, smoothing the front of her flowery wrap-around pinafore, she pulled her chair closer to Mary and sat down slowly. 'You read it, love.'

'OK but I'll have to have a wash first.' Mary dropped the pages on the table and hurried into the scullery. When she came back her mother hadn't moved. 'It's a long letter, for once,' Mary said, fastening her dressing gown.

Dear Mary,

I hope you are keeping well and everyone else is all right. Thought I'd let you know I've had a new cellmate since last month and we've become great pals. His name is Iori Griffith and he's a CO as well.

Winifred looked up. 'What did you say his friend was called?'

'Iori. I don't think I've said it right. Welsh, I think. I'll ask Tom how to say it when I see him next.'

He's doing his first stretch but he's so passionate about our cause that he seems to see it as a challenge and he says that one day people will see we were right to oppose this war. He writes for the 'Peace News'. He smuggles pieces out and he's told me if I want to write an article he will see it gets printed. He's also promised to ask his Mam to post this letter for me.

Winifred gave a low moan. 'He's going to get in awful bother. If he carries on like that he'll get caught and he'll get extra time again.' She rolled the hem of her pinafore round her fingers. 'They'll kill him before they're done.'

'He'll be careful, I'm sure Mam, try not to worry.' But Mary knew neither of them believed that Tom would back away from any danger his beliefs brought to him; he'd come too far for that. She'd waited outside the Courthouse in Bradlow every time he'd been prosecuted for refusing the compulsory fire-watching duties the authorities kept allocating to him. Three times she'd seen him dragged out of the building and thrown into the prison van, each time she'd had to go home and tell her mother he wouldn't be coming back. The last time Winifred had taken to her bed for a week. And she'd lost count of the number of times she'd turned up to visit him and been refused because he was in solitary or being punished in some other way.

But it all seemed to make him more convinced that he was right. Mary often thought that if his principles were going to kill anybody it wouldn't be Tom, it would be her mother. She reached up and stroked Winifred's hand. 'Do you want me to stop?'

'No, of course not.'

Mary began to read again.

He says she lives in a lovely little village near the sea in Wales ...

'You were right, the chap must be Welsh; they're a fiery bunch down there. He'll get our Tom in trouble.'

'Oh Mam, stop worrying.'

... and it takes her ages to get here but she comes every month without fail.

'Hmmm,' Winifred muttered, 'bet she hasn't got an awkward bugger for a husband.'

Outside the wind rattled the tin bath on the wall and the

50

cold draught from under the door swept over Mary. She moved closer to the range and held the letter towards the light of the flames. 'Where was I?' She scanned the page, reading the next few lines to herself.

We talk for hours at night, especially when there's a raid on – it stops you having to think about what's going on outside. Lots of the men make a right racket when the sirens sound and the planes come over. They shout and bang their plates and mugs on the bars and the warders go mad. But it's all right for the screws. We'd be the first to get it up here on this floor. During the raids they hide away downstairs in their own quarters. And to think they call such as me and Iori cowards. Once the all clear goes they're up here yelling and giving out all sorts of threats.

'Why have you stopped?' Winifred said.

'Just struggling a bit in this light.' She should have read this before she came downstairs. Did Tom think before he wrote half of this stuff? Didn't he realise how much it would upset Mam? She started to read aloud.

I still hate this place but as least now with Iori it's bearable – just. I'm sure the stink of it will stay with me forever.

Winifred rocked gently, her eyes closed and lips pressed tight.

'I'll skip the next bit,' Mary said, 'it's nothing important.'

'No, read it all.' Winifred opened her eyes. 'I want to know what he's written.'

'I'm a bit cold, Mam. I'm going to put more wood on.' She poked a couple of sticks into the ashy coals and as she started reading again they began to crackle.

'Come on, love, hurry up.'

The next bit made Mary heave. 'OK Mam but it's not pleasant.'

The food gets worse – there is a lot I can't eat. Sometimes we find things in it – fingernails, woodlice and, a lot of the time, hair. One of the chaps saw a guard spit in it the porridge can the other morning, so you can imagine how that made me feel.

'Dirty buggers.' Winifred scowled.

Luckily Iori's mother brings stuff in for us and as long as the warder on our landing gets his share we can have what's left.

'My God.' Winifred stopped rocking. 'They can't get away with that.'

'Who's to stop them, Mam?' Mary said. 'I can't read the next bit. Our Tom's writing gets worse.' She skimmed over the words, hoping her mother believed her. There was no way she was going to read what he had written next.

Last night we had our mattresses taken away again for the third time this week and we had to sleep on the boards, so I'm not getting much sleep, either. Half the time we don't know why they do it.

'I think he's saying he's sleeping OK. Hang on.' She'd leave the next few sentences out as well.

A lot of the men do wind the warders up but they don't need much of an excuse to give us a kicking. Some of the screws are OK – most are right nasty beggars.

The bullying amongst the men seems to be getting worse as well. Or perhaps it's because I see what Iori has to put up with. He's only small and they started on him the first day he got here. It makes me so angry. Another of the prisoners who's singled out is a chap called Sykes – he cries a lot. They make fun of him. At night they call out his name over and over again, louder and louder until the guards make them shut up. They've not tried it with me for a long time.

'He sounds cheerful enough about his new mate at any rate.' Mary smiled at Winifred. 'A bit of good company will make time pass quicker for him. He says:'

I think I've found a soul mate in Iori. I suppose that sounds a bit odd for a bloke to say that but when you're locked up at half five at night and not let out until seven the next morning, there's a lot of time to talk. Anyway, when you're both peeing in the same bucket ...

'He didn't used to be so coarse, our Tom. That place has a lot to answer for,' Winifred said. 'He always prided himself on speaking proper.'

'Oh Mam, don't be daft. Do you want me to carry on or not?'

'Of course I do. I was just saying ...'

... and taking turns to slop out, you can't really be standoffish, can you? I'm looking forward to your next visit. I hope everyone is OK – I don't get much news from anyone else but give them my love. Ask Ellen to write, will you?

'Then there's just the usual stuff about you going to see him sometime.'

Give my love to Mam, just tell her I'm fine.

'I'd like to, you know that. It's just ...'

'Dad,' Mary said. 'Well, perhaps I'll have a talk to him about it.'

'No, leave it for now. There's enough bother already in this house. What does Tom actually say?'

'Only,'

If she could bring herself to come and see me, it would be all I could ask for. Try to persuade her.

Your loving brother, Tom

'That's all.' Mary folded the letter and put it in her pocket. She could see Winifred was near to tears. 'Don't get upset, Mam, it's just that he wants to see you. Perhaps I shouldn't have read that last bit out.'

Winifred sighed. 'No, like I've said before, I want … need to know.' Pressing her hands on her knees, she forced herself to stand. 'Now I'm away to my bed.'

Mary watched her as she pushed her chair under the table, took off her pinafore and folded it tidily over the back, before shuffling through the curtain. The cinders were cold and black before she too climbed the stairs.

Lying next to the snoring form of Ellen three hours later, Mary was still sleepless, cringing by the way she'd felt so easily flattered by Frank's attention. She'd most likely joined a long line of other girls taken in by his charms. He was a good-looking chap who probably didn't have to try too hard to get what he wanted and she'd gone from thinking he was a smug beggar to almost hanging on his every word in a matter of hours. Mortified, she tossed around. She wouldn't have gone to the pub at all if he hadn't dared her; she'd never been able to resist a challenge. And, to be truthful, Jean's pettiness had really annoyed her. Not that it was her friend's fault she'd made such an idiot of herself. No she'd done that all by herself, helped by Ellen.

She gave up trying to sleep. Propping the pillow behind her she sat up. What if Frank thought she was like her sister? Mary remembered what he'd said about those two

54

girls in The Crown. What must he think of her family anyway? Ellen drunk, Mam smelling of the booze at teatime, her father and Patrick nearly fighting? Patrick!

Oh Lord, what if Frank tells Patrick about Ellen? He'd be bound to tell their father. Then there would be hell to pay.

Chapter 4

The shrill ring of her alarm clock forced Mary out of a restless sleep. It was still dark when she peeped through the curtains, but she knew if she didn't move quickly, she would be late for her shift. At her side Ellen lay on her back gently snoring, the smell of sick carried on every breath. Mary pushed at her shoulder, her tone curt. 'Come on, get a move on.'

Ellen groaned. 'I can't. Call in at the factory for me, our Mary. Tell Edith I'm ill.'

'Why should I lie to your forewoman? You got yourself into this state, not me.'

Ellen attempted to sit up but slumped back, shivering. 'It's no good. I can't.'

Exasperated, Mary flung the covers to one side and stood staring down at Ellen who curled herself into a tight ball. 'All right; just this once.' She pulled the eiderdown over her sister. How many times had she spoken those words to get Ellen out of trouble? From the moment she could walk, Mary was the one who'd followed her around and made excuses for every bit of trouble Ellen landed herself in, even taking the blame sometimes. Her sister might have forgotten the belting Mary had from their father for the time Ellen had thrown her school satchel across the yard in a temper and broken the kitchen window but Mary hadn't. She'd waited for days for her to own up but of course it never happened.

Downstairs, Patrick was already up and smoking his first cigarette of the day, his feet propped against the hearth where the fire gave out little heat and, in a large pan, a slab of belly pork congealed in water on top of the range. On the sideboard the wireless crackled and hissed as the valves warmed. Patrick was waiting for the War Report and he didn't speak as Mary entered the kitchen fastening the belt of her uniform. She perched on the edge of a chair and hastily slipped each foot into her black stockings. 'I'm off in a minute, Mam. Ellen's not feeling so good, so I told her I'd call in the factory and let them know. She might go in later.' She wouldn't, but Mary realised that Patrick was listening.

'What's up with her?' he said.

'Women's problems.' She knew he'd lived too long with his sisters to be embarrassed by mention of the 'monthlies', never even noticing the buckets of soaking rags that appeared on a regular basis in the scullery, and she saw him immediately lose interest. Bending forward, he took a last long drag on the thin paper that held a few strands of lit tobacco before flinging it on top of the smouldering coals and standing up.

Winifred appeared at the door between kitchen and scullery and stood drying her hands on a piece of towelling, watching her daughter clipping her stockings through the suspenders. 'You've got a ladder in the right one,' she observed.

'Drat. I'll sew it in my break.' Mary twisted the

stocking so the flaw was on the inside of her leg. 'Can you see it now?' Holding onto her skirt, she strained to look at it.

'No, I think you'll get away with it.'

'Anyone would think you were trying to impress a bloke.' Patrick scowled at her, combing his hair into two carefully arranged waves. 'You're only going to work at the bloody Jerry hospital … or are you trying to impress your bosses, the Jerry doctors?'

'Oh shut up Patrick, I'm sick of your sniping. I've told you before, it's the job of the Commandant to bring in German doctors for the POWs, we have no choice who we work with.' She took the cup of tea Winifred was holding out to her, 'Thanks Mam.'

The throat-clearing from upstairs was a warning that their father was getting up. 'I'm off out: strike meeting.' Patrick fastened his jacket. 'Back at teatime.' He wrapped his scarf around his neck and reached past his mother for his cap. 'Don't forget, it's my night for a bath, Mam, so I'll need hot water when I get home. Bring the bath in before then, will you? Warm it up a bit.' He slammed the back door behind him.

Winifred retreated into the scullery.

Fastening her cape, Mary watched her mother washing carrots and potatoes in the bowl in the sink. 'Our Patrick's gone worse. You should have told him to see to his own bath, Mam. Selfish pig.'

'Not worth having a row about it. He's in a funny mood these days,' her mother said. 'He was most put out his friend had left last night but, like I told him, what was the man supposed to do? Stand there like a fool until Patrick decided to come out of his room. He asked if you'd gone

57

at the same time. I knew what he meant and told him not to talk daft. I said, "Married to her job, is our Mary."'

Mary scowled. One day she'd do something that would surprise everybody. She didn't know what, something completely mad: get a job on the other side of the country, marry a doctor, just run away. Anything to escape. She heaved a loud sigh. Chance would be a fine thing. She knew she was trapped, she'd never leave her mother to cope with everything on her own, but she was so fed up with them thinking she was. She pursed her lips. 'Married to her job.' Her mother, oblivious to Mary's frustration, was still talking. '"She's got no time for tomfoolery," I said to him. "More sense than to get mixed up with anyone, let alone the likes of one of her brother's friends. Leave your sisters be," I said. Though I must say, I don't know what he'd have done if he'd seen Ellen last night. Are you going to tell me what happened or not?'

Adjusting her cap Mary said, 'I'll leave her to tell you, when she finally gets up.'

'Can you nip in the corner shop and see if we can have some bread on tick, on your way home? Patrick's just had the last.'

'No, Mam, but I'll buy some. Will later be all right?'

'Yes, I've enough porridge for your Dad's breakfast.'

'And I don't think Ellen will want anything to eat,' Mary said. They could hear Bill's heavy footsteps on the landing. 'I'll have to go too, Mam, I'm late. I'll see you later.'

The radio suddenly burst into life.

'Good morning to you, the nation. This is the BBC Light Programme. It's eight o'clock on Friday, the seventh of March. Here is the News. Casualties have been announced

by the Government...'

Mary slammed the door, silencing the doleful voice.

Chapter 5

Washes of pale blue had finally overcome the darkness of the night sky and, although it was still cold, the light dusting of frost was already disappearing from those cobbles not in the shadows. Mary stood still for a moment, her arms tucked underneath her cape. At this time in the morning only the low murmur of radios, hushed talk and the occasional wail of a fretful baby touched the quietness. A lot of the men were away. Those still at home were either like Patrick, working down the mines, or should be, she thought dryly, or like her dad, too old or sick to join up. In which case, they were still in bed or sitting in the kitchen getting in the way of their wives.

At the corner of Henshaw Street and Shaw Road a group of men lounged amidst a swirl of tobacco smoke, Patrick among them. Some of them, not her brother she noticed, inclined their heads at her and moved to one side so she could pass.

When she reached Moss Terrace, Jean's mother, a small thin woman in a black dress covered by a checked apron, was already on her knees at the front door step; the first on the street to be 'donkey-stoning' with her block of sandstone. Barely looking at Mary, and never breaking the rhythm of the sweeping strokes, she spoke in the high-pitched refined tone that she used outside the house. 'She's gone. And I don't blame her after last night. Fine friend you turned out to be.'

'Right, thanks Mrs Winterbottom.'

Elsie Winterbottom sniffed and sloshed a cloth around in the bucket next to her, wringing it out with vicious twists before smoothing the lines of sandstone into a yellow covering over the step. Mary grinned. She knew Jean's mother hated being burdened with what she considered a common name from a husband who had long since escaped his wife's sharp tongue.

'Jean's been a good friend to you for a lot of years, madam. Men come and go, as my daughter and I long ago found out.' With one final snort she lifted the bucket into the hall and striding over her work she closed the door.

Mary stared at the gleaming brass letterbox for a second, biting her lower lip. Oh hell, Jean's nose must be really out of joint if she'd already told her mother what had happened. She hitched her skirt above her knees and began to run, clutching her gas mask in its cardboard box, the back of her cap flapping on her neck. If she was reported to Matron for being undignified in public, she'd be in trouble, but she needed to catch Jean before they got to the camp. It would be an absolute nightmare working the shift with her friend sulking all day.

A cream and red double-decker bus passed her, half empty, and she wondered whether she should get on it and ride to the turning point just before the camp. At least then she could wait for Jean outside the hospital. The bus stopped farther up the road but as she dithered on the edge of the kerb she had to wait for the milk cart to go by. She smiled at the milkman. The everyday sounds: the solid clump of hooves on the tarmac, the jangling of bridle and bit and the rattling of the bottles in the wooden crates brought normality.

'Morning Mr Nicholls.'

'How do, lass. You're late this morning. I've just passed Jean. She's a funny one, no mistake. Head in the air today and not a word out of her.' The milkman stepped backwards out of the cart, the reins trailing out of his hands. The large carthorse clopped to a halt in front of Mary.

'We had a falling out, last night,' she said.

'Aye, well. Nothing you can't fix, I'm sure.'

'Let's hope so.' She stroked the horse's neck watching the bus set off again. 'Bye, Beauty.'

She was almost at the main gate to the hospital before she caught up with her friend. 'Jean, we need to talk.' Mary held her side; she had a stitch now and it was difficult to breath, let alone speak.

'Nothing to say.' Waiting for the guard to come out of the sentry box Jean stared fixedly across the road where rolls of barbed wire fenced in the group of allotments cluttered with small huts.

'Some of those sheds could do with a bit of fixing; the roof looks to be coming off that one on the right,' Mary said.

Jean pursed her lips.

Blast it, Mary thought, I could have a day of this. 'Please, Jean, listen.' She put out her hand. 'I'm sorry about last night but it wasn't planned, he just insisted on joining us.' She thought 'us' sounded better. 'We could go to the pictures again tonight.. I'll pay.'

Jean shook Mary's hand away. 'You made me look a right fool. I couldn't believe you'd gone off with him. I waited for you round the corner.'

They'd probably passed her as they ran for the pub. No

wonder she was so ratty.

'I'm sorry, really I am. I thought you'd left. I didn't see you when we – I – came out. If I'd known you were waiting…'

Jean blew out her cheeks out in a loud sigh, lifting and dropping her shoulders.

'Go on,' Mary said, 'let's try again tonight, my treat, and we'll have tea at our house first? Patrick will be home.'

'Perhaps,' Jean said, 'I'll have to see how I feel. And I'd have to go home and change first.'

Mary knew Jean wouldn't resist the chance to see her brother.

The guard lifted the barrier and they walked under it.

'I'm sure I've seen that chap from last night somewhere before though,' Jean said.

'Possibly.' Mary tried to sound nonchalant, ' Apparently he's been a guard here since Christmas.'

'And you didn't know? I find that hard to believe.'

'Well, believe it or not, I didn't,' Mary said, 'did you?'

'Suppose not.' Curiosity got the better of her. 'Where did you go, anyway?'

'The Crown.' Mary glanced up at the main gun post and with a mixture of disappointment and relief she saw that Frank wasn't on duty. 'We stayed in the cellar until the air raid was over,' she said, still trying to appease. 'You have no idea how mucky it was down there; I had to have a top to toe wash before I went to bed.'

Jean looked mollified but still couldn't resist saying, 'You should have gone home with me.'

'You're right, I should have.' Mary held out her arm for Jean to link. 'Let's forget it, huh? Water under the bridge?' She was getting a slightly annoyed now, but Jean was right. She should have gone home, then she wouldn't be feeling such a fool now.

But then what about Ellen? What would have happened to her with that bloody American?

Chapter 6

When they arrived at Henshaw Street at teatime Patrick wasn't there.

'I've brought Jean with me, Mam.'

'I hope that's all right, Mrs Howarth,' Jean said.

Winifred had her back to them as she spread the maroon chenille cloth over the table and flattened it with her hands. Her voice was low but friendly enough as she spoke. 'That's fine. It's good to see you, love.' She moved the chairs away from the table and pulled out a drawer from underneath that rattled with cutlery. 'Set the table, will you, Mary.'

'Can I help, Mrs Howarth? Anything I can do?'

Jean took Mary's cape and hung it on one of the pegs by the back door. The older woman hurried past her carrying the kettle. 'No, that's fine. Warm yourself by the fire, it's fair freezing out there.'

'Where is everybody, Mam?'

'Ellen's still in bed. She's been up twice to the lavvy and gone back, looking like death. Patrick hasn't come home yet. Apparently some of the men were meeting this morning, to decide on rotas for the picketing.' She reappeared at the door with the kettle, wiping drips from the spout with the corner of her apron. Putting it on the range she picked up a ladle and began to stir the stew. 'Mary, can you get the plates for this? Jean, if you're ready to eat, go and sit at the table.' As both girls moved, she turned quickly, her slippers slithering on the linoleum and went back into the scullery. 'Patrick said he was meeting his friend, sometime. That chap from last night? So he's probably called in The Crown with him. I can't remember his name...'

'Frank,' Mary said. Jean gave her a tight smile.

'And I bet your father's there too,' Winifred continued. 'Happen him and Patrick'll be the best of friends when they come home. At least until the ale wears off.'

Mary followed her into the scullery. There was something wrong. For a few seconds she watched her mother sweeping the flag floor around the wash boiler. Her hair, instead of being tightly pulled back into its usual large bun, hung untidily in grey wisps around her face. Mary her voice low. 'What is it, Mam, aren't you feeling well?'

Her mother didn't answer. She pushed the small pile of dust and bits of vegetable peelings onto a piece of newspaper on the floor and crushed it up, tossing it into a bucket under the sink. Straightening, she moaned softly under her breath, holding her side.

Mary put an arm around her. Seeing the ugly swelling on her mother's cheek and the red-rimmed eyes she scowled. 'Aw, Mam, not again. What was it this time?'

Winifred pushed her daughter away and turned on the tap to rinse her hands. 'There was only me here and he had one of his moods on him. It's Patrick really, as if we haven't enough to worry about. He'll have the police at the door, with all this trouble: picketing, striking, fighting the government. Your father says there's a right way and a wrong way to tackle the bosses and your brother's going about it all wrong.' She wiped her hands on a piece of towelling. 'He's furious because it's unofficial. You know what he's like.'

Like a bully and a bastard. Mary gritted her teeth, holding back the words. 'Why were you holding your side?'

'I banged into the table when...'

'When he hit you.'

Winifred glowered defensively at Mary. 'It's not his fault.'

'Of course it's his bloody fault. You can't keep putting up with it, Mam.'

'What can I do? Tell the police? ' Winifred gave a short ironic laugh. 'Sergeant Sykes is as bad. His wife often sports a black eye.' Tears slowly welled and spilled down her cheeks. Mary took the piece of towelling that her mother was twisting round her hands, ran a corner of it under the cold-water tap and carefully dabbed the puffy cheek. Then she held it out to her.

'Hold this to your face for a moment. I'll get the arnica, for the swelling.'

'No.' Winifred was horrified. 'Not in front of Jean. Go and eat. I'll do it later. I think I'll have a lie down.' She took the cloth. 'There's nothing you can do about it, nothing anybody can do.'

'You could leave. I'll help. We could find somewhere to rent, just you, me and Ellen. Leave those two to torment each other.'

Her mother stuffed the rag into her overall pocket. Her voice was hard. 'You're talking rubbish, girl. Go ... go on.

Don't leave Jean on her own. That stew's ready to eat now. Have some before they get in.' Winifred went into the kitchen but before going up the stairs she stopped, holding the curtain so that it partly covered her face. 'I've got a bit of a headache, Jean. If you don't mind I won't eat with you. I'm not really hungry.'

'Don't worry, Mrs Howarth. I hope you feel better soon.'

Mary could tell Jean was bursting with curiosity but she offered no explanation as her friend placed the warmed plates on the table. Mary tipped some of the saucepan's contents onto them and the two girls ate in silence.

Eventually Mary spoke. 'Jean?' She hesitated. 'Look, I'm sorry about this but do you mind if we don't go tonight.' Jean frowned but said nothing. 'Mam's not feeling well and I can't leave her. I'll have to wait until our Patrick's home.' Mary saw the barely disguised pleasure light up her friend's face. 'You do understand?'

'Course I do, forget about the film. We can go some other time.' Jean stood up, peering into the mirror by the back door, straightening the collar of her dress and fluffing up her short dark curls. 'I'll wait with you. Now, let's get these pots washed.'

'No. Honest. It's all right, I can do them.'

'Nonsense,' Jean said. 'It won't take five minutes.'

Together they tidied the kitchen in companionable silence; only the clunking of the clock and the sputtering of the flames in the grate broke the quietness. So it was easy to hear the drunken singing long before the familiar scrape of the gate on the flags; Bill's deep bass, at odds with his slight stature, harmonising with his son's tenor voice. The two women listened as the flush of the lavatory was followed by a scuffling in the yard and tittering, quickly hushed. Mary switched the scullery light out and both girls moved to the other side of the table to stand facing the back door as it crashed open, rebounding on its hinges.

Arms around the other's shoulders, the two men jostled in the doorway, each grinning, each trying to be first into the kitchen.

'Eh up, Mary. And Jean, begod. What a sight, lad, two smiling women waiting to get us our tea. But where's my lass, eh? Where's my Ellen?'

The resentment and anger was a lump in Mary's throat.

'No, I'm wrong. That there's a frosty face if ever I saw one.'

The sheepish grins evaporated. Bill and Patrick let go of each other's neck and, holding onto the doorframe, elbowed their way into the room.

'No, you're wrong, Pa, our Mary won't lose her temper. She's a right saint, aren't you, our kid?'

Mary didn't miss the sarcasm, but she didn't look at her brother. Instead she stared at her father until he flushed and, pushing Patrick to one side, grabbed at a chair and fell on to it, the legs screeching on the floor as he dragged it up to the table. He shoved his jacket off his shoulders and let it fall on to the seat of the chair behind him. 'Where's your mother? Why's my tea not on the table? She knows I'm on duty tonight.'

'Mam's not feeling too well.'

'What's up with her then?'

Mary didn't answer but she made sure he saw the contempt in her eyes before she turned away. Taking one of the plates from the range she scooped some stew onto it and slapped it on the table in front of him. He crouched low over his food, almost throwing it into his mouth. Mary watched in disgust.

'What about mine?' Patrick demanded.

'I'll get it.' Jean fussed over the food. 'Is that enough?' She showed the plate to Patrick. 'More? I can put more on.'

'No, thanks. That's fine.' He sounded suddenly sober. 'Thanks Jean.' Taking off his coat, he sat down at the table studying Jean and when he smiled at her, his eyes crinkling at the corners, Mary saw her blush but hold his gaze. Self-conscious for once, Patrick was the first to look away. Taking a quick look at Mary, he said, 'Off out again tonight?'

'No. We were going to go to the pictures but we changed our mind, didn't we Jean?'

'What? Oh, yes, we can go tomorrow.' Jean smiled tentatively at Patrick, who grinned back, then bent his head over his meal.

'Any more?' Bill demanded.

Silently Mary took his plate and refilled it.

After he'd eaten Bill shoved himself away from the table and lurched across the kitchen. Collapsing into her mother's rocking chair he was asleep in seconds.

Mary cleared away the crockery, leaving the other two talking and then went upstairs to check on her mother. She was asleep, the slant of light from the landing falling across her face, which was partly hidden by her hand holding the damp cloth to the bruise on her cheek. Mary crossed the room and smoothed Winifred's hair from her forehead. For a few seconds she stayed by the bed and then left, quietly closing the door. She opened her own bedroom door with more force, clicking the latch down with a snap. 'Are you awake, Ellen? Come on now, get up, I need to talk to you and Patrick. Come on, you've slept enough. I covered for you today at the factory but I'll not do it again tomorrow. If you're still feeling ill it's your own fault.' Ellen made a melodramatic snore. Mary pursed her lips. 'And you can stop pretending you're still asleep. You're pushing your luck.' She turned on her heel, leaving the door open, the glow of the small bulb filtering into the bedroom.

Downstairs, Jean was getting ready to leave. Patrick, his hair carefully combed back into style, was winding his white scarf around his neck. As he set his cap to one side of his head and adjusted the peak over one eye, he spoke with studied nonchalance. 'No bother at all. I'm off out to The Crown so I might as well walk with you.'

'Are you going out again, Patrick? We need to talk.' Mary nodded towards Bill who was slouched in the chair, snores bubbling from dropped jaw.

'We'll talk tomorrow. I'm meeting a few of the lads.'

Mary knew it was no use arguing in front of Jean; it would only make things worse. This was something she'd have to sort out without him, as usual. She whipped the tablecloth off the table and followed them to the door to shake it out in the yard. 'Turn the light off. We don't want the warden after us.' She spoke tersely but smiled at Jean, who, bright pink with suppressed happiness, gave her a little wave before going through the door that Patrick held open for her. Her brother left without looking back, pulling the gate behind him. Folding the tablecloth Mary heard her friend speaking in an unusually timid voice.

'I think you are really brave; standing up for your

rights. I wouldn't want to go underground. It's so dangerous and your work is just as much for the war effort as joining up, just as much …'

Mary closed the door.

The fire suddenly shunted in the grate. Mary stared into the flames, thinking about Jean and her brother. Her friend wouldn't let this opportunity pass her by; she'd waited a long time to be noticed by Patrick.

Behind her, Bill snorted, wriggled in his chair and smacked his lips together. She turned to look at him. All her life he'd watched her, criticising, waiting for her to fail, comparing her with Ellen. When he found out she wanted to be a nurse he'd been furious and the paltry wages she had brought home during her training had often been used to start a row.

Well, that had all changed since her promotion; now he needed her money. She turned away from him and went upstairs. In the bedroom she took off her uniform and removed her girdle sighing with relief, then she slipped on an old skirt and jumper.

Ellen pulled the eiderdown further over her head. 'Turn the light off.'

Mary had been trying not to think about Frank, but her sister's moan brought back the humiliation she'd felt. 'Don't you even dare to whinge.' She sat on the bed, pulling on a pair of ankle socks and rubbing the chilblain that had started itching during the day. 'Just get up and get downstairs. It's about time you stopped being so damn selfish and noticed what's going on around you.' Standing, she jerked the covers off Ellen, who drew her knees up to her chest and buried her face in the pillow. 'Get up.'

Downstairs the fire was struggling, a solitary column of

smoke drifted up towards the range chimney. Mary settled on her knees and took the poker out of the coal bucket and rattled it through the bars of on the grate. She could hear Winifred and Ellen talking on the landing.

'What? What?' Bill awoke with a startled jump. Mary took no notice, she felt calmer than she had done for months. As she dropped the poker back into the bucket, a few unburned clinkers dropped into the ash can and she pulled it out with the thick cloth that was kept especially for the purpose. Aware that her father was watching her, and knowing that he could hear the two women making their way down the stairs, she took her time, rehearsing the words that should have been spoken a long time ago. With the tongs she picked up the hot pieces of coal and threw them back into the dwindling flames. Pushing the can into place, she stood, folding the cloth over the rail of the oven. Then, arms folded, she waited for her mother and sister.

Winifred was the first to step from the bottom stair. Although her clothes were crumpled, her hair was back in place and a light dusting of powder concealed the shiny swelling on her face. She held the curtain back for Ellen, who stumbled into the kitchen, blinking in the light, still dishevelled in pyjamas and dressing gown.

'We can't go on like this.' Mary's words startled all three.

'What you talking about?' Thumbs tucked into the waistband of his trousers, legs outstretched, Bill squinted up at her, his face reddening.

'You know what I mean. Look at Mam's face.'

'Mary!'

'No, Mam, enough's enough. It's got to stop.'

71

'Just watch your mouth, girl.' Bill jumped up from the chair and raised his fist.

'Just try it, Dad, and I'll walk out. I'll leave, and I'll take my wages with me. And then where will you be? Your pension won't keep food on the table; you drink half of it away. Mam prays for the times The Crown runs out of beer. How long our Patrick'll be on strike, goodness only knows, so there's no money coming from that direction and don't think I don't know that Ellen keeps a good share of what she earns, so she can gad about. That'd have to change, if I left.'

Ellen, nervously biting the skin at the side of her thumb, gave a small cry of objection.

'Oh I don't blame you Ellen. With half a chance I'd keep some of my wages … if I ever got to go out on the town.' Mary said, keeping her eyes fixed on the man whose hand was only inches from her face. 'I'm fed up with being taken for granted, fed up with watching everything that goes on in this house and having to keep quiet about it. I'm sick to the back teeth of it all. Every day I'm cleaning up the results of this bloody war, all the vile things men do to each other. I see the brutality every time we have new patients and I will not – will not carry on living with it home. Look at Mam, just look at her face. You're a bully, Dad and it's got to stop!' Mary spat the words out. Something else needed saying. 'And another thing, next time I go to visit Tom, I'm taking Mam with me and there's nothing you can do about it' She was so close to her father she could see the thread veins on his nose and cheeks and smell the stale beer on his breath. She looked down and saw his fists, clenching, unclenching, then she lifted her eyes to his in silent challenge. Bill's lips narrowed. His breathing, shallow intakes through flared nostrils, quickened as a low growl began deep in his throat. Turning from her, he grabbed his jacket from the chair and reeled across the kitchen, pushing past Winifred and crashing out of the house. Mary leant against the table. When she looked up, she saw her mother and sister staring at her. Grabbing the chair, she fell on to the seat.

All three women listened as Bill's footsteps halted and then they sighed with relief at the sound of the gate scraping. Moments later they heard a hoarse deep yell. 'Bitch!' It echoed along the alleyway.

'Where would you go? Her mother's voice was small, scared.

'I don't know. Jean has a spare room. I could ask her.' Mary spoke wearily, 'I can't carry on with all this, Mam. Wondering what I'll find every time I come home; him and Patrick, the jibes about Tom, never knowing when he's going to hit you again.'

'That won't stop with just you leaving,' Ellen told her, moving towards the fireplace and pulling her dressing gown belt tighter. 'He's always clouted Mam, you know that.'

'Then you should grow up and help her to stand up to him,' Mary said. 'Or at least try to talk to him.'

Ellen glared at her.

'But you won't leave tonight?' Winifred said.

'No, Mam, not tonight. But if *you* think I'm sleeping in that pigsty,' she glared at Ellen, 'you've another think coming. You can go and change those sheets, before I go up. I'm tired and I'm on earlies again in the morning.'

Ellen left the kitchen, muttering.

Winifred moved closer to Mary and held her hands.

'You won't really leave, will you?'

Mary stroked her mother's fingers; the skin was rough beneath her own. 'Mam, do you honestly think I'd leave you in the lurch like that? But I had to make him think I would, he knows my wages are too good to lose. I just hope I haven't made things worse. You'll have to sleep in with us tonight.'

Holding on to the table, Winifred lowered herself into the chair next to Mary. 'No, love, I'll be all right. Remember, he's on duty all night at the church tower. He took his stuff down there this morning, so he could have a jar at dinnertime, and tomorrow he's down at the power station for range practice. Anyway, he won't touch me again for a while; he'll be feeling bad about it by the time he gets back home. I know him. I just hope Stan Green doesn't give him any more ale on the slate.'

'Don't worry, if he's on duty later, he won't be drinking any more. He's got his reputation to keep up,' Mary reminded her tartly. 'That's one thing you can be sure of.'

'His Home Guarding is the only thing he feels he does well these days.'

'You're not starting to feel sorry for him?' Mary couldn't believe it.

Winifred gave in to the misery she'd denied all day and cried. She plucked at the hem of her skirt in a futile attempt to lift it and cover her face. Mary wrapped her arms around the shaking figure, feeling the hot wetness on her neck.

Two streets away, outside The Crown, Bill rubbed roughly at his face with his hand, then wiped the damp palm on the front of his jacket.

Chapter 7

April 1944

Despite Mary's angry words to her father she hadn't been able to persuade her mother to come with her to visit Tom in Wormwood Scrubs; she'd been too frightened of her husband.

'What can he do, Mam?' Mary was exasperated. 'I told him I'd take you next time I went. He'll blame me not you.'

Winifred shrunk into her chair, the glass of stout in her hand. 'He'd wait 'til you're out and then I'd cop it.' She was so adamant that, in the end, Mary gave up.

'I've been on the go since five this morning.' The small woman in front of Mary in the queue stepped through the small opening in the large prison doors.

'Have you come far?' Mary followed her through the small door.

'From Wales.' She moved next to Mary, talking loudly over the clamour of movement along the drab passages. 'You visiting your hubby? '

'Brother…'

'Ah. My son, Iori, he says I don't need to visit every month, but I do. Well you have to really, don't you. You have to make sure they're all right.' Her eyes were anxious. 'Well, I do, anyway.'

Surely there couldn't be two men here with that name? 'Iori?' Mary asked. 'You're Iori's mother?'

'I am.' The women's forehead creased. 'Do you know him?'

'He's in the same cell as my brother. Tom? He wrote and told us.'

'Tom? Oh, I met Tom last month.' She touched her chest. 'I'm Gwyneth.'

'Mary.'

'Well, well, there we are then, *cariad*. Nice to meet you, I'm sure.'

The prison officer at the front held up his hand and shouted, 'Stop.'

Immediately a barrage of complaints began and children cried out, frightened by the sudden crush of people pressing forward.

A plump girl in front of them hitched her screaming toddler higher on her hip and reached forward to grab another child who was trying to escape. There was an immediate pungent odour of stale sweat.

Gwyneth wrinkled her nose. 'You get all sorts in here. Always best to keep yourself to yourself, I think.'

There was a sudden commotion at the end of the corridor. Two prisoners were fighting, yelling obscenities. Immediately surrounded by warders, they were dragged away. Soon the hollow tread of shoes on the iron rungs echoed above the waiting crowd.

'Visitors for Matthews and McClaren?'

Hands were held up.

'No visiting today. Back to the main doors.'

An old couple struggled through the crowd, followed by a youth angrily elbowing anyone who got in his way. He pushed the old woman and she stumbled. Someone grabbed the boy's sleeve. He yanked it out of their grasp and shoved his way past. The man gently put his arm around his wife and led her through the queue of people who stood to one side for them.

'You'd think the warders could at least be civil,' Mary said.

'They don't care. They're not human.' Gwyneth's words were lost in the mêlée as the warder signalled for them to move forward again.

Pulling at the knot of her headscarf, Gwyneth took it off and puffed up her hair where it had been flattened. 'How's that?'

Mary smiled. 'Lovely.'

They walked together into the room crammed with eight long tables. Mary blinked in the harsh artificial light; after the gloom of the passages it always hurt her eyes.

Tom was waving to her. Mary watched as he tapped the arm of the man sitting next to him and pointed towards her. Gwyneth was already weaving her way through the tables, holding her basket over her head at arm's length. Mary followed. The noise of chairs scraping on the concrete floor and shouted conversations increased to an almost unbearable level.

Sitting down, Mary immediately saw the likeness between mother and son, the slight build, the same dark hair, his flopping to one side of his forehead, identical brown eyes, except that he had a yellowing bruise around the left one. When they smiled at her, it was a mirror image, but the mother's lips trembled a little.

'Well,' Gwyneth Griffiths said. She looked from Tom and Iori to Mary. 'Well, isn't this nice, then?'

Then she began to cry.

Chapter 8

'She cried all the way through the visit,' Mary said, stripping the sheet off the mattress and dropping it into the linen basket. 'It would have been funny if it wasn't so awful. Tom says she does it every time.'

'Poor woman.' Jean was only half listening. 'Talking of time,' she said, glancing at the ward clock on the wall, 'it's nearly time for my break. Where is everybody?' She looked around the ward. There were no other nurses and the beds on the other side of the room were still unmade; some, empty, had the sheets thrown back. 'There're still another fifteen to do.' At the end of the ward two patients were perched on the end on one bed talking to its occupant, others were wandering around with wash bags and towels. 'It's chaos in here this morning. If Matron comes in she'll go spare.'

'I know.' Mary glanced down at her watch on the front of her uniform. 'I had to let Hetty and Olive go on their break and Elsie and Sylvia aren't in yet. There was a message to say Bradlow was hit again last night and they're having trouble getting in. I thought they'd be here by now.' She glanced towards the double doors of the ward where, through the small windows, she could see the German interpreter chatting to the sentry on the door. 'Get Sergeant Strausse to bring the orderlies back; at least we can have the floor cleaned. And we'll just have to move quicker. Do you mind going a bit late for your break?'

'No, so long as I get one eventually.'

'Good. Tell him first and then start on the other side. I'll carry on here.' Mary plunged the cloth into the steaming water then lifted it, dripping, from the bowl. The smell of Dettol enveloped her as she grasped each end of the material and twisted it tightly, the hot liquid scalding her hands. 'And tell those two patients to get back to their own beds.' She flung the cloth on to the bed, watching Jean hurrying down the long ward. It had been a fortnight since her friend and Patrick had started going out together and Mary was still not sure how she felt about it. Jean declared she was 'over the moon' and certainly walked around with a wide smile, but it was early days and Patrick would still be on his best behaviour. Eventually someone or something would bring out his volatile temper and Mary expected it would be her having to pick up the pieces; it was only a matter of waiting, she was sure.

She sighed, it was also two weeks since that night at the cinema and the debacle with Ellen and she hadn't seen Frank since. He hadn't even been near the house to see Patrick. So that's that, she thought, forget him: he'd probably moved on to some other girl by now. And Ellen had been giving her the cold shoulder since then. Mary wiped the plastic mattress with broad, almost angry sweeps. With both her sister and her father ignoring her, the atmosphere in the house was awful. She didn't care about him but she missed her sister. For days now, a cold misery had settled in Mary's stomach and, despite her reassurances to her mother, she knew if things didn't change, she'd have to get away, escape.

She was glad of the diversion when the ward doors opened and three men in navy dustcoats and carrying mops and buckets came in, followed by a plump middle-aged nurse who gazed around with a look of distaste. 'There are no minor ops today, so I've been asked to help out here. I'll start on the dressings … if that's all right with you?'

'Thanks.' Mary forced a brief smile, noting the unfriendly tone. She knew Hilda Lewis thought that she should have been given the Sister's post on this ward. Dear God, she thought, what next?

Mary lined up the bed with the wall and straightened up, holding the middle of her back. Stretching her neck, she moved her head from side to side to ease the tension that had been building since the start of the shift, suddenly noticing the three men standing at the doorway to the ward looking in her direction.

Tucking a stray strand of her hair behind her ears and adjusting her cap, she hurried towards them, smiling. She liked the Camp Commandant; although he was at the end of his army career he was fair with both prisoners and his staff, and the camp and the hospital had improved since he'd arrived a year ago. He took off his cap as he spoke. 'Sister Howarth, I've just spoken with Matron. This is Doctor Schormann and Doctor Pensch who are taking over the duties of Dr Müller.'

'Good morning, Doctors.' She acknowledged the men standing to attention in front of her. Both had the white patch sewn onto their uniforms to declare their indifference to National Socialism, so she knew they were regarded as trustworthy, but her only concern was their attitude towards the work they had been allocated. The last thing her nurses needed was another arrogant Müller. The smaller and older of the two men gazed back at her, nervously pushing the thinning grey hair back from his forehead with his fingers. Mary thought he looked tired already as he bowed his head and clicked his heels together; his eyes were bloodshot and underscored by dark shadows.

She turned her attention to the other doctor. She was as tall as he was, his pale blue eyes were on a level with hers, but, despite her direct gaze, he did not return it so she had the chance to study him. He was about thirty; fine blond hair cut very short, high forehead, high cheekbones and a long nose. Useful for looking down on everybody, Mary thought, her heart sinking. Damn, another Müller. He stood, confidently professional, broad shoulders held rigid with disapproval as he stared around the ward, his square chin lifted.

'*Gott in Himmel*,' he muttered to the man next to him. There was a cold arrogance in his features as he turned to Major Taylor. 'This is a British Army hospital, yes?'

The Commander shook his head. 'No, civilian.' He smiled at Mary. 'And Sister Howarth and her staff are very much valued here. If we didn't have the hospital next to the camp there would be many problems for both our men and the prisoners.'

Mary forced a small tight smile. 'I can assure you, Doctor, you will find all my nurses deal professionally and compassionately with the men here. We do the work we were trained for.'

The German raised his eyebrows, lifted his heels and snapped them smartly together before turning towards the Commandant. 'If you would be good enough to tell myself and my fellow doctor what you require of us, I would be grateful.'

His dismissal of Mary was obvious and she flushed with anger. She looked over his shoulder. 'Sergeant Strausse, I will take the doctors around and explain the daily routine of my ward. I would be grateful if, as interpreter, you would explain to them anything they do not understand.'

'*Ja*, Sister.' The Sergeant barely concealed his smirk of amusement.

'I'll leave things with you then, Sister,' the Commandant said. 'Doctors, when you have finished here, please ring through for an escort back into camp.'

Mary led the group of men to the first bed. 'You find us understaffed today, gentlemen. Two of my nurses have not reported for work yet. I believe the area they live in was the target of an air raid last night.' She emphasised the words. Neither man spoke. 'However,' she continued, 'I think you will find this has not affected our care of the patients.' She smiled at Dr Pensch. 'We simply work twice as hard. This is Nurse Lewis.' The woman looked up briefly, continuing to remove the soiled bandage from the man's leg and clean the skin with the solution of Picric acid. 'Did you sleep well?' Mary said to the soldier.

'*Haben Sie gut geschlafen*?' Sergeant Strausse said.

Out of the corner of her eye, Mary saw Dr Schormann look quickly at her as the man answered, 'Well, *danke*, I slept well,' and felt a twinge of satisfaction.

'Sergeant Strausse –' Mary inclined her head towards the burly Sergeant '– is very helpful, so that often, by the time the men leave here, they understand enough to answer "Yes or No" for themselves to routine questions.'

She left the two doctors to follow her around the ward, discussing each patient she passed and then led them into the cubby-hole that was her office. Indicating chairs on the opposite side of her desk she sat down. 'Now, gentlemen, if we could discuss our daily routine.' She was careful to keep her tone neutral but she was aware that only the older doctor had spoken to her so far. 'As I said, eight a.m.

82

is the start of the day duty shift.' She passed a sheet of paper to each of them. 'The reports of the night nurses are read and discussed. At nine I check the patients with my staff nurse and one of the prisoner orderlies.' The younger man straightened in his chair. 'You have a question, Dr Schormann?'

The man held up his hand. 'No, Sister. Please ... continue.'

'At nine thirty the Staff nurses and the orderlies dress the wounds, attend to the needs of the patients. At ten thirty the nurses and orderlies have their break, the German orderlies using the side room over there. ' She indicated one side of the ward, then the other. 'The nurses and British orderlies over there. At eleven the ward round is carried out. At least one of the doctors previously here were always present. I presume that will still be the case?' She looked inquiringly at them.

They nodded. 'We understand that is so,' the older doctor said. The younger man stifled a yawn.

'Good, thank you Dr Pensch.' Mary smiled at him. She tapped her pen on her teeth and continued. 'Lunchtime is twelve thirty. In the afternoon the patients are left to rest, occupy themselves with board games or if fit enough they are allowed into the camp to meet their comrades, take exercise and so on. Five o'clock the dressings are done again and sometime between seven and seven thirty the orderlies serve supper.' She spoke quickly. 'We have prisoner staff permanently here to clear away and wash everything and to clean the wards. After supper, if there is no one seriously ill needing peace and quiet, they have a singsong. I believe in not letting the men brood. They get better quicker if they are not depressed. Do you have any questions?'

'No, none, thank you Sister,' Doctor Pensch said.

Doctor Schormann lifted a hand. '*Nein*.'

Both men stood immediately Mary got up from her chair and walked to the door. 'The routine varies little, unless, of course, there is an emergency. Now, Dr Pensch, Dr Schormann, if you will excuse me, I will continue my duties.'

Sitting behind her desk again, Mary stared at the chair where the young doctor had been. Perhaps he was as exhausted as the older man but wouldn't show it. She'd been doing this job long enough to have heard all the horror stories of the long journeys the prisoners endured on their way to Britain and the POW camps; about the poor conditions of the makeshift transit sites where the prisoners were interrogated. Against all the regulations, Strausse had told her only last week that one of the new patients had told him how frightening the two-day journey from France inside the landing craft had been, how, in the crowded darkness, it was like floating in a coffin. She leant her elbows on the desk and covered her eyes. God in Heaven, what was happening to the world?

Chapter 9

Reluctant to go home, Mary made her way to her favourite bench by the lake. One of the boats had broken free of its moorings and was drifting aimlessly in the middle of the lake, its rope trailing behind. For once she was unable to bring back the happy times she spent there with Tom.

Instead her thoughts settled on Frank. Whichever

shifts he was on, they hadn't coincided with hers. Or he was keeping out of sight. Either way, if they did meet she wasn't sure what she would say to him and besides she had enough on her plate with her job and home. Nevertheless tears prickled the back of her eyes and she closed them; she must be more exhausted than she realised.

Mary lifted her face to the weak afternoon sun, smelling the faint whiff of smoke that permanently hung in the air. Resolutely she turned her mind to work.

According to Matron at the end of shift meeting, Schormann had been a general practitioner in civilian life who then became a captain with the Red Cross. As such, and in line with the Geneva Convention, he shouldn't have been taken prisoner, but he had been and Matron was pleased to have him in the hospital. She hadn't said much about Pensch, except that it was good that they now had two doctors to cover the four wards and, much to their annoyance, she'd added she expected each of the Ward Sisters to keep excellent order … as if they needed telling.

They'd all hurried away after that, eager to go home, so Mary hadn't chance to find out if Schormann had been as offhand with everyone else. Obviously he must resent what had happened to him, especially if Matron was right about the rules of war. Mary paused in her line of thought to wonder how anybody decided on what set of laws there could ever be for killing and maiming another human being.

By the time the doctors had left her office all her nurses were back on the ward and they'd had plenty to say about the two men. Leaving her door open she'd listened to the chatter afterwards and although she heard them all agreeing that the older doctor seemed all right – he'd greeted them with a tilt of his head and click of the heels – the younger man had won himself no favours with his cold attitude and his reluctance to acknowledge the group of young women.

'He looked straight through us,' Jean had said, indignant, 'with his bloody fish eyes.'

Mary had privately agreed with her friend but felt obliged to reprimand them. 'Let's keep things professional, please. The doctors have been transferred here to do a job, not make friends ... especially not to make friends,' she'd said, repeating Matron's mantra. 'As long as they are civil when they are working, that's all we should expect. And *I* expect courtesy from my nurses.'

Hilda Lewis, standing apart from the group, hadn't let that one pass. 'I hope you're not including me in your lecture on etiquette,' she'd said.

Mary's 'Of course not, Nurse Lewis' had been lost in the melodramatic groans of the others. Mary had ignored them; she knew the woman was not the most popular member of the hospital staff.

A young mother trundled a large wheeled Silver Cross pram across the grass and carefully pressed on the brake with her foot, before she sat next to Mary. Undoing the knot of her headscarf, the woman smiled at her. 'Just off duty?'

'Yes.' Mary smiled, watching the other child, a small boy, climb the wheels of the pram to peer into it and poke a grubby finger at the baby's stomach.

'Steady with her,' the woman cautioned. 'He's a really good brother, aren't you, love?' The boy beamed self-importantly. 'She's lucky to have you as an older brother, isn't she?' He nodded.

Mary stood. 'I'm sure she is.'

'Don't go because of us.'

'I've got to get home.' She'd had a brief recollection of Tom laughing and running full pelt down their street pushing that old pink pram with her hanging on for dear life. And, just as quickly she pictured him in that cheerless visiting room at Wormwood Scrubs. She felt sick.

When she got to the top end of their alleyway on Greenacre Street she had the urge to turn and run away. Lower down a gate opened and the large figure of their next door neighbour appeared and began to beat a mat against the brick wall. Through the dust, and the smoke that drifted up from the clay pipe clenched between yellowed teeth, the woman squinted curiously at Mary. 'All right, girl?'

Mary spoke shortly. 'All right, Mrs Jagger.'

The woman removed the pipe and gestured with it towards Mary's house. 'Quiet in your house, these last few days. You'd think there was no one in, most of the time.'

'Would you?'

Discomforted, Edith Jagger swung the mat back and forth from one hand and replaced the pipe in her mouth. She waited a moment and then wiped her forehead with the back of her hand, leaving a dusty stain. 'Well, I can't stand here all day nattering. I've lots to do.'

Mary went into her own yard and waited. She could see the top of the turbaned head of the woman hovering by the wall. She stopped by the tin bath, tapping her fingers on it and called out. 'Bye, Mrs Jagger.' There was a loud snort, a final small puff of smoke and the bang of a door closing.

Mary smiled, gratified for the small victory over the neighbour who had kept the gossip flowing when Tom had gone to prison the first time. She remembered the morning he was arrested, Edith Jagger waiting on the pavement outside to watch as he was led through the front door by the two policemen. 'Look after Mam,' he called over his shoulder. Mary had put her arms around her weeping mother and they'd stood in the kitchen doorway long after the front door had slammed shut. Her father had stayed in bed.

She made a slight movement of her head as though to shake off the memory. Holding on to the catch of the back door, she heard her father's cough. He was in the kitchen and there was someone with him.

'I don't know who I hated the most when I first went to France – the Huns or the army.'

Frank! What was he doing here? Mary held her hand to her throat. She could feel the pulse in her neck quicken.

'I joined up in April '39 and applied to be a driver in the Royal Artillery. Instead I finished up as a gunner in the 91st Field Regiment. We all had to take a test and the cheeky buggers said my score was low ... so that's what I had to be, a pissing gunner. Bloody sergeant had it in for me right from the beginning. Bastard ...'

He sounded different, harsher than before. She pushed the door slightly open and stood still.

'Come in, girl, you're letting the bloody cold in. You remember Frank, don't you? Patrick's mate? He's waiting for him an' we got talking.' Bill spoke impatiently as he looked up at her from the table and then back at Frank, who was sitting opposite him. No mention of the quarrel the younger man had witnessed. No indication this was the first time that her father had spoken to her for over two weeks.

'So I see.' She stepped into the kitchen and closed the door.

Frank kept his back to her and carried on talking. 'Our training was a farce. When they sent us off in September we were given what stuff they could find for us; bloody old service uniforms, light armour that wasn't worth using, and guns that had half the sodding range of the Jerries' artillery. I tell you Bill, we were a right sorry sight …'

Mary raised her eyebrows. Not only did he seem completely unaware of her presence, he was now on first name terms with her father. She couldn't remember any of her or her brother's friends calling her father Bill.

''Ang on a minute lad.' Bill looked out of the corner of his eye at Mary. 'Your Mam and our Ellen've gone round to Mrs Booth's. Her Ted's copped it.'

'Oh no.' Being ignored by someone she barely knew now seemed unimportant. 'Not Ted.' Mary was barely aware that Frank had swung round in his chair to watch her. She'd liked Ted Booth; a couple of years older than her, she'd known him all her life and he'd grown into a quiet and thoughtful man. She'd often sat at the kitchen table between him and Tom in the months before war was declared listening to her brother earnestly explaining why, as a Christian, it would be morally wrong for him to contribute to something that meant killing another human being. She'd heard them discuss what they would do if the Government brought in the Conscription Act. Then they did and one day Ted was gone, unable to follow Tom's actions. Now he was dead.

For as long as she could remember he'd been sweet on Ellen. There was even a time when Mary thought her sister would give in to his persistence and go out with him, but it hadn't happened and, despite his letters that had regularly arrived for her, Ellen very rarely mentioned him. Mary wondered how she'd reacted to the news of his death.

'Mary!' Her father's shout startled her.

'What?' She was close to tears.

Bill sucked greedily at his cigarette. 'I said make us a brew.'

'I'll get changed first, if you don't mind,' she snapped. Running upstairs she sat on the bed for a few minutes trying to work out what she felt. Sad for Ted, of course, irritated by her father, but angry at Frank as well and she couldn't work out why. Blowing her nose she changed into slacks and her favourite jumper; not that it mattered what she wore. She combed her fingers through her hair and checked her face in the mirror. She looked pale and tired. Blow it! Hanging up her uniform she noticed a dirty mark on her cap. When she went downstairs she took it with her.

Frank was still talking. 'We were part of the BEF that sailed from Southampton. You know how short transport was, in those early days? Well, *we* went in an old removal van. The blasted thing broke down before we were two miles from Cherbourg, so we left it there.' He sounded bitter, but as she pushed through the curtain and stepped down into the kitchen he winked at her. She stared, felt compelled to give a quick smile, and went through to the scullery. 'We marched to Laval singing the *Lambeth Walk,*' she heard him say, 'daft buggers that we were.'

Mary twisted the knob on the Ascot and watched the water run into the sink. She didn't know what to make of him; she didn't understand men, but then the only ones she'd ever really known were her father and brothers. Pursing her lips, she swished the small piece of carbolic soap around in the inch of warm water and then used it to scrub at the stain. If Bill and Patrick were true examples of manhood then, as she had told herself many times, she was better off not knowing. She dropped the cap in the bowl of cold water on the draining board and stood swirling it round with one finger. But perhaps Frank didn't know where he stood with her either; maybe he was too embarrassed to say anything in front of her father. Somehow she doubted that. She picked up the kettle to fill it but stopped as she heard her father's voice.

'Same for us … Infantry … part of the Ashford mob.'

Mary waited. Her father never mentioned his war. She held her breath. What would he say next? But he didn't speak again. She turned the tap on, the pipes shrieked as the water gushed out then clanked as she shut off the flow. She carried the kettle across the kitchen and, going round the back of Frank's chair, put it on top of the range. 'The fire needs more coal,' she said.

It was as though she hadn't spoken. Bill was shaking his head and studying his fists, his knuckles pressed tightly together. '*We* marched out of town singin' *Tipperary* to Ashford's brass band.' His sigh came from deep within his chest and finished with a breathless whistle. Mary realised they weren't even aware she was listening. 'Loaded up like mules with all sorts of shit.'

He slapped his hands on the table and pushed himself up. Grasping the poker he stabbed at the coals before throwing a few more bits on. Grey ash fell into the can below the grate. The fire began to breathe small yellow flames so that their shadows wavered on the back wall of the kitchen.

Mary took two mugs from the hooks under the shelf on the wall and put them on the blue checked oilcloth. In the scullery she emptied out the sludge of leaves from the last brew and rinsed the pot before carefully spooning out a small scoop of tea leaves. All the time she listened and watched through the open door as Frank talked and Bill listened. Every day she patched up the injuries men did to one another in war, but she would never experience what these two men shared.

'When we got to Belgium we were told we would have two, maybe three weeks to get ready, but the Jerries were on us in four bloody days,' Frank said. 'At least the damn Luftwaffe was.' He leaned back on the chair until it rested on two legs and clasped his hands behind his head. 'They didn't attack us though. They just let us know they were there and we soon found out why. They were waiting for the rest of the buggers to catch up, the ground forces.' He tugged on his earlobe, his mouth twisted into an embittered line.

'Bloody thousands of them.' He banged the chair legs back down onto the floor and stood up. 'We should have known.'

When she came back into the kitchen, Mary saw he was watching her.

'All the time we were going further into Belgium, people were flooding past us, getting out. All loaded up to the gills carrying everything they owned.' He moved restlessly around the table, stopping to light a cigarette.

'We hadn't a clue what was going on, not a clue, and they wouldn't tell us.' His voice was bleak. 'The women stared like they hated us … and the wailing … all those kids.' He whipped round towards Bill. 'The soldiers just shuffled past with their heads down. We didn't realise they were retreating, until we collared one who could speak a bit of English.' He flopped back down in his chair, blowing out cigarette smoke through clenched teeth. 'We heard nothing from the bloody bigwigs. Our orders were to just keep going. We had no idea what was in front of us. And them in charge hadn't a clue either.'

In the silence, the lid on the kettle lifted and fell back with a soft click, at first slowly, then faster. Steam gushed out of the spout and sputtered on the hot plate. Mary wrapped the towel around the handle of the kettle and poured the water into the teapot, stirring at the same time.

Both men watched. Then Bill spoke. 'Aye lad, it were the same for us. They were useless then. Gave it a grand title, mind, 'The Big Push'. They even ordered fuckin' bagpipes to play somewhere. I dreamt about that sodding miserable noise for years.' He coughed and, leaning over, spat into the middle of the fire. 'Our lot started shelling to get rid of the Hun's front lines but what with the bloody smoke and dust we couldn't see a thing.' He waited until Mary poured the tea into the mugs and moved away from the table. 'We couldn't keep up the artillery fire an' when we stopped the Germans left their lines and set up gun posts, cool as you like. It were like a wall of shells exploding all over the place, coming at us, and behind them their infantry. We didn't stand a chance.'

In the pause that followed, each man picked up their mugs of tea and slurped. Bill banged his down on the table. Tea slopped out and both men watched the thin brown liquid spread over the oilcloth, turning the blue checks into a mucky green.

When her father spoke again, it was almost as if he was talking to himself. 'The mustard gas got me, bloody gas masks were neither use nor ornament. My skin came up in great sodding blisters.' Mary squeezed her hands tightly together. 'Burns your eyes, you know ... Christ, that hurts. In the end it did my lungs in. I've been a useless bastard ever since.'

For the first time in her life she wanted to go and put her arms around her father, but when he looked up at her there was something, almost a warning in his eyes that stopped her.

On the range, the kettle, almost empty, spluttered – a hollow boiling. Without moving they all stared towards the noise.

'That'll burn through,' Bill said, but he didn't get up. He blew his nose loudly and shoved the handkerchief back into his trouser pocket.

Mary moved quickly and grabbed the handle. It was hot and as she shifted it to the side of the plate a bubble of air burst out of the spout and sprayed boiling water. She jumped, flapping her hands.

'Are you OK?' Frank leapt up. 'Here, stick them under the tap.' Grasping her arm, he ushered her into the scullery.

'I'm fine. Honestly, it's fine.'

'Stop your damn fussing, man. You heard what she said. She's OK. She's a nurse, she knows what to do.' Bill pushed himself off his chair. 'Anyhow, I'm off to The Crown, see if I can get in by the back door. Are you coming or what? Our Patrick might be there.'

'No, thanks, I said I'd wait here. He's supposed to be off the line by five.'

'Suit yourself.' Bill slapped his cap on to his head and grabbed his jacket off the hook. He was pushing his arms into the sleeves and winding his scarf around his neck as he left; it was as though he couldn't wait to get out of the house.

Mary was the first to break away. Turning the water off, she picked up the towel and, carefully drying her hands, walked into the kitchen. 'I haven't seen you at the camp for a few days.'

Frank followed. 'No. I had leave owed so I took it – my knee was a bit crock.'

'I'm sorry. That was our fault.'

He put his arm over her shoulder. 'It was worth it.'

Mary tensed, told herself not to be stupid, yet she was aware at the same time that she was on her own in the house with a man she hardly knew; not a situation she'd been in before. Frank moved the pad of his thumb on her skin just above the neck of her jumper. It was too much, too familiar. She moved away.

On the mantelpiece the mechanics inside the clock softly whirred as the spring tightened, then the hammer struck against the metal band, six muffled beats. 'Oh heavens, is that the time?' Mary walked over to the fireplace and picking up the clock, wiped it with the towel. 'I wonder when Mam and Ellen will be back. And Patrick!' She replaced the clock and walked to the other side of the table from Frank, forcing herself not to touch the part of her neck he'd stoked, reluctantly acknowledging the stirrings of an unfamiliar excitement.

She held on to the back of the kitchen chair, her face burning.

Frank smiled, watching her. 'I'll let you into a secret, shall I? I haven't seen Patrick all week. I just needed an excuse to see you.'

He was lying. He'd talked to her brother a couple of days before in The Crown. And if it was true what Patrick had said about her never having had a boyfriend as far as he knew, she was probably still a virgin. The thought excited Frank.

Mary was stuck for words. God she was hopeless; for someone who gave orders and could run a hospital ward with her eyes shut, she was bloody useless in this sort of situation. 'I've never heard Dad talk to anyone about his time in the war before,' she said eventually. 'You were honoured.'

Frank shrugged. 'I like your dad. I think he's easy to get on with.'

The words hung between them, the angry figure of her father on the night she stood up to him an unwelcome image for Mary.

'I will have another brew, if that's all right with you,' Frank said.

'Right.' Mary hurried to the scullery, relieved to be doing something that broke the tension between them. 'Build the fire up a bit, will you? Use the wood in the bucket, there. Mam'll probably be frozen when she gets in.'

They sat drinking the tea on opposite sides of the table. Frank's other arm stretched out across the surface, so that his fingers almost touched her hand.

'So it's just you and your mother at home?' Mary said.

Frank shuffled in his chair, his ruddy complexion deepening. 'Yeah.' He rubbed the bump on the bridge of his nose and looked across at her. 'My father buggered off years ago so there's just me and Ma, most of the time. We rub along all right. She takes in washing for the big houses on Manchester Road and with my bit of an army pension and wage from the camp we manage OK. We rent a little two up, two down on Barnes Street. It's enough for us. George, that's my brother, he's in the National Fire Service in Manchester, comes home when he can, kips on the sofa. He … can be a bit hot headed, but can't we all? Next time he's home you'll have to come and meet him and Ma.'

'Yes, perhaps.' He was very sure of himself. Mary wasn't certain if it excited or annoyed her.

'All right if I put some more coal on the fire?'

Mary nodded. 'We'd better keep it going 'til Mam gets back, but use that wood in the bucket first, they're bits that Dad scrounged from a bombed-out house in Atherton Street. Save on the coal.' She picked up the two empty mugs. 'I hope Mam and Ellen are all right. I bet she forgot to take her torch. Perhaps I should have gone round to Mrs Booth's earlier.'

'Do you want me to walk you round there?'

'No, it's too late now, they could be home anytime. I'd better clear these pots away.'

When she came back into the kitchen, Frank had put the two wooden chairs side by side in front of the fire and was sitting smoking a cigarette. He pointed towards the seat next to him. 'Come and sit down, you look all in.'

'I am tired,' she admitted.

'Do you want me to go?'

'It's up to you.'

'I'll wait with you then.' The wood crackled in the heat of the fire as it began to burn. 'Ted?' he asked. 'Where does he fit in?'

'He's a family friend, we all grew up together. Well, really he was more of a friend to Tom, they were nearer in age.'

He stared into the flames for a couple of minutes and then said, 'Tell me about your brother.'

Mary hesitated. 'Well,' she said, 'he's tall, got light hair, blue eyes, just like Mam's. He doesn't fuss as much as Patrick about how he looks, but he's just as handsome.'

'Patrick told me he's a Conscientious Objector. There doesn't seem much love lost there.'

The anger flared immediately. 'Patrick has a big mouth. Tom's a lovely bloke and entitled to his own beliefs.'

Frank held his hands up. 'Whoa, I was only saying.'

'Yes, well,' Mary said, 'for some reason, Patrick's been jealous of him for as long as I can remember. Stupid really, Tom was fourteen when he was born, but Patrick could never stand him getting any attention. He used to play up all the time.' She smiled, trying to lighten the moment. 'Generally being a nuisance really, typical younger brother.' Her voice faltered. 'Look, I know what people think about COs. I'm not expecting you to feel any different. Let's leave it for tonight.'

'No. I want to know.' Frank was insistent. 'Tell me.'

Mary's hands, pressed palm to palm, were held tight between her knees and she hunched her back, feeling the clench of her stomach muscles. 'Tom was always the odd one out, the only one in the family who still went to church when the rest of us lapsed years ago. I think I still believe, but these days I find it difficult. Not Tom though.' How many times had she tried to understand the depths of Tom's unquestioning faith? 'His beliefs rule his life. It would have been easier for him if they didn't. After it all came out, we discovered he'd belonged to a group in Manchester for ages. You know, meetings, talks on pacifism and so on and distributing leaflets about how he felt about violence, how he felt it wrong to get involved with the war. When he first refused to sign up, he was given exemption, provided he continued to work in local government; he was in the Stationery Department. But he turned that down. He said he wouldn't work for a government of a country at war.' Mary leant back in her chair and met Frank's stare. 'He was sent to London to Wormwood Scrubs and he's been there on and off ever since. They keep trying to make him do fire watching and he won't do that either. They've extended his sentence loads of times. Dad won't have his name mentioned in the house, won't let Mam visit him, wouldn't let him come home the times he's been released.'

A memory of the last grubby bedsit Tom lived in flashed into her mind. It had been in a part of Bradlow she didn't even know existed, a maze of narrow streets lined with shabby back-to-back terraced houses and filled with gangs of dirty kids and barking dogs. She'd studied the bit of paper with the address written on it before pushing her way past the two women smoking on the bottom step of a flight of stairs. The door to Tom's room was open and for a moment she'd watched him sitting on the edge of the bed, his head in his hands, his arms sticking out of the sleeves of a jacket too small for him, his back shuddering with sobs.

'They keep saying he has to do work that involves the war and he refuses. I think they do it for spite.' Sparks flew from the fire on to the hearthrug and Frank reached out with his foot and stamped down on them. She couldn't tell from his expression what he was thinking. 'I admire what he did. I think it took a lot of courage.'

Frank leant forward, his hands clasped in front of him. Then he pressed his thumb against the first knuckle of each finger until it cracked. The noise jarred in the silence between them.

The back door latch clicked loudly. Winifred and Ellen ushered the cold night into the kitchen. Ellen was pale, her eyelids pink and swollen. She barely glanced at Mary and Frank as she hung up her coat and took off her shoes. Her voice was hoarse when she spoke to her mother. 'I'm going up.'

Winifred didn't seem to hear her. She sat down in the chair Frank offered without comment and sighed, holding her hands out to the fire. 'It's such a shame, Mary, so unfair. Hannah Booth only had her Ted since her hubby died. Now he's gone too. It's just not fair.'

Ellen gave out a loud wail and ran upstairs. After a moment her mother gestured with her head towards the ceiling, her voice broken with fatigue. 'She's taken it bad. I thought she would settle for Ted one day, when she was ready. But coming home she tells me she'd written to him, telling him she'd met this American soldier – silly little fool – and that she'd only ever thought of poor Ted as a friend. Wishes she hadn't now. I told her, if wishes were horses, beggars would ride. Can't undo what's done.'

'That's true,' Frank said.

Winifred looked up at him and then at Mary.

'Patrick's friend, Mam, remember?' Mary said. 'He's waiting for him.'

Winifred shook her head. 'Our Patrick'll still be picketing. Some of the men are going back into work tonight, so they're going to be ready for them. He'll not be home until morning.'

'In that case,' Frank said, 'I'll get out of your way.'

Winifred gave him a faint smile.

'I'll see you out.' Mary stood up. 'I'll put the kettle on in a minute, Mam.'

'I'd rather have a stout, I think, Mary. Get me a mug, will you?'

At the door Frank bent his head and whispered, 'See you tomorrow?' His lips brushed her cheek.

There it was again; that small thrill of excitement. 'Probably,' she said.

Mary carefully slid her arm from under Ellen's shoulder and folded the eiderdown around her neck, listening to the gulps and gradual slowing of her breath. Ellen had allowed Mary to comfort her and it had taken a while for her to calm down. Mary wasn't sure whether it was genuine grief or guilt from the way she'd told Ted about the American soldier. She had suspected she was still seeing the Yank, tonight her mother had confirmed it.

She turned onto her side and tucked her hand under her cheek. Ellen's ability to attract and keep the attention of boys, even if she was disinterested in them, had always baffled Mary. Ted had only ever had eyes for Ellen. Poor Ted … and poor Mrs Booth. She'd go and see her tomorrow; she must be in a right state.

Ellen hiccupped and moaned in her sleep. Mary

carefully rolled onto her back staring into the darkness. Perhaps her sister hadn't ruined things after all with Frank. He'd made it obvious today that he fancied her and that he thought it worked both ways. And it did; she did like him, she liked how he made her feel, as though she was really alive for the first time in her life. But there was also something about him she didn't understand, something she couldn't quite put her finger on.

She closed her eyes but the thought wouldn't go away.

Chapter 10

'I'm just not sure about him. I thought he was too full of himself that first time at the house but he was different last night.' Mary folded the crisp white sheet under the mattress. 'I know he's had a rotten time, I heard him telling Dad about it, but …' She shook the blanket and it billowed over the bed. Jean caught hold of the corners and between them they spread it out and folded it under the mattress. 'I just don't know what to make of him.' Picking up a pillow she held it to her and looked across the bed at Jean. 'I told him about Tom … about him being in prison and why.'

'What did he say?'

'He didn't get a chance to say anything. Mam and Ellen got back from the Booths' just then, so I'm not sure how he felt.' She handed the pillow to Jean and took another off the cupboard at the side of the bed.

'Perhaps he'll tell you next time you see him,' Jean said, tucking the pillow under her chin and easing the case over the end of it, her voice muffled.

'If there is another time. He could be as bad as the rest of that lot.' Mary looked out of the long windows towards the guardroom. The northerly wind was whipping the bare branches of the trees, so that, with each gust and splatter of rain, they rapped against the panes. 'When they first found out about Tom being a CO, they had a field day with their snide comments.' She wondered if Frank was on duty. She could just make out the figures of three soldiers lounging on chairs in the guardroom. Frank wasn't one of them. 'Everybody has an opinion about COs and it's usually unrepeatable.' As she watched she saw Frank stride towards the small brick building, head bent against the weather. One of the other soldiers left and Frank reappeared just inside the doorway, smoking. Mary watched him gazing towards the hospital, his eyes following the span of the wards above hers and then along the length of the building until he came to the window where she was standing. He saw her and nodded. Mary lifted her hand and moved away from the window.

Jean gave the pillow a good shake and dropped it on the bed before saying, 'Give him a chance, Mary. Patrick says he's a decent bloke.'

'Patrick could say the moon was made of green cheese and you'd believe him. He's only known him five minutes.'

Jean flushed. 'That doesn't mean he's wrong. Personally I think Patrick is a good judge of character.'

'I know.' Mary smiled. 'After all he likes my friend.'

'And, as you know I've liked *him* for a long time.' Jean was oblivious to Mary's teasing. 'But I thought I was too old for him.'

'You're all of what … three years older? Quite the old maid.'

'OK, OK.' Jean smiled. 'But I meant what I said, give Frank a chance.' She looked down at the patient, who had been waiting in a chair nearby. 'Right, Egon, ready?' The young man stuck his thumbs up, and they helped him on to the bed.

'*Danke.*'

'You're welcome.' Jean patted him on the shoulder. 'Sleep, now.'

'The age thing doesn't bother Patrick though, does it?' They moved to the next bed, Jean pushing the trolley that carried the two bowls of steaming water and disinfectant and the clean sheets.

'Doesn't seem to. He's not mentioned it, anyway.'

'Good. And you're sure about him, how you feel I mean?'

'Why wouldn't I be? I know you two don't always get on…'

An understatement if there was one, Mary thought. 'We have our differences.'

'But he and I get on like a house on fire.'

'You mean blazing rows?' Mary laughed again, but when Jean pulled her lips into a tight line she said, 'Sorry, couldn't resist.'

'I'm happy, Mary. Be happy for us?'

Mary lifted her hands. 'OK.' But she frowned, thinking back to the short conversation she'd had with her brother shortly after he'd started courting Jean.

Patrick was in front of the kitchen mirror, leaning back with his knees bent so he could see his reflection and carefully arranging the natural waves of his dark hair.

'Out with Jean again tonight?' Mary was mending

104

the umpteenth ladder in the same stocking and wishing that, just for once, she could be like Ellen and always find someone to buy new ones for her. She'd gone off gallivanting as well. It seemed Mary that she was the only one with no social life.

'What's it to you?' Patrick was staring at her, his brown eyes narrowed.

'Nothing.' Mary moved her shoulders, breaking the thread with her teeth and putting the needle back in the case. She stopped. 'Well, actually, if you must know, I wondered why the interest in her after all this time.'

Patrick stretched his lips back over his teeth and examined them in the mirror; they were white and even. Mary knew he thought them his best feature and often used his smile to his advantage. He rubbed his forefinger over them. 'She makes me laugh.'

Well, that's a first, she thought.

'And she's good to talk to.'

For that read good at listening. 'Met her mother yet?' Mary asked.

'Her Ma?' He straightened up and turned towards her, fastening the studs on his shirt collar. 'Yeah, course I have. I knew who she was. I'd seen her around before. I've been to the house a few times.'

'You're honoured. She doesn't normally let men in that house since Jean's father left.'

'Well, she's no choice really, has she? What with the house belonging to Jean.'

'Jean?' Mary was startled. Her friend had never mentioned that.

He grinned. 'Yeah, didn't you know?' He put his overcoat on. 'Her father arranged for it to be put in her name when she was twenty-one.'

'Her father left years ago.'

'Yeah, but the house was still his. Jean said he'd done it through a solicitor.' Patrick smirked. 'Thought she'd have told you.'

Before Mary could say anything else he was gone.

Keep out of it, Mary told herself, mind your own business.

She and Jean worked efficiently. Chucking soiled bedding into the linen basket, wiping mattresses and working with newly starched sheets, they mirrored each other's actions until, stopping at an empty bed, Jean glanced at the other two nurses on the other side of the ward and whispered, 'Patrick told me about Frank the other day. About him being injured at Dunkirk. In confidence, of course, he doesn't want it bandying around. Patrick says he doesn't want anybody to know at the camp.'

Mary raised her eyebrows.

Jean saw her expression. 'What?'

'He told Patrick in confidence?'

'Yes?'

'And Patrick told you?'

'Patrick tells me everything. We've agreed not to have secrets from each other.'

'And now you're telling me. I don't think Frank would be too pleased, do you?'

'I just thought it would help you to understand him better,' Jean huffed, 'I only wanted to help. Sorry I spoke, I'm sure.'

'I just think if something's been said in confidence, it

shouldn't be passed around.' Mary dropped her cloth on to the mattress and rubbed at a stubborn stain, ignoring the glower Jean was sending at her.

The ward doors swung open, an orderly pushed his way in carrying a mop and bucket and began to shift the bedside cabinets of the first two beds before slopping hot water over the floor,

'We'd better get a move on, we're running late,' Mary said. They finished the bed in silence.

When Jean spoke again, her voice was cool. 'Anyway, like I said, Patrick thinks he's a decent chap. He wasn't too happy when I told him about that first night at the pictures, but I think he'll be OK about you being friendly with him now.'

'That's big of him.' Mary folded her arms and leaned against the basket.

'I think you're spoiling for a row today.' Jean stood with her hands on her hips.

'No … no, I'm not.' Mary couldn't be bothered. Her friend had been different since she'd been going out with Patrick; influenced right away by him. 'Let's just get on, shall we.'

'Yeah, well, there's only three more, anyway.' Jean smoothed her apron and pushed the trolley to the next bed. A minute later she burst out, 'I can't believe how much Mother's taken to Patrick. He's the first person she's allowed in the house for ages.'

'He …' Mary wondered if she should tell Jean what her brother had said.

Jean misunderstood her hesitation. 'Yes, he's been a lot to the house. When he turned up that first night I could have died. I thought she'd have a fit, but before I could say anything, there he was, sitting at the kitchen table unloading stuff off the black market; eggs, marmalade, biscuits.'

'Oh, was he?'

The sarcasm was lost on Jean. 'Well, after that he could do no wrong. You know her, anything for nothing. She says she can't believe he's brother to …' Jean stopped.

Mary saw the confusion in her face. 'The one who's in prison? The conchie?' She finished the sentence for her, a bitter smile twisting her lips.

'I'm sorry,' Jean mumbled. 'She can be a right old cow, sometimes. Well, most of the time, really.'

Mary went over to the washbasin in the corner of the ward and picked up the small green bar of soap. She was angry at Jean's mother, angry at Patrick. She couldn't remember a time when his ability to play the black market had benefited his family. Now he was using his talent to get his feet under Jean's table. She finished washing her hands and took a small towel off the rail under the basin. Well, who could blame him? Obviously he'd worked out a way of escaping from home. 'Come on, we'd better hurry up. Matron will be here on her rounds before we can turn round.'

Drying her fingers she crossed the ward and looked out of the window again. The rain was heavier on the window and now the outline of the old mill was a blurred shadow. 'We're going to get wet, going home.' She dropped the towel into the basket. 'Right, let's get this lot to the laundry room and finish our reports for Matron.' She surveyed the room. Everything in its place. Patients back in bed, pinned down by immaculately white sheets. One or two of the men grinned at her and gave a thumbs-up sign. She smiled.

Sometimes, most of the time to tell the truth, she forgot they were the enemy.

'Who's on with her today?'

'Schormann.' Mary pulled a face. 'Worse luck.' She gestured to the other nurses to help Jean to move the basket. The wheels squealed in protest as they pushed it through the swing doors of the ward.

'Sister?'

Mary turned. The German doctor was standing by the first bed, a clipboard in his hands. Oh hell, how long had he been there? She felt her face grow hot. 'Doctor Schormann?'

He moved from one foot to the other, fidgeting with the stethoscope around his neck. 'May I have a word?'

'Can I help you, Doctor?'

'I am hoping.' His voice was low. 'We had an unfortunate first meeting. I was rude. I offended you.' He ran a hand over his short hair. *'Entschuldigung Sie, bitte.* I am sorry.'

'It really doesn't matter, Doctor.' Mary studied him, saw the humiliation in his eyes. They weren't, as Jean had described them, like the eyes of a fish. They were a clear blue and framed by long blond lashes. She felt a flicker of sympathy for him.

'It is important that we ... how do you say ... are in harmony, *ja*?'

'I agree Doctor.' At least it would make her life easier if they could work together with professional respect.

'My name, it is Peter.'

'I can't.' Mary lifted a hand to soften the words.

'Of course.' He clicked his heels together. His black shoes gleamed through the muddy rain marks. 'I understand.'

'I meant ...'

His mortification was almost painful to watch. 'I understand,' he repeated, turning away from her.

Mary gazed thoughtfully at the ward doors gently swinging long after he'd left.

Chapter 11

Mary unpinned her cap and threaded it through the belt of her uniform, before fastening her cape.

'I thought she was never going to let us go.' Jean pulled the hood of her waterproof cloak over her head, trying unsuccessfully to tuck both her cap and her black curls inside it. 'And I wanted to get away today. Patrick's promised to take me dancing. There are two new bands on at the Palais in Bradlow.' They stood outside the main entrance to the hospital watching the rain slant across the compound.

Jean waved to Patrick, who was sheltering under one of the trees on the opposite side of the road. Then she nudged Mary with her elbow. 'Good grief, look who's there.' Standing by her brother Frank hunched his shoulders against the driving rain.

Mary followed her across the road. Without speaking Patrick opened his overcoat so that Jean could shelter against him. As she ran towards him and wrapped her arms around his chest, her head burrowed into his neck, Mary knew instinctively that things between them had gone further than she had realised. She stood, the discomfort palpable between her and Frank. They watched the couple as they walked away, stopping now and again to kiss, oblivious to the weather.

'Well, they're getting on all right.' Frank pulled at his collar. 'Would you mind me walking with you?'

'No, that's fine,' Mary said, glad to move; the rain was already soaking through her stockings. 'Though I'd rather take the shortcut if it's all the same to you; under the bridge, along the canal and across Skirm. I don't particularly want to follow those two all the way home.' They began to walk. 'I thought you were on duty?'

'I've just finished.' He held out his hand. 'How's it gone today?'

She hesitated and then took hold of it, the warmth of his skin somehow familiar.

'All right. It was the new young doctor. I thought he was going to be as difficult as the last one but I'm not sure now.'

'The last one?'

'Doctor Müller, he was so full of himself. Really rude to the nurses. I'm hoping this doctor will be better to work with.'

'Just remember it's him that's the prisoner,' Frank said. 'He's the same as the rest of the arrogant sods.'

'It's different in the hospital, Frank,' Mary said. When she'd watched the doctor leave the ward she'd been aware of how hard the apology must have been for him; she'd almost felt sorry for him. She wondered whether to tell Frank what Matron had said about Schormann and his Red Cross status but the thought was immediately quashed by his next words.

'It's no bloody different, Mary. He's a POW and that's the end of it and he has to do as he's told. We …' He stopped. 'The Commandant will make sure of that.'

'The Commandant has appointed him as *Lagerführer*,

amongst the prisoners,' Mary pointed out. 'Surely that means he deserves some respect?'

'Being Camp Leader for the buggers means nothing.' They turned down towards the canal. 'Hold on to the rail. These steps are lethal.' Frank went first. The stones, covered in moss, were slimy.

Mary noticed how carefully he moved and as they turned under the bridge saw that his limp was more pronounced. Obviously the damp affected his knee. And his temper. She felt she should try to make him understand how the hospital worked; perhaps it would make him less harsh. 'He's a doctor, Frank. A lot of the camps in the country use German doctors when they can. We need them and it makes it easier for everybody.'

'Who gives a damn about them, they're prisoners. You don't have to take any shit from them. Just report him if he gets too bloody chopsy.'

'I can't do that, there has to be mutual respect in the hospital. We're working together to achieve the same thing; to make the men fit.'

Frank scowled. 'Fit to kill one of our own again.'

Mary felt the exasperation rising in her. 'You know they're not going to do that; they'll be prisoners until the war's over.'

'Providing they don't escape.'

'Well, that's up to you isn't it? That's your job, to guard them.' She spoke sharply; it was like listening to Patrick.

Frank's face changed. He gave a short laugh and held up his hand. 'Whoa. Talked myself into that one, didn't I? Daft thing to say, anyway, they'll not get out with the lot we've got at Granville; they're a good crowd.'

'I've heard rumours that some of the younger guards

can be a bit rough on the prisoners.' In fact, Mary knew the Commandant had had to discipline one section of the guard force for excessive violence.

'That's rubbish. If anything it's the old guard, the lot from the last shindig and the civilian patrols that we have to put up with, that are the soft buggers. Places like Granville need proper discipline to keep the sods down.' He squeezed her fingers. 'Let's not waste any more breath on the bastards.'

They walked on.

However appalled she was by Frank's bitterness, Mary knew he was bound to be resentful. He'd been badly injured: so much so he'd been unable to carry on as an active soldier in the war. She wished she knew him well enough to talk about it with him. Best to leave it for now, she thought.

Bowing their heads against the rain, they walked along the canal path. Mary suddenly realised that the water, reflecting the grey sky, was becoming increasingly pockmarked by raindrops: and, as they splashed through leaden puddles, that Frank's immaculate boots were covered in mud.

'Sorry about this. I never thought.' Her own shoes were sodden.

'Doesn't matter.' Frank negotiated a large pool of water. 'Look, how about going out somewhere tonight?' He walked backwards in front of her, studying her.

Mary was conscious that the rain had plastered her hair to her scalp and she was wearing no make-up. 'You'll fall over if you don't watch out,' she said, playing for time yet annoyed with herself. Wasn't this what she wanted? Was it the conversation they'd just had that was making her hesitate?

Frank spun round and grabbed hold of her hand. 'So, what do you say?' he persisted. 'Just a drink?'

They'd reached the next bridge, the steps at the side led up to the park. Water seeped through the stones and fell, unnoticed, in heavy drips on to them. For a while they watched the line of rain that rippled the surface of the canal outside the shelter of the arch. Mary was conscious of his impatience. He turned her around to face him and held her at arm's length. 'Well?'

Uncomfortable under his intent gaze, she looked down as she shifted her feet and, for the first time, noticed they were standing in water. 'If we stay here much longer we'll catch our death of cold.'

Frank waited for an answer.

Mary stifled her doubts. He'd been intolerant because of the pain in his knee, and wasn't that partly her fault, hers and Ellen's? She laughed in exaggerated exasperation. 'Yes, all right, I'd love to go out tonight. Just for a drink and only if you promise to go back now. There's no point in you getting any wetter and I'm nearly home.' She freed herself. 'I'll meet you at the end of our street. Eight o'clock!'

'Seven.' Frank said, catching hold of her arm and giving her a quick peck on the cheek. 'Can't wait 'til eight. Seven ... tonight ... and tomorrow ... and the day after that.' Mary laughed, her cheeks flushed.

He let go of her, turned and went back along the path, one arm raised above his head, his hand making circles in the air. '... and the day after that ...' Frank let his voice fade away as he walked, but in his mind he still spoke, '... and the day after ... and the day after ...'

Chapter 12

May 1944

'Kapitän Weiser? Mary leant over the bed of the man whose eyes were covered by bandages.

'Es ist Zeit?'

'Yes,' she said, 'it is time.' Doctor Schormann was making his way towards them, stopping at each bed to speak to the patients. Mary was aware how popular he was with the men and, she acknowledged, how easy he was to work with. Much better then Doctor Pensch who dithered over everything, creating confusion in the ward. In contrast the younger doctor was efficient and professional and Mary knew he had gained respect amongst the nurses.

Mary checked the contents of the trolley: Dettol, gloves, gauze, cotton wool, sterilizing bin, waste bin, drop bottle with warm water in it, and the silver nitrate. She pointed to each one, nodding as she listed them.

'Good Morning, Sister.'

'Doctor.' Mary nodded, noticing his glance over the trolley and the faint smile of approval. She was also aware of the pleasure it gave her.

He touched the patient on the arm, *'Guten Morgen, Herr Kapitän, Vorbereitet? Ready?'*.

'Ja.' Kapitän Weiser was pale and his skin glistened with sweat. Mary squeezed his shoulder as the doctor gently removed the bandages from the man's eyes.

'Beiben Sie ruhig ... Stay still,' he said.

The Kapitän was clutching hold of Mary's hand now

and she moved closer to the bed. The last of the bandages fell away and the doctor lifted the dressing. *'Lassen Sie die Augen verschlossen.* I've told him to keep the eyes closed,' Doctor Schormann said.

Mary gave him a brief smile. There was still a lot of bruising on the man's face, but the stitches that closed one eyelid were a neat line. Not for the first time she admired the doctor's dedication.

'Those can come out today.'

'Right.' She smiled openly at him now. 'I hope you don't mind my complimenting your work.'

He coloured. 'Thank you, Sister.' He leant closer, examining the wound. 'I too am pleased. *Sie wissen schön, Herr Kapitän, daß Ihr linkes Auge ganz geschädigt worden ist, und wir das Auge weggenommen haben..'* Kapitän Weiser's hand tightened on Mary's. She stroked his fingers. 'I've explained what we have done, Sister,' Doctor Schormann said. 'That the shrapnel badly damaged his left eye, that we had to remove it. *Doch hoffen wir daß Sie im rechten Auge noch sehen können.* He should still have the sight in the right.' He glanced up at Mary. 'Sister?' She handed him a retractor and he hooked the ends of the instrument over his thumb and middle finger of his left hand and slowly stretched the spring. *'Bleiben Sie ruhig* … stay still.'

The Kapitän flinched as the doctor gently lifted both lids to examine the eye. *'Gut*! Sister.'

Mary dripped the lukewarm water from the drop bottle into his eye. 'Close again,' she said.

Peter spoke in German again to the Kapitän, then glanced up at Mary. 'I've told him his sight will be blurred at first, at least until there is adjustment. So he must stay still, he must not panic.'

Kapitän Weiser forced his eyelid open and blinked.

'Wie geht es jetzt? OK?'

'Ja!'

Mary noticed the doctor's hands were shaking slightly as he stripped off his gloves and dropped them on the trolley.

The patient's eyes flickered and finally settled on Mary. He said a few words to the doctor who smiled.

'Doctor?' Mary looked from the man to Peter Schormann.

'Herr Kapitän says he fell in love with your voice the first time he heard it and now he sees you he is absolutely in love.'

Embarrassed, Mary tugged at the cuffs of her uniform and checked her watch. But when she looked up she smiled. She wagged a finger at the Kapitän. 'Enough!'

He spoke again. *'Sie ist ganz schön, glauben Sie nicht, Herr Doktor? Jemand würde sich in sie verlieben.'*

From the way Peter Schormann looked at her, Mary knew they were continuing the same conversation. She understood the word *'verlieben'*, Sergeant Strausse had once translated it for her when one of the German prisoners, a submarine officer, if she remembered rightly, made a nuisance of himself by declaring himself in love with one of her nurses. He'd been rapidly transported to Canada. Now she put a finger to her lips. 'Shush!' Tucking the sheets tightly around the Kapitän, she said, ' *Schlafen Sie jetzt.* Sleep now!'

He settled against the pillows with his eye closed again. *'Danke schön.'*

'Thank you, Sister,' Doctor Schormann said. 'I think

117

we did well this morning.' He held her gaze.

Such kind eyes. The thought came unbidden. Mary glanced around. Had she said that aloud? But nobody was taking any notice of them. She looked back at him. 'Yes.' She smiled. 'We did.'

He made a slight gesture with his hand towards her and she thought he was going to speak again. She straightened her shoulders and when she spoke made sure her voice was coolly professional. 'Was there something else, Doctor Schormann?'

'No … yes … I am glad we are colleagues, Sister.'

The ward doors swung open again and Matron bustled towards them. 'Apologies, Doctor. I intended to observe the procedure with Kapitän Weiser this morning, but I was called to Ward Four. Did everything go well?'

'Yes, Matron. I have asked Sister Howarth to remove the stitches of the left socket. I have prescribed drops of silver nitrate solution twice a day.'

'Good.' Matron barely acknowledged the information. 'I'm sure Sister knows what to do. Doctor Schormann, would you come and look at the patient with the influenza on Ward Four?' She turned on her heel and spoke over her shoulder. 'Doctor?' There was an impatient note in her voice.

Peter Schormann and Mary shared a look.

'Doctor!'

Peter followed her. Before he let the door swing to, he glanced back at Mary, raised his eyebrows and grinned.

Chapter 13

The sun was not yet at its highest point in the sky as they walked slowly alongside the grim walls of Wormwood Scrubs and it felt chilly in the shade. Winifred gripped Mary's arm; she was shaking.

'Are you cold?' Mary pulled Winifred's collar up round the back of her neck.

Winifred shook her head.

'I told you we'd be too soon,' Mary said. It had been no small triumph to get her mother this far. Mary thought she'd never be able to persuade her, but she'd persisted and this month Winfred had plucked up enough courage to defy her husband.

Now she was staring up at the brick-patterned towers as they walked towards the medieval-looking doors. They cast a long shadow and in the centre of each there were what looked like laurel wreaths. She squinted to see the carvings in the centre. 'Who do you think they are in the middle of those things?' she asked.

'I don't know.' There were few people mingling around outside. Mary set her bag down and flexed her fingers. 'I said we were too early.'

'I just wanted to get here. I wanted to see where they're keeping my son,' Winifred said quietly. 'I've waited a long time to get here, too long, thanks to your father. And now I am here … I'm frightened.' She looked at Mary and tapped her forehead. 'In my mind I had this picture of where Tom was. He's never described it, has he? So I had this picture.' She looked up at the towers. 'This is nothing like what I thought … this is … this is … worse.'

'I know, Mam.' Mary couldn't think what else to say.

She remembered the first time she'd seen the prison. They stood in silence. Winifred blinked hard. She pulled her chin in and wiped her fingers over her eyes.

'We've still an hour to wait,' Mary said.' Do you want to go to a café to get a cup of tea?'

'I'd rather have a glass of stout, just to settle my stomach,' Winifred said. 'I feel awful, Mary.'

'I'm not going in a pub, especially at this time of day,' Mary put her arm around Winifred's waist and hugged her. 'Anyway you don't want to go in smelling of ale, do you? You know what Tom thinks of drink.'

'It's just that it's been such a long day already, Mary and I'm gasping.'

'There's a little place down one of these streets,' Mary said. 'A cup of tea will set you up, Mam.'

They walked out of the shade of the wall to where it was a warm day.

When they got back, an hour later, a queue was haphazardly forming and people were shuffling through a small door in the large gates.

'You OK, Mam?'

'All these people, Mary.' Winifred shook her head. 'All these people.'

Mary knew the last twenty-four hours had been difficult for her mother. It was a long journey, her first time in London with all the hustle and bustle and their lodgings last night had left a lot to be desired. 'It'll move pretty quickly once it gets going. Let's find the end, shall we?'

They walked past the queue and tagged on at the back. A group of women and children soon joined them and they were jostled and pushed forwards. Mary put her arm around Winifred. 'All right?'

'I just want to see my boy.'

'Our visiting order says we've got an hour.'

'What's it like, Mary? Will we be able to see him on our own?'

'No, Mam, we'll be in a room with all the others.'

'All this lot?' Her mother was shocked.

'Yes.' Mary said.

'Do they keep … do they keep the … ones like our Tom … separate?'

'You mean the COs?'

'Yes.'

'No, they lump them all together.'

'And that's all right? I mean the … others are all right with them?'

'Yes.' For once Mary wasn't honest with her mother; she'd told no one about her first visit to Tom all that time ago.

She remembered the feeling of being completely overwhelmed by the place, the incessant noise, the smells, the crowds and being knocked from side to side by people pushing past her as she scanned the visiting room, looking for her brother.

'Come on, ducks, out the way,' a man said, giving her a sly pinch on her bottom. 'What's up? Can't find who you've come to see?'

'Happen he's escaped,' someone else joked, followed by another voice, 'Fat bloody chance, we'll be lucky to get out, never mind them.' The trickle of laughter flowed around Mary as she searched the room for Tom. Her glance passed over him twice before she realised it was him.

She sat down slowly unable to take her eyes away from his face; his eyes were dull slits in the swollen bruised flesh that spread across his face from cheekbone to eyebrow like raw liver. Mary covered her mouth with her palm. 'Oh my God, Tom, what happened?'

When he spoke, a cut in his lower lip split open and seeped blood. He licked it. 'You don't need to know, Sis,' he said.

Mary was aware that some of the men at the tables around them were watching. One, a thickset young man with a red face and small eyes, waggled his finger in an obscene gesture at her. She flushed and turned away. 'Who did it?' she asked.

'Take your pick,' Tom said, 'but don't worry, I'll be ready next time.'

'Report whoever did it,' she demanded.

'Who too?'

And then she understood. She stared at the warder who'd smiled at her at the door; he wasn't smiling now.

'You mean ...'

He bent his head towards the table. 'Some of them are worse than the prisoners,' he said, 'and we have the lot in here: murderers, thieves, gangsters, black market runners.' He rubbed his face over the backs of his hands. Mary heard someone snigger. 'I was talking to one of the other COs about how we feel ... we were overheard ... it's not encouraged.'

She reached across the table.

'No touching.' The shout made her jump.

'I've learned my lesson,' Tom said.

'Yes.' Mary said again, 'the others are all right with him.'

122

They moved forward. 'What about these potato cakes I've made. Will they let us take them in?'

'Well, I've brought stuff before and they've let me.' Mary leant towards her. 'It's OK. Tom will be over the moon to see you.'

Winifred lowered her head, took a deep breath and tried to smile as they stepped through the small entrance in one of the huge doors.

Inside the prison they were led through the narrow corridors by three wardens to the visiting room. Mary wrinkled her nose; every time she visited this place she was left with the memory of this smell, of sourness, stale sweat, rancid food and cigarettes. Winifred glanced at her, an expression of disgust on her face. 'My God.'

'Shush.' Mary looked across the room and pushed her mother's elbow. See … Tom, he's there.'

'Where? Where? Oh dear God.' Winifred faltered.

Mary gave her a small shove in the back. '*Smile*, Mam.'

Her mother smiled. She moved slowly towards the table where Tom waited. This time Iori wasn't by his side; it was another prisoner, who was already quarrelling with his visitor, a weary-looking old man. Mary and Winifred sat at the opposite end. Without looking at them, the old man shifted his chair sideways to make room.

'Son.' Winifred's voice was weak. She put her hand on the surface of the table as though she would try to reach out to him. 'Son.' Her fingertips rubbed at the rough wood.

'Stupid bastard, I asked you for cigarettes,' the other prisoner shouted.

Winifred glanced at the old man, at Mary, at Tom. She opened her mouth but no sound came out.

'No Iori today?' Mary raised her voice.

'No, he's … he's not well.'

'Oh. How are you Tom?'

A shadow crossed his face. Mary saw the bleakness in his eyes. She smiled, encouraging him to talk, afraid of what he would say.

Winifred blew her nose. 'I didn't realise how thin he'd be … that uniform … nothing fitted him … his trousers … halfway up his legs … his sleeves. Did you see how dirty, how filthy that man next to him was?' Her voice rose in a wail. 'How grubby most of them were?'

'Not Tom, though.' Mary took out her own handkerchief and wiped the tears that traced the folds of her mother's cheeks.

'Oh, Mary, what a horrible … That stink was worse than next door's lavvy. He shouldn't be in that awful place.'

Mary helped her mother put on her coat. She was angry with herself; she shouldn't have insisted her mother should come with her.

'I didn't think I'd ever say this but I wish to God I'd never come now,' her mother said. 'But I'll tell you something else and all. I'll never let on to that old bugger at home. I wouldn't give him the satisfaction.' She pulled a handkerchief from her coat pocket and blew her nose. She set off walking. 'Tom wouldn't be there if they'd given him a proper choice of a job,' she said. 'He wouldn't have minded going down the mines. He'd have done that. It would have been better all round. Patrick could have gone into his precious army and Tom would be the one coming home every day.' She stopped and looked in horror at

Mary. 'I didn't mean that. I didn't ...'

'I know,' Mary said. She caught up with Winifred and took hold of her arm. 'I know.' She turned her mother around. 'We're going in the wrong direction. The station's over that way. If we can, we'll find somewhere to stay nearby so we won't have so far to walk in the morning.' She looked anxiously at her mother. 'OK?'

'As long as it's clean, Mary.' Winifred shuddered. 'What am I saying? I don't think I'll ever feel clean again.' She stopped walking and put her hat on. 'Mind, Tom fair bucked up when he was telling us about the chats he has with his friend; that Iori, didn't he,' she said, jamming the hatpin firmly into her hair.

Chapter 14

June 1944

'Oh come on, I've hardly seen you outside of work for weeks.' Jean shook Mary's arm. They watched the bus rattle away. 'You haven't told me yet how your visit to Tom went last week.'

'I'd rather forget it. It was awful. Mam was so upset and by the time we got home she was out on her feet. I feel bad I persuaded her to go.

'You didn't make her go, She wanted to see Tom, you know she did. You said your father was stopping her.

'I know but ...'

'It was her choice, Mary, just as it was Tom's choice to do what he did; he wouldn't be in prison if ...'

'If what?' The skin on Mary's neck started to prickle.

She heard the bus brake on the corner of Shaw Street and Bridge Terrace, saw an old man struggle to plant his walking stick on the pavement and step on the platform at the back. 'If what, Jean? His choice? Hell's bells, I can tell who've you've been listening to.'

'It's just that I can understand in a way how your dad … and Patrick … feel about what Tom did.'

Mary glared at her. 'So it's Tom's own fault he's being treated like an animal?'

'I'm not saying they're right, just that I understand how they feel,' Jean spoke hastily. 'It's like I said to Patrick, we can all have different ideas about things.'

'And I'm sure my brother agreed,' Mary said. 'After all, he's so tolerant.'

'Sorry, that came out all wrong. Forget I said anything.' Jean linked her arm through Mary's.

'Just promise not to discuss Tom with Patrick again. He's always been jealous of Tom and I'd hate to think it would spoil things between me and you.'

'I promise, honest.' Jean lifted her hand in a Girl Guide gesture. 'Now, a girl's night in, hmmm? Just us?' She squeezed Mary's arm. 'You can give Frank a miss for one night, can't you? Like I said to Patrick, surely you don't have to see Frank every day do you, not every day?'

There she goes again. Mary took a long breath. 'It's a shame you and my brother don't have anything else to talk about other than the rest of us.' Jean's reliance on Patrick's opinion aggravated her, especially when it was about her and Frank. Even more so because she knew that, in this, they were right. Although initially flattered by Frank's insistence that they met at least once a day, she had begun to feel stifled, swept along at a hectic pace that she had no control over. 'Anyway you're a fine one to talk. We don't see Patrick at our house from one day to the next, he's always with you.'

They walked the few yards to the end of Moss Terrace. 'Please Mary,' Jean pleaded.

'All right, all right, I'll tell Frank I can't see him tonight.' He'd sulk but so what? 'Anyway, I could do with a break from men. Doctor Pensch really got on my nerves today, dithering about on the ward today; he's so slow.'

'At least he's pleasant enough, not like Schormann. Now he *is* a right pain,' Jean said. 'He's too big for his boots and I don't think he's ever said more than two words to me on any shift.'

Patrick's influence again. Mary kept her thoughts to herself. 'The other nurses seem to get on with him,' she said.

'Well, not me.' Jean looked sideways at Mary. 'What are you thinking?'

'Nothing really.' She wasn't about to tell her friend how the more she worked with the younger doctor the more she respected – no, she corrected herself, the more she liked him. Nor that in her mind she now thought of him as Peter.

And it was especially important that Jean had no idea that Mary believed her feelings to be reciprocated.

She thought back to the first time she'd realised that.

She was standing outside the hospital when Peter arrived to make a routine check on one of the patients. The outline of the mill and the countryside in the background were dense black shapes against a sky pierced by millions of stars and holding the slightest sliver of a moon. She felt awkward being alone with him. She tilted her chin upwards to indicate the sky. 'Beautiful night,' she said. 'So clear … the stars … so brilliant … Makes you forget all your troubles.'

'I can never forget,' he said in a low voice.

'No, of course not: I'm sorry, Doctor.'

'I hate this war. I hate what it makes of men.'

'Yes.' There was nothing else to say. A sentry strolled past on the other side of the fence. It was Quarmby, one of Frank's mates. When he was directly opposite them, she heard him clear his throat and spit. Then he walked on.

'It seemed …' She stopped and then said, 'It was as if he did that on purpose.''

'Ja, soll der Teufel ihn holen! It happens often.'

'To all the men or just to you?'

'Mainly at me, I think.' He paced back and forth, taking short edgy drags on his cigarette.

'I must go in,' Mary said. 'I only came out for fresh air.'

He stopped moving. 'I will come too. May I finish this before we go inside?'

She glanced towards the compound; the two guards were talking. 'I think I should go.' She could see the pale blur of one of the men's faces turned towards them. She shivered. 'Has something happened, Doctor?'

He blew out a puff of smoke. 'You know I am the *Lagerführer*?'

'Yes, of course.'

'I try to make sure the men follow all Camp rules.'

'Yes.'

'I took this role because I thought I could help make things better, easier for the men. But some of the guards do not want things to be easy for the prisoners. They make sure there is always trouble. I have complained to the Commandant.'

Mary remembered something Frank had said once; she wouldn't put anything past some of the sentries. 'It must make things difficult in there.'

'Yes, since then ...' He wafted a hand towards the guard who was now retracing his steps. 'That ... and worse.

'Sometimes, a lot of the time, I am sorry I became involved in this war, it is not right and I could have avoided ... this.' He gestured towards the compound. 'I could have continued to work at the hospital in Berlin where I had qualified, but my father thought I had a duty to my country to use my skills to help those who fight.' He dropped his voice even lower. 'I would be beaten by the Nazis amongst us if they heard what I am saying now.' Peter carefully squeezed the end of the cigarette and dropped it into his jacket pocket.

A ginger cat slunk past, low to the ground. Within seconds another followed, growling, and vanished towards the side gate in the security fence a few yards away. Almost immediately there were piercing shrieks and yowls, followed by a man shouting and the clatter of something being thrown. The cats flashed past again. Peter ignored them.

'I would even have preferred to stay at home,' he continued, 'helping my father and brothers on the farm but that was not allowed. So I was sent to use my skills where it was thought they would be most needed.' He raised his chin. 'And I am proud to say that I saved many lives throughout the years. I gained much respect. I was valued by the army.' He straightened his shoulders.

'That all changed when I was captured. In El Alamein. The soldiers, they were ... *schweine* ... pigs. They took no notice of my Red Cross status. I became officially a prisoner of war. Even though I was vigorous in my protestations that I was the medical officer, I was still treated like the others. I still had to put up my hands. They marched us to an assembly point. All our personal possessions were taken from us,' he pushed his sleeve up, 'including my watch. We were interrogated. Oh!' Mary watched the muscles in his jaw move. *'Ich war böse*, I was angry, furious, they would not believe who ... what I was. We were all locked in a building for days. Then we were brought to Britain. I have been moved from one camp to another with no recognition of my status. Here, at last, I am recognised as a doctor. I have the so-called status of *Lägerfuhrer* but even so, some of the guards ...' He faced her, taking in an unsteady breath. 'With some of the guards, *es gibt keine Rücksicht*, there is no respect.'

'You have my respect and that of my nurses: you are highly esteemed on the ward.' Even as she spoke Mary was aware of the recklessness of her words. And that they were standing too close. She stepped back.

He acted as though he hadn't noticed. 'And for that I am grateful, especially after I was so ill-mannered the first time we met.'

Mary dipped her head. 'That's forgotten now.'

'Even so...'

She cut in, 'You should tell the Commandant what has happened since your complaint.'

'It would cause more trouble, make matters worse. Difficult perhaps even for you.'

'Me? Why me?' Mary stopped abruptly, remembering

Quarmby. Peter Schormann was talking about Frank. How did he know about her and Frank? She touched her throat, feeling the heat against her fingers. The nurses were always gossiping on the ward, he'd probably heard about them through that. 'Whoever is the instigator, Doctor … whoever is causing the problems that make it difficult for you to carry out your role here you should report them. Whoever it is.'

And whatever the consequences, she thought.

'Well?' Jean asked.

'Sorry?'

'I think I've been talking to myself for the last five minutes. Are you coming round tonight or what?'

'I was just thinking what to tell Frank.'

'Just tell him you want a night off.'

'Right,' Mary paused. 'Yes, you're right. I'll do that.'

'Good. Seven o'clock and don't be late.'

Chapter 15

By seven o'clock Mary was glad to get out of the house. Almost every day over the two months since the Union had given in to Government pressure forcing the strikers to return to work, Patrick and Bill had quarrelled. Tonight had been no exception.

'Hey, wait for me,' Patrick shouted. He caught up with her as she crossed to walk along Shaw Road, his shoulders hunched with tension.

'I was supposed to meet Frank at eight but I'm going to Jean's instead,' Mary said. Will you be seeing him?'

'Should do.' Patrick shrugged. 'He'll be in The Crown. Usually is at this time of night, if he's not working'

'Can you let him know?'

'Aye, OK.'

'I do wish you wouldn't get Dad going like that, especially when we're leaving Mam on her own with him. You know he's been spoiling for a fight since she went with me to see Tom.'

'Yeah, OK, he just gets me so wound up, crowing about how we lost the strike. We fought so bloody hard to get a decent wage and now they've beaten us. The men should never have given in so easily.'

'What set him off tonight?'

'We've got another meeting before we go on shift now. He has to stick his two penn'orth in, telling me what to say.' He took a last pull on his cigarette and gave a snort of laughter. 'Anyway, you don't need to worry about Mam, he won't be clouting her again; you put the fear of God in him last time. Besides he's on duty tonight, I heard him talking to Ellen before she went out.' He hunched his shoulders higher. 'But I'll tell you this, Mary, I've had enough of him poking his bloody nose in. I'm going to find lodgings somewhere. I can't stand his bloody pick, pick, picking all the soddin' time.' He strode away.

Mary caught her lower lip between her teeth. Here we go again, she thought, muggins here will be left to pick up the pieces. She turned into Moss Terrace. Jean was already on the doorstep, waiting for her.

Chapter 16

Jean's news that she was pregnant hadn't been too much of as surprise but Mary worried about the repercussions on the family. Her father would go mad when he found out; he really would lay into Patrick this time, perhaps even the strike would pale into insignificance compared with the prospect of an illegitimate baby. One thing was sure, if her friend's belief in Patrick was right and he did marry her there'd be less money coming into the house and that would be the first thing her father would cotton on to. Either way he'd be unbearable. She curled her arm above her head and closed her eyes. She'd just have to give Mam more of her own wages. She sighed loudly.

'What?' Ellen lifted her head off the pillow, her voice petulant.

'Sorry.'

Ellen turned over and bounced to the edge of the bed, dragging the covers with her.

'How long are you going to keep this up?' Mary said. 'It's been weeks since that business in The Crown and, except for when we got the news about Ted you've barely spoken a word to me since.'

'Just shut up.'

Mary heard the quiver in Ellen's voice. She knew her sister still visited Mrs Booth but whether it was still from guilt or genuine compassion she wasn't sure. 'Oh grow up, you're like a big kid. I'd rather we were friends, Ellen, but if you want to carry on sulking you can; I've other things to worry about.'

Ellen grunted.

'Things that will affect you as well.'

'What?'

That got her interest. 'It's time you listened to a few home truths, my girl. If Frank and me hadn't brought you home that night you could be in the same boat now as …'

'As?' Ellen turned her head, now wide-awake.

'Jean. She's over two months pregnant.'

'Who by?' Ellen propped herself on her elbow.

'Well, who do you think?' Even as she spoke Mary knew Ellen's question was genuine. 'If you opened your eyes as to what's happening in this house, you'd know.'

'Patrick?'

'Patrick.'

'My God!'

'And it'll be you next, if you're not careful.'

'I won't be that stupid.'

'You think you're so clever, Ellen, but you're not.'

'If something did happen Al would look after me.'

'And pigs might fly,' Mary said. 'You wouldn't see him for dust.' She turned her face towards Ellen. 'You're such a selfish little cow. This isn't about you. Just for once, think about someone else. Think about it. They'll get married. It'll be one less wage in the house with Patrick gone. There'll be ructions, Dad'll hit the roof, Mam will cop it.'

'Not my problem.' Ellen lay down again.

'You're unbelievable.' Mary leaned low over her. 'And it will be; you're going to have to stump up more of your wages.'

'Not on your life.'

'I could make it your problem. You do know that, don't you? Who do you think covers up for you when you don't bother to come home at night. Mam and me, that's who. What do you think Dad would say if he knew what his precious little girl gets up to? Do you know what he would *do* if he heard you were messing around with an American? You've heard him often enough once he gets on his bandwagon, going on about the "bloody Yanks", he doesn't think they should even be here.' Ellen burrowed deeper under the covers. Mary pulled them off her, relentless. 'You know that any mention of them he goes berserk, you know he thinks they not interested in helping us; that they only got into the war because of Pearl Harbour. So what do you think he'd do if he found out about you, eh, on top of Patrick's news?' She sat back, pulling her share of the eiderdown up to her chin. 'He'd take his strap to you. And for once in your life, I'd let you deal with your own mess.'

Ellen bounced over to her own side of the bed.

Mary closed her eyes, leaning against the iron bedstead, thinking about Jean earlier in the evening. Mam will go spare when she finds out, she thought. On the other hand Mrs Winterbottom will be in clover. And it hadn't taken Jean's mother long to realise it.

'I can't believe Mother.' Jean perched on the end of her bed after hustling Mary upstairs as soon as she arrived. 'She's actually excited about it, even planning the wedding. She says there's no point in putting it off.'

'Does Patrick know?'

'Not yet. I'm going to tell him tomorrow.' Jean was confident. 'He did say ... when we first, you know ... he did say he'd look after me, so I'm sure everything will be all right. And Mother says she'll buy us a double bed as a wedding present. And we can have the front room to ourselves. She's being so good about it all. I can't believe it!'

Mary could; Patrick would be both an added income and a useful source for extra rations.

'I'm meeting him after work tomorrow. I'll tell him then. It'll be fine,' Jean said. 'Listen, I know you're not too keen on dancing but let's all go to the Palais tomorrow.' She giggled. 'I'll be too fat to move soon, so I'm going to make the most of it.'

There was no doubt in Jean's mind that Patrick would accept what had happened. For a moment Mary felt a stab of envy; they'd be planning their future while she'd be still stuck in Henshaw Street. What chance did she have as long as Mam relied on her wages?

Chapter 17

Jean was right. Patrick seemed to be floating when he and Mary walked to Jean's house, the following evening. 'I suppose I knew it might happen but I was a bit dropped on when Jean told me. Once upon a time I would've gone bloody mad but, to tell the truth, I'm over the moon. I think we should get wed as soon as we can.'

'When will you tell Mam and Dad?'

From his short and determined answer, 'When it's all sorted,' Mary knew that her brother had already dismissed their home and was looking forward to married life.

At least there'd be no more rows between him and her father.

They were late meeting Frank. Mary quickened her footsteps. 'How we're doing for time?' she said.

'We set off soon enough.' Patrick fumbled around in the pocket of his waistcoat for his watch. 'We're OK.'

They quickened their steps. Even so, Jean was waiting for them by the time they got to the end of her street. 'Hurry up, we'll miss the bus,' she chided, linking Patrick's arm and giving him a kiss.

'She's a right bossy boots.' He grumbled, but squeezed her arms and began to sing, 'Oh, Merzy Doats and Dozey Doats and Little Lambs Eat Ivy...' His voice was muffled when Jean clapped her hand over his mouth.

'What's he like?' she laughed.

The bus passed them.

Mary groaned. 'Frank'll hit the roof; he hates it when I'm late.'

'Tough,' Jean and Patrick chorused in the same breath.

Chapter 18

The dance hall was packed and the loud music made talking impossible. Blue cigarette smoke coiled upwards. The huge glass globe hanging high above on the ceiling twisted and turned, casting a kaleidoscope of coloured rays and mirroring the crowds below. Patrick led Jean on to the dance floor as soon as they'd hung up their coats. Mary and Frank leant against the wall. She knew he was still simmering with resentment at being kept waiting at the bus stop.

'Can't do these fast dances,' he shouted, 'my leg.' He glared at the GI's who made up the bulk of the jivers.

'Don't worry,' Mary mouthed the words and clicked her fingers in time to the Benny Goodman tune. She smiled wryly; *In the Mood* was apt. 'I don't much feel like dancing anyway.' Looking around she saw some empty seats and, touching his arm, pointed to them just as the jive session finished. 'Let's talk.'

He shook his head and gestured in the direction of the stage; the female vocalist was beginning a husky rendition of *We'll Meet Again.* 'Slow waltz, come on.' Grabbing Mary's hand he pushed his way through the group of girls and American soldiers who were drifting back to their tables. Shouldering into one of the men, he tripped and almost fell. Someone laughed.

'Take more water with it next time, fella.' It was Al, Ellen's boyfriend. Mary looked over his shoulder; her sister was standing behind him. Her giggles turned to screams as Frank dived at Al, bunching his fist into the man's face. The force propelled him backwards through the crowd and Frank followed, knocking Ellen over. He dived on top of the American and, lifting him up by the shoulders of his uniform, head-butted him. Blood splattered from Al's nose, covering both men, and in seconds other men appeared from nowhere and joined in.

In the background the singer left the stage and the band struck up a loud version of *Kiss Me Goodnight Sergeant Major.*

'Ellen.' Mary fought her way towards her sister and yanked her to her feet.

'Get that bloody lunatic off Al.' Hopping around on one foot, Ellen took off her shoe and began to hit out at the struggling group of men.

Outside the clang of bells grew closer. 'Police!' In seconds the chaos stopped and the crowd dispersed as quickly as it had formed. Patrick dragged Frank out of the ballroom.

Ellen pushed Mary away. 'Happy now?' She dropped to

her knees at the side of Al. 'You and that bloody lunatic.' She shook her head, almost in tears. 'Always bloody interfering.'

Mary held out her hand. Ellen flicked it away and, with some of Al's friends, lifted him on to a chair. He fell forward, his head between his knees, blood steadily dripping. Ellen knelt by him, dabbing at his face with her handkerchief. 'Just go away Mary. Go on, bugger off.'

Mary picked up her coat and ran out of the ballroom. In the dim foyer Patrick had Frank pinned to the wall. Jean huddled, crying, a few feet away.

'Get him out, Patrick, before the bobbies get here.' Mary gasped for breath. 'Jean, you all right?'

'I just want to go home.'

The clatter of bells rose to a pitch and then faded as an ambulance sped past the building. 'It wasn't the police,' Mary said, 'but let's get out of here.'

'No. Mary. Wait.' Frank tried to push himself off the wall. 'Get off,' he yelled at Patrick. 'Fuck off.'

'Calm down, you mad bugger. What the hell's wrong with you?' Mary's brother held on to him. 'You're going nowhere till you calm down.'

A laughing group of young people, swarming through the doors of the Palais, quietened as they passed. Frank lifted his hands suddenly and knocked Patrick's arms away, gingerly touching the reddening skin around his eye; it was already beginning to close. He turned towards the inner doors to the dance floor and shouted, 'Bloody Yanks. Think they're God's sodding gift to women.'

Mary threw him a look of disgust and led Jean outside. The pavement in front of the Palais was crowded with people, but further away the footpaths in front of the shops were empty.

When Patrick appeared at the side of them she said, 'You look after Jean. I'm catching the next bus.' She looked past him at Frank. 'Just leave me alone.'

'Don't worry, he will,' Patrick said. 'Believe me. Take care, Sis.'

'Thanks, I will.' It was the first brotherly gesture from Patrick for a long time. Mary felt the burn of tears.

'Let me see you home,' Frank said. He was rubbing his knuckles but his deep breathing was steady now.

'She told you to leave her alone.' Patrick barred his way, fingers flat against Frank's chest.

'I'm going home.' She made a sharp movement with her head to emphasise the last word. 'Alone.'

There was a rumble of engine and a double-decker bus loomed out of the shadows and past them. Mary ran after it. When it squealed to a halt a few yards away at the next stop she jumped on to the platform at the back and clung to the rail as it slowly revved up and set off again.

'I'm sorry,' Frank yelled. 'I'll see you tomorrow, yeah?'

Mary sat down on the bench seat just inside the bus. A middle-aged woman was at the other end, clutching a large basket. She crossed thick ankles and grinned, showing large nicotine-stained teeth. 'Had a row with your young man then?' she asked. 'You not speaking to him?' She chewed for a few minutes, pushing a wedge of tobacco around her mouth with her tongue. Her foul breath, even from a few feet away, wafted over Mary. She turned to look out of the back of the bus. Frank was still standing in the middle of the road. The woman coughed; a throaty sound. When she spoke again her voice crackled with thick saliva. 'Well, make the most of it lass, 'cos once he gets that ring on your finger, it'll be him that calls the shots, mark my word. Your life'll never be your own again.' Her laughter ended in a long wheezing breath. 'Nope, you won't be half so clever then.'

Chapter 19

'What the hell was wrong with you last night?' Mary swung her arm out of Frank's grasp. 'Let go, I've got to get to work.' Despite the heat of the midday sun she was cold and she wrapped her cape around her.

'It was your fault.'

'What?' Her mouth opened. 'What?'

'It was your fault,' he repeated. 'You kept me hanging about like an idiot at the bus stop waiting for you and the night before you stood me up for that bloody fat cow of a friend of yours. I don't know who you think you are but I won't be made a fool of.'

He'd turned it all around to her! 'You're mad, Frank.'

A hiss of breath escaped through his tight lips. He grasped her wrist under her cape. 'Don't ever call me mad.'

Mary prised his fingers off her and backed away. Her stomach was churning. 'Leave me alone, Frank, just leave me alone.' She wondered whether to run to Jean's house, it was only a couple of minutes away. Then she remembered it was her day off and would probably still be in bed and there was no way she wanted to see the smug face of Mrs Winterbottom anyway.

'I'm sorry.' Frank was following her along Shaw Street, one hand held out. 'I'm sorry, I didn't mean to hurt you.'

His voice was conciliatory. 'I just get … I don't know … I just get …'

Mary spun round. She felt safer now she'd put some distance between them. 'Mad, Frank, that's what you get, mad. And so, for no rhyme or reason, you decide to beat the living daylights out of someone you don't even know?'

The net curtains in a couple of the houses twitched. A woman came out of her front door and began to clean her living room window with a sheet of screwed up newspaper, her face angled in their direction. Mary cringed from embarrassment, but a part of her was glad people could see them; she felt less vulnerable.

He moved towards her, speaking low through clenched teeth. 'Course I fucking knew him. The bastard made me to do my knee in that night I carried your stupid sister home. Remember?'

For a split second there was a flash of guilt. Mary remembered how he'd struggled that night, but then she squared her shoulders. 'No, no, I'm sorry Frank, you're not shifting the blame on me or on Ellen, not for what you did last night. You said it yourself, you were in a bad temper because I was late and you wanted to take it out on someone. The bloke was the convenient punchbag.' Her chest was tight and she was struggling for breath. 'You were vicious for no real reason.' Images of her mother's face suffering the consequences of her father's frustrations and anger over the years flashed past her; the familiar fear of his raised voice a childhood memory. 'I've lived with one bad-tempered man all my life. I'll not put up with another.' She turned and ran.

Frank took a few paces before his leg gave way and he staggered. He glanced around, made crude two-fingered gestures at the woman cleaning her window. 'Fuck off, you nosy bitch.'

She banged the door after her,

With a faked casual manner he strolled on until he got to the old gas lamp at the end of Moss Terrace and he leaned heavily against it. There was no sign of Mary's cow of a friend. His fingers shook when he took out a Woodbine and it broke, scattering flecks of tobacco over the front of his uniform. He brushed them off with the back of his hand: he couldn't brush away her words.

Much of what had happened in the dance hall was blurred by the familiar uncontrolled fury that often overtook him but he did remember that bloody bastard American laughing at him and he pulled his top lip back from his teeth. 'I'll not let you go, girl, you wait and see,' he muttered, pushing away from the lamppost. He was late for his shift.

Crossing the top of Newroyd Street, Mary saw the usual group of old men on the benches outside The Crown. She shuddered and held her cape closer. I've lived with one bad-tempered man all my life, she said it again to herself, I'll not put up with another.

Chapter 20

They were words she repeated a week later to Frank's brother, George, when he met her at the top of the steps to the canal path. The low sun cast a pearly glow on the oily surface of the water.

'But there's a reason for what he does … how he is.' The man walked alongside her. She would never have guessed they were brothers; he looked nothing like Frank. A pale man with curly ginger hair, he was almost a head shorter than her. Only his grey eyes, now fixed on hers, were the same.

Unease made her voice harsh. 'Look, I'm sorry, I don't know you, it's been a long day and I'm tired. Why should I believe anything you say? If he thinks he can send you to explain away what he did, he's mistaken.'

An old man stood in their way, feeding three ducks that darted around, snatching noisily at small chunks of bread. He grinned toothlessly at Mary. She smiled at him and quickened her step to get in front of Frank's brother. They walked in single file until they'd passed him.

'Surprised they're not on somebody's table by now,' George joked, catching up with Mary.

Mary tried to shut off from him.

'Frank doesn't know I'm here. I've been waiting outside the hospital for ages. I asked one of the guards to point you out. The least you can do is to listen to what I have to say.'

'Why? I don't owe you or him anything.'

He offered her a cigarette; his fingers were thick, stubby. When she shook her head he lit his as he carried on walking. Like her dad, like many short men, he had a bouncy arrogant walk; her dislike of him was instinctive. 'I've been home for over a week now and I knew right away there was something wrong. He only told me about you last night and … well … me and him are quite close. When we were kids it were only us; we didn't need anybody else, especially after our dad left.'

Mary wished he would shut up. He had nothing to say that she wanted to hear.

'He's proud, you must know by now. He doesn't say much about what happened to him in France?'

'He's actually told me quite a lot,' she said. Too much for his own good sometimes, she thought, he'd revealed a lot about his bigotry.

'But not this, I bet.' He sucked hard on his cigarette. 'Ever since he got back from France, every now and then, it's like he's going to explode. He can't stop it.'

Mary made a small clicking noise on the back of her teeth with her tongue. She'd heard the same excuse from her father when he was drunk and maudlin. He thought it excused the bouts of temper, the brutality.

'He was ill when he first came home.'

'I know that.'

'No,' George waved a dismissive hand. 'I mean really ill.' Tapping his head he said, 'He cracked up. Our Ma says it used to be called "shell shock"; there's a fancy name for it now.' He had to take quicker steps to keep up with her. 'He always says he doesn't remember much about being in hospital, only bad headaches and pains in his leg, but I think he remembers a lot more and won't admit it.' His cigarette gave a slight hiss as it hit the surface of the canal. 'And then, when he actually went home … they were in Rhyl then … Ma says he had nightmares. She had a right time with him.'

Mary stopped by the steps leading up to Skirm. 'This is where I go up to the road.' She held on to the rail, still warm from the day's sun. 'It makes no difference.' She glanced towards the top of the steps. 'I have to get home.'

'I might as well come with you as far as The Crown; I'm supposed to be meeting him there.' He batted at a swarm of midges. 'God, let's get away from this lot, shall we? We'll be bitten to death.'

They crossed the bridge. 'Our Frank means a lot to me, Mary, and I know how much he thinks of you. So it's up to me to make sure you know all the facts; why he gets bad moods, why he's so short tempered, the nightmares … before you decide to get rid of him.'

'I've not changed my mind. I've told him there's no point in carrying on.'

'But he's getting better all the time. Honest.' George rubbed the side of his nose with his forefinger. 'He won't tell you this but he still sees the doc and *he* says it's just a matter of time.'

Oh hell, Mary hesitated, her innate sense of fairness seesawing with the urge to escape from this man. 'These nightmares?'

'They've always been the same. His mate, Arnold, was killed in that first spat they were involved in. When Frank was in hospital, he used to say he saw him. He said Arnold would sit at the end of his bed and smile at him, that he had a little blue hole in his neck. And then Arnold would laugh and get up and walk away and Frank would see that the back of his head was blown off.' Mary closed her eyes briefly. George nodded. 'When he came home the nightmares carried on. Don't happen as often these days, but I think he still dreads them. And I think he's ashamed of them, like it makes him weak or something. He doesn't want anybody thinking he's soft.' George walked alongside her as far as the churchyard wall and stopped. 'So there you are. Ma says he's been a lot more settled since you started going out with him. She says she'd like to meet you.' George blew out a small sigh. 'To thank you for making our kid easier to live with.'

146

Mary moved her head, she could feel herself being sucked back in. 'No, she said, side-stepping him, 'no, I'm sorry, I don't think I can.' She walked away. 'Like I said to him, I live with one moody bloke, I don't need another.'

She slowed down when she got to the lake. The water was calm and the boats were still. She sat down on one of the benches, wrapping her cape around her. There was no one else about and the only sounds were the occasional engines of vehicles on the road and the mutterings of birds settling down for the night. The light was fading fast and shadows darkened under the trees around her. Mary shivered; the more she thought about what Frank's brother had told her, the more uneasy she became.

Chapter 21

July 1944

'What did Tom say about me and Patrick getting married?' The sterilizing room wasn't hot but Jean was sweating as she stood at the sink scrubbing the dissection forceps. .

'Leave those,' Mary said. 'Have a rest. I'll do them in a minute.'

'No, you've got enough to do and I want to get these finished before we go on our break. Go on, tell me what Tom said.' Jean rinsed the instruments under running cold water.

'He was pleased for you, said he always knew you were sweet on Patrick.' Mary pulled the towel off the rail.

'Was I that obvious?' Jean laughed, placing the forceps

into the sterilizer.

'Of course you were,' Mary grinned, 'but not to Patrick, so that's OK.' She dried her hands.

In fact Tom was worried. Despite her occasional brusqueness, Mary knew he liked her friend who'd always been pleasant with him even after knowing he was a CO.

'Has she seen his nasty side yet?' he said.

Mary lowered her voice. 'Doubt it but I think she'll be able to handle him. Anyway, it's a bit late for that now. She's almost four months.'

'Do they know at the hospital yet?'

'No, Jean says she always knew there'd be a perk to being plump.' Mary gave him a small grin. 'She's not really showing yet. She's hoping she'll be able to carry on working until after they're married.'

'Well, he should be able to keep them anyway with all his contacts.'

Mary pulled a face. 'You're right.' She directed a look at Iori and Gwyneth. 'Has Iori been in the wars again?' she whispered. His left eye was closed and there was a large lump on his forehead.

Tom's face closed. 'Bastards,' was all he said.

Mary knew him enough to leave it at that. She went back to talking about Jean and Patrick's wedding. 'It's all planned … courtesy of Jean's mother.'

'Do they know at home?'

'Mam does now. Dad's too busy with his Home Guard to see beyond the end of his nose.'

'Has he been behaving?'

'Yes. He avoids me though.' She spread her fingers on the scored surface of the table. 'Suits me down to the ground.'

'Be careful, Mary. He'll go mad.' Mary flinched at his words. 'Or at the least he'll have a good rant when he does find out and you can bet, if he can't get at Patrick, he'll take it out on Mam or you.'

'Well it won't be Ellen, that's for sure.' Her voice was grim.

'How are things between the two of you?'

'We don't talk much these days. She's still holding a grudge because of what Frank and I did that day she got drunk.'

'What's happening with you and him?'

'Frank? I haven't seen him lately.' She traced one of the scratches with her nail. Out of the corner of her eye, she saw him studying her but didn't look up.

Tom breathed in and leant back in his chair. He ran the palms of his large hands along the edge of the table. 'I had a letter from Ellen,' he said.

'Really? Well, that must be a first.' Mary felt a twinge of resentment

'Um, she feels bad about Ted. I wrote and told her there's nothing she can do now. Did you know she goes to see his mother a lot?'

'I knew she went sometimes.'

'Yeah.'

'Well if it makes her feel better ...'

Later, walking towards the railway station, Mary wondered if anyone else had notice how close Tom and Iori were sitting, how they looked at each other. She didn't care – it was good that Tom had someone in that place – but she prayed they would be careful.

Mary was conscious she was frowning; she draped the

towel over the rail.

'Mary? I said is there anything else to go in?'

'No.' Mary checked the work surfaces. 'No, that's the lot. We'll have our break now. They'll be ready to be dried when we get back.'

'Great, we'll be able to catch up on all the gossip. It seems ages since we had a proper natter.' They hadn't spent much time together since that night at the Palais.

Mary signalled to the nurse sitting at the ward desk. 'Five minutes? I'm in the rest room if the doctor wants to start his rounds before I get back.' The woman nodded.

'I'll get the boiler going,' Jean said. They crossed the corridor to the rest room. 'There's something I've been meaning to ask you.' Jean was still rubbing the base of her spine. 'I want you to be my witness when we get married.'

'Me?'

'Well, I wouldn't want anybody else, would I?'

'I'd love to.' Mary hugged her, feeling Jean stiffen. 'You OK?'

'Yes, of course.'

'You look all hot and bothered.' She held her at arms' length. 'So sit down while I make the tea.'

Jean unfolded the card table propped up against the wall and dragged two chairs up to it. She squeezed past Mary and sat down. 'I could do with a rest,' she admitted. 'I'm tired today.'

'Well, take it easy.' Mary opened the cupboard on the wall and searched the shelves. 'Who's Patrick asking to be his witness.'

'One of his union mates, Jack Radcliffe?'

'Nope, don't know him,' Mary said. 'Mind you; I don't know many of his friends these days.'

'He seems all right. I've seen him once or twice.'

'Good.' Mary brought out two cups. She kept her voice offhand. 'Will Frank be there?'

'Not if I've anything to do with it.' Jean scowled. 'Have you seen him since that night?'

'No, I'm avoiding him; the extra night shifts have been useful.' Mary opened a container of dried milk with her name on it and shook it. 'Do you know, this is nearly empty again,' she said. 'I swear someone's dipping in.' She rattled the spoon around and broke up a few lumps of the powder in the bottom of the box. 'His brother, George, collared me the other day though.' She kept her voice neutral. 'He told me Frank had some kind of breakdown after Dunkirk.'

'Did you believe him?' Jean shifted in her chair.

'Well, it answers a lot of questions, doesn't it?'

'Perhaps.' Jean spoke in short breaths.

The boiler hissed and spat steam. Mary rinsed the cups in the rush of water from the tap. 'These cups never seem clean.' She spoke over the noise. 'I'm not sure he'd listen to what I have to say anyway. It's over.' She startled herself by actually saying the words out loud. The boiler automatically stopped and Mary shut off the tap. In the silence that followed she heard the gasp and whirled round. 'Jean?'

She was clutching the edge of the table, her eyes closed. 'Pain … a pain …' Jean's skin was sickly yellow. She slumped sideways.

Mary dropped the cups and lunged, catching Jean before she fell. Grabbing the towel she put it under Jean's head and lowered her to the floor. 'I'll get Matron.'

'No.' Jean grabbed her hand. 'No, you can't, she'll see

... she'll know. I'll get the sack.' She drew her knees up and rocked, taking deep gulps of air. 'I'll be ...'

Mary flung the door open. Across the corridor Peter was talking to Matron in her office. 'Doctor! Matron!'

He was on his feet before Matron looked up.

'It's Jean, Nurse Winterbottom. I think she's losing her baby.'

'What?' Matron stood up, holding on to her desk. 'What are you saying, Sister?'

Mary ignored her. 'Doctor?'

The doctor bent over Jean and gently lifted her.

Matron's lips were compressed so tightly there was a white line around them, but after a perfunctory glare the scene she recovered her composure and took over. 'This way, Doctor Schormann, this one.' She led the way to an empty side ward.

Peter pushed past her and lay Jean on to the bed. She curled up, sweat beading her top lip with each spasm of pain.

'I'll get some clean sheets. You stay with her, Sister, I'll get cover for your ward.' Matron hesitated at the door. 'I will only be a moment, Doctor Schormann.'

It was as though he hadn't heard her. He talked to Jean. 'You will be fine, Nurse ...?'

He looked up at Mary.

'Jean,' Mary said, 'it's Jean.' She held her friend's hand. 'She's about seventeen weeks now.'

'Thank you.' He bent over the girl, his hand on her shoulder. 'Jean, listen to me.'

She jerked her head from side to side. 'It hurts.' She began a high keening wail, her pale face now bathed in sweat.

'I know it does … listen, please … I need to see … *Ich werde sanft sein* … I will be gentle, *ja*?' He signalled to Mary. 'Sister, her clothes?'

Mary worked from the other side of the bed, unbuttoning the neck of her uniform. He talked as he washed his hands with Dettol solution. 'We lift her legs,' he said. 'Put the pillows under, *ja*?' He looked at Mary. '*Ja*?'

'Yes.' Mary pushed the skirt of Jean's uniform as far as her waist and eased her camiknickers down her legs.

Jean made a small noise of protest.

'No time for modesty, love,' Mary said. 'Like the doctor says, we need to see what's happening.' She caught his eye. 'Ready,' she said.

He made a slight movement with his head and went to stand at the other side of the bed. 'OK now, Jean, we will move you. We will be gentle,' he said again. Mary waited until he threaded his arm under Jean's knees and elevated them before pushing the pillows under Jean's thighs. Her fingers touched the back of his hand. She froze, unable to prevent the sharp catch in her breath, and darted a look at him. His eyelids flickered; she knew he'd felt it too.

Then she saw the dark red blood seeped from under Jean's thighs and on to the white cover and the moment passed.

'We need to stop the bleeding,' he said. 'Jean, take the long breaths, try to relax.'

'No.' She arched her back and gave one long scream.

'Oh my God,' Mary whispered. The flow of blood increased mixed with large clots of tissue and then a small creamy coloured sac of membrane. 'Oh my God.'

Matron reappeared carrying an armful of sheets and

towels. 'Doctor?'

He shook his head.

'I need to get back on the ward, it's chaos out there.' Matron thrust the bundle at Mary and left, closing the door behind her.

Always careful to cover up scandal, Mary thought bitterly. She slid a towel under Jean's thighs and went to the washbasin to fill a bowl with warm water. She felt Peter's hand briefly on her shoulder before he turned back to Jean.

'No!' Jean cried, tilting her head to look at Mary. 'No,' she said softly.

'I'm sorry,' Mary whispered. She put the bowl down and dropped to her knees by the side of the bed, pressing her cheek against her friend's.

Jean turned away.

Chapter 22

'I'm sorry, Patrick.' Jean's voice was husky, her eyelids swollen. She plucked at the eiderdown.

Mary touched Patrick's arm. 'I'll be downstairs.'

Patrick's eyes told her nothing. He stroked Jean's cheek. 'Hush. It'll be OK.'

'We don't have to get married now. We don't. I don't want you to feel you have to.'

'I don't want to hear any more of that rubbish. We'll just alter the date with that Registrar. You've just got to get back on your feet.'

Mary hesitated, hearing the anguish in his voice. Reluctant to leave, she waited, willing Jean to say something. The bedroom window was open, but no fresh air moved the closed curtains. Dust motes floated in the chink of sunlight on the ceiling. A bus passed the end of the street and changed gears noisily. Mary could hear Mrs Winterbottom sweeping the pavement outside the house, banging the brush head hard against the front step. Jean started to cry, loud gasping sobs. Mary closed the door, pinching the bridge of her nose; she was weary. The guilt she felt for the quarrel between them the week before Jean lost the baby had haunted her for the last two days.

When Patrick came downstairs, she and Jean's mother were sitting in the kitchen with the back door open. His eyes were red. Mary lifted a hand towards him and then, when he ignored her, let it drop. 'We're still getting wed,' he said.

Jean's mother covered her face with her hands. 'Thank you, Patrick,' she said. 'Oh thank you.'

Chapter 23

Mary was in her bedroom when the back door opened. Running down the stairs, her uniform over her arm, she called out, 'Mam?'

It wasn't her mother, it was Frank, sitting in her father's armchair, feet up on the fender in front of the fireplace. Not taking his eyes off her, he finished his cigarette and standing up, threw it onto the bare grate. 'Thought I'd just drop in,' he said, 'seeing as how we've not seen much of one another lately; more than made up for it now though.' He smiled, slowly looking her up and down.

Mary could feel the heat rise from her neck. 'What are

you doing here, Frank? I'm due at the hospital in an hour.' She held her dress in front of her.

'Plenty of time then, more than enough for a ... chat.' Frank crossed the kitchen, pulled her uniform out of her hands and dropped it on one of the chairs round the table. He leant over her, his hand moving from her buttock to her thigh, his fingers tracing the top of her stocking through the thin material of her petticoat.

Mary could smell the beer on him. She pushed both hands against his chest. 'Stop it Frank.' Panic made her voice shake. 'I don't want ...'

He shoved her away. 'Always you; always what you want.' He leant against the fireplace, chewing on his thumbnail.

'I'd like you to get out. Now!'

'Not yet. Not 'til I know where I stand with you.'

'I told you. I told your brother. Look, I don't know how else to say it.' She picked up her uniform, her hands shaking. 'We can't ... I can't ... I can't think about anything else but my job at the moment.'

'Your job! Nursing bloody Huns?' Frank hit the mantelpiece with the flat of his hand. Mary moved to the other side of the table. 'There were no bloody German nurses to look after us in Arras. I was in agony and there was no bloody nurse to mollycoddle me.' He slapped his palm down again.

'Stop it, Frank. What I do ... the nursing ... is important to me. I'm needed and I trained hard for years.' Mary fastened the buttons down the front of her dress and picked up the clips that had fallen out of her hair onto the floor. Pinning them into place she said, 'While this war continues I want to do my bit. It's the only thing I can think of at the moment.' She held on to the back of one of the kitchen chair. 'Surely you understand that?'

'Understand? The only bloody thing I understand is that you're just the same as that sodding Conchie brother of yours. It's about time you decided what side you're on in this bloody war; ours or the bloody Jerries.'

'Get out.'

He took a step towards her.

'Get out.'

'You'll not get rid of me that easy.' He pointed his finger at her. 'You'll not.' He made a strange choking sound before turning from her and almost running across the kitchen. When he slammed the door behind him, it bounced back from the doorframe and hit the wall. The mirror fell from its hook on to the linoleum and smashed.

Chapter 24

'You're quiet today.' Jean lay on the settee in the front room. 'Have you had another row with Ellen?'

'We don't even speak these days, let alone row. Ellen knows I don't like her boyfriend.' Mary smiled wryly at her. 'I think he's trouble. She stops out most nights, goodness only knows where because he's supposed to be in barracks over in Upcross. When she does come home, more often than not she's drunk. I don't know what's going to happen to her, Jean.' She hesitated. 'But it's not that,' she said. 'It's about the baby. I want to know if you and Patrick blame me for what happened with the baby?'

Jean lifted her head off the arm of the settee, a look of surprise on her face. 'No, do we heck. Is that what you've been thinking? That it's your fault? No, honestly Mary, I'd been feeling rotten for a couple of days. I thought you knew that.'

'It was just that business with Frank. I'd wound him up that night being late.'

'We were all late for the bus.'

'I know but I should have realised what he'd be like. And then the fight. You were really upset. And you and me had argued the week before.' Mary held out her hands. 'I've felt awful.'

'Don't be daft, it wasn't your fault,' Jean interrupted. 'Get that right out of your head. The fight wasn't your fault and Patrick didn't know we'd argued. Him and me, we're all right together. That's all that matters.'

'If you're sure?'

'I'm sure, honest.' She glanced at the clock on the fireplace. 'Hey, aren't you supposed to be on duty soon?'

'Yes, I'll go in a minute.'

'There was something I've been meaning to say though,' Jean said. 'I didn't get the chance to thank Doctor Schormann. He was so good to me that day, and afterwards, while I was still in hospital; so kind.'

'I don't think he'd expect you to thank him. He's a doctor. He did what he was trained to do.'

'But he didn't need to persuade Matron to let me stay at Granville, especially when I think how I was with him.' Jean rolled the tassel of the blanket covering her between her thumb and finger. 'She was desperate to get me away from the hospital after I lost – after it happened. She told me in no uncertain terms that I'd brought shame on her and on –' Jean stressed her next words '– "our profession". I think she'd have me hung, drawn and quartered, given half a chance. She said I should have been transferred to Bradlow but Doctor Schormann insisted he could look after me as well as his other duties.'

'He's like that. He's a good … I mean kind … man.'

Jean's eyes widened, her mouth opened. 'You like him, don't you Mary?'

'Well, yes I suppose I do. He's a good doctor.' And he likes me, she thought; I know he does. Even though she was slightly ashamed that it had happened at the same time as Jean had lost her baby, she still remembered the warm feeling she'd felt when his hand was on her shoulder.

Jean took a quick glance over the back of the settee towards the half open door. Her mother was singing as she clattered around in the kitchen.

'I meant you really like him,' she said in a whisper.

Mary kept quiet, her face red.

'Oh God, Mary, no!'

They heard footsteps in the hall, the tinkle of spoons in saucers. Jean raised her voice. 'So don't forget to thank Doctor Schormann for me. I feel awful because I was always really off-hand with him.' She looked up as her mother came into the room, pushing the door wider open with her backside.

'I bet he didn't even notice,' Mary said. 'I don't think he sees anyone but the patients when he comes on to the ward.'

Mrs Winterbottom turned to face them, a cup and saucer in each hand. 'Tea?'

'Thanks, Mother.' Jean pushed herself into a sitting position whilst her mother fussed with the cushions behind her.

'Carry on, don't mind me.' Elsie Winterbottom moved around the room, repositioning ornaments and opening the window wider. 'It's stuffy in here.' She straightened the curtains. 'Don't mind me,' she repeated. When neither girl said anything she pursed her lips and went out, stopping momentarily to pull a duster out of her overall pocket and rub the door handle vigorously. As soon as she'd gone they grinned at each other.

'She's all right really,' Jean whispered. 'In fact she's been wonderful.' She pulled a face. 'But she's so nosy. What Patrick and me'll do when we're married and I get back to rights, I don't know.' She lifted her chin towards the door. 'Close it.'

'How is Patrick?' Mary asked, softly turning the doorknob handle.'I've barely seen him for ages, at least not to talk to.' She stayed in her room when he was having his baths after shifts and, usually, by the time she went downstairs, he'd dressed, dragged the tin bath outside and emptied it in the backyard and left the house.

'He can't do enough.' Jean sipped her tea. 'He's really looking after me. I'm so lucky. I don't think I've ever been happier. Except for ...' She sighed.

'I know.' Mary balanced her cup on her lap and covered Jean's hand with hers. 'It'll get better, you'll be all right.'

'Which is more than I can say for you if you carry on like this,' Jean whispered. 'Just what's going on? What are you playing at?'

'Nothing, I'm not playing at anything,' Mary said. 'I just think Doctor Schormann's a decent bloke and seeing how much I hated him when he first arrived at the camp, it's a relief to know I can work with him.' She stood and went over to the window so her friend couldn't see her face. What she had started to feel over the last couple of months was nothing like the heady turmoil Frank had provoked in her. His pursuit of her had been flatteringly hasty. Her attraction to Peter had grown steadily from respect to … what? She hesitated to give her emotions a name, she was too afraid. She wished she could tell Jean but it was impossible; it was too dangerous to voice the words, ever. 'Don't make mountains out of molehills, eh love?' She tapped her clenched hand against her thigh. 'OK?'

'OK.'

Mary composed her face before turning her back to the window and leaning against the sill, holding on to it. She could tell Jean was reluctant to change the subject and stared stubbornly at her until her friend spoke again.

'There's something else, isn't there?' Jean put her cup and saucer on the floor.

'It's Frank,' Mary said. 'I've decided it's definitely over.'

Jean studied her for a moment. 'Good, he's a pig. Have you told him?'

'Yes, I'm not sure he believed me. I shouldn't have let it get this far.'

'Has something happened?''

'He came round to the house when I was on my own,' Mary said. 'He wasn't very nice; in fact he was horrible. He thinks I've been leading him on. I was frightened he was going to … you know.' She pulled a face.

Jean gasped. 'Do you want me to tell Patrick?'

'No. No! He'd only want to go and thump him.'

'It'd be no more than he deserved. My God, Mary, anything could have happened. I wouldn't trust Frank

Shuttleworth further than I could throw him.'

'He wouldn't really have hurt me. I was just a bit scared.'

'You don't know that. Look at what happened at the Palais, he totally lost it. Let me tell Patrick.'

'No please. I'll sort things out myself. I'll make sure Frank understands we're finished.'

'Just be careful.'

Mary picked up her cape. 'I will. Now, I'll have to go or I'll be late and we're short-staffed at the moment.'

'As if I didn't know,' Jean said. 'I'll be glad to get back to work, that's if Matron will let me come back.'

'I'll talk to her. With the way things are I'm sure she can put her offended feelings to one side. After all you are one of our best nurses.'

'Thank you, ma'am.' Jean smiled. She glanced towards the window. 'Do me a favour before you go will you, Mary. Pull the sash down a bit. Mother always insists on having it wide open. Flies get in and Patrick goes mad about them.'

Mary lowered the window. 'That better?' She rubbed dust off the palms of her hands.

'Thanks.'

'If it was up to me I'd be glad to have you back, but not until you feel up to it. It's only been a couple of weeks.'

'The doc says I could be up and about by next week.' Jean looked towards the door and whispered, 'Mother's driving me round the bend with her fussing about the wedding.'

'Let her get on with it.' Mary gave Jean a kiss on the forehead. 'Just make sure it's what you want. Now, rest … nurse's orders. No telling Patrick about Frank.' She hesitated. 'Or the other thing.' She wrapped her cape around her and fastened it. 'Please?'

'Just promise to be careful … about everything.'

'I will.'

Running along Shaw Road towards the camp, Mary hoped her friend would keep both her promises.

Chapter 25

The doors swished open and Peter Schormann hurried into the ward. His white coat was unbuttoned and for once he was not wearing his uniform jacket, his shirtcollar was undone. He combed through his hair with his fingertips. It was longer now. Mary thought it suited him. A wave of happiness tightened her skin and she felt light-headed. This is so wrong, she told herself; she had no right to feel this way. Peter kept his eyes fixed on her as he approached, his face carefully arranged to reflect his professionalism, but she saw her pleasure answered in his eyes.

Mary looked around the ward. The nurses on duty were busy changing dressings. She unhooked the notes from the end of the bed and studied them to stop the impulse to smile at him. Swallowing hard, she moved to the head of the bed, patting the arm of the patient who watched every movement she made. Under the heavy swathe of bandages he looked terrified. 'Doctor Schormann, thank you for coming. Before we do anything could you please reassure this man. I think he is frightened.'

Peter leaned towards the patient and spoke a few words. The man sighed and moved his head from side to side.

'He has extensive shattering of the lower jaw and has the original Barrell bandage on at the moment,' she said. 'He needs examining before we change it.' She signalled to one of the nurses. When the girl was beside her she said, 'As soon as the doctor has finished his examination I want you to put on a fresh Barrell bandage. You've done one before, Nurse Blackstock?' The girl nodded. 'Good.' Mary faced Peter again. 'Also, Doctor Schormann, as you can see, his right arm was amputated before he was shipped here. Extra pain relief?' she asked, handing him the notes. Their fingers touched.

'*Ja.*' Peter scanned the patient's records. 'Morphine, another two grains a day,' he said, 'no more.' He countersigned the prescription, his hand unsteady, and smiled briefly at her as he handed back the board.

'Thank you, Doctor.' Mary didn't look at him. She spoke to the nurse who was carefully undoing the ends of the bandage. 'I'll be back in a minute.'

'Yes, Sister.'

Peter and Mary moved away. Speaking quickly she said, 'I called to see Jean, Nurse Winterbottom, before I came into work. She asked me to thank you for helping her.'

'I did nothing. It is a sad thing, one my wife herself experienced.'

He clamped his lips together. The words were a barrier between them.

'I'm sorry.' Mary kept her voice even. 'Do you have other children?'

'No, we were married only the six months.' He shoved his hands in his pocket. 'We did not … we met only a few times before … she also was having the child before we

164

married. Then I left.' He gave a rueful shrug. 'We agreed we had made the mistake … it was for the best that I left. At least that is what I thought then.' He pulled a face. 'But not when I was captured.' Then he stared at her, first her eyes and then her mouth. 'But I have again changed my mind these last few months.'

Mary licked her lips. 'Jean …' It was all she could think to say.

'Ah yes, Jean.' Peter made a movement; an unconscious gesture as though to pull himself together. 'She is well now?'

'A lot better,' Mary said, grateful they were on safer ground.

'Good.'

'Your kindness meant a lot to her.' She hesitated. 'And to me.'

'For that I am glad.' In an undertone he spoke again. 'I would do anything for you, Mary.' He pulled his shoulders back and rising slightly, clicked his heels. When he next spoke it was loudly. 'If there is nothing else, Sister?'

'Nothing else, Doctor.'

'Then I will return to my barracks.' He inclined his head, speaking quietly again. 'I am tired. Last night … it was, as I think you would say in your country, a disturbed one.' He moved away and then half turned and opened his mouth as though to continue. He caught his top lip between his teeth.

'What?' Mary tilted her head, mouthing the word, holding his gaze for the few seconds it lasted. She watched him as he left. What was it? What had he been going to tell her? She became aware that Hilda Lewis had come on to the ward, followed by one of the orderlies carrying an oxygen tent. The woman was staring at her.

On sudden impulse Mary pushed past her and left the ward.

Peter was standing outside the main doors of the hospital, staring across the compound towards the block of asbestos buildings that held the Commandant's office.

'Peter.' Mary stopped a few feet behind him, her body turned to one side so that, from a distance, it was impossible to see she was speaking to him. 'What is it? What's wrong?' She became aware that groups of prisoners were huddled together beyond the fence. 'Those men, what are they waiting for?'

There was despair in Peter's voice. 'They expect me to act on something that happened last night. But your friend has … advised me there will be more trouble if I do.'

'My friend?'

'Shuttleworth.' He threw the name over his shoulder, his eyes still on the prisoners. 'He ordered a strip search at three of the morning. I was on duty in the hospital when I heard the commotion outside in the dark. There were rows of the prisoners standing in the compound: they were naked. Some of the guards, they walked along the lines of the men, they bounce thick cudgels off the palms of their hands.' Mary gasped. 'I asked on whose command is this happening.' He stumbled over the English words in his anger. '*Verdammt!* Three of the morning! I asked, is there emergency? He says as the senior rank on duty he finds it necessary to hold the search.' Peter took a deep intake of air. 'I say I know the regulations. Strip searches must be carried out on the orders of the Commandant only. I say that, as *Lagerführer*, I have been informed earlier in the day that the Major was away visiting another camp so I

166

know this is illegal.'

'But why? Why did Frank … why did Frank Shuttleworth do this?' Mary felt sick; this was her fault, it must be. She had thwarted Frank, rejected him. In true cowardly fashion he'd taken it out on those who were helpless against his cruelty. The anger in her was reflected in Peter's face as he gave her a fleeting glance.

'He says one of the men had an automatic pistol and ammunition sewn into the back of his greatcoat. *Dummkopf!* A warm day in summer and this man wears a greatcoat on. Stupid. Of course he is caught.' When he spoke again, Mary heard the weariness in his voice. 'So he punishes all those in the same block. The men, they are nervous, even though they fear the Nazis in the camp they secretly read the *Wochenpost.* They believe the war is lost. They are afraid of the guards, especially Shuttleworth and his … friends, of what they will do to them. I promised them I will report Shuttleworth to the Commandant as soon as he returned. So now they wait for me to keep my word. But I know if I do it will be the worse for them. They will suffer.'

'I'm sorry.' Mary felt helpless. There was nothing she could say or do that would help.

Peter spoke softly. 'Just then, when I came into the ward, when I saw you there, I almost forgot how much I was in despair. I love to look at you, Mary. But you must tell me the truth. Is he … is he your friend?'

'No,' Mary said quietly, 'no, he's not, not any more.'

Chapter 26

The back of Mary's cotton dress clung between her shoulder blades and although it had only taken her twenty minutes to get from home to the street where Frank lived, sweat beaded her forehead and tendrils of hair had escaped from the roll she'd pinned at the back of her neck. She pushed open the small gate and took two steps to the front door. Number four; this was it.

Her heart thumped remembering the last time she saw Frank, but she was determined not to let him see she was nervous; after all she'd been dealing with bullies at home all her life. She wanted him to know that she would report him if he carried on with his maltreatment of the prisoners and then she would make sure he understood he and she were finished. But was she being stupid just coming here? She decided that if he answered the door and no one else was in the house she'd stand on the step and tell him.

She glanced up and down Barnes Street. The houses had an air of past affluence. Although terraced, they were stone fronted with bay windows and low walls enclosed small areas of tarmac in front of each one. There wasn't a soul around; no one sat on their doorsteps, no one leant against the walls gossiping and there was no noise: no shouting, no radios, no cries of children. The only sounds Mary heard were the rumble of vehicles from Shaw Road and the shouts of male voices. It sounded as though there was some sort of game, perhaps a football match, at the camp.

Mary turned to look at the house in front of her. Amongst all the others this one stood out in its neglect. The paint on the door, once black, was dull and flaked and the oblong leaded window in the upper panel was filthy. Out of the corner of her eye she saw a movement in the net curtain in the window next door. Taking a deep breath she grabbed the brass knocker and hammered. She waited, re-pinning her hair and straightening the collar of her dress.

The door was tugged twice before it opened. The woman who stood in the doorway gave her a toothless smile. 'I know who you are; you're our Frank's Mary? I'm Nelly. Come in, out of this heat. I'll give him a shout. He's still asleep in his room, being on nights like.' Mary followed the stout figure down the hall. The back of Nelly's slippers were flattened and slapped against her feet. 'I'll make a brew in a minute, pet, but you'll have to come through to the wash house, I'm just mangling some clothes.'

'I only wanted a word with Frank if you don't mind, Mrs Shuttleworth.'

'Nelly!'

'Nelly. It's just that I'm on shift at two o'clock.'

'Plenty of time.' The older woman stood over a copper tub and stirred the washing one last time with the long wooden dolly-stick. 'I'll have to get this out on the line. First lot's already dry.' She lifted a white sheet out of the soapy water and fed it through the rollers by turning the large wheel on the side of the mangle. The muscles under the skin of her bare arms bulged. She gave Mary another gummy grin. 'I take washing in from the big houses. Keeps the wolf from the door.'

'I'm sorry, I don't have much time and I still have to get back home to change.'

'Well, if it's that urgent ...' Frank's mother was

obviously disappointed that Mary wasn't going to have time to chat.

'It is.'

'Tell you what, then. I'll rinse these and make a cuppa. You go and wake him up. Up the stairs, first right.'

'OK.'

Mary waited a moment outside Frank's bedroom and then, slowing her breathing, knocked.

'What?' He yelled. 'Ma?'

'It's Mary.'

She heard the springs on his bed crunch and then he opened the door. 'What are you doing here?' She stepped back. He was wearing only his trousers and he scowled at her as he fastened the fly buttons and tugged fiercely on his belt, his arm muscles flexing under the skin. 'What's up with you? What d'you think I'm going to do? In my own house?'

'After the other day? In mine?' Mary shrugged. 'I need to talk to you.' She avoided looking at him. Hitching her bag further onto her shoulder and crossing her arms, she stepped into the room, wincing as he slammed the door. Hearing his mother singing outside in the yard as she pegged out the sheets made Mary feel a little less anxious.

Frank went to his bedside table and picked up a packet of cigarettes. He sat down on the edge of the bed and lit one. 'Sit down.' He gestured with his thumb towards a chair in the corner of the room piled high with clothes. 'Shift that lot.' He blew smoke out, making an impatient clicking noise with his tongue on the back of his teeth.

'I won't, thanks.' Mary crossed to the window and watched his mother hook the wooden prop under the washing line and hoist it higher. Steam began to rise

170

instantly from the sheets. Now she was here she couldn't think where to start. Without turning around she blurted, 'I know you resent Tom and, especially after the other day, I don't really care.' She heard the crack of his knuckles. 'What you said about him and about me just showed how nasty you are.' The headboard of the bed creaked and then bumped softly against the wall as Frank leaned against it.

When he answered her, his tone was surly. 'What do you expect, you and your flaming brother? I'm sick of everything. I should be out there fighting the bloody Jerries, part of this invasion that's going on and here I am looking after a bunch of Nazis.'

'I've heard all this before, Frank.'

'Aye and you look at me as though I'm a rotten smell under your nose half the time.'

'I don't.' She took a quick look over her shoulder at him. He was biting his nails. 'But it's … it's not worked out, Frank. Even before you did what you did in our house you wanted too much, too soon.' She heard his snort of derision and took a deep breath. 'We're finished. I want you to understand that before I leave here.' She rushed on before she ran out of courage. 'And the other thing is I've heard about some of the things you and the other guards do.' She flinched as she heard him launch himself off the bed to stand behind her.

'What! What're you talking about?'

Her skin crawled when she felt his breath on her neck but she carried on. 'They won't let you get away with it, you know. They'll complain.'

'Complain? Complain?' His voice trembled with suppressed rage. 'They've got the life of bloody Riley up there. Half of them got sodding captured the first time they saw some action. You haven't a bastard clue! Besides it's none of your business. Poking your nose in ...' Mary drew away. He stank of stale beer and cigarettes. 'I could complain ... complain about how bloody knackered I was ... being told to stand and fight ... but not being allowed to fire on the Boche planes that flew over us,' she heard the sneer, 'in case we warned the Panzer division that was coming up behind them. I could complain about being bombed left, right and sodding centre.'

He moved to the side of her. Mary shifted away from him again. She watched his mother balance the washtub on its rim and empty out the dirty water. It sloshed over her feet but she didn't seem to notice and paddled through it to feel the hems of the drying sheets.

'Like I said before, you've told me this already, Frank. I know it was horrible.'

He interrupted, 'What do you know? Sod all! You didn't have half your bloody leg torn to bits. You weren't stuck on a truck for bloody days on end, a sodding sitting target. So don't tell me you bloody well know.' He was almost touching Mary. She flinched away from him. 'You know nothing!' He spat out the words and walked back to his bed. She heard him crush his cigarette in the saucer he used as an ashtray and then light another, adding to the fug of blue smoke.

She tugged at the lock on the frame and lifted the casement open. When he spoke again his voice was so low Mary had to half turn to hear him. 'On the beach I was on a stretcher near a Red Cross flag. They'd to put Skipper next to me. They'd no choice.' Frank smirked. 'He had good teeth and a bad temper, that dog.' He began to pace the floor behind Mary, banging one fist into the palm of his other hand. She listened to cold hatred in his words. 'A Red Cross flag, but the bastards still strafed us. I still dream about that … men yelling … screaming … shouting for water … no one daring to come near us.' He raised his voice. 'Shells whining and bursting all around. Bastards. Bastards.' He stood close behind her and hissed the words. 'And you wonder why I hate the bleedin' lot of them.'

Mary sighed. 'I know – I think I know how hard it is Frank. But you can't keep using it as an excuse. If the Commandant knew how you felt, you'd be taken off your duties. Thousands of men are going through what you've been through. It's not that I don't feel sorry for …'

'I don't want your ruddy pity.'

Mary watched his mother emerge from the outside lavatory in the yard, her skirt up around her waist as she adjusted her pink bloomers. She stared up at Mary who turned from the window and went to stand in front of Frank.

'Every time something goes wrong, every time,' she emphasised, 'you blame what happened to you. But you can't carry on like this, Frank. And I'm sorry but neither can I. Like I said, it's finished.'

'It's that bloody doctor, isn't it? I've heard the rumours.'

Mary went cold. She stepped back as he stood up, punctuating each word with a poke of his finger into her chest. 'The so-called sodding *Lagerführer.*' He sneered. '*Schormann*; mouthpiece for that festering lot.' Mary watched the speckles of spit gather at the corner of his mouth. 'Well, you can tell your precious friend to watch his back.'

'I don't know what you're talking about, Frank. There

are no rumours because there's nothing to gossip about.' She walked as steadily as she could to the door. 'I have to go now, I'm due on shift.' She paused. 'I didn't want it to be like this, Frank…'

'No, I bet you bloody didn't.'

She was halfway down the stairs when he shouted again. His words sent a shock of fear through her. 'Remember! Tell him … tell that *precious* Schormann to watch his back. Tell him, I'll be watching him. Tell him, I'll make sure the Nazi bastards are watching him as well.'

Chapter 27

August 1944

The wedding party piled off the bus, a rowdy giggling crowd, leaving it almost empty. 'That bus driver had a shock seeing us lot,' Patrick laughed.

'The conductor sent his best wishes,' Mrs Winterbottom said to Jean, peering from under the brim of her hat which had been knocked crooked in the crush. She straightened it and followed at a sedate pace as they crowded into The Crown. The groom's father was already there. He sat in his usual place in the corner of the room by the large stone fireplace, pint pot in hand. There was no fire in the hearth; instead a large aspidistra filled the space, Betty Green's contribution to the celebrations.

It was a gloriously sunny day. Some of the guests, mostly Patrick's workmates and a few off-duty nurses from the hospital, collected their drinks from the bar and made their way outside to sit on the benches. Except for Ellen, the family stayed inside.

'I don't know why you couldn't have come to the Registry Office.' Winifred stood over her husband, brave enough to challenge him in a roomful of people.

He didn't answer. Instead he raised his glass. 'Cheers, you two,' he shouted across the room, 'mine's a pint.'

Mrs Winterbottom, resplendent in her matching floral hat and dress, once the curtains in the back bedroom of her house, looked at him with distaste and turned her back.

Mary watched Patrick carry the foamless beer over to her father. Wedding or no wedding, Stan Green wasn't going to let sentiment get in the way of business. If anything the ale looked more watered down than ever.

'You're feeling generous,' she said to her brother as he passed her.

'I told you, nowt's going to spoil today. Master of my own house now, our kid.' He winked at her. She supposed he was right, Jean's home was his now, though it didn't seem quite right. She hoped when her friend realised that it wouldn't be too much of a shock

'What're you having, Mam? Stout, sherry?' Mary said, pulling out one of the chairs at her father's table. 'Sit down, it'll be a crush once they bring the food out, so you'll be better off over here.' She put a hand on her father's shoulder. 'You're OK with that aren't you, Dad?' She made the warning clear. 'You'll make sure there'll be nothing that spoils the day for Patrick and Jean, won't you?'

He waved his hand, refusing to meet her eye. 'Just keep the drinks coming.'

'I wish out Tom could be here, Mary.'

'And me, Mam.'

Bill glowered into his glass.

At the bar Mary stood next to Jean and her new husband. Although Jean was paler than usual, the weight Mary's friend had lost suited her and she looked lovely in the fitted powder-blue silk and wool crepe mix two-piece that she'd bought from the Co-op for eleven coupons; six of which were Mary's, her wedding gift. She still gripped the prayer book that she'd carried for the ceremony and every now and then touched the artificial spray of white carnations on her lapel. Her dark curls escaped from the short lace veil and the swathe of pale blue net across her forehead accentuated her eyes. Mary grinned. Mrs Winterbottom could certainly work wonders with curtains and Dolly Blue.

She'd also made Mary and Ellen's dresses.

'Could have been a bit fancier,' Ellen had grumbled, the first time they'd tried them on. 'She just doesn't want us take any attention away from Jean.' The girls had been standing on kitchen chairs in the front room of Moss Terrace.

'Sshhhh, stop whinging and stand still,' Winifred had hissed through a mouthful of pins. 'I might not like the woman but she's done you both proud. Now let me finish this hem or we'll be here all day.'

Elsie Winterbottom had come through from the kitchen holding a large tray with a pot of tea, a plate of biscuits and four china cups and saucers that Mary had never seen before.

'Patrick,' Ellen had mouthed, pointing at the biscuits.

Mary shrugged and frowned.

'Your Patrick got the parachute silk for us,' Mrs Winterbottom had said, 'I cut it on the bias across the weave of the fabric so that it fits nicely'.

It did. It clung closely to their slender figures and now Mary pulled self-consciously at the waist, smoothing it down over her hips and watching Ellen blatantly playing to the admiring glances of Patrick's friends.

'Look at that lot gawking at her.' Jean nudged Mary, who turned her back to the group of men following her sister to the bar.

'Silly devils! I hope the wedding photographs turn out well,' Mary said deliberately. It would be a good day to remember out of all the dark times they'd had.

'I could have killed you lot for watching us through the window when we went into the studio for that photo.'

'Well, you have to admit it was a scream.' Mary grinned.

'We were supposed to be driving away on our honeymoon,' Jean said, 'that's why we had the country scene in the background.'

'Sitting on two chairs behind a cardboard car?'

Jean giggled. 'I'll have you know that was a Lanchester Convertible.'

'Best bit was when Patrick fell off his chair and knocked the whole thing over.' Mary laughed.

'Oi, watch it.' Patrick punched her lightly on the arm. 'It was a bloody silly idea anyway.'

'He bent one of the headlamps, the photographer was furious.' Jean joined in the laughter. 'It was good of Tom to send money to Patrick to pay for the photographs out of his prison wages.'

A shadow crossed Mary's face; whatever Patrick

thought about him, she knew Tom loved his brother. It had probably taken months for him to save the six shillings they cost. She just hoped Patrick appreciated it.

'Hope you remember to write and thank Tom, Patrick,' Mary said.

The laughter faded. 'I will,' he said, 'don't worry, our Mary, I will.'

'Grub's up.' Stan Green carried in long wooden tray filled with salad, potatoes and bread and put it on the line of tables covered with blue-and-white checked tablecloths, alongside the elaborate wedding cake.

'Cake's lovely,' Winifred called to Mrs Winterbottom. Jean's mother sniffed and pushed the cake to one side to make room for the plates of food Stan was unloading.

'Hey up, you'll have it over,' Winifred shouted again, finishing her third sherry. The cake tilted to reveal a small sponge underneath.

'I thought you'd splashed out,' Mary whispered to Jean, who giggled and clutched hold of Patrick's arm, pulling him closer to her.

'It's a model, isn't it Patrick?'

'No!' Mary said in mocked surprise.

'We hired it from Hirst's bakery.'

Patrick waggled his eyebrows. 'Only the best cardboard for us today.'

'Ice cream for afters,' Stan called.

'You really pushed the boat out today for us, Mr Green,' Mary said.

'Got an allowance for extra food,' he said. 'You know, dried egg, margarine, cheese and a few other bits and bobs.' He gathered up the long strand of greasy hair that had fallen over his ear and stroked it back across his head.

178

'And your Patrick got us some stuff as well.'

Mary blocked her immediate response. If her brother couldn't use his black market connections today, when could he? Holding her plate aloft, she pushed her way through the groups of people, smiling and adding to the babble of conversations. 'You had enough to eat, Mam?'

'I have, love, I've had your dad's as well; he didn't want any,' Winifred said. 'It was a lovely spread.' She smiled and patted her navy handbag that matched her dress. 'I've put some by for tomorrow.' Then she lifted her chin. 'What's Ellen doing?'

Mary looked over to where Ellen swayed around in front of Jean. 'Show me your wedding ring then.' Her voice was shrill. 'God, I bet that cost a fortune.'

Mary could tell she was being sarcastic; she hoped Jean couldn't.

'Twenty-five shilling and ninepence from Wright's in Bradlow.' Jean twirled the ring round her finger with the pad of her thumb. 'It's a bit big at the moment but Patrick says when I get a bit of meat on my bones it'll be just right.'

His smile softened the angular lines of his face.

'Al says he'll give me his grandmother's wedding ring,' Ellen boasted. 'It's twenty-four carat. He inherited it.' She smoothed her hands over her blonde hair that, like Mary's, had been carefully rolled to frame her face. 'He says when we get home to Philadelphia …' She obviously liked the sound of that as she repeated it. 'When we get home to Philadelphia, we'll have the biggest, fanciest wedding, one that will beat any over here into a cocked hat. He says when he takes me to America we'll have servants. He says all American wives have servants.'

179

He says a lot of things from the sound of it, Mary thought, edging past the scrum of people at the food table. Her sister was heading for a fall with that American, she was sure of it. She touched Ellen's elbow. 'Come and have something to eat.'

'Not hungry.' Ellen was surly; she stood with one hand on her hip, head poked forward. 'And I still don't know why Al wasn't allowed to come to the wedding, since we're as good as engaged, he's almost my fiancé.'

'We don't know him. None of us do. And how would you have explained him to Dad?'

'Oh, bugger off, Mary.'

'The 'appy couple are leaving now,' Stan Green bellowed. Everyone cheered and swarmed outside. The brightness of the sun caused the sky to shimmer, the tar between the cobbles glistened and heat radiated from the walls of the pub.

'Couldn't have been a lovelier day.' Jean's mother linked arms with Winifred, who was fanning her face with her hat.

'By, it's a warm one all right.' Four sweet Sherries each and they were best friends, at least for the day, as Winifred confided to her eldest daughter later.

Jean clasped Mary to her. 'Thanks for everything.' Tears threatened to spill over, but she grinned. 'Especially for persuading Matron to let me back to work now I'll be a respectable married woman and all that'

'You are very welcome, sister-in-law.' Mary beamed. 'And I'll take your wedding presents back to our house and look after them until you can pick them up.'

They giggled; the couple had been given seven hand-knitted tea cosies and two lots of egg cosies. 'You guard them with your life,' Jean warned. 'I'm expecting them to last until our Silver Wedding Anniversary.' She grabbed hold of her husband's hand.

Some of the nurses had been collecting bits of paper from the office paper punch at the hospital for the last month and now they scattered them like confetti over Patrick and Jean as they ran up the street, Jean's hand flat on top of her head to hold on her veil.

'Don't forget, I'll be back from Aunty Florrie's on Friday,' Jean's mother called.

'Thanks for reminding us,' Patrick shouted. 'I'll be sure to lock the door.'

Even as Mary joined in the laughter, a cold sadness filled her. Whatever she'd felt for Frank it wasn't love, she knew that now. And, as unbearable as it was, she could never reveal her feelings for Peter.

Chapter 28

Mary looked around. Through the trees she could see children crowded into the boats on the lake, their laughter shrill as they rowed in circles on the water. She sat down on the grass and unfolded Tom's letter. From the postmark, this one had come through the official channels and, as usual, huge blocks of words had been blacked out.

Dear Mary,

Things have been difficult here. ███████████

████████████████████████████████████

████████████████████████████████████

████████████████████████████████████

███████████████ *go mad*

██████████████████████████████████████

████████████████████████████

Mary held the paper up towards the sky. It was impossible to see the words through the censor's ink.

████████████████████ *I enjoyed hearing all about the wedding in your letter – it sounds as though you all had a great time, even sounds as if Dad behaved himself for once. I just wish I could have been there.*

There was a loud hollow bump followed by laughter. She looked up. Two boats had collided at the edge of the lake. An older boy was standing in one pushing the other away with his oar while the two girls in it tried to grab hold of the end of the paddle. Mary smiled, remembering her own attempts at learning to row with Tom. She began to read again.

Iori and I have talked a lot about families - he has no brothers or sisters ████████████████████████

████████████████████████████████████

████████████████████████████████████

████████████████████

Mary frowned. Why had that been blacked out? What had Tom said? Sometimes she thought it was only done for spite.

I am worried about Frank Shuttleworth. I've talked it over with Iori and he agrees with me, you need to be careful, love, we think he's dangerous. Also I am worried about the other matter you mentioned in your last letter – your friendship with the 'doctor' – and I hope you don't mind but I have told Iori about it.

She caught her breath.

The hours are long during the nights when we can't sleep, Mary. I hope you can forgive me for sharing my worries with him. We talk about all sorts of things. Anyway, please be careful. You could get into trouble – you know what I mean!!!!

There is a lot of panicking here since the ▓▓▓▓▓*s have come on the scene.* ▓▓▓▓▓▓▓▓▓ *bad enough when the sirens went for the air raids and we could see enemy aircraft at night in the searchlights and hear all the bombs, and anti aircraft guns on Wormwood Scrubs Common but you can't hear these things coming. And, as always, some of the chaps create a fuss; banging plates and, mugs because they're locked in and then the wardens go mad and*

▓▓▓▓▓▓▓▓▓▓▓▓▓▓▓▓▓▓▓▓

can sense the fear as soon as rumours go round that the things are being sent over.

Iori and I spend a lot of time planning what we will do after this lot is over. It takes our minds off the brutishness ...

Someone had made a mark over the word and written 'of the prisoners' over the top of it.

... we see every day in here. I've told him what it's like in Ashford and he's told me about the village, Llamroth, where he grew up. It sounds very pleasant, a lot better than Ashford – somewhere to escape to perhaps?

He wants to write a book when we get out of here; he says his ambition is to be an author. He laughs when I say there's enough going on in here to write ten books. I suppose the last line will be censored!

There was a loud yell. Mary glanced towards the lake. The boy had fallen in and was standing chest deep in water with lumps of weeds on his head and shoulders. The two girls were clutching each other, convulsed with giggles, until he grabbed the side of their boat and began to rock it. A man shouted. Mary looked over her shoulder. Alerted by their screams the Park Keeper was striding across the grass, waving his stick.

They're ███████████████████████████
████████████████████████████████████
████████████████████████████████████
████████████████████████████████████
████████████████████████████████████
████████████████

There has been a lot of restlessness here since what they called D Day on the ████████████████ *last month. We weren't allowed to read it in the newspapers, of course, but were told by one of the screws on our block. Now the* ████████*vasion in Europe has happened things might move quickly and you never know I might get lucky and be released from* ████████████████████████ *hopefully.*

Always in my thoughts.

Your loving brother, Tom

'So this is where you're hiding. I've been looking for you.' Frank pushed her shoe with the toe of his boot.

Mary folded the letter quickly and shoved it in her pocket. She leant backwards, one hand on the grass and shading her eyes with her other hand as she looked up at him. Outlined against the bright sky she couldn't see his face, but his voice was slurred and she knew he'd been drinking.

'What you got there? Love letter?'

'No. Go away.' Mary pulled her knees up under her chin and wrapped her skirt around her legs. 'How many ways do you need telling? We're finished.'

He crouched down and overbalanced, falling against her. 'Not until I say.'

She shoved him away. 'Get off. I'm not arguing with you, Frank.' As she stood up he grasped her ankle. 'Let go.'

Frank rolled onto his front and struggled to his feet. 'Why, Mary. What did I do wrong?'

'You mean besides your moods, your temper?'

'You know what I've been through, I told you.'

'You're a bully, Frank, I doubt it was the war that did that, I think that's something you've always been.'

'It's that bloody doctor, isn't it?'

'I'm not discussing my work with you.'

Frank lurched towards her. 'Oh yes … your work! Got a soft spot for the enemy, haven't you?'

'How dare you!'

Frank shrugged. 'Not just me saying it.'

'I don't believe you. And if anyone was, it would only be because of your vile accusations.' An elderly couple strolled past. The woman held on to her companion, looking at Mary with inquisitiveness through wire-rimmed spectacles. Mary breathed deeply, trying to calm her anger. She walked slowly in the direction the couple had gone, keeping her voice reasonable. 'Look, Frank …'

He pulled at her coat.

'What are you doing?' Mary struggled as he shoved his hand in her pocket and dragged out Tom's letter.

'Bet this is from lover boy.' Staggering sideways onto

the grass and then back to the path to stand, feet wide apart, in front of her he rocked backwards and forwards as he unfolded it. 'Oh no, it's not. It's from that soft sod of a brother of yours, the yellow-bellied bastard.' He hiccupped and slurred over some of the words. 'The bastard who won't fight for his country. What's he saying, the soft bastard? Moaning about what he has to put up with in prison? Wouldn't surprise me if he wasn't a shirt-lifting bastard as well – him and his Conchie mates.'

Mary moved swiftly. In one movement she took a step, slapped him across his face and grabbed at the letter. He pushed her away and, without hesitation, retaliated, swinging his arm upwards. The back of his fist hit the side of her head and she fell. He straddled over her, treading on her cape. 'Learned your lesson yet?'

Mary felt sick and dizzy. She tried to sit up, but he shoved her back to the ground. 'Let me go.' She pushed at his legs and rolled over, forcing herself to kneel up. Frank moved in front of her, watching and waiting to see what she did next.

Mary dug the toes of her shoes into the ground, willing herself to stop shaking. Then she hurled herself forward at his midriff. He dropped to the ground and rolled over, hands between his legs. She'd caught him in the groin.

She fell alongside him, lying still for an instance. Then her fingers closed around Tom's letter and, staggering to her feet and hoping the fracas hadn't been seen, she walked unsteadily towards the park gate without a backward glance.

Chapter 29

'Patrick will be furious when I tell him. You know what his temper's like.' Jean held up her hand, fingers spread wide. 'Don't even try to stop me, Mary. Frank's gone too far this time. God only knows what he'll do next.'

'I wish I hadn't told you.' Mary rubbed her forehead. 'It's been two days and I haven't seen him and he hasn't been to the house either. I'm sure he'll keep his distance.'

'He will. He will when Patrick's finished with him.' Jean's face was grim. From her front doorstep they watched the milk cart stop and start in front of the houses. The horse shook its head, lifting and stamping its front hoof. The bottles clattered and the wheels of the cart jerked forward.

'Whoa, you daft beggar,' the milkman roared. 'Morning girls, beautiful for this time of year, eh? Morning, Mrs Winterbottom.' The milkman passed two bottles over Mary's head to Jean's mother, who appeared behind them. 'Two as usual? You feeling better, Jean?'

'Yes thanks, Mr Nicholls.'

'Well, this stuff will get you back on your feet, lass. Fresh this morning, no dried muck at your house, eh?' He laughed and jumped up on the metal step at the back of the cart. 'Go on girl. Go on, Beauty.'

They listened to the horse's hooves growing fainter as it trotted along Shaw Road.

Mary looked over her shoulder into the hall to make sure Elsie Winterbottom had gone. 'Don't tell Patrick, Jean. It'll only cause more bother.'

Jean pursed her lips. Mary knew there was no point in saying anything else. And at least they'd managed to keep off the subject of her and Peter.

Going through the main gate the following evening for the night shift, Mary passed Frank as he went off duty. He turned his head away but not before she saw the swelling around his eyes. Now what? Not Patrick, she hoped.

Chapter 30

Mary studied Peter's profile. His fair hair stuck out at odd angles and there were dark smudges beneath his eyes. He looked older tonight. Or perhaps it was only that the close glow of his cigarette shadowed his features, showing the lines on his forehead and by his mouth. The doctor wasn't wearing his white coat. His uniform hung crumpled on his frame revealing the amount of weight he'd lost.

She handed him a mug of tea, letting her fingers brush his and he smiled at her. 'The new patient had just been admitted when I came on duty tonight,' Mary said. 'His temperature was very high and I was concerned about the infection in his wound. Still, perhaps it could have waited until morning, Peter. I'm sorry; I should have dealt with it myself.'

He smiled at her. 'Do not worry, I was not sleeping. Today I was called to meet with the Commandant about two prisoners, the two pilots who were recaptured this morning.'

'Yes, I'd heard about the escape,' Mary said.

'It is every man's duty to try to escape and if recaptured it is the correct punishment under the Geneva Convention for them to have the thirty days in the cells.' Peter nodded as he spoke. 'But as *Lagerführer* I must make sure they are well treated; it is my duty, *ja*?'

'Yes, of course.'

'Some of the guards do not see the importance of that. As you know I have had need to complain before to the Commandant.' He frowned. 'Still I am not sure, so I do not sleep well.' His lips twisted and he took a long gulp of tea.

'The Commandant is a fair man; he will make sure they are safe.'

'Yes, you are right, I hope.'

They stood in easy silence in the darkness outside the main door of the hospital. Mary leant against the wall and watched the tip of his cigarette flame as he drew heavily on the nicotine laced smoke. 'Is there something else wrong?'

Peter shrugged. 'For us –' he waved his hand in the direction of the building that loomed in front of them, the cigarette between his fingers sparking '– the war is over. This time next year, who knows? I read in the *Wochenpost* that de Gaulle has led an armoured unit into Paris. She is … as they put it … liberated.'

Mary peered into the darkness, nervous that he would be overheard, but saw no one. She blew on her tea and sipped. The night was punctuated by the hoarse coughs of the prisoners and the occasional shout. Further away the shunt of trains on the railway line blended with the low hum of the camp's generators.

Peter stubbed out his cigarette before it was finished. 'For later,' he explained, folding it into a piece of paper. 'The last,' he said ruefully.

'I can get more for you,' Mary said, thinking of Patrick.

'You would do that?''

'I *will* do that.'

He moved his hand, curled his little finger around hers. She held her breath, felt the now familiar thrill in the pit of her stomach. 'At this time of year ... at the end August,' he said quietly, 'I think always of home. Almost all the crops will be ready to be gathered in. My father and brothers they will be happy if it has been a good year. If not ...' He lifted her hand to his face; she briefly touched his smile before pulling his arm down. Even though they were in the shadows, she was afraid they would be seen, more than afraid. 'If not, then my father will be glad that still he has two of his sons with him and my wife to help in the house.' He shut up, embarrassed. Pushing his sleeve up, jerked his chin in self-mockery. 'I forget ... no timepiece. How much longer have we yet?'

Mary put her mug on the nearest windowsill, took her fob watch between forefinger and thumb and lifted it from the bib of her apron, peering closely. 'Five more minutes, then I must get back to the ward,' she said, adding, 'have you heard from your wife at all?'

'No, no,' Peter said, 'I was allowed to send the card, you know, the one to say I am safe?'

'I know.'

'But I hear nothing since. As I said before I was married only the six months. I knew my wife only shortly. Sometimes ... most times, the marriage ... it is not feeling real. My life then, not real.' He gesticulated towards the mill. 'Yet all this ... sometimes I wake and think all this is a nightmare.' They were standing so closely that Mary could see his Adam's apple move up and down in his throat as he swallowed. Then he said, 'Except I met you.'

A lorry drove into the compound and stopped. A low light shone from the kitchen stores in the basement of the mill as a door was opened and closed. Mary felt incredibly sad. Gripping his fingers she said, 'I know, I feel the same. But there is nothing we can do.' She peered into the darkness. There was a low murmur of voices from the guardroom and, in the dimmed light she could see the heads of three men. That meant there was only one patrolling. She listened for the sound of footsteps crunching on the gravel of the compound: nothing. She raised her face, pressing her lips to his, feeling his mouth move under hers, his body respond before she unwillingly pulled away. They didn't speak; each heard the other's quickened breathing.

Mary spoke first, thrilled at the risk she'd taken. 'There's something I've been meaning to tell you.'

'Yes?' He waited for her to continue, standing as close to her as he dared, his hand wrapped around hers.

'I have a brother who also thinks the world's gone mad. He refused to fight and he's in prison because he wouldn't answer his conscription. He isn't a doctor though.' The main hospital doors swung open letting a dim shaft of light across the entrance and two orderlies struggled through with dirty laundry. At the same time one of the guards sauntered past on the other side of the fence.

Mary let go of Peter's fingers and tucked her hands under her armpits, giving the two men a small smile as they bumped the basket down the steps and across to the gate to the compound. She waited a while and then said, 'It's different for him; he doesn't believe in war at all. He's … he's a Conscientious Objector. Because of his faith. My father hates what he stands for.' She stopped, the memory of her fear for Tom suddenly overwhelming.

Though some days had a hint of spring that day hadn't been one of them. Despite a weak glimmer of sunlight a dismal greyness draped the streets, a reminder of the threat of war that hung over the country. Her final exams were coming up: between studying and working on the wards in Bradlow General, Mary was exhausted.

She'd heard the angry voice of her father as she walked down the alleyway to the house and pushing through the group of women standing by her back gate, had run across the yard and into the kitchen. 'By God I'm glad he's not my son … dirty yellow coward.'

Even now Mary could picture her father pacing the kitchen, his braces dangling down on either side of his trousers. His face was blood red with rage while her mother's was grey and impassive. But Mary saw the distress in her eyes.

'Dad, the whole street's listening outside!'

'Well, bloody let them. You know what's happened? What your Nancy boy of a brother has done now?' He rolled up the sleeves of his collarless shirt, usually a precursor to one of then getting belted.

'Dad!'

'Only declared himself a bloody Conchie at a bloody tribunal, the soft-arse. A bloody Conscientious Objector; been all the way to Birmingham to do it and all. Now he's going to jail. And this one here knew all about it and didn't tell me.' Bill jerked his head towards his wife and glared at her.

He wrenched a small crumpled packet of Woodbines from of his shirt pocket, took one out and put it between his lips. 'You buy more fags today?' Winifred moved her head once. 'Bloody useless. I'll have to go to the pub for more, now. How will I hold my head up in there, I ask you.'

'What bothers my father more than anything is what people would think of us, of him,' Mary said.

'He believes this war is right?' Peter asked, so close she felt his breath on the side of her face.

She shivered. 'No. Yes, I suppose so, although he hates the Government, the politicians.' Mary hadn't intended for the conversation to go in this direction. Peter was one of the enemy after all. But not mine, she thought, not mine. 'In fact he hates anyone in authority. It's just that he's a Home Guard. He takes himself very seriously and he's ashamed of Tom. He tried to join up himself but they said he was too old, and ill. He was gassed last time. That made him very bitter. He's a hard man who thinks he's always right. I just wish he would let everyone else have their own beliefs, live their own lives.'

The two orderlies returned with the empty basket. Peter moved to the other side of the steps to let them pass.

Mary watched them go back into the hospital. 'My brother, Tom, he's been in and out of prison for the last four years, since he refused his call-up papers. They let him out after about a year, but they put him on fire watching and he said it was war work so he went on strike. It's happened twice since; they let him out, give him something to do that they know he'll say is war work and will refuse to do, and then they arrest him again. The Home Office – the Government says the COs should be given other work to do, but someone's got a grudge against our Tom. And he's stubborn.' Mary's voice was bitter. 'They've tried to break his spirit: solitary confinement, bread and water, extra work until he was almost dead on his feet. But they haven't beaten him. Yet.' She looked at him. 'So you see Peter, the war is a nightmare for him too.'

He nodded and touched her fingers, a fleeting contact this time. 'I understand,' he said, shifting on his feet and moving closer. She could smell the antiseptic soap on his hands. The door to the kitchen stores opened again, the dim glow illuminating the figure of the driver as he ran across the loading bay and jumped into his vehicle. The engine coughed into life and the lorry juddered towards the gates, it's dipped beams lighting the way. After an exchange of words between driver and sentry, the truck edged under the barrier of the main entrance. Mary heard the scrape of gears and the chug of the engine fade away. She could think of nothing else to say.

'I must go now,' Peter said.

'Yes.' He squeezed her hand and she watched him walk away to the connecting gate between hospital grounds and compound. At least he was still doing the work he believed in. What had Tom achieved other than to say he wouldn't fight because he wouldn't kill, wouldn't be a party to the killing? Was that ever enough, a gesture towards his philosophy? For the first time she doubted it; Tom might be standing up for what he believed was right but what did it achieve?

At the end of her shift, Mary took a long breath of the fresh air as she looked around and waited to be signed out by the guard at the main gate. The sun, rising above the hills in the distance, glinted golden on the windows of the greenhouses and sheds of the allotments.

In the compound, a few of the prisoners had been let out and were grouped together Peter was leaning against the fence, eyes closed, face upturned to the sun. She coughed, hoping he would hear her. Instead a shadow came between her and the sun and, shading her eyes Mary looked up at the sentry post. Frank returned her stare and then turned and pointed his rifle down into the compound, moving slowly, deliberately. Mary followed the direction of the barrel of the weapon, instinctively knowing what he was doing. She saw him grin and held the weapon steady, still trained on Peter. Then he glanced over his shoulder and winked at her before lowering the rifle to his side.

Mary's legs shook as she ducked under the barrier and hurried away from the camp. She was, she realized, frightened of Frank, of what he might do, what he might be capable of if pushed. She didn't want to think about it.

Chapter 31

September 1944

'I'm telling you, Ellen, it was Al.' Mary held her blouse up towards the scullery window before laying it on the draining board and scrubbing at the collar with the block of Sunlight soap. 'He was in the park smooching with this other girl and if you must know, it's not the first time I've seen him with her. I thought I'd made a mistake last time, but I know it was him today. And he had his hand down her blouse.'

'Oh, shut up.' Hunched over the kitchen table, Ellen flicked the pages of her *Woman's Own* magazine. 'You're just jealous.'

'I am not.' Mary dropped the blouse into the bowl of cold water in the sink. 'Look I don't want us to fall out again.'

Ellen gave a short laugh. 'Give over.' She lit a cigarette.

Mary came to the kitchen door. She brushed a wisp of air from her cheek with the back of her hand. 'You've changed, Ellen.'

'Yeah, yeah!' Ellen reached over to the sideboard and turned up the radio. 'Oh, I do like this song.' She tapped her fingers and hummed as Anne Shelton belted out *Over There.*

Mary spoke loudly over the music. 'No one wants to make you miserable.'

'Huh!'

'Or stop you doing what you want to do. I know how fed up you get at the factory. I know you want to do more with your life, but you're only young and there's plenty of time. This war won't last forever. Just think about what I've said. He's no good for you.' Ellen turned the radio louder. Exasperated Mary went back into the scullery. 'OK, have it your own way, but I'm telling you, I saw him with this other girl. If you don't believe me, ask him yourself.' She lifted up the blouse and wrung it out. Her voice strained with the effort as she said loudly, 'Ask him, ask him tonight. I presume you are going out with him again later? And try coming home before morning. Dad's going to find out sooner or later.'

Her sister's next words shocked her. 'Who cares? Al has asked me to marry him like I always said he would, so there. And, like I said before, he'll take me to America.'

Mary whirled round from the sink. 'Oh Ellen!'

'Oh Ellen,' she imitated Mary's voice, flipping the magazine closed. 'For your information he loves me. He gets me anything I want from the Post Exchange, stockings, nail varnish. Even perfume. When was the last time a bloke bought you perfume, Mary?'

'Buying stuff from the army shop doesn't mean he loves you, you idiot,' Mary flared at Ellen's last sentence. If she had to answer it would be never and for a split second that stung. 'Especially the pay he's on. He gets over twice as much as our lads. He'll have what he wants from you and move on to the next daft girl. If you think you're going to be a GI bride you've another think coming.'

Ellen stood up, rolling the magazine in her hands. 'And you're just a dried-up old spinster. If you must know I've signed on for a lecture on transatlantic customs at the town hall. I'm going to be the best wife that I can be for Al.' She flounced up the stairs.

Mary lowered the clothes rack from the ceiling and folded the blouse over the bars. 'Dad's going to hit the roof,' she muttered.

Chapter 32

'Dad'll hit the roof, Jean.'

They trod carefully over the long grass that had spilled from each side of the canal path and now lay flattened and slimy underfoot. Mottled grey clouds, filled with more rain, brooded low in the sky. The water moved slowly, sucking up debris from the banking as it floated.

'Do you think she's told your mother?'

'Doubt it, no. Mam would have told me. No, Ellen will keep this plan close to her chest.' Mary remembered the last time her sister had attempted to leave home; the offer of the job in that London theatre two years ago had caused major ructions. In the end her father had won. Mary always wondered if Ellen's wildness had worsened because of that. She'd had dreams thwarted before; she wouldn't let it happen again.

'Will you talk to her about it?'

'Mam? Yes, suppose I'll have to sometime. Can't say I'm looking forward to it, though.'

'Well, it's not really your problem, is it?'

'You can bet Ellen won't be around to make it hers. She'll scarper like she always does.'

'Then you'll have to do the same,' Jean said.

'Chance'd be a fine thing,' Mary grumbled. She picked up some stones from the path and skimmed them, one by one, across the water. She watched the ripples circle outwards. 'What am I going to do, Jean? Ellen won't listen to anything I say these days.'

'Look, you've done your best. She'll have to make her own mistakes. She'll come round eventually.'

'From America?'

'It won't come to that, trust me. She'll have to wait until after the war anyway. According to Marion's mother next door but one to us, you know, Marion Cartwright?' Mary shook her head. 'The one with big teeth ...?'

'Oh yes.'

'Well she's been told they won't let their servicemen take British girls back to the States just like that, even if they are married. The men will go home first and then

198

it'll take months of paperwork, all sorts of forms, to get permission and what have you. Ellen will have got fed up with the idea long before then.'

'It would be a relief to think you're right.'

'I am.'

'Nothing has been right since that first time I saw her with Al.'

'Well, I think you did the right thing then and all.' Jean looked upwards.' It's going to rain again. We'd better get a move on.' They quickened their steps. 'One of the few things Frank Shuttleworth was useful for, if you ask me.'

'I was glad of Frank at the time, true enough.'

'Talking of the devil, have you seen him lately?'

A man on a bicycle rang his bell behind them. Mary flinched. Jean cocked her head to one side. 'You're jumpy.'

They stood to one side to let the cyclist pass. He raised his cap to them, said, 'Ladies,' and pressed harder on the pedals, his gas mask and 'snap' bag bumping together on his back.

Jean persisted. 'Mary? I said have you seen Frank lately?'

Mary linked arms with her and sighed. 'Everywhere, Jean, I swear he's following me. Yesterday I was in the queue at the butcher's and he was stood right behind me, pushing up against me.'

'Now that *is* your problem. So what are you going to do?'

'Nothing. What can I do? Last week, when I was going to work he trailed behind me all the way. I knew he wasn't on shift – I'd changed so I wouldn't see him – and there he was. Every time I stopped, so did he, I told him what I thought of him but he just laughed at me. Honestly Jean, he's giving me the creeps.' Mary didn't tell her friend about the whispered threats each time he came near her, or the way he looked at her.

'I'll tell Patrick,' Jean said. 'He'll deal with him.'

'No!' Mary was adamant. 'No, Jean. *I'll* deal with it. Frank wouldn't let Patrick get away with another beating; he'd get some of his mates behind him. I don't want you two to get involved again. Right?'

'Right' Jean pursed her lips.

They stopped at the steps leading up to Skirm. 'Let's get home,' Mary said, 'we're both on earlies tomorrow. She heard a scuffle of stones further down the path. As she looked back a man disappeared into the bushes, but she knew Frank meant her to see him.

And he wasn't her only problem. As Mary left Jean at the end of Moss Terrace, she thought back to the conversation they'd had earlier on their break. 'Be careful, Mary, please.'

'What d'you mean?' But Mary knew what she meant, she seen Jean watching her and Peter after they'd finished the round of the ward. As he left he'd touched her hand, twined his little finger in hers.

'Just be careful,' Jean repeated, 'you're playing with fire.'

'I can't help it, Jean. Peter says we ...'

Jean held up her hand. 'I don't want to discuss it, Mary. I don't know how I feel about it all and I hate keeping anything from Patrick. I owe Doctor Schormann for his kindness when I lost the baby but ... but he's a *German*.' She stressed her words. 'You seem to have forgotten that but I can't; it worries me and I'm frightened for you.'

'Don't be.' Mary put an arm around her. 'Please don't be. I know what I'm doing.'

'Well, I don't think you do, it's madness.' She didn't relax against Mary. ' So don't tell me anything, all right? And be more careful in work.'

'You wouldn't say anything, though, would you? Not to Patrick … not to anyone?'

'You shouldn't need to ask that.' Jean scowled. 'But keep me out of it. That's all I'm asking, keep me out of it.'

Chapter 33

October 1944

My dear Mary

Only a short note, I'm afraid. Gwyneth is coming to visit Iori so she'll get this out for me as well as my article for the Peace News. *Mary, I want you to promise me something. If you won't report Shuttleworth to the Commandant or the police, I want you to promise you'll never go anywhere on your own. It makes me so angry that I can't be there to look out for you, though what use I'd be I don't know, I can't even protect Iori from the bullies in here. He gets pushed around all the time and won't let me do anything about it. He's not like me, Mary, he hasn't an angry bone in his body – just this belief that violence is wrong whatever the circumstances. He thinks words will always solve a problem and I'm ashamed to say that, sometimes, my temper gets the better of me. And then I question if I really am a pacifist. Anyhow, enough of this heart-searching, I need to finish now as Iori is going*

down to the hall for visiting time. Take great care, dear,
and remember what I've said – go nowhere on your own.
There are no signs of my getting out yet. Perhaps in a few
months time I will be up for review again. Iori promises
to show me Llamroth eventually. Perhaps all three of us
will see it together one day.

Keep safe, Mary. Love to Mam.
Tom

Chapter 34

The night air carried a fine drizzle that darkened the stone
outside the entrance of the hospital. Mary held her hand
over her mouth as she yawned; she was exhausted.

'You are tired?' Peter, huddled inside his overcoat,
collar turned up, looked at her.

'Not sleeping well these days.' She swallowed her tea.

'Yes, that can be a problem if one is troubled.' He took
a long gulp from the mug he cupped in his hands, his eyes
anxious over the rim. 'You are troubled?'

Mary shrugged. 'It's nothing.' She stood a few feet
away from him, casually looking across to the other side
of the porch where three orderlies were grouped, the
smoke from their cigarettes settling around them and
mingling with the drizzle. She wondered if Frank was
watching from somewhere in the darkness.

A nurse opened the main doors and said, 'Yes, it's still
raining.'

Another female voice answered, 'I'm not that desperate
for a fag. I'll wait till the end of the shift.'

The doors slowly closed. In the dim light that escaped

from inside the hospital, Mary saw one of the orderlies lift his cup in a gesture of acknowledgement to her and she raised her hand, turning back towards Peter. 'I'd better go in.' She hesitated.

'What is it?'

'Nothing.'

'There is something wrong.' He kept his tone neutral as the men passed them and ran down the steps towards the compound, heads bent against the rain. '*Gutenacht Herr Doctor.*'

'*Gutenacht.*'

The sentry had opened the gate, let the orderlies through and returned to the guardroom before Peter spoke again. 'Tell me, please.'

'It's Frank.'

Peter shifted so that he faced the hospital doors. He took hold of her hand and held it to his chest. She could feel the quickened beat of his heart. 'Shuttleworth?'

'Yes.' She paused. 'I shouldn't…'

'Please, *leibling.*'

'You know I was seeing him for a while. Going out with him.' She heard the suppressed curse, felt the sudden squeeze of his fingers.

'Yes,' Peter said. 'You … he … were courting…'

Mary's voice cracked. 'I suppose you could say that. Just for a very short time. Before I found out what he's like.'

'And you found out?'

'Yes.'

'And now?'

Mary stared towards the fence where the guard had vanished into the darkness, her breathing uneven. 'Now I'm not, haven't been for a while.' Her relationship with

Frank had been acknowledged by them both but not spoken about.

The main doors opened again releasing muted light and voices. He let go of her hand.

'I must go in,' Mary said, 'we've been here too long.'

'What? There is more. You have more to say.' Disregarding the half open doors, Peter held on to her arm. 'What is it?'

'I shouldn't …'

'Mary.' His voice was sharp.

'He's following me,' she said. 'Everywhere I go he's following me.'

Peter's eyes narrowed.

'And I'm frightened. He scares me.'

Chapter 35

'You're wet through.' Her mother took Mary's cape from her and hung it on the back of one of the kitchen chairs in front of the range.

'It's still absolutely pouring out there.' Mary shuddered.

'Third day in a row.' Winifred pushed the iron poker into the fire and gave it a jiggle. 'Get upstairs and get changed. There's some vegetable soup on the range.'

'For a change,' her father grumbled, scratching his stomach through his vest as he appeared at the bottom of the stairs.

'If you don't want it, you know what to do.' Winifred pulled out the table drawer and took out some spoons.

'Aye, I will and all.' Bill went back upstairs. They could hear him grumbling to himself.

'He's more miserable than usual these days,' Mary said, draping her cap over the rack and drying her hair.

Her mother made a face. 'He's lost heart since they announced the Home Guard's going to be disbanded in December. That's his excuse to go The Crown; he's drowning his sorrows because the Home Guard parades end this week. You know him; he likes all that marching about.'

'As long as he doesn't take it out on you.' Mary stripped her stockings off and rubbed her legs and feet then draped the towel over the rail on the range. 'I'll be down in two shakes of a lamb's tail.'

She waited at the bottom of the stairs until her father stepped down into the kitchen and ran upstairs, stopping on the top tread. The door to her bedroom was closed but she could tell Ellen was inside; there was a thin slit of light showing underneath the wood and noises of drawers being opened and closed. She bit her lip. She didn't feel up to dealing with Ellen's moods. Being on nights for the last week had made things easier; at least she didn't have to lie in the same bed being careful not to touch her, listening to her breathing, knowing Ellen was doing the same. But now it was back to the oppressive silences.

There was a worse draught than normal on the landing; her brothers' bedroom door was open. Tom's room now, she corrected herself. Pushing the door wider she clicked the light on. Piles of clothes littered both beds: Ellen's clothes. Mary spun round and lifted the latch on the opposite door. Ellen had her back to her. Wearing only her petticoat she was taking dresses out of the wardrobe and tossing them onto the bed alongside a jumble of underclothes. When Mary walked into the room Ellen stopped but didn't say anything.

'Can't decide what to wear?' Mary tried to joke but her voice was strained. 'What's going on?'

'I'm moving into the boys' room.' Ellen's tone was curt.

'Tom's room, you mean. Why?'

'Why not? It's empty.'

'But it won't be. They'll let him out sometime'.

'And you think Dad will let him come back home?'

'You've still no right.'

'The days when you could tell me what to do are long gone.'

Ellen picked up her clothes and barged past her.

When Mary got downstairs she almost cried out; Frank was hunched over the fire talking to her father who sitting on his chair fastening his bootlaces. She glared at him and then pulled a face at her mother. Winifred raised her shoulders and went into the scullery. Mary followed. 'What's he doing here?' she hissed.

'Says he's come to take your Dad out for a pint.'

'I don't want him here. Doesn't Dad know I'm not seeing him anymore?'

'Does your father care about anything or anybody if there's a free pint in it?'

'I don't believe this!' Mary stood with her arms crossed leaning on the doorframe, glaring at Frank; she wasn't going to allow him to upset her in her own house.

Bill had his face turned sideways, listening as Frank talked.

'We had German prisoners on the train with us when we were being brought home.' Frank leaned back and linked his hands behind his head. 'That was until some of the men found out and threatened to beat them up. The guards stopped the train and they were taken off. If I'd known and I'd been fit enough I'd have killed the bastards for what they did to me.' Frank waited a moment, rubbing the palms of his hands up and down the back of his head. 'And here I am, stuck in a job with a load of other rejects, keeping watch over the bloody scum.' He sneaked a look at Mary before speaking again. 'There's a girl in our street in trouble for fraternizing with one of the Krauts she worked with on a farm somewhere down South. She's been sent home and boy, is she in big trouble now.'

'Should be fucking tarred and feathered.' Bill lifted the cushion on his chair and then stood looking around the kitchen. 'I can't find my jumper. Where's my blue jumper?'

'If you mean the one you've had on your back for the last fortnight, it's in the wash. It walked there by itself.' Winifred opened the sideboard and got out four bowls.

'I need it. I'm going to The Crown.'

'Your red one's in your drawer upstairs. And if you must go out again, you could at least bring me a bottle back.'

'I will if you've got some brass.' He went back upstairs.

Frank turned to look at Mary and smirked. 'Haven't seen you for ages, Mary, how are you keeping?'

Chapter 36

November 1944

'Have you borrowed my green cardigan?' Mary held on to the door handle of what was now Ellen's bedroom.

'Ever heard of knocking?' She had her back to Mary.

Rain blew against the windowpanes and gathered in lines along the wooden frames. Through the smeared glass Mary saw the curtained lights of the houses on the opposite side of the street. 'The curtains should be closed,' she said.

'My room, my business,' Ellen retorted. 'I like them back. Anyway, blackout finished two months ago, if you care to remember.'

'There are still restrictions,' Mary said. 'The "dim out" means we can use ordinary curtains instead of black-out ones … not none at all. But it's not that. They can see you in your underclothes from across the street.' She went over to the window, pulled the curtain across the wire and, out of habit, tucked the material onto the windowsill to make sure no light escaped.

'God, you have to interfere, don't you?' Ellen stepped into her skirt. 'Miss bloody goody two shoes.'

Mary reached past Ellen into the wardrobe. 'Mine I think,' she said, taking the green cardigan from a hanger. 'I'll have it back if you don't —' She glanced at her sister struggling to fasten the buttons on her skirt and stopped before she finished the sentence. 'Ellen? Oh God, no, Ellen, you're not—'

'Pregnant. I'll finish the sentence for you.' Ellen glared at her. 'I'm pregnant. So what?' She stretched her arm past Mary and slammed the bedroom door closed.

'What has Al said?'

'He's gone. He's gone back to America. That should please you, Miss high and bloody mighty.' Ellen took a jumper from the wardrobe and shoved her arms into the sleeves. 'Except you're not so high and bloody mighty, are you?' She pulled it over her head, her voice muffled. 'You do know what it's called, don't you?'

'What?' Mary frowned. 'What what's called?'

'It's called fraternization.' Ellen smoothed the jumper down. 'At least that's what they call just getting friendly with a German. But you've gone one better, haven't you Mary? You sleep with one.'

Mary's legs buckled; she sat on the bed. The window frame rattled with a blast of wind. Downstairs Mary could hear her father coughing as he moved about the kitchen. 'I don't know what you're talking about.'

Ellen folded her arms. 'Frank told me.'

'Frank told you what? When?'

'Never mind when. I just know, that's all.'

'Ellen, you're wrong. You've got it all wrong,' Mary said. 'God, do you know what trouble you'd get me in if you go around saying things like that?'

'True though, huh?'

'No, it's not true. If that's what Frank's said, it's only one of his many nasty lies.'

'Well you would say that, wouldn't you?' Ellen went to the window and opened the curtains again.

'Look, whatever rubbish Frank's told you is –' Mary struggled for the word '– is rubbish. What is real is what's happening with you, Ellen. How long did you think you could hide being pregnant?'

'As long as I needed to.'

'I don't understand.' Mary held out her hand towards her. 'What are you going to do, love?' Ellen didn't move. Mary let her hand drop. 'Have you'd tried to contact Al? His unit?'

'Me and Al finished. He doesn't know.'

'Oh! I didn't know, you didn't say.'

'Why should I? Why should I tell you anything?'

'Don't, Ellen. Don't push me away. What are you going to do? They'll have to be told,' Mary nodded towards the floor. 'You'll not get away with it forever; you'll be showing properly before long. You'll have to tell them.'

'Why?' Ellen lifted her chin. 'I've found out about a place down South. I'll tell them I've got a job, go there.'

'Dad won't let you go.'

'I'm not a kid anymore, I'll go where I like.'

'What kind of place?'

'Somewhere where girls like me,' she said, her mouth twisted, 'girls like me … can stay there until it's … until afterwards … and then they take it away … for adoption.'

'You can't, Ellen, please. You mustn't think about giving your baby away. We'll manage somehow. I'll sort Dad out.'

'And give that lot round here something to gossip about? Old Ma Jagger? Not bloody likely.'

'Sod them. Who cares what anybody thinks?' Mary caught hold of her hand.

Ellen squirmed away from her. 'Who cares? Who cares?' Her voice rose. 'Him downstairs for starters, he'll bloody kill me if he finds out.' She pulled her arms tight to her body and crumpled on to the bed. 'Oh God, oh God.'

'Shush, shush.' Mary pulled her into her arms. 'Come

on now, love, it'll be all right. We'll sort something out.'

Ellen tucked her face against Mary's neck and sobbed.

'How far gone are you?' Mary asked.

'I've missed two periods … I think it must be about eleven weeks. Oh God, what am I going to do?'

Mary stroked her sister's hair; it felt dry and brittle.

The window rattled again as the back door banged. 'That's Dad gone out.'

Ellen sat up. 'What am I going to do?' she said, her voice hoarse. 'He'll kill me.'

'He won't. I won't let him. We'll find a way.'

'I'm sorry I've been so horrible to you.' She leaned on Mary and began to cry again. 'I just wanted to believe Al would take me back to America and every time you said something I remembered how you hated him from the first time you saw him and …'

'Hush now.' Mary rocked her.

'… and I knew it hadn't worked out with you and Frank. So I didn't care …' She stopped.

'Sshhhh.' Mary stopped swaying. 'What, love? You didn't care … about what?'

'Nothing.' Ellen moved her head against Mary's shoulder. 'Nothing.' Ellen wished things hadn't changed between her and Mary. She wished she'd never met Al. Most of all she wished she hadn't been so stupid as to think Frank Shuttleworth was interested in her when all the time all he'd wanted was to hurt her sister …

He'd grinned at Ellen when she opened the door.

'What do you want?'

'Well, that's a nice welcome I must say.'

'Mary's not here.'

'I know,' he said, 'it isn't her I want to see. She obviously hasn't told you we're not going out any more?'

'Oh. No, she hasn't. More fool her then; you were the first bloke that had looked at her for … well forever, as far as I know. Is it Dad you wanted then?'

'Yes.'

'He's gone to The Crown.' Ellen waited a moment. 'You'll probably catch up with him, he's only just left.'

'Mind if I have a word first?'

'Why?'

'Couple of things I want to tell you.'

'What about?'

'Why don't you let me in and then you'll find out?'

Ellen opened the door wider to let Frank in. 'You can't stop long. I'm going out in a bit.' She closed the door and stood with her back to it. 'Mary and I don't talk much these days. You probably know why,' she said, her tone petulant. She watched Frank slowly raise one eyebrow as though he was making fun of her and then noticed his expression change to one of appreciation. His gaze moved over her long slender legs, the curve of her hips under the thin material of her dress. She pulled her shoulders back, thrusting forward her breasts. 'She doesn't like Al.' Ellen pushed her lower lip out in a provocative manner. 'Hasn't since the first time she saw him that night in the pub; since you both saw us. Remember that night, do you?' she said, unable to resist the slight stab of resentment.

'Probably more than you do, love.' Frank smiled. Laughter lines crinkled around his dark grey eyes and the dimple in his chin deepened.

He was very attractive when he smiled. Ellen wondered why she hadn't noticed before. 'Won't be a minute.' In the scullery she took a small mirror out of the pocket of her coat, quickly applied some lipstick and pinched both cheeks. Pulling the grips out of her blonde hair, she shook it free. A feeling of excitement fluttered in her stomach. She wasn't sure what was going on but it had made her feel good to see the look of pleasure on his face. And it'd be one in the eye for Mary if she went out with Frank. Mary must have been crazy to dump him. When she returned Frank was sitting at the table with his leg held stiffly out in front of him, his jacket slung over the back of the chair. She sat down opposite him. 'What happened to your knee, then?'

'Just something I picked up at Dunkirk,' he said shortly.

'If you don't want to talk about it, it's no skin off my nose.'

'Let's just say it buggered up my life and have done with it.'

'Fine by me.' She bit her thumbnail.

'You've got my bad habit.' Frank said

Ellen tilted her head. 'What's that?'

'Biting your nails. I always do that when I'm worried … or nervous.'

'I don't know what you mean.' She tossed her hair away from her face.

'You look worried.'

'I don't, I'm not.'

'Seems to me you are. Trouble with this boyfriend of yours?'

The tears came all at once. 'Our Mary told me he's got another girl on the go.' She looked defiantly at him. 'I think she's out to cause trouble between us.' A hint of uncertainty came into her voice. 'Anyway, if he's been

213

messing me around, he'll be sorry.'

'Poor chap.'

Ellen gave a defiant laugh. 'No man messes me about.' She stood up. 'I have to go, I'll be late.'

He caught hold of her hand. 'Hang on a bit. You can't go out all upset. He'll think you're desperate and that won't do, will it?'

Ellen suddenly realised she was going nowhere.

Frank took hold of her other hand. 'Come on, sit down for a minute. If you don't want to talk about your Yank –' he grinned, disarming her '– we can talk about something else.' He gave her fingers a slight tug. 'We've never really talked, you and me. Never had the chance, have we? What do you say? I know … you choose a subject, any subject.'

At that moment a familiar low whine began in the distance.

Afterwards, for weeks afterwards, Ellen often wondered if things would have gone as far as they did if the air raid hadn't happened. As the warning got louder and louder, Frank cursed. 'What's the point of Moaning Minnie these days? We wouldn't know where the V2s are going to land anyway, we can't soddin' hear them, so why warn us? Bloody bombs could be anywhere.'

Ellen was panicking. 'We have to get under the table,' she said. 'Quick, drag the hearth rug under.' She ran to the back door and clicked the light off; for some reason it made her feel safer. By the light of the fire, they shifted the chairs and pushed the rag rug under the stout oak table. Frank propped himself up against one of the table legs and eased Ellen back so she was leaning on him. He put his arms around her. She was still trembling. 'No point in being scared,' he said, 'we're as safe here as anywhere.'

She snuggled down as though it was the most natural thing for her to do. Wonder what you'd think of this, Mary Howarth, she thought. 'I know but I just hate it,' she said. 'I hate everything about this bloody war.'

'Bloody Germans,' he said.

'Yeah, bloody Germans.'

'And your sister's sleeping with one.' The frown lines on Frank's forehead furrowed for an instant but when Ellen pulled away from him his face was expressionless.

'What? No! I don't believe you.'

'Why would I lie?'

'I don't know.' Ellen paused. 'Anyway, how could she be? The only ones she sees are POW patients at the hospital.'

'And the doctors…'

'One of the doctors? My God, how could she?' Her voice lowered to a whisper. 'She could get done for fraternizing.' Ellen was silent, a slow anger growing inside her. After all Mary had said about Al, she was carrying on with one of the enemy – a bloody Jerry. She couldn't take it in. 'How do you know though? Have you seen them?'

He closed his eyes as though in confirmation. 'So, who is she to judge anyone, eh?'

'Just wait until I see her.'

It was then he'd stopped Ellen talking. Leaning over, he covered her mouth with his. She opened her lips to let his tongue explore. Slowly unbuttoning her blouse, he freed her breasts from her brassiere and lowering his head, sucked on one nipple. Immediately Ellen felt the heat radiate from her thighs. She moaned and arched her back, sliding down on to the rug. Unbuttoning her

215

skirt, Frank lifted her slightly and tugged it down. He stroked the smoothness of skin between stocking top and camiknickers. She touched him, felt him respond. Shrugging out of her blouse, she dragged the brassiere straps down her arms. He fumbled with his braces and buttons and pushed his trousers past his buttocks. Tracing his tongue over her lips, he gently circled one nipple with his palm before trailing his hand along her hips, pulling her camiknickers over her thighs and down to her ankles. She flicked them away and, as he moved his mouth up over her stomach, breast, throat, she groaned again and curved backwards. From what she knew of Mary, she wouldn't have let this man do these things to her. Well, as she'd thought earlier, more fool Mary. She had him now. Ellen wound her arms around his neck and drew him towards her, feeling his hands down her body, stroking the soft blond hair between her thighs, and cautiously sliding a finger into her. She was ready for him.

'What is it?' Mary said again.

'Nothing.' Ellen buried her face against her sister's neck. What had happened during that air raid wasn't something Ellen wanted to remember, let alone tell her sister about.

They'd both dozed until the all clear began its wail. Frank jumped up. 'Blast!' He pulled on his trousers and hauled his braces back over his shoulders. 'Come on, get up,' he said curtly, 'if we get caught they'll go mad.'

'You needn't worry. I told you, I'm not expecting Mam back for ages.' Ellen's words were automatic; she knew he couldn't wait to get away from her. She could feel the hard lumps of the rug underneath her back and turned on her side. In the ashy glow of the fire, her skin, gleaming with perspiration, revealed the roughness of his lovemaking, ugly bruised swellings against the paleness. Sitting up, she pushed her arms into the crumpled blouse and looked around for her discarded camiknickers and skirt. 'Does this mean we're going out, now? You've definitely finished with our Mary?'

She would never forget his words. 'You must be joking! I haven't finished with her yet. Not by a long way.'

The burnt out coals settled softly in the fireplace, smothering the last tiny flames. In the dark Ellen felt rather than saw him move away from her. She turned her head as the harsh snap of the latch broke the silence, watched his shadowy figure as he shrugged on his coat. Tears scalded her eyes and she gave a loud hiccupping sob. How could he? How could he lie? Bastard …

He didn't look back as he closed the door.

Mary waited a few more minutes but the moment had gone; whatever Ellen had intended to say, she'd obviously decided not to. It wasn't important. After a while Mary said again, 'It'll be all right. But we've got to tell Mam and the sooner the better.'

Chapter 37

December 1944

Jean tucked Mary's scarf into her coat and adjusted her hat lower on her head. 'You look after yourself. You're bearing the brunt of all this. Now, mind how you go, it's slippery out there.' She opened the front door. 'Remember what Patrick said about us helping out.'

'I meant it; if you need anything just ask,' her brother said, leaning over Jean's shoulder. 'And when you do decide to tell Dad about Ellen, let me know and I'll be there in case he kicks off. Just remember, huh?'

Marriage had certainly improved Patrick. 'Thanks.' Mary gave him a quick smile but doubted she would; another fight was all they needed and perhaps all her brother wanted to prove to his father was that he could no longer rule the roost unopposed. She pushed away the cynical thought, no, it was that, perhaps for the first time in his life, Patrick was content. Still she wasn't chancing anything. Jean had been through enough, which was why she hadn't told Jean that the business with Frank was getting worse and she was becoming more scared. Patrick might seem calmer, but she knew he would beat the living daylights out of his former drinking pal if he knew. It must be bad enough him seeing Frank and Bill together in The Crown.

'I will. But keep it to yourselves for now, won't you? I tried talking to her, but we still don't know if she'll keep the baby yet and if she decides not to Dad doesn't need to know. It seems to be a decent place from what she said and she sounded all right. I think it helped making friends with her roommate so quickly. I'll let you know more when she rings next week.' Mary stepped on to the pavement clutching the wall of the house to stop herself sliding. 'Don't stand on the step, you two, you'll freeze.' She smiled at them. 'And don't leave it too long before you tell Mam your good news either, it'll cheer her up.'

'We just want to leave it until we know everything's going to be fine, especially after last time,' Jean said. 'You sure you don't want Patrick to see you home?'

'Don't be daft, no point in him going out in this as well.'

The sleet, driven by a biting wind stung her face. She pulled the woollen scarf up over her nose, gingerly picking her way along Shaw Street.

It would be nice for Mam to have some good news after the last two weeks; Mary knew she'd been frantic with worry. Ellen had left home, leaving her parents a note to say she'd had the offer of a better-paid job in a factory in Shrewsbury, but Mary was still unsure whether she would keep the baby.

'God I'm frozen,' Mary said, resting Ellen's suitcase on the porter's trolley and stamping her feet on the platform. 'We've been here nearly an hour.'

'I couldn't stand it in the house any longer. I was terrified Dad would come home and catch us.' Ellen chewed the skin at the side of her thumbnail and looked up at the large station clock. 'It should be here in ten minutes, anyway.'

'We could have gone into the waiting room.' Mary jigged up and down and banged her gloved hands together. 'Aren't you cold?'

'I can't remember the last time I was warm.' Ellen glanced towards the steamed-up window of the little building that was crammed with people. 'But I'm not going in there to be skenned at.'

'Nobody would be looking at you, why would they? Anyway you're muffled up to the eyebrows; nobody could tell.'

'Huh!' Ellen puffed out a small cloud of white air, nodding towards the suitcase. 'Somebody would have something to say.' She wrapped her arms around herself. 'I'll miss you, Mary. I am sorry about … everything, you know.'

'I know, love. And there really is no need to go yet,' Mary said. 'You're only four months, you're hardly showing.' An unwelcome thought rose up: look what had happened to Jean at this stage of her pregnancy. Please God, don't let me wish that on Ellen, Mary thought.

'Showing enough.'

'Are you sure the home will take you in this early?'

'Yes, I checked.'

All at once a shrill whistle accompanied an increasing regular pound of metal on rails.

'Mary!' The expression of panic on Ellen's face reflected on her sister's.

'You'll be all right.'

'I'll be all right.'

They spoke together and gave a strained laugh.

'You do know you can come home if you don't like the place?'

'Give my love to Mam, promise not to tell Dad, tell Tom I'll write. Was he very cross with me?'

'I'll tell Mam … I promise … course he wasn't,'

There was no more time; the wheels grated, screeched to a halt. The waiting room door was flung back and people pushed past the two girls standing together, arms around one another.

'Come home.' Mary pushed a strand of Ellen's hair behind her ear. Her cheek was icy cold.

'I can't.' Tears poured down her face. 'I can't.'

'If you change your mind about keeping the … it …'

'I won't.'

'Write!'

'Write, too!'

Then Ellen was gone. Mary watched the train struggle away from the platform. Steam covered her feet.

Thinking about it now Mary could almost taste the acrid smell of smoke left behind by the train.

It wasn't that far from Moss Terrace but by the time she turned into the alley Mary was frozen and breathless and her scarf was stuck to her mouth. Jean was right, she would be taking the responsibility for everything, but she had no choice. She'd promised Ellen it would be all right, but she knew that the consequences of her sister's actions would, as usual, affect them all.

She paused for a moment, looking along the terrace. The blackout curtains had been removed with a collective sigh of relief and the cloak of darkness driven away by flickering fires and forty-watt bulbs.

It also meant there were less shadows for Frank to hide in.

Next door's bedroom light lit up the back gate which hung drunkenly on one hinge. Mary stepped cautiously over the splintered wood and looked around the yard.

Although the corners were crusted white, the flags were slushy with melted sleet and in the centre the sunken grid was overflowing. As though her feet weren't wet enough, she thought. There didn't seem to be anything else wrong but, unusually for this time of night, the house was in darkness.

Her father and mother were sitting at the table. The fire was out and the room felt as cold as outside.

'Mam? What is it? Is it Tom, Ellen?' Mary switched the light on. She could see her mother had been crying. 'What's wrong?'

Bill shoved his chair back and it crashed to the floor. 'What's wrong? What's bloody wrong?' he yelled, 'I'll show you what's soddin' wrong.' He leapt at her, fist raised, and knocked her to the floor. He stood over her. 'Don't get up,' he bellowed. 'Don't get up or by God I'll kill you; you and that slut of a sister of yours if I ever get my hands on her.'

'That's enough.' Winifred pushed him. He grabbed her, his fingers round her throat and forced her backwards until she was pressed against the sideboard.

Holding the back of her head, Mary got on her knees, squeezing her eyes closed. She hung on to the armchair and hoisted herself to her feet; looking around in bewilderment. She saw the two figures struggling and launched herself across the kitchen at him. 'Let her go.' She clung round his neck, taking him by surprise and they swung from left to right as they staggered backwards around the kitchen, banging into the furniture. He was smaller than her but she felt the strength in his fingers as he forced her arms apart and flung her away. She tripped over the hearthrug and fell, half under the table. As he came at her again, she scuttled backwards, reached up and grabbed the back of the cutlery drawer, pushing it forward as hard as she could. It hit him in the crotch. As he doubled up, Mary scrabbled on all fours to Winifred. 'Mam?' They clutched one another. 'Mam? What's happened?'

'He's found out about Ellen having a baby, God only knows how.' Winifred's voice rasped in her throat. 'And Frank Shuttleworth's been telling him some tale about you and one of the German doctors.'

'Oh my God Mam, what's he been saying?' Mary put her hand on her mother's face and turned it towards hers. 'Frank's not right in the head, Mam. He won't accept we're finished and he's been following me for months. He won't let me alone. Whatever he's said, he's made it up. It's not true.'

'Did you think I wouldn't find out?' Bill rolled on the rug gasping, his hands between his thighs. 'He's been hinting about it for fucking weeks and tonight he came right out and said it. If he hadn't told me, I'd have found out sooner or later. I have eyes in my arse, you should know that by now. Nowt gets past me.'

The two women watched him. The clock springs whirred and the hammer struck seven times. Bill crawled towards them. In panic, Mary reached above her head and groped along the top of the sideboard. She brought the bread knife down within inches of his face. Her hand quivered, but she kept her eyes on his. 'Don't come any nearer,' she said. 'I mean it.'

He fell back on his haunches. Then without speaking he staggered to his feet and reeled across to the stairs, still holding himself with one hand. Hanging on to the curtain he turned to look at them both, but the hatred was directed only at Mary. 'Bleedin' sluts,' he said. 'You and your dirty bloody sister. Just like your mother, I should'a known ...'

They listened as, step by step, he went slowly up the stairs.

Grating sobs woke Mary the following morning. Her mother, sitting up straight in the bed, stared towards the door as Mary looked in. She opened her mouth but no sound came. Mary watched as she ran her tongue over her thin dry lips.

'Mam, what is it?'

The pinched face turned to the figure lying beside her. Bill, still seeming to be asleep, he was snoring, but as Mary approached the bed she saw that his face was distorted and slack.

'Dad?' She touched his cheek; his skin was cold and clammy. She knelt down by the side of the bed and held his wrist between two fingers and thumb. The pillow was wet under his head, saliva dribble from the corner of his mouth. 'It's a stroke, I think,' she said slowly to the weeping woman sitting motionless at his side. 'He's had a stroke.'

Bill Howarth didn't die that day or during the following week, but an expectant hush fell over the house. Patrick brought a bed downstairs for him. The days dragged in monotony and Christmas came and went unnoticed.

Chapter 38

January 1945

'Come on Dad, just try some more.' Mary tipped the mashed potatoes mixed with the precious ration of butter into the toothless mouth. Bill's lips clamped shut at an angle and some of the food dribbled out. She scraped it up from his chin with the spoon and tried again. He turned his head away. 'Enough? OK then. Do you want to sit up?' One eye closed. 'Right, hold on.' Mary put the dish on top of the sideboard. She glanced at the clock. Her mother should be back in a minute. At least she hoped so, she only had half an hour to get ready and be at the hospital in time for her next shift. And she wanted, needed, to see Peter even if it was only a glimpse of him. For some reason, they always seemed to be on different shifts these day.

She eased her father up on the pillows, feeling the sharp boniness of his shoulder blades, and gently pulled the sheet up to his chin. 'There!' She tucked the bedding under the mattress on both sides. 'Tucked up like a boat.' Mary laughed quietly. 'Do you remember that? That's what you used to say every night.' At least that was what he'd tease after he'd pulled the sheet taut on Ellen's side. Mary took the dish into the scullery and ran cold water into it. Now, where had that come from? she chided herself. She'd never been jealous of her sister, not even the times when they were little and her father had swung Ellen onto his shoulders so she could see more of the Ashford carnival or Father Christmas' procession. Mary remembered looking up and laughing with Ellen, never expecting that it should be her he held.

She wondered if her sister would come home when she got the letter. Tom obviously couldn't, but Ellen? No, perhaps it would be better if she didn't.

She went to the doorway of the scullery. Bill was agitated, jerking his head from side to side, and the strands of grey hair trailed down the side of his face, getting in his eyes. Mary opened the cutlery drawer and took out a pair of scissors. Standing at the side of the bed she smoothed his hair back into place. 'It's annoying you, isn't it?' She stroked his cheek with the back of her fingers. 'How about we cut it?' She bent down close to him.

Anger darkened his eyes. He pushed with one shoulder at the sheets. His arm swung in an arc and hit her hard across the side of the head. The movement prompted his body to react and a stench leaked into the air. He glared at Mary, humiliation mixed with despair.

Mary's eyes watered with the blow, but still she said, 'Don't worry, it can't be helped. I'll clean you up.'

The back door opened and an icy blast of air swept into the kitchen. 'I've posted both letters. They should get them in a few days.' Winifred's nose wrinkled involuntarily. Her husband's eyes met hers and then she turned to Mary. She laid a hand on her arm and gently pulled her away from the bed. 'I'll see to him.'

Mary nodded. 'I'll go and get ready for work.' Stepping onto the first stair she stood for a moment to watch them. Her mother held his hand close to her cheek then carefully turned his palm upwards and kissed it. He watched her, expressionless. Mary heard the whisper, 'I love you,' the words sounded strange, unused; her mother's voice that of a young woman.

Mary let the curtain slip back into place and slowly walked up the stairs. She didn't understand; she could, *did,* identify with the care and compassion her mother gave to him, after all it was part of her own make-up, something innate in her so that she could do the work she loved. But had her mother forgotten everything? All the regrets, the disappointments, the humiliations and the violence she'd endured, that her children had grown up with? Or did she remember them yet was still able to utter those words.

Mary breathed in a long deep breath and let it escape through tightened lips. No, she didn't understand that kind of love. The image of Frank's face flashed into her mind. She couldn't imagine she ever would.

Chapter 39

Although the fire baked the kitchen and the bed was piled high with eiderdowns taken from the other beds, Bill still shivered uncontrollably.

'Do you want the radio on?'

Bill moved his head on the pillow. Mary watched his lips struggle to form the words. Eventually he muttered, 'Talk.' The effort was too much for him. He collapsed into the pillows surrounding him.

'Talk? I would've thought that with all the visitors you've had over the last two weeks you'd had enough of hearing folk talking.' Mary turned the sleeve of the dress she was ironing on the kitchen table. 'OK, what shall we talk about then? Jean and Patrick having the baby, that's something to look forward to, isn't it?' She hung the dress on a wooden hanger, hooked it over the scullery door and took a pyjama jacket out of the wash basket. 'And Ellen? We'd a lovely letter from Ellen yesterday.' Mary kept the fixed smile on her face. Seeing the vagueness in his eyes, she put the iron down on the asbestos mat and walked over to the bed. 'It's all right,' she said.

'Ell …?' he gasped, 'where …?'

'He can't remember what's happened.' Her mother, dozing in her armchair, had woken up. She got up. 'Don't remind him,' she whispered. She moved nearer to the bed. 'Ellen's gone away for a few days. Bit of a holiday.'

Bill frowned. 'Want.'

'She'll be back before you know it,' Mary said. 'Shall I make a brew?'

'No, I'll do it. I need to go out to the lavvy first though.' Winifred wrapped her shawl around her head and folded it across her chest. 'Tempted though I am to use your father's throne. It's freezing out there.' She clutched the ends of the shawl in her fists. 'I should shift it; he'll not be able to use it again, will he?' She peered under the bed. 'It's full,' she exclaimed. 'He hasn't …?'

'No, he hasn't. I emptied the bedpan into it.' Mary said. 'He's been too twitchy for me to leave him. Sorry, I'll take it to the lavatory now.'

'My job, I think.'

Mary opened the back door for her and closed it as Winifred carefully carried the pot out. When she turned, Bill was still looking at her. 'What is it Dad?' Walking over to him she clasped his cold hand as his face contorted. 'Take your time.' Tears escaped and rippled over the skin on his cheeks.

228

He closed his eyes. When he opened them again, they searched her face. She could tell he was frightened. But there was something else. She watched the tongue flop out of his mouth, slide along his lower lip and curl back into his mouth. 'Sorry.' The word, lisping, spilled out. His Adam's apple moved under the skin on his neck. 'Sorry.' He raised his forefinger slightly and pointed at her. 'Frank … no … good.'

'Frank? No good? Well, I know that,' she said. 'Does that mean you believe me and not Frank?'

He moved his chin up and down. 'Mmmm.'

Mary dropped to his knees and covered his hand with both of hers. 'Oh Dad.' She rested her forehead on their hands before looking up at him.

His eyelids drooped leaving a thin line of white showing. 'To … Tom …' he stammered.

'Tom?' She searched his face. 'You want me to tell Tom you understand what he had to do.' She waited. 'That you're sorry you fell out. I can write and tell him. He'll be so …'

'No!' The word exploded from her father's mouth.

It was the last thing Bill Howarth said. He died that night.

Chapter 40

January 1945

… so now you know the truth, Mary, and you'll see why I can't keep this baby. I have to give it up. There would be too many bad memories and every day it would remind

us. I couldn't stand it and I know you wouldn't be able to either. I hope you can forgive me.

Ellen.

'You were to blame for Dad's stroke.' Mary glared at Frank, who was on duty at the side gate.

'Crap.' Frank sauntered towards the fence, rifle slung casually over his shoulder.

'He used to like you,' she said, 'thought you were the son he should have had; the son he thought he wanted.'

He sniggered, drawling the words out. 'Well, who wouldn't?'

'But then he found out what you were really like. He got himself into a state and he had a stroke because of you and your lies.'

'Lies?' Rocking up and down on his heels, a sneer distorted the lower half of his face.

'Yes, lies.' Mary waited a moment, studying him. How had she ever imagined herself in love with this man? 'Lies about me.' He raised an eyebrow. 'And the lies you told about being injured at Dunkirk.'

Frank's jaw jutted forward. 'What?' The word clicked against the back of his teeth.

Mary glanced towards the guardhouse at the main gate where the sentry was watching them with curiosity, only yards away. She stepped closer to the fence. 'Remember Barry Gates? His dad drinks at The Crown. Barry came home on leave.' She tilted her head, questioning. 'Mam told me last night that his father came to see my dad before he died.' Her heart was beating so hard she felt she moved with each pulse. She steadied herself as Frank came closer on the other side of the fence. 'Barry

230

was in your unit. He remembers you only too well,' she said. 'You and your temper. He also remembered the fight when you were shot in the knee when your own gun went off accidentally.' Mary looked sideways. There were two guards at the main gate watching them now. 'What lies did you tell the MoD to get this civilian post, Frank?' Mary raised her voice.

Frank glanced to his right at the two men. 'Shut it,' he said.

'Well, you must have said something for them to get you a job as a guard.'

'If you don't shut your mouth …' He took a backward step and, gulping in air he leant against the sentry hut. 'What d'you think you can do about it?' He held his hand steady as he lit a cigarette.

'Nothing. Not much anyway.' She wasn't going to tell him she'd spoken to Barry Gates and his father and asked them not to tell anyone. They hadn't understood, but they'd respected Bill and agreed to let Mary deal with Frank, so she repeated, 'I'm not going to do anything for the time being. It's what you're going to do: you're going to stop following me. Leave me alone. Leave my family alone. Leave Doctor Schormann and the other men alone.'

'Schormann?'

She kept her eyes on him. 'Yes.'

'Fucking knew it. I fucking knew you were in with him.'

'No,' she said, 'I'm not. I just don't like bullies and that's what you are.' She tossed a glance towards the two guards watching. 'You and your cronies.'

She threaded her fingers through the wire of the fence, speaking softly, 'And there's something else, Frank. Ellen.'

231

Frank's mouth worked. 'What about her?' His eyes narrowed.

'I had a letter from her.'

'So? Sod all to do with me.' Frank threw his half-finished cigarette to the floor and ground it underfoot, moving closer.

Mary didn't move. For the first time in months she wasn't afraid of him. 'She's having a baby.' His head jerked upwards, his mouth slack. 'She says it's yours.' Frank made a guttural sound. 'Oh, don't worry, she wants nothing from you. She's not keeping it.' Mary felt a twist of pain as she said the words. 'I just wanted you to know … that I know what you did to her … to me.'

'You can't pin it on me. What about her Yank?'

'She says she hadn't slept with Al for weeks … before you … you …' Mary swallowed. 'Before he was posted home and I believe her. It's your child.'

'You'll get nowt out of me,' Frank blustered. One of the two guards began to saunter towards them.

'Like I said, you don't have to worry on that score.' Mary didn't bother keeping the contempt out of her voice. 'And I won't be telling anybody.' She saw the look of relief flash across his face and felt sick. 'Except, of course, my brothers, if I need to. You do understand what I'm saying, don't you?'

'Brothers? Brothers?' Frank sniggered. 'You're joking. That coward in prison?'

'Don't underestimate Tom, Frank. He'll be out one day and he has a fiery temper; especially if someone he loves is getting hurt. So remember, he'll want you to leave me alone and he'll want you to leave Ellen alone. If you don't you'd better watch your back.' The man walking towards them had stopped and was kneeling down fiddling with his shoelace. 'But not just him, there's Patrick too. I don't suppose it will be long before Patrick finds out about Barry Gates; knowing how that lot talk in The Crown. But that's your problem, not mine. Perhaps you'd better start thinking about getting another transfer well away from Ashford.' Let him stew on that, she thought and forced herself to walk confidently towards the hospital steps.

Chapter 41

'Bring her through to the kitchen; it's warmer in there than in the parlour.' Mary put her shoulder to the front door and forced it open. 'This always sticks in winter; we should have sorted it before the funeral.'

'I thought we'd have to carry him out through the back,' Patrick whispered. 'I could just see us marching down the alley with him.' He raised his voice, 'Come on, Mam,' and helped Winifred up the front step and along the hall. 'Leave the door, I'll come back and see to it in a minute.'

Jean helped Mary to get the older woman out of her coat before taking her own off and unpinning the small black hat tilted to the side of her head.

'I've never seen so many at one funeral,' Mary said, putting the kettle on the range and thinking that her father must have been a much nicer man outside the house than he was to his family. 'You are stopping for a brew?' She flung her coat over the back of one of the kitchen chairs and looked at her mother. 'Mam, I'll help you with your shoes now.' She crouched in front of her. 'Let me take them off and then you can have your cup of ...'

'I should have been with him,' Winifred cut in. 'I should have been there.'

'Mam?' Mary undid the laces.

'When he died.' Winifred looked at each of them in turn. 'When he died I should have been with him.'

'He didn't know, Mam, he died in his sleep.' Mary slipped the shoes off and put them at the side of the chair.

'It was my turn to sit with him. You should have woken me up.'

'No point in worrying about that now, love.' Mary leaned back, opened the range door and took out a newspaper-wrapped parcel. She shook it and her mother's slippers fell out. 'Let's get these on you, they're nice and warm.'

'More than he is. He's not warm.' Her voice was flat. 'He's cold … cold in that box … in that hole …'

'Oh Mam.' Patrick knelt by her side and put his arms around her.

She stroked his hair, staring into the fire and then at Bill's armchair. 'I'm tired. I want to go to bed. Take me upstairs, our Mary.'

'I've got some bottles of stout for you Mam. Don't you want one?'

'Not at the moment, maybe later. I just want to sleep now.'

When Mary came down Jean had already poured the tea and she and Patrick were sitting at the table.

'We should have had a bit of a send off for the old man,' he said.

'Mam didn't want a do, Patrick. You can always have a pint on him at The Crown. I'm sure Stan will set something up.'

'Aye, you're right.' He looked around and then towards the hall. 'I'll try and fix that door before I go.'

'Just make sure it's properly closed and locked, that's all. We won't be using it again for a while.' As soon as he'd gone into the hall, Mary said quietly, 'Did you see me talking to Frank's mother outside the church?'

'The big woman?' Jean said. 'I wondered who she was.'

'It was good of her to come. She's a nice woman. She said his brother, George, is living with her as well now, since he got demobbed from the National Fire Service in September.'

'He's the one who tried to persuade you to stay with Frank?'

'Yes.'

'Hmm, how did she find out about your father?'

'Guess.' Mary made a face.

'Did you tell her what Frank's been doing? You know, following you?'

'No. She wouldn't be able to do anything and it might make him worse if she tried.'

The front door thudded.

'How, Mary?' Jean said. 'How could things get worse? From what you say he's still following you everywhere.'

'He might change now. I told him to leave me alone. Now Dad's died there's no need for him to come anywhere near the house or us ...'

'Do you think he'll take any notice? He hasn't so far, so what's so different now?'

Mary didn't answer. She hadn't told Jean about Barry Gates or Ellen's letter.

'I don't care what you say, you should let me tell Patrick.'

'Tell me what?' Patrick stood in the doorway.

'Nothing, love, did you manage the door?'

'Yeah, I'll come back with my carpenter's plane and scrape a bit off the top edge. I'll do the back gate as well.' He looked at the girls, his face guarded. 'We off now? I'm due in work.'

At the back door Mary said, 'I'm going to see Tom next week. Let him know how everything went. Will you sit with Mam, while I'm gone, Jean?'

'Of course. Does he know about us?' Jean said. 'Having a family?'

'I thought you'd have written to him.' Mary looked at them both in surprise.

'No,' Jean said. 'We thought you would.'

'It's your news and he'd have appreciated a visit from you, Patrick. You could have told him yourself.'

Patrick shook his head. 'Been too busy lately.'

Mary closed the door behind them. As far as she knew Patrick had never been near The Scrubs. She sighed and collected the mugs off the table and took them into the scullery. Obviously the old animosity still rankled in her youngest brother. Even with Dad gone it seemed the family was always going to be split.

Winifred was still asleep three hours later. Mary peeped in at the bedroom door. The room was shadowed orange and black from the small fire that she'd lit in the grate earlier. She waited for the harsh coughing to split the silence of the house before she remembered she would never hear it again. Her mother was still curled in the foetal position that she'd been in when she fell asleep but Mary must have disturbed her; she straightened her legs,

236

shivered and drew them up again.

Mary backed onto the landing but not before she heard the whisper, 'Bill?' She saw Winifred run her hand over the well-worn dent in the flock of the pillow where her husband had lain his head for so many years. 'Oh, Bill.'

Chapter 42

February 1945

Mary leant forward on the bed, sliding the envelope backwards and forwards between her fingers and staring at the window. Through the ice-patterned panes the light was a bright pearly grey. She could hear the hooves of the milkman's horse slipping and scraping on the road and the laughter of children sliding down the footpath but her thoughts were on the letter she'd just read. She read the cramped handwriting again.

My dear Mary

I guessed from what you were saying that Mam's drinking a bit.

That's quite an understatement, Tom, she thought.

I know it's hard but you'll have to let her grieve in her own way. Just accept it for now and keep an eye on her. I know her and Dad rowed a lot but she must be really missing him – they had been married a long time. And, in an odd sort of way, I'll miss him too. I've spent years resenting him but when you told me what he'd said, that he finally understood how I felt – well it meant so much.

Mary's lips formed a wry smile. She could imagine the fury on her father's face if he knew what she'd done. She reached down and absently rubbed her toes; her chilblains were worse than ever this year.

I've been thinking a lot about Ellen. When you first told me about the baby I presumed the American was the father. It was a shock when you said it was Shuttleworth. I think you're right not to tell anyone else in the family, although I have to admit it makes me sick to my stomach after all he's done.

And me, the bastard.

If Dad had his stroke the night Shuttleworth told him about your 'friend' then, as far as I'm concerned he caused it. For that and what it's done to Mam, he will pay one day.

It must be hard for Ellen to hear about Patrick and Jean starting a family. Iori and I have talked a lot about her baby and we've a suggestion. Do you think it would make her change her mind about keeping the baby if we all offered to help? Sooner or later I'll be coming home and Iori's said he'll give Ashford a try. We're both bound to get jobs so we can help in that way as well. It doesn't matter that Ellen's not married. I know what it's like to be ostracized and I've learned not to care and she mustn't either.

Easier said than done, Tom.

As long as the baby's loved by all of us that's all that matters. And it will be, won't it?

Mary closed her eyes. Of course the baby would be loved, the circumstances of its birth wouldn't be the baby's fault, he couldn't think they'd blame it for that. Was he asking because the baby was Frank's or because he thought she was still angry at Ellen? Either way he should know her better than that. She'd told him she'd made her peace with Ellen months ago. And she couldn't care less about Frank. Although there was no sign of him getting a transfer, as far as she could tell, he wasn't following her anymore, so she didn't care. At least that was what she kept telling herself.

To be honest we'd both have preferred to go to Llamroth to start a new life but I've told Iori you'll make him welcome ...

But would anyone else? Tom had been detested for his beliefs for years now, how much worse would it get, how would people react if they saw him with Iori? If it was obvious to her they were too close, it wouldn't be long before others saw it too. People could be so cruel. Tom and Iori would be hounded at the very least; at the worst they would be prosecuted. How would Mam cope with that? Or Patrick?

God she was so tired of having to worry about everybody else in the family.

I doubt either Iori or I will ever get married, Mary, so I think between us all we could help Ellen to make it work.

Because, of course, I'll never get married either, will I? The thought was an automatic acerbic reaction to Tom's words, but Mary knew what he wrote was a reality. The muscle in her jawline quivered as she clenched her teeth. She had to face it; there could never be any future between her and Peter. Her eyes were hot with angry tears. She hated this bloody war!

Mary had said the same thing to Peter the last time they'd been alone together, the week before her father had his stroke. For once careless, she'd hurried along the dimly lit corridors and down the stone steps to the boiler house in the hospital basement where he waited for her.

'But then we would not have met, *mien Liebling*.' Peter held both her hands in his against his chest. 'We would not be here now.'

'I know. I should not ask you to meet me here. I'm putting you in such danger, Peter.'

'Doing this we are both in danger, sweetheart,'

'Shall I go then?'

'No.'

They stood still, each savouring the closeness of the other in the light that escaped from around the doors of the large furnace at the other end of the room.

'I love you.' Mary lifted her face to his. 'I can't bear it, Peter, it's so unfair.'

'And I love you, *ich liebe Sie* Mary.' He released her hands and pulled her to him, slowly touching each part of her face with his mouth until his lips were over hers. They were still for a moment and then they kissed.

For Mary, even her fear of everything she could lose couldn't stop the intense craving to have this man's body against hers. She pressed herself against him, her eyes closed, moving slowly with the rhythm of his hands on her.

'You are sure?' Peter drew away from her, spoke softly.

'Sure,' she murmured, unbuttoning first the white apron bib and then the bodice of her uniform.

He freed her breasts and flicked his tongue around her nipples. She ground her hips against his, pulling at his shirt, and ran her palms over the smoothness of his skin, realising how strong, how muscular he must have been in his former life. Even now, despite the privations of camp life, his arms were strong enough to lift her off her feet and press her against the wall. He kissed her, one arm still holding her around the waist so her breasts were crushed to his chest. He lifted the skirt of her uniform with his other hand and, hooking his thumb around the waistband of her camiknickers, tugged until they fell around her ankles.

Her lips still brushing his, she struggled with the buttons of his trouser. 'Oh hell,' she breathed, 'I can't ...' She tugged again.

Peter laughed a low hoarse sound and putting his fingers over hers helped to release the buttons. He lifted her, cradling her head against his neck. *'Ich liebe Sie*, I love you Sister Howarth,' he whispered as she wrapped her legs around his waist. He guided himself gently into her. For a moment she stiffened, a small gasp escaping her lips and he hesitated.

'No,' she moaned, tightening her thighs, 'don't stop ... don't stop.'

Sometimes the unwilling thought came into her mind: Had someone seen them? Was that why Frank had finally told her father? But then surely he would have reported them. It would have been the quickest way to split them up, to get rid of Peter. He would have been transported to Canada within days. And that hadn't happened.

What did happen was that Matron insisted she take time off from the hospital at home to help the family cope with Bill's illness and subsequent death. And when she was in work, now, Peter was always on a different shift.

She pressed her fingers to her eyelids The only time she felt alive was when she was near him but she had barely seen him for two months. Coincidence or contrivance:

the question swirled constantly in her mind. At night she dreamt that someone was biding their time, waiting to denounce them. But as yet no one had.

Through the thin bedroom wall the monotony of muffled gasps and sobs had stopped for the time being and once or twice Mary thought there was a chinking noise of glass on glass. Mam had started early today. She put the letter on the bed and read the rest of it quickly while she got dressed.

I'll have to close now. One of the blokes on our landing's being released today and he's promised to get this out for me. One day that'll be us. I can't wait to get away from this god-forsaken hole.

As always, you are in my thoughts and prayers.

Be strong Mary, we are all depending on you.

All my love, Tom

Mary folded the paper and pushed it back into the envelope. She opened the top drawer of the tallboy and dropped Tom's letter into it. Partly closing it, she stood still, holding on to the handle and biting hard on her lower lip. Then she gave the drawer a final shove and it snapped shut. Oh yes Tom, she thought, I'll be the one to look after everybody. I'll be strong, just like everybody expects, but who's going to be strong for me?

Chapter 43

It was almost dark enough to draw the curtains for the night. Against the floodlights of the compound, the windowpanes were patterned with diagonal threads of golden raindrops.

Mary surveyed the ward; except for the young soldier with both legs amputated and a couple of others too ill to move, it was empty. The other patients had been escorted outside for a roll call long before she'd come on duty. And with both doctors and the German orderlies also instructed to participate in the count, the hospital had been quiet all day. She began to load up a small trolley with bowls, solutions and bandages.

As she picked up a kidney bowl full of used dressings, a double thud of gunshots made her jump, dropping the tray with a clatter amongst the other bits and pieces. Mary's stomach lurched. She peered through the window but could only see confusion as men, guards and prisoners, ran about. 'That sounded like firing.'

'It did.' Jean hurried to stand next to Mary at the window. 'Can you see anything?'

'Not much. Looks like something's happened though.'

'Well, we'll soon find out, no doubt,' Jean said. 'Do you need help here?'

'No, see to Harald, will you?' Mary nodded towards the youth, who was moaning loudly. 'He's due for his next morphine.' She pushed the trolley towards the first bed and forced herself to concentrate on the man lying in it. She unwound the dressings around his head and slowly lifted the gauze mask from his face, watching his reaction. 'Nearly done now,' she reassured him.

'*Dank sei Gott*,' he muttered, his lips pressed tightly together in pain.

Dropping the soiled bandages into a bin near the sink, Mary washed and dried her hands, glancing out of the window as she walked back to her patient. Across the compound guards were marshalling crowds of prisoners through the wooden door of the mill entrance.

Dipping the cotton wool into the solution of tannic acid, she smoothed it over the damaged features before replacing fresh gauze.

Jean came and stood beside her. 'Sure you don't want me to take over?'

'Nearly done now. Did you give Harald his pain relief?'

'Yes, he should sleep shortly.'

'Good. We'll have a cup of tea in a minute.' Mary wrapped the open weave cotton bandages over the gauze. She stroked back the lock of hair that flopped over the dressings on the man's forehead. 'All finished.'

'*Danke.*'

She settled the patient into a more comfortable position and straightened up. Outside the ward there were shouts, a scuffle of boots and the doors crashed open. A British orderly staggered backwards carrying one end of a stretcher, two German orderlies following. The first man called over his shoulder. 'Two more for your ministrations, girls. Where do you want them? There's been a right to-do out there today. We've taken one to the morgue. If you ask me we're in for trouble.'

Mary hurried towards him as a second stretcher was brought in. Her tone hid the sickness in her stomach. 'We didn't ask you, Mr Hampson, and may I remind you there are poorly men in here. Please keep the noise down. Put the first one there.' She gestured towards a bed. 'The other at the end of the ward.' She spoke quietly to Jean. 'Nurse, please help here. Let the orderlies do the lifting,' she warned and then looked back at the man. 'Would you find the Commandant, say we need at least one of the doctors.'

He left. 'Can any of you tell me what has happened?' The German orderlies were prisoners newly allocated to the hospital; they didn't understand her. Exasperated Mary looked for Jean. 'All right? Can you find out if Sergeant Strausse is anywhere around yet, instead, please, we need a translator.' As Jean left, Mary helped to move the man from the first stretcher on to the bed. She recognised him as one of the guards.

He gave her a weak grin. 'Busted my leg, I think,' he muttered. 'Got soddin' knocked over in the bloody rush to stop one of the bleeders from getting away. Pardon my French.'

'Get him ready for the doctor, please, Nurse Blackstock,' Mary said to the other nurse. 'When he gets here, that is.' She glanced at the doors as they quietly opened. Jean held on to one of them, the sergeant behind her. They both looked past her.

'What is it?' Mary turned. At the end of the ward, the man being lifted on to the bed was facing away from her but she saw his hand, the long slender fingers. She felt she was moving in slow motion until she was by his side. He was unconscious. Automatically she noted the blood pumping out of his shoulder, the flesh torn and open. She swallowed hard. 'Let's get his shirt off and see what we're dealing with.' She deliberately kept her voice impersonal. 'We can all see that it's Doctor Schormann, but for now he's simply a patient.'

The bullet had gone straight through his shoulder. Mary gestured at the two German orderlies and they lifted him so that she could see the exit wound. 'Get these wet clothes off him.' Sergeant Strausse barked an order and they worked quickly.

'We'll have to wait until Doctor Pensch comes before we know if there is damage to the bone,' Mary said. 'There's a cut on the back of his head as well.' She saw slivers of bone and grey matter in his hair. 'Oh God!' She blanched.

Jean bent closer. 'They must be remnants of the skull and brain from the dead prisoner.' She touched Mary's back, speaking quietly. 'Keep calm, Mary, he's just a patient, remember?' She raised her voice. 'But it's a bad laceration. I can start to clean it up.'

'Thanks Jean, I'm fine.' Mary's murmur was appreciative. She stepped away from the bed. 'No, it's all right, Nurse Howarth, you see to the guard,' she said. She turned to the other nurse. 'Get me some saline, please.'

Left alone Mary looked around before leaning over the doctor as though examining the grazes on his face. 'I love you, Peter Schormann,' she whispered. 'Don't you dare die, do you hear me? Don't you dare.'

Chapter 44

'Doctor Pensch says he's out of danger.' Mary handed the notes to the sister on night duty.

'What happened, do you know?'

'Not exactly. Apparently there has to be an inquest.'

They'd finished walking from bed to bed discussing each patient. Now they stood in front of Peter.

'We're keeping him sedated.' Mary picked up his wrist and studied her fob watch, his skin hot under her fingertips. 'He's lost a lot of blood.'

'What's happening about replacing Doctor Schormann?'

Mary kept her voice steady. 'Matron says they're going through records at other camps. The first two they found were Nazis so, of course, they were ruled out. We've enough of those of our own. We'll have to muddle through until it's sorted.' It was all she could do to keep control of herself. She wanted to go home to the safety of her room, yet she felt she couldn't bear to leave.

'Are you ready?' Jean appeared with their capes over her arm. 'At least it's stopped raining.'

When they got outside the ward she threaded her hand through Mary's arm and, merging with the other nurses going off shift, led her to the main entrance. 'Keep yourself together, love,' she murmured and, out of sight of anyone, put Mary's cape around her shoulders and fastened it. 'Best foot forward now. Remember the sentries.'

'Oh, Jean, I'm so glad Matron let you come back to work. What would I do without you?' Mary walked with stiff legs along Shaw Road.

'Well, that's one thing about being at war, love, hospitals need all the help they can get. Including married women.'

'The orderly said it was Frank. He said it was him that did it.'

'So I believe,' Jean said. 'But they're saying it was an accident, that he fired from the west tower overlooking the road while they were doing the count. The sentry I spoke to said one of the prisoners had been playing up all day and finally tried to rush a guard. Doctor Schormann simply got in the way.' She stopped at the next lamppost pretending to tie her shoelaces. 'Can I be honest?' She kept her head down until the last of the nurses had gone past. 'I know you like the man, Mary, but if you're not more careful it will look as though there's been something going on.' She straightened up, adjusting her gas mask on her shoulder. 'You know what it's like, what they're like.' She nodded in the direction of the nurses, the pools of dimmed light from their torches growing smaller. 'There's always tittle-tattle.' The silence between them spread out. Eventually Jean moved nearer. 'Mary?' Jean clicked her own torch on so she could see her.

'I couldn't tell you.' The words were barely audible. 'We … I didn't plan to get involved with Peter,' she said, 'it just happened.'

'What? What on earth do you mean?' Jean spoke in a fierce whisper. The bobbing lights had disappeared but the muted chatter of the women still floated through the darkness. 'Involved? How involved?' Her head was poked forward, her face only inches away from Mary's. 'Are you telling me there really is something going on?'

Mary could hardly breathe. 'He's a good man. He's gentle, honest.'

'Honest? He's a bloody German. Hell's bells, Mary, you're supposed to be the sensible one in your family.' Jean faltered to a halt before saying. 'That time at our house, just after I lost the baby, when you first said you liked him, I was worried but this…' She held her hands out in bewilderment. 'Have you completely lost your senses?' She shook her head and walked away, Mary followed. She felt as though her throat was closing. She tried to swallow but her mouth was dry.

When Jean spoke again, her voice was deliberately restrained. 'Remember what happened to Hetty Crabtree from Clarence Street? She was caught fratting with that POW she worked with on Tanner's Farm. She was prosecuted under that Act. He was sent away. People were vicious; made her and her mother's life hell, if you remember. None of the shops would serve them. They had horrible words painted all over the walls of their house. She couldn't even walk down the street without getting things thrown at her. They had to move away in the end.' She turned so quickly Mary almost fell over her. 'How could you be so stupid?'

'It was only the once.' Mary's skin shone pale in the darkness. 'And I've scarcely seen him since Dad died, let alone...' She shut up as Jean threw up her hands again.

'It shouldn't even have been once,' she hissed, moving closer. 'You could finish up in prison, your whole life, your career down the lavvy.' Her eyes suddenly widened. 'What if you're pregnant?'

'I'm not. I've had my monthly since.' Mary felt the despair changing to anger and tried to curb it. 'Peter could die, Jean, so I'm not going to be made to feel guilty for what I feel, what we did. I know you don't approve.' She paused. 'No, it's more than that ... you judge and condemn, just as everybody else would if they knew. You don't trust me, don't understand what it's like, any more than they would.' She moved round Jean and walked on. They were at the crossroads of Huddersfield Road and Shaw Street before she spoke again. A car approached, its lights muted, and they had to wait until it passed. Standing still, Mary's legs began to shake so much she couldn't move and she held on to the wall of the end house. 'No one needs to know; not unless you decide to report us.'

Jean whirled round at her. 'How could you?' she said, her voice strained. 'How could you think I'd do that, despite everything.'

'I'm sorry, Jean. I had to know. I'm frightened.'

They stayed in the shadows of the house until both were calmer. Jean was the first to walk on. Gathering her cape around her she said, 'I don't approve, you know that. I won't say anything, course I won't, but promise me you'll be careful.' She blew her nose. 'This is something I never thought I'd have to deal with. It scares me. It's too close to home.'

'I'm sorry, Jean, it just happened. Sometimes I wish it hadn't and it frightens me to death, but I can't help loving Peter and he loves me. I've even wished it had worked out with Frank … that he had been different …'

Jean put her hand over her mouth. 'Frank? Does he know about Peter?'

'He's guessed, I think.' Mary bit her lip.

'My God,' Jean whispered.

'There's something else.' A car came from behind and splashed through a puddle in the road, spraying water over their feet but neither noticed.

'What?' Jean pressed Mary forward again. 'Keep walking.'

'It's Ellen.' Mary spoke in a rush. She'd let the one secret out she might as well tell Jean the other. 'She's written to me. She and Frank … they … made love … just the once and she says the baby's Frank's. She thinks he just used her to get at me.'

'Hell's bells, poor Ellen.' Jean stared into the dipped low lights of the double-decker bus approaching. She waited until it had droned past. 'What a bastard. Does he know that as well?'

'Yes. I confronted him about it. Had to.'

'Does Ellen know you've told him?'

'No, I know I shouldn't have. But he's so bloody arrogant I couldn't help myself. She'll probably go mad.'

They walked on in silence. There was nothing more to say.

Chapter 45

Winifred was huddled by the range and the fire was almost out. She didn't turn round but said in a low voice, 'There're two letters on the table for you,' and pulled her shawl further over her face.

'Mam. You all right?'

Her mother slowly moved her head up and down and shifted in her chair, knocking over an empty bottle that rolled across the linoleum. Mary stopped it with her foot and picked it up. There were two others by the sink in the scullery. Mary closed her eyes for a second. How much more could she take today? She turned off the tap, which was dripping water on to a jumbled collection of dirty cups and plates. She stretched her neck from side to side, trying to loosen the tightness in her shoulders.

Walking back into the kitchen, she unclipped her cape, took off her cap and dropped them on to the table. She turned the envelopes over. 'They're both from Tom.' Her mother didn't answer. 'I'll read them to you later. I'm going to have a lie down. It's been a bit of a bad day.'

Winifred lifted her shoulders, still didn't speak.

Mary crossed to the fire, picked up two pieces of old chair legs from the scuttle and laid them on top of the grey smouldering coal. She waited a moment, watching smoke creeping around the wood. 'Mam?' The older woman grimaced but said nothing, just stared into the grate. Mary saw her eyes were red rimmed and puffy. She squeezed her shoulder gently.

Holding the letters she went slowly upstairs and flung herself on the bed. She pulled Ellen's pillow to her, smelling her perfume. She hadn't wanted to wash it, wanted the reminder. Revealing the truth to Frank about the baby was perhaps the most stupid thing she'd ever done, well, next to telling Jean about it all, anyway. Please God she didn't let it slip to Patrick: then the trouble would really start. Mary groaned and, still in her uniform, dragged the eiderdown over her and slept.

When she woke one of the envelopes crackled under her cheek. She ripped it open and held it towards the light from the landing. It was just two words.

Iori died.

Chapter 46

March 1945

'Tom must be feeling dreadful, Jean.' Mary gnawed on the inside of her cheek. 'They were … were good friends, really good.'

'And he hasn't replied to your letters?' They stood back from the rest of the nurses, waiting to be allowed in through the main gates.

'No. I've written three times now. I've even written to Mrs Griffiths, Iori's mother, to send my sympathies and ask if she knows what happened, but she hasn't replied yet.' Mary pulled her cape tighter around her. 'And I've telephoned the prison. I pretended I wanted a Visiting Order so they had to tell me what'd happened,' she said. 'They wouldn't tell me anything about Iori, of course, because I wasn't a relative, and all they said about Tom was that he was all right.'

'And Tom said they'd been beaten up?'

'Yes, in the other letter.' Mary struggled not to cry. 'He must be in an awful state. He said it was the same group of men that'd been making Iori's life hell for ages. They'd beaten him badly and Tom lost his temper and took them all on.'

'And the prison said ...?'

'*They* said Tom and Iori'd been in a fight.' Mary made a small huffing noise through her lips. 'Honestly, Jean, Iori looked as though he couldn't fight his way out of a paper bag, he was that skinny. I lost my rag with the chap on the phone. I asked him when they intended telling us about Tom. He said, "*There is no legal entitlement for us to inform you about such incident.*" Snotty bugger.' Her voice rose. 'I couldn't believe it. I asked if I could see Tom and he said no, they'd put him in solitary.'

She thought of him and Iori sitting so close together the last time she visited. She'd been right to worry. And now Tom would be alone in that god-forsaken place. He must be going mad. It was a nightmare and she could do nothing about it. She felt sick. She needed to see him and she needed to find out what had happened. Surely the prison had to report it, didn't they? Weren't they supposed to tell the police? Was it all going to be hushed up? It was ironic that there might be an inquest about the shooting in camp and not into what had happened to Tom and Iori.

As soon as the thought occurred to her she felt guilty, but it didn't seem right that there seemed to be one rule for one set of people and a different one for others. Anyway, it wasn't Peter she was thinking of; it was the man who'd been killed, the man known to be a troublemaker. And just as quickly it flashed into her mind: perhaps that's how the authorities at the Scrubs saw Tom, as a troublemaker.

A sob escaped without warning. One or two of the other nurses looked curiously in their direction. She glared at them until they turned away.

'Move to one side please, girls.' The guard waved his arms at the group.

A large black car drove up to the main gates. After a cursory check of the document that the driver pushed through the inch of open window, the sentry waved the vehicle in. Everyone watched as it stopped and then was allowed to drive through the gates of the compound.

'Who was that?'

'Who knows through all that dark glass,' one of the other girls said.

'Who cares?' someone else said. 'Let us through, can't you?' she shouted at the guard. 'We'll be late.'

Jean took hold of Mary's elbow and moved them further away from the others. 'It'll be all right. I'll ask Patrick to telephone. See if he can find out what's happening.'

Mary squeezed her eyes tight to stop the tears.

'Have you told Mam?'

'Only that Iori's died.' Mary dabbed at her eyes. 'She didn't ask how and I didn't tell her. I'm not sure it's sunk in.' She blew her nose. 'Between that and – you know.' She gestured towards the hospital. 'I'm going out of my mind. It's just one thing after another.'

'You have to pull yourself together,' Jean whispered.

I'm terrified Peter's going to ramble … talk about me … about us.' Mary said. 'I know it sounds selfish but …'

'They'll put it down to the fever,' Jean whispered. 'Look, you've been working with him for months now. We all have. And we *all* get on with him and Doctor Pensch. It's not as though you're ever on your own with him.' Jean stared at her with a determined look. 'Is it? Are you listening, Mary? That's what you say, OK? You've never been on your own with him.'

'The investigation into that shooting starts today.' The guard announced with self-importance.

'Come on, Quarmby,' one of the girls said impatiently. 'What makes you think we're interested? Just let us in, will you?'

He ignored her. 'That lot were representatives of the Swiss ambassador.' His voice became sour, the burn on the side of his face made his mouth twist even more as he grumbled. 'They going to look after the Jerries; make sure their side of the story's told about how Bock and Schormann got shot.'

'Is that the name of the man who was killed?' Nurse Lewis asked. 'We weren't told.'

'Bloody hell, woman, what does it matter? One Hun's same as another.' The guard shepherded them through.

Mary and Jean lingered behind.

'I'm more bothered about what Frank's going to say,' Jean said.

'He seems to be keeping his head down,' Mary said. 'I haven't seen him at all this week. In fact he hasn't followed me since he was suspended from duty.'

'Come on, girls. I haven't got all day.'

'Says he,' a sarcastic voice intoned.

'Obnoxious man.' Nurse Lewis bristled. 'Who does he think he is; calling me *woman.*'

'Who indeed?' One of the girls murmured. There were a few titters.

Quarmby lowered the barrier. 'Yeah, Hans Bock he was called, a right bother causer. Well known for trouble. Spent more time in the cells than out. I don't think he was that daft, mind,' he continued to talk as they walked towards the hospital doors. 'Meals brought to him … books to read … no standing out in all weathers for roll call.' He raised his voice. 'Got his comeuppance in the end though, didn't he?'

'I hate it when Bernard Quarmby's on the main gate,' one of the girls complained. 'You can never get away from him. Standing around in the cold, that wind went straight through me.'

'I hate these early starts; it's like coming to work in the middle of the night,' another said.

'Too much partying, my girl,' Nurse Lewis said. 'Early to bed, early to rise; that's my motto.' The young nurse pulled a face at her friends as they bent over to write their names in the signing-in book and they giggled, furtively peering up at a group of civilian police who were milling around.

Mary looked through the windows in the ward doors. She couldn't see Peter for all the pillows around him. She went into her office. The Staff Nurse who was going off duty was sitting at the desk finishing her reports. Taking off her cape Mary asked, 'What's that lot doing in the corridor, Staff?'

The woman scowled. 'They've put the major who's in

overall charge of the investigation in one of the side wards without a by your leave,' she grumbled. 'The police've been hanging around for the last hour, disturbing all the patients, disrupting things. I'll be glad when it's all over and we can get back to normal.'

'Whatever that is these days,' Mary said. Despite her determination to concentrate on her work, she found herself taken back to Tom's words in his first letter.

... I wanted to kill them when I saw what they were doing to Iori. I know I'll never forget what I saw...

She shivered. She didn't think anything would ever be normal again for her brother. Or her.

The woman fastened her cape. 'Hmm, you're right there. Oh, and by the way, there's one of them waiting to talk to Doctor Schormann.' She frowned. 'He's sitting right at the end of his bed, getting in everybody's way. Won't shift. Says the doctor is an important witness.'

Chapter 47

'Let's just hope they get this inquiry over and done with soon,' Jean shouted over the noise of the wind rattling the tin roof on the coal shed in her backyard. 'Now get home and have something to eat. You're looking dreadful these days. All pale and thin. Positively scraggy, in fact. So go … eat. I don't want my child to have a scraggy auntie.'

Mary laughed. 'You're only saying that because you're getting fat.'

Her smile faded as soon as she walked away. Jean's words had brought an instant image of Ellen, now almost eight months pregnant. Her weekly letters home were full of chitchat about the regimental routine of the home and how she and the other girls enjoyed breaking the rules, but Mary sensed her misery beneath the jokes. She wished Ellen would let her visit her but she wouldn't. She often wondered if Ellen thought she would try to persuade her to keep her baby.

She hurried along the alleyway, for once relieved to be home. It had been a difficult day but at least Peter's fever had broken and he had slept most of the time, much to the chagrin of the official waiting to speak to him.

She reached over the top of the gate and unlocked it hoping Mam had lit the fire; mostly she didn't and by the time Mary got home it was usually too late in the day to make it worth bothering. She was glad to see the flicker of flames through the kitchen window tonight. She pushed the lavatory door open.

When she came out the kitchen light was on. She could see her mother standing in front of the fireplace with three men, looking anxiously towards the back door. Mary hurried across the yard.

'She's here now.' Her mother pleated her apron between her finger and thumb, looking at Mary. 'I was just saying you'd be in any minute from the hospital.'

'Detective Yeats, Miss, Bradlow CID.' The man held out his hand. Mary shook it and stepped back, forcing a smile on her face. 'We have a few questions we need to ask.'

Mary's heart missed a beat.

'It's Tom … he's escaped,' her mother said. 'They were at some hospital …'

'He was having problems, Miss. Apparently he'd been involved in an incident?'

'He was beaten up.' Mary was terse. 'What kind of problems? What happened?'

'I'm afraid we don't have any details other than he's escaped and we were contacted by the authorities.'

Winifred sat down with a thud into her armchair. There was a chink as her foot knocked over a glass.

Mary moved swiftly. Bending over Winifred she put her arms around her, pressing her cheek to the side of her mother's head. 'Please sit down,' she said to the men, looking up at them. 'I need to get some water for my mother. She's not been well.'

In the scullery she heaved dryly over the sink. Without lifting her head she reached sideways and pulled the piece of towelling off its hook. She wiped the cold sweat from her face, waiting for her stomach to settle, the relief of realising they hadn't come about Peter for a moment overwhelming her fear for her brother. However she justified what they felt for each other, she knew the shame she would bring to the family would destroy her mother. She picked up a mug from the draining board, filled it with water and carried it through to the kitchen. The men stood up as she came through the door and didn't sit until she perched on the arm of her mother's chair.

'We haven't heard from Tom for a month.' Mary saw no reason to mention Iori's death. Winifred sipped the water, said nothing. 'And the last time I saw him was in January when I went to the prison after my father died.'

Winifred gave a small sob. Mary put a hand on her arm. 'He certainly hasn't been here.'

The detective stared intently at her. It wasn't until one of the others coughed that he breathed in deeply, letting the air out in a long sigh. 'Right-oh Miss. I think that'll be all for now.' He looked at them both. 'But it'll be in his best interest if you inform us when … if … Mr Howarth turns up. Better all round he gives himself up.' Tipping his hat at Winifred, he glared at the other men until they did the same. 'We'll leave you for now, Mrs Howarth.'

'I'll show you out.' Mary closed the front door behind them. Her mother was crying.

Mary stroked her hair. 'I'll make a brew.'

'I'll have some of that potato wine that Mr Brown gave to us when your father died. It's in the sideboard. I'll have a drop of that.'

Mary picked up the glass from under the chair. The bottle in the cupboard was almost empty. 'I didn't know we'd opened it,' she said, tipping it up to get the last drops.

'I have a little drink of it, every now and then,' Winifred said defensively.

'I didn't mean anything, Mam.' Mary handed her the glass. 'I simply said I didn't know we'd opened the bottle.'

'*We* didn't,' Winifred said, 'I did. And when that one's finished Mr Brown says I can have another.'

She avoided Mary's eyes but turned as Patrick burst through the back door. 'I've been to see Ellen,' he said aggressively.

'Did she know you were going?'

'No, I didn't need permission.'

Mary took a deep breath. 'How is she?' She bent over the pan of black peas she'd left simmering on the range that morning and stirred them, trying to sound calm. Poor Ellen, that's all she needed, she thought, him turning up like a bull at a gate. 'I hope you didn't upset her, Patrick, she's enough to worry about.'

'Why didn't you tell me the kid's Shuttleworth's?'

'What?' His mother whipped round to look Mary and then back to him. 'I thought the father was that American she went out with? How can it be Frank Shuttleworth? I don't understand?'

'So you didn't know either Mam?' He stopped in front of her. Folding his arms he rocked on his heels. 'Kept this one all to yourself then, our Mary. Oh no, I forgot, you told Jean, didn't you?'

Damn you Jean, she thought, you and your big gob. 'No, I didn't tell you. One because I knew what you would be like and two because you didn't need to know. And I wish I hadn't told Jean now.' Her mother slumped smaller into the chair. 'I'm sorry Mam, I thought it best not to say anything; after all she's not going to keep the baby.'

Her mother stared blankly at her.

'Like to keep secrets, don't you?' Patrick said. Mary straightened up and looked at him. Fear dried her mouth. The spoon dripped water on to the hot hearth where it sizzled and evaporated. 'I'm Jean's husband and Ellen's brother … and yours. I've a right to know everything that goes on.'

'And you're also a hot head.' Mary's words were dismissive. She tried to prevent him seeing her apprehension.

Patrick stood in front of her, glaring around the kitchen, snapping his finger and thumb together before flinging out, 'Does Shuttleworth know?'

'Yes, he does and I'll tell you what I told him.' Mary turned away from him to lift the lid off the saucepan again. 'She's giving it up for adoption, she wants nothing from him.'

261

'I'll swing for the bastard.' Mary saw his face flush then blanch with rage. 'He'll fucking pay for this, for everything he's done.'

She glanced quickly at him. 'What do you mean … everything?'

'Never you mind. He'll be bleedin' sorry he ever met me.'

'Not everything's your business, Patrick.' Mary had her back to him. 'This family's had enough trouble, you'll do nothing.'

He watched as she took a spoonful of peas and prodded them with her finger before dropping them back into the water.

'Or what?' He glowered at her. 'Who put you in bloody charge, huh? I'm head of this family now Dad's gone.'

Winifred whimpered.

He began pacing again. 'Does Tom know?' He saw her hesitate. 'He does, doesn't he?' he shouted. 'He knows about everything, doesn't he?' He wiped the spittle from his chin with the heel of his hand. 'Bloody hell, Mam, just you and me left in the bleedin' dark then.' He turned and grabbed hold of the latch on the back door and opened it. The draught lifted the oilcloth on the table and billowed the stairs curtain.

'Patrick. Just let it go … just listen.'

'No, I've heard enough. I'll bloody show you who's boss.' He left the door wide open.

Both women turned to look at one another. 'You didn't tell him about Tom,' Winifred said. 'You didn't tell him about Tom being missing.'

Dear Gwyneth,

I'm sorry to have to write this letter to you but it is important that you know. Tom has escaped. I have a feeling that if he doesn't come here he will try to get to see you. My mother is out of her mind with worry. If he does come to you please try to persuade him to give himself up. Tell him to think about what this is doing to Mam. He is only making things worse for himself.

I'm sorry I didn't manage to get to the funeral. My thoughts are with you. Have you had any more news about what happened?

Kind Regards

Mary

Chapter 48

April 1945

'And now, to repeat the special bulletin from the United States of America: the death has been reported of the President, Mr Roosevelt. He has been replaced by Mr Teddy S Trueman. Further details will be reported, as they become known. This is the BBC Light Programme and that was an extra news bulletin on this, the thirteenth of April nineteen forty-five.'

Jean switched the wireless off. 'Funny having the BBC news read out with a local accent after all those years of a toffee-nosed one. Bit like having a friend in your living room,' she said. 'Still can't figure out why they've changed it.' She sat on the settee.

Mary wiped her eyes and blew her nose loudly. She

didn't care who read the news; it was all bad anyway. She stared out of Jean's front room window. Above the roofs of the houses across the street, the sky merged pale blue with fast moving grey clouds.

'What's wrong?' Jean's voice was cautious. 'I doubt it was the news about the President of America. You've got too much on your plate to be even interested in that, so what is it?' She poured tea into two mugs.

Mary watched the woman in the doorway of the opposite house exchange some rags for a slab of donkey stone from a man with a small cart. 'I don't know. Where shall I start? Everything's wrong. Tom still missing, God knows where and in what state. Ellen in that place, Peter, Mam, her drinking … everything.' She was still too scared to voice the question that had been hovering on her lips since she had arrived. She turned away from the window. 'The rag and bone man's here.'

'Mother's not in. Anyway, she says she's making her stone last: doing her bit for the country.' Jean laughed uncertainly. 'Only doing her step every other day.' She put the teapot down, held one mug out to Mary and picked up the other. 'You've heard nothing at all about Tom?'

'No, that detective from Bradlow keeps calling but there's still no news. I feel sick with worry but Mam won't talk about it. Where can he be, Jean?'

Jean shook her head. 'I don't know, love. I've tried talking to Patrick about it but he's too obsessed with Shuttleworth.' Jean stopped abruptly.

'Jean. About Peter?'

It was as though she hadn't spoken. 'Your Mam, how is she?' Jean said.

'Still drinking, I could kill Mr Brown and his potato

wine.' Right at this moment she meant it: last night had been the third time in a row she'd had to help her mother to bed. She didn't understand it. Her mother had always enjoyed a tipple but it had become a real problem since Dad died. Even the odd sort of friendship that had developed between Arthur Brown and her mother didn't appear to stop Mam feeling lonely. It was as though her mother only remembered the young man she had first married, not the bully he'd turned into. Mary felt guilty but she thought she would scream if she had to listen to one more maudlin story about the way Bill had courted her; it just wasn't how she remembered her father. Couldn't really imagine it.

'Patrick said she was worse for wear when he called round the other day. He ...' Jean stopped.

'He?'

Jean didn't answer. There was a difficult pause.

'Jean.' Mary tried again. 'About Peter ...'

'I thought he looked more like himself yesterday. Now he's up and about, most of the time.' Jean tucked her chin in and blew on the surface of her tea, watching a line of tea leaves circle.

'He'll be discharged anytime, I think. He's going to talk to the Commandant about when he can take up his post again.'

Mary thought about the few minutes they'd had together the previous day. When she arrived for her shift one of the orderlies had taken him to sit outside on the low wall at the side of the hospital steps for a smoke and Mary had stopped to talk with him as the rest of the nurses streamed past calling out, 'Morning, Doctor Schormann.' 'Hello Doctor'.

'You're a right Mr Popular,' she'd laughed.

'Of course, I am the perfect patient.' Peter stubbed out his cigarette. Keeping his head low, he said, 'I have missed you. This is the first time we have been alone since that night.'

'I know.' The memory quickened her pulse. 'I miss our talks; there is so much I need to say.'

'We have not the chance to speak properly since then … your father, my accident.'

'It wasn't an accident,' Mary said, 'we both know that.' She turned her back on the compound and balanced her gas mask on the wall, close enough to touch his hand. He curled his little finger around hers.

'Yes, but it is not that of which I want to speak.' It was as though he was caressing her with his voice. 'It was your first time?'

Mary blushed. 'Yes.'

'Then I will treasure it even more, *mein Geliebter.* I have the memory locked in my heart.'

'And me, my darling.'

'I will go in now you have arrived.'

'You were waiting for me?'

'Of course.'

'Come on then.' Mary put her other arm around his back as though helping him to his feet, her face close to his.

His hand tightened on hers. 'Be careful who watches.'

Mary glanced up and took a quick intake of breath. Frank's friend, Quarmby, was standing by the guardroom. 'Ignore him. He can't do anything. I'm just helping you back to the ward.' But until they got inside the main doors she felt as though their every step was watched. There was no one in the reception area.

'It would be for the better if you let go of my hand, *ja*?' Peter said, a mixture of anxiety and amusement in his voice.

'Oh!'

'You forgot something.' Quarmby's voice cut through their laughter. He stood in the doorway dangling Mary's gas mask from his fingers. 'You should be careful,' he warned. 'Carelessness gets you into trouble.'

His words had frightened her.

'I said it might be a bit soon for him to start work,' Jean was still talking. 'Though we'd be glad of him, wouldn't we? Being a doctor short is difficult and we're understaffed as it is.'

Mary sat next to Jean and cut into her chatter. 'Jean, there's something I need to say, well, ask, really.' She knew her friend enough to realise Jean was immediately nervous. 'I know you told Patrick about Ellen and the baby.' Jean started to speak. Mary shook her head. 'You shouldn't have told him about Frank, you promised not to.' Jean lifted her chin, the corners of her mouth tightened. 'But I understand; you needed to talk to him. We all have to confide in someone. I honestly don't know what I would have done, if I hadn't got you.' She smiled, but it was a small worried stretching of her lips. 'And I know you don't like having secrets from him, but I need to know if you've also told him about me and Peter.'

'No, I haven't, Mary.' Jean looked down into her mug again, swirled the tea around. 'Don't you think I know what would happen to you if that got out?' She paused, frowned. 'But even if Patrick knew … even if he put two and two together and realised that Shuttleworth shot Peter on purpose because you and he are ... because of how you feel about Peter.' She spoke in short breathless bursts. 'And even though he's so angry about Ellen he could give Frank a good hiding ... he wouldn't report him for the shooting. I do know that, honestly. Because that would mean ...'

'That would mean it would come out about me and Peter. I'd be prosecuted.' Mary put her hand on her friend's arm. 'I'd lose my job.' Her fingers slipped off as Jean shuffled forward on the sofa, leaning towards the small table in front of them.

'And more, Mary ... and more. Your reputation as well, remember that.' Jean picked up a plate with a cake on it. 'Look, I don't want to talk about it, right?'

'But would I lose you, our friendship, if it got out?' Mary tilted her head to one side, trying to see Jean's face, but she kept her head down, slicing a large chunk off the cake.

'It won't get out, I'm sure. But if it did it'd be difficult – you have to admit that – with the way Patrick feels about the Germans. You know how bitter he is about not being able to fight.' Jean stopped, holding the knife up and pointing in the air with it. '*I'm* glad he couldn't go. We might not have got together if he'd gone in the army.' She lifted the slice of cake and slid it on a plate. 'Not that I'd dare tell him that, of course. Here eat some of this, please, I'm sick to death of it. Mother read somewhere that carrots are as good as sugar and she found a recipe book with a picture of this mad thing in spectacles ...'

'Doctor Carrot.' Mary gave up trying to talk to Jean about her fears and her relationship with Peter. It was obvious she wouldn't say any more. Mary balanced the plate on her knee. 'There are loads of pamphlets in the corner shop about it. Ministry for Food leaflets.'

'Yes, well, she's got this idea we should save on sugar. I asked her, why, when we have Patrick and his never-ending supplies? That reminds me, there's some biscuits for you somewhere. He brought home two more packets last night.'

'Thanks, Jean. Mam likes sweet stuff. She's eating precious little else.' Mary took a bite of the cake and chewed slowly. She had no appetite and it was dry in her mouth. She wondered if Tom was eating properly, wherever he was. 'It's good, it's really tasty.'

'Until you've eaten it at least once every day for a week.' Jean sat back in her chair, her hand resting on the slight swelling of her stomach. 'Dear God, what a world to bring a child into.'

'It'll have two good parents.' Mary sighed. The moment had gone. She could only hope Jean hadn't said too much to Patrick.

They sat in silence until Jean said. 'I haven't heard any more about the inquest, have you?' She concentrated on pouring more tea into their mugs.

'No. With it being held in the police court in Bradlow, I didn't expect to. They did say the verdict would be in this week so it should be in the *Reporter* sometime soon.'

'I did hear they'd had experts examine Bock's skull and they said the damage showed he was killed at close range,' Jean said, 'which means that Shuttleworth didn't kill him. It had to be the guard on the ground.'

'We both know Frank wasn't aiming at Bock.' Mary willed her to look up. 'He was shooting at Peter.'

269

'We'll never be able to say that to the police.' Jean arranged Mary's mug so that the handle was turned towards her and carefully picked up her own. 'They would ask why ...'

'And we can't say, can we? It would get Peter transferred right away to another camp and me in trouble like we just said.' They were going round in circles and getting nowhere, Mary thought, at least I'm not.

Jean's hand shook and the tea spilled onto her skirt. 'I'll get a cloth.' She jumped up and went out of the room.

In the silence, the scrape of wooden wheels sounded loud on the road, as the rag and bone man trundled away. Mary looked towards the window and then at Jean as she came back into the room, rubbing at the stain. 'I'd better get home. See what Mam's up to.'

'Shuttleworth will always say it was an accident, you do know that, don't you?' Jean said, not looking at Mary. 'As far as everyone else is concerned he has no reason to single Peter out.'

'I know.' Mary put the mugs and plate on the tray.

The front door banged. Jean stood up. 'That's Mother.'

'Like I said, I'd better go anyway.' Mary put her coat on and buttoned it.

'Don't forget the biscuits.' Jean said. 'I put them on the stand in the hall just now.'

'Thanks. And I'll try not to tread on the front step.' Mary smiled. 'I wouldn't want your mother using up her donkey stone because of me. I'll see you tonight, end of the street, usual time.'

But on Shaw Street Mary turned in the opposite direction of home, telling herself she needed to think. If she was right, if Jean had told Patrick everything, then things were going to get even worse. His resentment that she had confided in Tom and even his wife about Ellen, but not him, was bad enough. If he also knew about Peter, she was in trouble, one way or the other. He wouldn't report her, Mary knew that, but how far would his temper take him? What would he do? Mary pushed her hands into her coat pockets. She could only hope she was worrying unnecessarily. Perhaps she was completely wrong.

She turned up Newroyd Street towards Skirm. At the lake she sat on one of the benches and leaning her elbows on her knees, she put her face in the palms of her hands and wept. She told herself she was crying for her family, for Tom, for Ellen, for her mother. But she was also weeping for the hopelessness of her own life, for her and Peter. If the inquest ruled that Peter's shooting was an accident, Frank would be cleared. And knowing him as she did, Mary knew it wouldn't end there; he was too sure of himself. Peter was never going to be safe. And neither was she.

Chapter 49

'May I have a word, Sister Howarth?'

Mary looked up from the notes she was writing. 'Will it take long, Nurse Lewis, I need to finish this paperwork before I go off shift?'

'No, not long.'

Mary frowned as the woman stepped further into her office and closed the door behind her. 'Sorry, I did say I only have a minute …'

'I rather think this is something you might not want the

rest of the staff to hear.' Hilda Lewis sat on the chair in the corner of the tiny room.

'Now really, Nurse.' Mary put the top on her pen and resting both arms across the desk, leant forward. 'What is it this time?' she sighed, making no attempt to hide her irritation. 'Who has done what now?'

The small overhead light bulb shone on the lenses of Hilda Lewis's spectacles so Mary couldn't see the expression in her small dark eyes, but she could see the triumphant sneer in the thin lips. Somebody is definitely in trouble, she thought again, watching Hilda tidy tiny wisps of greying hair under her cap before folding her hands neatly in her lap and recognizing that any hope of halting what was surely malicious gossip had not worked.

'I have something to report.' The nurse glanced round at the door in an exaggerated fashion and bent forward. 'Well, perhaps not to report, Sister Howarth, perhaps just to say to you.'

Mary lifted her chin, an involuntary movement. The woman's breath was sour. She sat back in her chair, winding the pen through her fingers.

'Yes, it's probably best you listen carefully.' Hilda Lewis moved her head slowly up and down.

Mary shifted, a sense of foreboding moved under her skin. 'What is it?'

'As you know I've been helping on the ward today.'

'You were detailed here, Nurse Lewis, because you were not needed on your own floor today. Get on with it, please.'

The lenses flashed as Hilda flung her head back and sniffed. 'Right! I was finishing the dressing on the patient in bed fourteen when one of the guards came into the ward.' She paused, now visibly enjoying herself again. 'It was Shuttleworth, the man who was involved in the incident when Doctor Schormann was shot?' Mary dropped the pen. Annoyed with herself she flattened her hand over it before it rolled off the desk. Hilda nodded. 'Well, he walked straight up to the Doctor's bed.' She lowered her voice. 'I was going to say something but then they started talking and, seeing as how I was behind the dividing curtains, I thought to myself, if I come out now they'll think I was listening, so I stayed where I was.' She paused.

Mary didn't move. Her mind raced but she could find nothing to say.

'I thought at first they must be on friendly terms and I was thinking I might have to report that … I mean, as my duty … you know how Matron's always going on about how wrong it is for anybody to get too friendly with the prisoners.' Hilda paused. 'I've always made a point of keeping my distance. I hope you've noticed that, Sister?'

Mary moved her head automatically.

'Good! But then,' she stressed the word, 'then, Shuttleworth started going on about the shooting, about the findings of the inquest, and I have to say he had a very nasty tone on him. He was saying about the verdicts being justifiable homicide and accidental wounding. He said the words really slowly; especially when he said the accident part of the findings was the bit about him shooting Doctor Schormann.' Hilda shuffled to the edge of the chair, her hands clasped together on her knees.

'Just get on with it, please Nurse,' Mary said. She pressed her thumb on the back of her fingers until they were white.

'Then he said something really odd. He said he'd got away with it and he would really have preferred justifiable homicide in Doctor Schormann's case too. Don't you think that's an odd thing to say, Sister?'

Mary tried to swallow, her throat dry. She took her hands off the table and clenched them in her lap.

Hilda Lewis watched, waiting for a reply and made a slight shrug. 'Well, I did. Then Shuttleworth said that the man who'd died had been warned about jumping in and out of line. Shuttleworth said he'd been ordered to watch out for him and that's why, when he charged at that Gunner, he shot him, his duty, he said … which I suppose it was,' she added. 'He then said that Schormann …'

'Doctor Schormann,' Mary corrected

'Yes, well. He said the doctor just got in the way.' The woman lowered her voice even more. 'I had to really listen to hear what he said next.' She paused. 'He leant closer to the doctor and whispered … I remember the exact words because I couldn't believe my ears when I heard them and you'll be the same …'

'Just get on with it,' Mary snapped.

Hilda Lewis raised her eyebrows. 'Manners cost nothing, miss.'

Mary let the deliberate slight pass. 'Just tell me what he said, please.'

'He said, "And if you know what's good for you; if you don't want another accident, you'll stay away from Mary." And then he did that horrible cracking of his knuckles that men do sometimes … and then …' She'd leant so far forward now she was holding on to the edge of the desk. 'And then he said, "I'll be right on target next time, believe me."'

274

She leant back, her eyes invisible again, but the sneer openly widening her mouth. 'That was when you came on to the ward with Doctor Pensch. I saw you notice what was happening and the orderly going off. At the same time Doctor Schormann said something.' Her nostrils flared. 'It sounded like he was swearing in that horrible language of his.' She gave a long gusty sigh. 'I didn't hear any more but I did see Doctor Schormann do something though, he made a gesture ... like this.' She crooked her forefinger. 'Shuttleworth leaned towards him.

'That was when Matron came into the ward.' Hilda sniggered. 'She told him, didn't she?' Her gaze never left Mary's face. 'I didn't hear what Doctor Schormann said, but it really made Shuttleworth mad, though, even though he kept the smile on his face. He said something like, "I can see we'll have to have words, Mary and me." And then he checked his watch. Oh, he was mad all right, even if he did do that stupid swagger when he left ... just like all the guards do.'

Mary could feel the bile curdling in her stomach. She understood now, thinking back to when it happened, she knew why he'd pretended to be so cocky. That was why it felt so threatening: she knew it had been pretence. She tried to remember exactly what happened ...

'What are you doing in my hospital, may I ask?' Matron's voice was icy cold.

'Just seeing how the doctor is, Matron.' Frank leapt to his feet, the chair legs scraping the polished floor. He tightened his belt and, stretching his neck upwards, straightened his tie.

'You have no right to be here. Please leave.' Matron

fixed a baleful stare on him.

Frank winked at Mary and swaggered out, feeling in his tunic pocket for his cigarettes. Through the window in the door she saw him light it in the corridor, ignoring the disapproving look from Nurse Lewis, who, seeming to appear from nowhere, followed him out.

Matron turned to the bed. 'Doctor Schormann, are you all right?'

'I am well, Matron, thank you, and ready to start my duties.'

'Not yet, I think.' Matron allowed herself a small smile. 'But you're well enough to go back to your own quarters whenever you wish. As long as you let Doctor Pensch keep an eye on you.' She moved down the ward, but Doctor Pensch lingered by Peter's bed.

'Ja, mein Freund, wie geht's?'

'Well, Wolfgang.' Peter kept his voice steady. 'Well enough to get out of this place.'

He didn't look at Mary. There was a strange, almost angry tone in the words, but she supposed he was being careful in front of Doctor Pensch. Either that or Frank's appearance had shaken him. She left the two men and went to the ward door to make sure Shuttleworth had gone.

He hadn't. She watched him pace the floor in the reception area taking quick gasping drags on his cigarette. Suddenly he turned and punched the wall with his fist.

'I just thought I'd let you know,' Hilda Lewis took off her glasses and began cleaning them on a small white handkerchief. She looked myopically in Mary's direction. 'I told myself, Hilda, it's your duty to tell Sister Howarth what these two are saying about her, so I have. It was just a good thing there was no one else around, there's not many in this place as discreet as me, if I say so myself.' She wound the wire of her spectacles around her ears and adjusted the nosepiece. Giving Mary such a sympathetic smile that Mary was tempted to slap her, Nurse Lewis stood, straightening the creases in her white apron. 'Perhaps you'll let me know what you decide to do?' She opened the office door. 'These things need nipping in the bud.'

Chapter 50

The puddles on the towpath gradually mirrored the weak dawn sky. Frank slouched against the wall under the bridge. The splash of water dropping into the oily canal and the occasional scream of a cat-fight had been the only sounds during his long wait. He heard her on the gravel path of the bridge above, then her light tread on the steps and threw the half-empty beer bottle into the canal where it bobbed alongside three more. Still leaning, he uncrossed his ankles and shifted his feet so his good leg took his weight.

Then he pushed one shoulder off the blackened stone and swung around the corner to face her. 'You just won't be told, will you?'

Through the light drizzle of rain, Mary saw the flushing of anger in Frank's upturned face, the bloodshot eyes. Oh God, no. She stopped, watching him warily. The iron handrail, fastened to the wall, was cold and wet under her fingers. 'What are you doing here?'

He raised one leg, placed his foot alongside hers on the step and pushed his face towards hers. 'I'm waiting for you.' He prodded his finger at her chest. 'I hear you're in love?' He emphasised his words with five more pokes of his forefinger.

'I don't know what you're talking about.' Mary stepped off the last step and tried to push past him, suppressing the rising panic in her throat. 'Get out of the way.' Shifting closer, he grabbed hold of the end of rail, trapping her against the wall. She glared up at him smelling the beer fumes on his breath. She turned to go back up the steps but he put his other arm past her, his hand flat on the stones. 'Get out of the way, Frank.' She kept her voice low, strong; determined not to let her fear show. 'If you don't let me past I'll tell Patrick.'

'I don't care about your fucking brother. He'll get his soon enough, just you wait and see.'

'Let me pass.' Mary forced herself to sound angry.

'How about I go and see the Camp Commandant? You'll be in big trouble then. That bastard'll be transported to Canada.' He rocked forward. 'I can do that … no trouble, don't think I won't. And you … everybody will know about you … Mary Howarth … the fraternizer … the collaborator.'

'Oh, don't be so stupid.'

Mary shoved his arm and he stumbled against her. Her head jerked backwards and struck the rough surface of the slimy stone. She felt the burst of sharp pain and when she opened her eyes she was dizzy, the pale sunlight, breaking through the clouds and glistening on the wet leaves above, blurred, cleared and blurred again.

Frank regained his balance and grabbed her wrist.

She dug her nails into his flesh, trying to prise away his fingers, but he was too strong and he pulled her under the bridge. Using one arm to shield her body, she pressed herself against the wall and twisted away from him. His whiskers scratched as he sucked at her neck. Forcing his chin against her jaw, he searched for her lips and thrust his tongue down into her throat until she gagged. He drew back to stare at her, his breathing rapid, flecks of spittle in the corners of his mouth. 'You're my girl,' he said, teeth gritted and forcing his arm behind her, crushed her against him. 'It's about time you learned that.'

'Let me go.' Her arm was still trapped between them. She tried to dig her elbow into his stomach but he was too close, so she thrust the heel of her hand upwards into his jaw, pushing his head backwards. He moved to free himself and brought his forehead down on to the bridge of her nose.

Mary heard the crack inside her head and the sudden pain brought tears. Without a sound she slumped against him, blood streamed over her mouth and chin and she swallowed, choked, as he tightened his grip on her waist, almost lifting her off her feet. Her head flopped back, her blood spraying over Frank's chest. 'Get off me.' The words were spat out along with the metallic salty taste of her blood that made her retch.

He didn't speak. The canal lapped against the banking. One of the bottles disappeared with a plop. In the distance a dog barked and a car passed on the road above them. The sounds were barely distinguishable through the rushing sound in Mary's ears.

He pressed his hips hard against hers and pushed her cape aside, ripping the buttons off the bodice of her uniform and pulling it down over her shoulders. Her arms were trapped. Pushing his thumbs under the straps of her brassiere and petticoat, he pulled them out of the way and grabbed her breasts.

Mary gasped in pain. 'No.' She brought her knee up and, for a moment, his leg gave way and he cursed, viciously pinching one nipple. She squeezed her eyes shut and twisted her head from side to side; she didn't want to look at his face so close to hers. The pins that fastened her cap to her hair snapped on the stones. The skin on the side of her face scraped across the stones on the wall.

Mary thought she heard the crunch of footsteps on the bridge and lifting her head yelled, 'Help! Please, help me.' The scream echoed along the water and was choked off as he held his forearm against her throat. Seizing her between the legs, he moved his hand over her stomach and grabbed the waistband of her camiknickers. The material split along the seam and they slid down to Mary's ankles. 'No!' She fought to free her arms, as the bodice of her uniform cut into her skin.

Using his head and shoulders to hold her, he fumbled with the buttons on his trousers, covering her body with his. Mary struggled, her face squashed against him and fresh blood gushed from her nose again. She cried out, 'Get off me,' light-headed with pain, but Frank ignored her and, balancing himself, he stood on his stronger leg and used his other knee to force her legs apart. He plunged first one, then all his fingers deep inside her.

'Come on, Mary, enjoy it,' he panted. His sweat mingled with her blood, her tears.

'Get off! Stop it … Frank, please … no!' The sickening rush of sound, the flashes of bright light and blackness consumed her: she was going to faint. Her feet slid sideways and with one heave Frank grasped her buttocks, lifted her so he could enter her and thrust upwards. She cried out, the pain bringing a fleeting bitter recollection of Peter's gentleness. Seconds later, Frank groaned and shuddered.

Then he was gone. Mary was barely aware that someone was gently laying her on the path, cradling her head and brushing aside the rain-drenched strands of hair from her face. Eyes still closed, she rolled on to her side and drew up her legs, wrapping her arms around them. As though from a distance she heard the crunch of footsteps, the sound of blows, and then Frank's shout, 'You! You f–'

Somewhere behind her Mary sensed more movement and then someone spat; a great gathering and explosion of phlegm that reminded her of her father. There was a loud thud, a wheezing expulsion of breath followed by smaller duller sounds, each followed by gasps until finally there was a loud splash. Mary tried to open her eyes but it was too much effort. She lay still and listened to the thrashing of water, the choking and spluttering. Someone was struggling in the canal but the tiniest movement, the smallest shift, caused a spasm of pain that took her own breath so she lay still and waited and heard Frank's voice again.

'Bastard.'

So it was Frank in the water. His voice was high and thin, Mary could tell he was frightened. Nearby the short quick breaths of the man, Mary was sure it was a man, gradually evened out.

Frank again, gulping for air. 'I can't …' There was almost a rhythm to the splashing now as though he was treading water but then there was silence.

Mary's eyelids flickered. She tilted her head back and saw a pair of black boots before the light caused a spasm of pain behind her eyes. Whoever was by her moved quickly away from the shelter of the bridge. She heard the squelch of mud, a snap of a branch, the return of footsteps and then, all at once, more thrashing in the canal. The man, yes it was definitely a man, knelt by her and there was a swish of leaves. Mary was splattered with drops of rain.

Frank was screaming now, 'I can't swim, I can't swim,' over and over again, each cry cut off by watery choking. And then, 'Bastard.' The angry outburst must have left his lungs empty because he sank each time he spat out the word, 'Bastard.' Mary imagined the blackness waiting each time for him, each time lasting a fraction of a second longer than before. She heard him the last time he broke the surface. 'Bastard,' he coughed. And then he was quiet.

Mary lay motionless, the pain hitting her simultaneously across her cheekbones and between her legs. Sounds came and went in waves; shouts, boots scrabbling on loose stones, the splash of water, voices. Someone knelt by the side of her, tried to hold her. 'No.' She flailed her arms, squeezed her eyelids tight and waited until the darkness took her to an unreachable place.

Chapter 51

May 1945

The rich smell of leather mixed with lavender polish. The Coroner sat behind the long mahogany table. A large man with thinning grey hair and spectacles, he filled the upholstered chair which he gently swivelled from side to side as he read the notes in his hand. Every now and then he glanced over the top of glasses at the dozen people scattered about the six rows of chairs in front of him.

Sitting between Jean and Patrick, Mary closed her eyes, although most of the swelling around her nose and eyes had gone, the bruising, now mottled purple and yellow, still hurt and the heat in the large room was oppressive.

The Coroner – Mary had been told he was the same man, a solicitor from a large firm on Bradlow, who'd had a role in the inquest when Peter was shot – now leaned forward, his arms resting on the desk. 'To sum up,' he said, 'this inquest was convened to look into the death of Frank Shuttleworth on,' he glanced at the papers, 'on the 27th April 1945 at Ashford and to seek and ascertain the cause of his death.'

There was a moan from the other side of the room. Mary looked behind Jean along the row to where Nelly Shuttleworth was clutching a wicker-shopping basket to her chest and resting her forehead on the handle. Frank's brother, George, was sitting next to her, one arm around her ample shoulders, and he was glaring at Mary. She felt a frisson of fear; his eyes were flint grey, darker than Frank's, but it was the same baleful stare.

She turned away, forcing herself to concentrate on the

Coroner's words. He appeared to be as uncomfortable as her in the stifling heat. He was wearing a shirt and tie under a thick tweed suit and now he was sweating. He removed his spectacles and wiped a large white handkerchief over his red face as he spoke.

'I would like to thank the three witnesses, Mr Baxter and Mr Stokes, for their accounts of what they saw from the bridge above the canal after the incident and Miss Howarth for her clear account of the sequence of events leading up to the deceased's death.' He paused, cleared his throat. 'So far as she can remember them. I have noted that at the actual point of his death she was only partially conscious and has therefore only limited recollection. I wish her a speedy recovery from the injuries she incurred.' He looked at Mary, his lips twitching into a small smile.

'The pathologist established the cause of death as drowning. However witness statements and the injuries sustained by Mr Shuttleworth immediately before death indicate without doubt that he suffered a violent and unnatural end.' His gravelly voice deepened. 'A death instigated by a third party or third parties and it is my view that there is a strong possibility that he was first beaten and then thrown or pushed into the canal.

'Therefore my verdict must be unlawful killing by person or persons unknown.'

'Huh! I think we all know who the bloody *third party* was.'

The Coroner removed his glasses and looked at George. 'And you are?'

'The brother of the poor bugger what's been murdered.' Nelly tugged at his jacket as George stood. 'Murdered by one of her bloody family.' He pointed at Mary. Mary heard the stifled exclamation from Patrick.

'You have some evidence that you wish to present?'

'Ah, what's the sodding use?' George Shuttleworth jerked his coat from his mother's grasp and flung himself out of the room, leaving the door open and letting in a cool waft of air. Mary breathed deeply, noticing that her brother was doing the same.

The Coroner nodded to a policeman at the back of the room who closed the door. Then he coughed and replaced his spectacles. 'To continue, I am satisfied that I am now able to instruct the Registrar to register the death of Mr Shuttleworth and to issue a Burial Order. However I have been informed that thus far the police authorities have been unable to discover the identity of the third party or parties and investigations will continue.'

The words echoed in Mary's mind as she stood on the steps of the Town Hall.

'Come on, let's go to Lyons' for tea.' Jean held Mary's arm. 'It's all over, no more worrying. The Registrar will issue the death certificate, they can get the funeral over and done with and then you can forget all about it.'

'I'm off back to work.' Patrick circled his cap in his hand. 'OK?'

'OK.' Jean nodded.

'Thanks for coming with me, Patrick,' Mary said.

He looked down at his boots and then up and down Manchester Road. 'Right.' He clumped down the steps and, without looking back, jumped on the platform of a passing bus.

'Jean, now he's gone, there's something I need to ask you. Peter –'

'Shush,' Jean hissed.

'What?' Mary glanced around. 'Nobody knows who I'm talking about. I just want to know if he's all right, if he's said anything about me?' She put a hand to her throat. 'Does he know Frank raped me? And if he did, how did it make him feel?'

'I'm not doing this, Mary.'

'Jean –'

Her friend sighed. 'He's fine as far as I can see. He's back on the ward full time and no.' She held up her hand as Mary started to speak. 'No, he's not mentioned you to me lately. I told you before, after the … attack he asked how you were and I told him. Twice. And then I had to tell him not to ask again. I've said it before, Mary, don't involve me, Patrick would go mad.' Jean put her hand on Mary's arm. 'The whole hospital knows what happened, Mary, so Doc –' She stopped. 'So Peter must too. No one blames you for anything. It wasn't your fault.'

'Except for Frank's cronies,' Mary said bitterly.

There were footsteps behind them. 'Mary?' Nelly Shuttleworth stood on the next step.

'Oh God, what next?' Jean tugged her arm. 'Come on.'

Mary let herself be led away. Looking back at the woman she said, 'I can't … not yet.'

She knew she would have to talk to Frank's mother sometime; to explain how it had ended up like this. But not yet.

Chapter 52

'I hope you don't mind me calling. I was on this side of town and I wanted to see if Mary was all right.'

Winifred looked the woman up and down. Dressed in black the large figure filled the doorway. 'She's not up to visitors.'

'I know.' The woman fingered the clasp of her handbag and looked past Winifred. 'I just wondered if …'

'Who is it, Mam?' Mary stood in the kitchen doorway.

'Well, it's not the police again, thank God.' Winifred moved to one side.

'Mrs Shuttleworth,' Mary couldn't prevent the shock in her voice.

'I was just saying …'

'Mam this is …'

'I heard.' Winifred started to close the door. 'I don't want you in this house.'

Nelly's face crumpled. 'I know how you must feel, Mrs Howarth.'

'It wasn't her fault, Mam.'

'She brought him up.'

'And I'm ashamed for what he did,' Nelly said. 'He always had a temper, just like his father.' She fumbled in her handbag and brought out a handkerchief. 'He was worse since he came back home. He said it was Dunkirk. I always thought something would happen.' She blew her nose loudly. 'But not that, never that.' She put out her hand towards Mary. 'I am so sorry. I haven't known what to do.'

'It was his funeral today, wasn't it?' Mary said quietly. 'That's why you're here.'

Nelly looked down at the step. 'We had him buried at St John's. He wasn't religious, he didn't believe in it, but he was christened C of E so I thought it only right.'

Winifred snorted. 'There was nothing right about that bugger.'

'There was nobody there, just George and me.' Nelly's shoulders shook.

'Come in.' Mary moved back. 'Let her in, Mam, she shouldn't have to stand on the doorstep.'

'I don't want her in the house.' Winifred stood firm.

'Well, I do,' Mary said. 'Let her in.'

There was disgust on Winifred's face as she stamped down the hall. She was just closing the sideboard door when they walked into the kitchen.

'I'll be in my room.' Wrapping her shawl around her arms she pushed through the stair curtain. Mary sighed, looking from Winifred to the sideboard. 'All right?' her mother challenged.

Mary shrugged and, crossing the kitchen, sat on her father's chair.

'How are you?' Nelly stood near the table, twisting the handkerchief. 'I tried to ask last week.'

'I know, I'm sorry, it was difficult,' Mary said.

'I know, lass.'

'But I'll be fine,' she faltered. She saw Nelly flinch. 'I'm OK. If it wasn't for the nightmares.'

'I shouldn't have come.' She was close to tears.

'I'm glad you did,' Mary said. 'I've been wondering how you were.'

Nelly glanced at her, surprised. 'I thought you'd hate me.'

'It wasn't your fault.' Mary said. 'I should have gone to

the police when he started following me all the time.'

'Following you?'

Mary kept her voice low, 'And threatening me.'

'I had no idea.' Nelly sat down hard on one of the kitchen chairs, her hand over her mouth. 'I didn't know. I could have done something.'

'There was nothing you could do. I've thought about it a lot lately.' Mary smiled at her. 'Frank was ill; we both know that, don't we?' She hesitated, wondering whether to say the next thing. 'Have the police spoken to you since the inquest? Have they any idea who it was?'

'No.' Nelly sighed. 'And you didn't see?'

'No,' Mary said, 'it's like I told the Coroner, I just heard the fight.' She shifted in her chair. 'And then lots of shouting.'

Nelly stared down at her hands. 'Can I ask you something?'

'What?'

'Just now your mother said something about the police. Was it about Frank's murder?'

'No,' Mary said, 'they were here about Tom, my elder brother. He's in prison: Wormwood Scrubs. He's a Conscientious Objector.'

'Oh.'

'He'd escaped. The police came to tell Mam he'd been caught.' She put her hand in her skirt pocket, fingering Tom's note and the letter she'd received from Gwyneth that morning.

'Where was he found?'

Mary thought she heard a thread of suspicion in Nelly's voice. 'He'd hidden at a house in Wales. A friend of his had died in prison and Tom was very upset. But it was a stupid thing to do and got him in a lot of bother.'

'Grief affects us all in one way or another. I'm having awful bother with George. He's drinking a lot at the moment.'

Mary thought about her mother upstairs. No doubt she'd be well into that bottle by now.

'You were right about Frank's mind,' Nelly said. 'He frightened me with his temper sometimes.'

The back door opened and Jean came in. 'It's quite pleasant out there today, Mary. We could sit in the yard if you want.'

'Jean, remember Mrs Shuttleworth?' Mary said. She frowned, warning her friend not to say anything.

Jean spoke slowly, staring at Nelly. 'I just came round to see how you are.' She looked at Mary pointedly.

'I must go.' Nelly picked up her handbag and pushing down on the table, stood up. 'Don't get up.'

'Bye.' Mary smiled.

'Bye then.'

Jean banged the front door having seen the visitor out and came from the hall, bristling with indignation. 'Well I never! How dare she come here?'

'I thought it was a brave thing to do. He was still her son and someone killed him.'

'How can you think like that? God only knows what would have happened to you if he hadn't been stopped.'

'I know,' Mary said, 'I know, but I feel sorry for her.'

'Don't waste your sympathy on her.'

'Just think if you had a son like that.'

Jean placed her arms protectively over her stomach.

'Anyway I like her,' Mary said. 'I've met her before and she's kind-hearted. And she saw Mam take a bottle of Mr

Brown's wine from the sideboard before she went upstairs and she didn't say a word. I could have died from shame.'

'Have you thought what you're going to do about Mam?' Jean said.

'No, not really.'

'Well, something will have to be said before long.'

'And I suppose that the one doing the saying will be me,' Mary said resignedly. 'But forget Mam for now, I've something to show you'.

Chapter 53

'I've had a letter from Tom,' Mary took it from her pocket. 'It's only a note really. Here, read it.' Jean sat at the table and skimmed through it. 'Well?' Mary said.

'I don't know.'

'It was this bit here …' Mary took the letter from Jean and studied it. 'Here: *I've had a visit from Patrick. I've been very low and it was difficult, but for the first time ever I feel we really understand each other. Now the War is coming to an end maybe we can put our differences to one side.* What does that mean?'

Jean stared at the words and then abruptly stood up. She walked across to the door and leaning against it, looked out at the yard.

'Jean? Patrick's hated what Tom's done, he's despised him for being a CO, so why has he been to see him now? The war's more or less over. Tom should be released in the near future, even taking into mind the pettiness of some of them in charge of him,' Mary said quietly. 'He must have visited Tom as soon as he came out of solitary.

So why? And why didn't you tell me?'

'I don't know, honest. I meant to tell you.' Jean turned to face Mary, her arms crossed. 'I just didn't want to worry you.'

'Worry me? After all the nagging I've done to get Patrick to go and see him, after all these years?' Mary was incredulous. 'You must have known I'd be glad that he finally went, especially after what Tom's been through. Why should I be worried?' Suddenly she knew. 'Oh my God, it's something to do with what happened, isn't it?' She said. 'It's about Frank, that's why you're not telling me.' The kitchen started to tilt.

'No. I don't know.' Suddenly Jean had her arms around her. 'Honestly, Mary, Patrick didn't tell me. And he won't talk about it.' She faltered for a moment then spoke quickly, her words running into one another. 'But think about it.' She shook Mary's arm. 'Tom *was* interviewed by the police. He *was* out same time Frank was murdered.'

'So? He was in Wales.' Mary forced herself to breath evenly.

'Not all the time. Apparently he was trying to get to see you and Mam, but he saw some policemen on the railway station at Bradlow. He was that close to Ashford. He said he thought they were looking for him so he hid on the train and didn't get off. But Mary, he has no alibi.'

Mary looked at her in dismay. She knew it was the truth. She had read and re-read Tom's note and felt he was trying to tell her something. She forced herself to stay calm. 'He said that to Patrick?'

'Yes.'

'So Patrick told you that much at least,' Mary said slowly. 'Has he been interviewed as well?'

'Well, yes but only as a matter of course.' Jean said. 'Loads of the men round here have been seen by the police.'

'And where was he when it happened?'

'He was with me. He'd been on nightshift.'

Mary stared at her. 'He would have been coming home at the same time as me, then. I didn't see him. Surely I would have seen him?'

'What are you trying to say?' Jean stood up, her hand cradling her stomach.

'I'm not saying anything. I'm just trying to understand what it all means, why Patrick went to see Tom.'

'I've no idea.' Jean shrugged. 'But I do know Patrick was with me that morning.'

'Why are you being so defensive?'

'I'm not. I'm just saying he was with me and I'd say that to anyone.'

'Anyone? Even me?' Mary frowned. 'Jean, he's my brother. These are *my* brothers we're talking about. I'd do anything for them. Even lie. So … are you lying for Patrick now?'

Jean flushed. 'No,' she snapped, 'I'm not.'

'I'll tell you what I think, shall I?' Mary clasped her hands tightly, resting them on the table. 'I think one of them killed Frank.' She lifted her head and held Jean's gaze. 'I'm not sure which one. Patrick has a temper. Tom worries about the people he loves and he can be very protective, too much so, sometimes. I'd told him about Frank. If he'd been brooding about what Frank was doing …' Mary's voice cracked. 'But if I'm wrong, you have to tell me.'

Her hand shook as she reached out to her friend. Jean

held on to it and sat down again.

'Frank was badly beaten before he died,' Mary continued. 'The police said they knew I couldn't have inflicted that amount of injury. So, was it Patrick? Did he do it? They'd fought before. You did tell Patrick about him following me, didn't you?' Jean nodded reluctantly. 'And you know he's always had a short temper, it's been worse since they made him go in the mines.'

'He's not been as bad since we got married,' Jean protested.

'I know, love, but he's still the brother I've always known and if something doesn't suit, he still reacts with his fists.' Mary squeezed her friend's fingers. 'So, please, if you know something, you must tell me.'

'I don't, I swear. Patrick says he doesn't want to talk about what happened.' Jean's voice trembled. 'He just says Shuttleworth's dead and he's glad.' She shrugged in a helpless gesture. 'But there is something …'

'What?'

Jean jerked around in her chair as the toilet was flushed next door and, seconds later, a door banged.

'Oh hell, I'd forgotten Mrs Jagger was on the prowl. She collared me about the celebration party they're holding on our street. She wants to go. Apparently she fallen out with a couple of your neighbours and won't come to the one they're holding here. Peace on earth, eh? Except for her.' Jean put her hand over her mouth. 'Oh God, do you think she heard us talking?'

'No,' Mary said, first with uncertainty, then more firmly. 'No. But just check she's not still in the yard.'

Jean stood up. When she came back into the kitchen she shook her head. 'She's gone.'

'What were you going to say?'

'That morning Patrick was late home. He had marks all over his hands.' Jean sat down carefully and spoke in a whisper. 'First he said he must have done it in work ... and then that he admitted he'd been in a fight. We had a row; our first proper set to. Things were difficult between us for a couple of weeks. Then he disappeared for over a day. I was frantic. When he got back he said he'd been to see Tom. He says it's nothing to do with me. There were things they had to sort out, stuff they'd never talked about before.' She looked at Mary, pleading. 'It could have been anything, couldn't it? Perhaps he sorted out how he feels about Tom; perhaps he's tried to understand why Tom feels as he does about the war?'

Mary shook her head. 'Doubt it.'

Jean felt her sleeve and produced a handkerchief. 'Well I don't know. I will tell you one thing, though.' She blew her nose fiercely. 'I'd not let him go to prison for killing scum like Shuttleworth. I'd lie through my teeth. I don't care about the consequences.' She leant forward across the table, her tone defiant. '*This* baby has a father and I want him with me. He promised he didn't do it and I believe him ... I have to ... and so do you.'

'I'm not sure.' Mary folded Tom's letter, pressing it down on the table and sharpening the creases with her knuckles. 'But I do know we haven't heard the last of it.'

Mary couldn't get her breath. Frank was holding her down. She could smell his sourness; feel the harsh rasp of his rough chin on her as he pressed his head against her neck. He grasped her wrists with one hand and she felt him inside her, his weight crushing her. She fought back, the nightmare of the rape all too real.

She woke drenched in sweat, her heart racing. She sensed her cries were lingering in the room although the sound had gone.

She listened to hear if she had woken her mother. Nothing. Winifred must still be sleeping off the excesses of the street party that had gone on until the early hours. A bonfire had been built on the site of the bombed house at the far end of Greenacre Street and the screeching of fireworks drilled into her brain worse than any noises of sirens or bombing had done over the last six years. Mary had pressed her hands over her ears in an attempt to shut it out but she still heard people cheering and singing. At one point she thought that if she heard *Auld Lang Syne* one more time she'd scream. The thought had brought back a faded memory of Ellen saying something similar once about the girls where she worked and *Workers' Playtime,* but she couldn't be bothered pursuing the recollection. Instead she'd wrapped a pillow round her head to shut out the banging of dustbin lids and blown whistles that started each time the singing stopped. And at one point someone had even climbed up the lamppost outside her window and banged on the pane, shouting for her to come outside. She'd thrown the pillow then and screamed at them to go away. People outside were celebrating freedom and she was trapped in her own hell.

Mary pushed the covers away, her arms and legs entangled in the sheet and her mind a jumble of images: Frank, the sluggish canal, rain sliding off the leaves above her, the glowering early morning sky. The horrific scenes had been a regular occurrence in the nights that followed the rape. Now they'd returned and it could only be because of her talk with Jean today. But this time there was a difference, this time there was the addition of an image of her brothers beating Frank repeatedly until he was a bloody mess lying on the canal path.

But then the face of the battered body became Peter's.

Mary laid back clutching her arms tight across her chest and taking shallow breaths in an effort to control the pain that had started under her ribs. Her eyes stretched wide, staring upwards at the faint fingers of dawn light that played across the ceiling. Cold sweat trickled between her breasts and although the air was soft and warm on her skin she couldn't stop shaking. Tears stung, she blinked rapidly and the image disappeared. 'Peter,' she whispered.

Chapter 54

When Mary next struggled to consciousness it was to the clatter of clogs on the pavement followed by the urgent thwack of wood on glass as the 'knocker-upper' made his way from house to house, hoarsely calling to wake those men who were on early shift in the mine.

She listened to the twang of bedsprings through the thin wall and her mother's stumbling descent down the stairs. 'Oh Mam,' she whispered. Jean was right: there had to be a way to stop her drinking; they couldn't carry on like this

The water pipes rattled as Winifred banged the kettle against the tap in the scullery and Mary listened to the tank gurgling in the loft above her for what seemed the hundredth time in the last six weeks.

Six weeks! It had been six weeks since she was raped

by Frank, six weeks since his death. And the police were no nearer to finding out who'd killed him. Every time Mary thought about it her stomach churned. Did she want them to find out: what would the truth be? She just wanted all the worry to go away.

The doctor had said she could go back to work on light duties in a fortnight, but how could she leave her mother like this, drinking day and night? Mary flung the sheet off her and lay with her hands by her sides. But she needed to get back to work, back to Peter; to see the look in his eyes when he first saw her again, to know that he didn't blame her for the rape and that he wouldn't turn away from her.

She curled up and buried her face in the pillow, smothering the hot rush of tears. She wouldn't think about that. Think about what to do about her mother.

But her mind was in a whirl, her mother wasn't the only person to be dealt with. She had to sort things out with her brothers. She lifted herself up onto her elbows. She'd go to see Tom first; she hadn't been able to see him since Iori died, since his escape, since her … attack. His whole life had fallen apart and despite all that had happened to both of them and all the letters she'd sent, the only contact she'd had from him had been that one short note. It wasn't like him. He was her big brother, the one who looked after her, who shared her secrets. She should have gone to see him as soon as he came out of solitary, before Patrick got to him.

Mary rested her chin in her hands, hardly breathing; why had that thought come to her? She frowned, trying to work out why she was so suspicious of Patrick, why she couldn't believe he'd visited Tom to see if he was all right. Because it wasn't like him, that's why, she told herself; he'd resented Tom all his life, he wasn't going to start caring now. So why? She sighed and gave up – it was all too much. There was so much to worry about: Peter, Mam, Tom, Patrick. And Ellen. She wondered if Tom had written to Ellen offering his help before Iori died. And if he had done, would that have changed her mind about keeping the baby? But of course that didn't matter now. Everything was different.

The misery in the letter she'd received from Ellen was stark and desperate. The baby was due anytime in the next week, Ellen was adamant she would sign her rights to the baby away and then she wanted to come home. True to form, in her reply to Mary's letter that told her everything that had happened, she hadn't mentioned anything about Frank's death or what he's done to Mary.

Mary shrugged. Perhaps Ellen couldn't cope with anything other than her own problems right now. Perhaps afterwards they would talk. Mary slowly sat up, an idea forming. Ellen would need something to take her mind off everything. For the first time in her life Mary put herself first. She'd written back immediately telling her sister she'd be welcomed with open arms. Now Mary realised Ellen could be the answer. Even if she couldn't do much at first, she'd be home. Mary refused to listen to the inner voice that had always guided her, that automatically told her she was being selfish. Her desperation to see Peter pushed everything else to one side. Ellen's presence would solve everything. She could look after the house and their mother.

Swinging her legs over the edge of the bed, she stood up and wrapped her dressing gown around her. She'd go down and talk to Mam, sort everything out once and for all, try to find out properly why her mother was drinking so much, make her see that it wasn't the answer to her misery.

Now she'd made the decision she felt better than she had for weeks.

Chapter 55

June 1945

'I want to come back to work, Matron. I know you're short staffed. Jean, Staff Nurse Howarth, has told me you are, especially as she's now finished work, with the baby due in a few weeks. She said there's been chaos in the camp.'

'Not in my hospital, Sister,' Matron said sharply.

'No, I didn't mean that. She said since Germany surrendered in Berlin and the prisoners were shown the films of those horrible concentration camp places that have been all over the news, there's a lot of unrest in the compound and fights.' Mary shrugged. 'I just want to help. I want to get back to work. Please Matron.'

Matron smiled at her. 'I appreciate what you are saying, Sister, but are you well enough? We've lost all the German orderlies; they've either been transferred to other places or given work outside the camp. The nurses, even the Ward Sisters, have to do a lot of the heavy work themselves. I doubt you're up to that yet. You've lost a great deal of weight and you are looking rather flushed. Have you exerted yourself today? Did you walk here?'

'No, I came on the bus. Honestly, Matron I'm fine.' Mary had caught a glimpse of Peter as she'd passed the ward and her heart was still thumping. 'I'd be an extra pair of hands. I want to get back to work. My sister comes home tomorrow. She'll look after my mother.' Mary hoped she didn't sound as frantic as she felt. She had to be where Peter was. It had been so long since they'd spoken. Even a snatched conversation here or there was better than nothing; was something to hold on to. And any guilt she felt for leaving Ellen with their mother was balanced against the hope that her sister would make Mr Brown stop bringing his bottles of wine into the house every day.

'Ah yes, your sister. She's been working away? Is she back for good?'

'Yes.'

'And your mother?'

'She's fine, Matron.'

Mary really did think her mother was trying to cut down on her drinking since they'd had that first talk. Of course it helped that Mr Brown had been away, staying with his son in Birmingham, but at least Mary understood a little of why she drank so much.

'I'm lonely Mary,' Winifred said, hugging the beaker of tea. 'I miss your father.'

'I know that Mam but Dad was such a bully.' Mary said, her forehead furrowed in puzzlement. 'And you're free to do what you want now.'

'That's just it, love. I don't know what I want,' Winifred said. 'I've done what's been expected of me for so long I don't know what I want now. I suppose, if I think about it, it's not so much that I miss your father as I miss being needed. Even if no one noticed what I did.' Fat tears plopped on to her hands as she drank. 'I thought that after

301

what happened to you, you'd need me but you don't. Jean and Patrick have taken over. And Ellen … she could have stayed at home, kept the baby. I'd have helped her to look after it. My first grandchild, Mary, and it'll be brought up God knows where by God knows who.' She brushed the tears off her face with the back of her hand. 'And Tom … I miss Tom. Every time I think they'll let him out he seems to do something they can pounce on; something that lets them keep him in.' She put her beaker on the table and looked at Mary, her eyes bleak. 'No one needs me, I'm no use to anyone.'

'That's not true.' Mary grabbed her hand and squeezed it. 'That's not true, Mam. We all know how much you did for us. It's just different at the moment, but in our own way we still need you. I have to get back to work, we need the money, so you'll have to keep the house ticking over; look after things like you used to. And once Tom and Ellen get back you'll feel better. And then there's Patrick and Jean's baby coming soon, they'll be glad of some help then.'

'Happen,' Winifred sighed, 'happen.'

'I want you to be the Mam we used to have. I know you've always liked the odd tipple, and heaven knows you deserved it with all you had to put up with, but it's too much now. You're drinking too much, love, and you know it.'

'Aye, I know you're right. It's just so hard.'

'Just try, eh Mam, just try.'

'I will, love. For you Mary, I'll try.'

And Winifred had. But, as Mary reminded herself, Mr Brown was away.

'So, if you're sure you're ready?'

'I am, Matron. Thank you.'

'Well, I'm sure we can find plenty for you to do.' She tapped a pencil on her desk, giving one last sharp rap before she said, 'I hope you don't mind me asking but there is something else. Private Shuttleworth.' The unexpected mention of his name sent a shock through Mary. 'Because he was a guard here the police informed the Camp Commandant as to what happened and he received a copy of the Coroner's Inquest for the records. It must have been dreadful for you and as far as the Commandant and I are concerned that is an end to the matter, except there is something I have to ask. I'm aware it must be a painful subject for you.' She hesitated.

Mary swallowed and clenched her hands behind her back. 'Yes Matron, it is. But, please, if you have anything to ask?'

'I believe your brothers have been subsequently questioned? Hospital gossip, I'm afraid, Sister, but I need to know there will be no distractions from your work, if you come back. Were any charges brought?'

'No.' Mary frowned. Matron had plainly heard about Tom's escape, why otherwise did she ask about both of them? Well, she'll get nothing from me, she thought. 'They were cleared of being involved in any way.' She didn't think it necessary to tell Matron that she'd been refused her last prison visit to Wormwood Scrubs, with no good reason given. Or that Detective Yeats had actually told Mary that his men had more to worry about than the death of a rapist; they had their hands full dealing with the riots caused by the resentment of soldiers returning from the war, jobless, and seeing German POWs working on the building sites and roadworks in Bradlow. Investigations into Frank's murder were on hold and unlikely to be reopened.

'Well then, if you're sure you're ready, Sister Howarth, I'll be very glad to see you back on the ward. But not for another week or so.' She held up a hand as Mary started to speak. 'That's my final word, Mary. It will give you more time to recover; you've been through a lot. So, I will see you on,' she consulted her calendar, 'the seventeenth. Start you on days.'

'I would prefer night shift, Matron.'

'Give it a little time to get adjusted and then let's see, Sister.'

Outside Matron's office Mary grimaced. Another week!

Peter was waiting in the corridor, reading a bulletin on the notice board. He didn't look at Mary as she walked towards him. 'Good afternoon, Doctor Schormann,' she said in a loud voice. 'How are you?'

He turned towards her and clicked his heel. 'Matron, she watches,' he murmured.

'I'll see you next week,' Mary whispered.

'You are back?'

'Yes. I love you. I have missed you so much.'

Peter raised his voice. 'I am well. Fully recovered, thank you Sister.' Then he muttered. 'She is gone. I too have missed you. And I love you, *mein Geliebter*.' Their hands brushed as Mary walked on. He'd met her gaze, his eyes hadn't wavered and they'd told her everything she needed to know.

Chapter 56

Mary had been watching Peter all morning. This was the second time she'd seen him since she came back to work two days ago and he was different somehow. What if she'd got it wrong last week? What if he did think she was partly to blame for what Frank did to her? Her skin prickled. 'Is there something wrong?' She collected the notes from ward round off the trolley and joined Peter, who was sitting at her desk, filling out forms.

'It is nothing.'

Mary shuffled the files, pretending to put them in order. 'Is it me? Do you feel differently about me?' She made herself sound calm. 'Is it us? Has someone said something?'

Peter sighed and looked past her at the other nurses on the ward. He spoke quietly. 'No, it is not us. I have received threats from … certain people; about something that I wrote in the *Wochenpost*.'

Mary balanced the notes on top of the filing cabinet and began to search through them. They didn't look at each other.

'While you were … ill, not here, we were shown some films of the KZs, the concentration camps. Those poor people; their suffering.'

Mary stopped filing. 'I know,' she said, 'I've heard it on the radio, read about them in the papers. It's horrible.'

'For weeks I was unable to remove them from my mind. I could not sleep. The creatures that carried out such horrific crimes are not part of the Germany I know and love. They are a cancerous growth. I needed to say how much, as an honourable German, I am ashamed. But my writing has caused harm to others. There have been beatings of those who dared to agree with what I wrote.'

'The Nazis?'

He moved his head slightly.

'So, it is the Nazis who are threatening you?'

'Ja. They are young SS thugs. I care nothing for politics but they seek to weaken my position as *Lagerführer*; show others that I cannot protect them.' He spread his fingers. 'That I am unable to make sure they are looked after by the authorities here. They are determined to demonstrate what will happen if anyone dares to oppose their doctrines.'

'You must report them.'

'I cannot. It will make things worse.'

'Then I will.' Mary opened a drawer and began arranging the files in the compartments. 'As a doctor you are part of this hospital and you are entitled to protection.'

'No, please Mary. You must not draw attention to yourself. It is dangerous for you. Your people …'

'I'll not stand by and see you beaten like some of those poor beggars in there,' Mary interrupted, waving her hand towards the ward.

'You must not. You will put yourself in danger.' Peter watched a nurse walking down the ward towards the office. 'Staff Nurse Lewis is coming. Please, Mary, say nothing, for your own sake.' He stood up. 'And there are too many of the SS. If one or two are sent away, there are others to replace them.' He moved away from Mary's desk. 'I must get back to camp, to my other duties.'

'Be careful!'

'I will, but I must also do what I can to prevent more beatings. I have to reassure the others, tell them, as you say, to keep their heads down.'

When Hilda Lewis walked into the room he inclined his head and snapped his heels together.

'Is everything all right, Sister Howarth?'

'Fine.' Mary returned her gaze. She thought back to the last conversation she'd had with the woman. Since she'd returned to work she'd avoided her. From what the other girls said she'd become even more insufferable since her promotion. 'Why wouldn't it be?'

'I just wondered.' Hilda Lewis hovered by the door. 'We haven't spoken since you came back and I just wanted to say I was so sorry to hear what happened. It was dreadful. I was shocked. I do hope it was nothing to do with what we'd spoken about?'

'I'm sorry, I can't remember.'

'Oh surely you must. I told you … about the conversation I heard.'

'You *thought* you heard, Staff.'

'I know I heard, Sister. So I wondered …'

'Instead of wondering, Staff, you would make better use of your time if you supervised the second Urea Concentration Test on the patient admitted this morning. We need to see if his kidneys are working as they should.' That should keep her busy for a while, Mary thought. 'I have to leave the ward for a few minutes. I'm taking some notes to Matron.'

As she left Mary could almost feel the hatred that Hilda Lewis was directing at her back.

Chapter 57

'You're settling back in all right, Sister?'

'Thank you, Matron, yes.'

'Good. And you would rather wait until the Commandant arrives before you tell me what this is about?' Matron's mouth was pursed.

'Please. Only so I don't have to repeat myself, Matron.'

Mary wasn't told she could sit down. She clasped her hands in front of her.

'And there are no problems with my hospital or the running of my hospital?'

'No. No, it's nothing like that.'

'Hmm.' Matron picked up a pen and began writing. Mary knew she wasn't mollified.

The door opened and the Commandant strode in. 'I hope this won't take long Matron.' He was unusually impatient. 'I have a delegation of angry POWs waiting to see me about the cut in rations.' He flopped down in an armchair in the corner of the room.

Matron pointed at Mary with her pen. 'Sister Howarth has something to share with you, Major Taylor.' She stressed the 'you'.

'With both of you, Matron,' Mary said.

'Well, sit down, girl, and get it over with. As you heard, the Commandant is a very busy man.'

Mary hadn't thought about what she wanted to say; she'd acted on impulse. Now she knew she should be careful. 'It's Doctor Schormann.' Both raised their eyebrows but said nothing. 'I overheard him telling Sergeant Strauss today that he was being threatened by some of the Nazis for a piece he wrote in the Camp newspaper. When I asked him about it he refused to discuss it with me.'

'Quite right too,' Matron said. 'Your conversation should extend only to hospital matters.'

'I know, Matron, and I'm sorry. It's just that he only returned to his post a few weeks ago because of his injury and –'

'Which was an accident,' the Commandant broke in.

'Yes, of course, Major, I was only trying to say he perhaps is not as strong because of the accident.'

'I am not sure how that concerns you, Sister.' Matron fiddled with the pen and leaned back in her chair.

Mary laced her fingers together to stop her hands shaking. 'My only concern is the hospital, Matron. You said yourself last week that we were short staffed and when Doctor Schormann was a patient they couldn't find anyone to replace him. We can't afford to lose his services again, especially as Doctor Pensch isn't too well either.'

'All right, all right. Perhaps you should tell Major Taylor why you are concerned.'

'You know how things are at the moment Major; we have a ward full of men as a result of the beatings and bullying by the Nazi faction within the camp. And then there was that murder, just before I returned to work; that prisoner hung in the wash house as a supposed traitor.'

'A one-off incident, Sister.' Major Taylor said, frowning.

'But it could happen again ... Doctor Schormann ...'

'Sister,' Matron warned.

Mary didn't stop. 'His piece in the *Wochenpost* could be misconstrued by the Nazis.' She saw them glance at one another. Matron was looking increasingly agitated.

Mary knew she had said too much. Her words tailed off. 'It was only that I thought we're so busy we can't afford to lose him.' She waited for one of them to speak.

Matron rapped her pen rapidly on the arm of her chair, scowling at Mary.

The Commandant leaned forward, his hands steepled, and he tapped his fingertips together before standing up. 'Right, Sister, leave it with me.' Holding the door handle, he responding to the older woman's stiff smile. 'Matron.' He studied Mary. She thought he was going to say something else, but adjusting his cap, he opened the door and left.

'Close the door after you, Sister,' Matron said coldly.

Mary stood up. 'And, Sister.'

'Yes, Matron?'

'You are treading on very thin ice. I'm not a fool and I'm neither deaf nor blind. I know what goes on in my hospital.'

'I don't know what you mean, Matron.'

'Oh I think you do, my girl. In fact I know you do.'

'No, Matron, I don't. If I could go now, the ward is busy?'

'Then you should have thought about that before you came to me with concerns that are none of your business.'

Mary bit back her retort. 'Matron.'

The woman waved her away. 'Don't make me regret taking you back, Sister Howarth.'

Mary pulled the door to behind her. She couldn't let go of the handle, even though she realised that Matron would probably be watching her through the glass panel. Finally she took in a huge gulp of air and moved away. Walking back to her ward, she knew she'd made a terrible mistake.

Chapter 58

July 1945

The backyard was a suntrap. It was hot and it wasn't even midday yet. Mary had dragged what they still called her father's armchair out from the kitchen and now sat next to Jean, who was perched on a wooden chair, her hands folded over her stomach. Neither mentioned the faint but still unpleasant smell that lingered over next door's lavatory. Mary tilted her face to the sky and narrowed her eyes; iridescent particles of dust danced above her head. She tried to relax but a headache lurked behind her eyes. She hadn't slept properly for days, not since the interview with the Commandant and Matron.

'There's no way you should have got involved,' Jean said, wiping her forehead with a handkerchief. 'Now you've got on the wrong side of Matron, she'll be watching you like a hawk. It's as though you've lost all reason. The man is a POW.'

'Shush.' Mary peered over her shoulder towards the house. Ellen was in the scullery emptying the wash boiler.

Jean followed her glance. 'Should she be doing all that lifting? It's not two months since she had the baby.'

'I know. She came home as soon as they took the baby apparently and she won't talk about it. It's as though it never happened.'

'I don't know how she could part with her, poor little girl. What will happen to her?' Jean stroked her stomach.

Mary felt a twinge of irritation. 'I don't know but I do know Ellen felt she had no choice. But I am worried about her. What with her and Tom.'

'No visit yet?'

'No, I don't know what's going on, it's a worry.'

'You seem to be worrying about everyone but yourself,' Jean said. 'You should be thinking more about what you're doing. If you take my advice you'll stay clear of you know who.'

'I've not seen him anyway,' Mary said. 'He seems to be on different shifts all the time. We've had Doctor Pensch on the ward for the shifts I'm on.' Mary circled her fingertips over her temples.

'I thought Doctor Pensch wasn't well?'

'Stomach ulcers apparently; he's being given extra rations. Why are we talking about Doctor Pensch?'

'It was just that you said you hadn't seen Peter.' Jean stopped and sniffed. 'Smell?' she pointed towards next door.

'Lavvy, stinking.' Mary nodded.

'No, the pipe smoke.' Jean mouthed the words, 'Mrs Jagger.'

'All right, Mrs Jagger?' Mary called. There was exaggerated coughing and the lavatory flushed. The girls listened to her shuffling across the yard.

'Nosy old bag,' Mary said.

'But that's exactly what I mean,' Jean whispered. 'You have to be careful. They didn't stick those "Walls have Ears" posters up for nothing.'

'Not sure they were thinking about old Jagger though.' Mary smiled slightly.

'It's not funny.'

'I know, I know,' Mary said, 'I just didn't think …'

'Bit like you not using your head about Peter. The war might be over, just about, but we don't know what's going to happen and you can't carry on like this. Anyway, you told me he's married. He'll go back home, once he's released. Back to his wife.'

Mary closed her eyes. 'He might not. I've heard they're allowing some to stay if they want. I just need to talk to him.'

Ellen came out into the yard. 'I'm going to have to move you two,' she said. 'I'm putting the sheets out.' She unfurled the line off the hook on the wall and carried one end over to a large nail in the doorframe of the lavatory where she fastened it with a bulky knot. 'Get me the prop, our Mary. I'll need some help putting this lot out before you go to work or the sun will be off the yard. Mam's no use. She's sneaked out the front door. I think she's gone up to Mr Brown's.'

'Oh Lord, not again.'

'Still having trouble?' Jean said. 'I thought she'd stopped.'

'She's better than she was,' Mary said. 'It's him, it started again as soon as he came home. Ellen being back has helped a bit, but Mr Brown's a really bad influence on her.' She put her arms around her friend and heaved her out of the kitchen chair they'd brought outside. 'God, you're a lump now. Are you sure it's not twins?'

'Cheeky beggar,' Jean giggled then gasped and held her side. 'There's something going on in there today: feel.'

Mary held her hand over Jean's stomach; there was a rippling motion under her fingers. She laughed and caught Ellen watching, misery etched on her face. 'Ellen.'

Ellen shook her head. 'I'm all right.'

'I'm sorry, Ellen.' Jean stood still, waiting to get her balance. 'I didn't mean to upset you.'

'It's fine.' Ellen set her lips and dumped the wash basket of wet clothes on the chair Jean had just left. A rhythmic thumping began and clouds of dust rose above the adjoining wall between the back yards. Ellen climbed on top of the dustbin and scowled at the woman beating a hearthrug on the washing line. 'Mrs Jagger, you've done this for as long as I can remember. Every time we put our washing out you beat your bloody rugs. Why can't you wash on a Monday like everybody else?' There was a mumbled reply.

'Well,' Ellen declared, 'carry on and you'll find out what I'll do about it. I'm not my mother and I won't stand for it.' She climbed down. 'It's taken me all morning to do that lot. I'm not letting the old cow muck it up again. Help me move the mangle out of the way, Mary, and then we can peg out.'

'It's heavy. We should leave it until Patrick comes back. He can shift it again. We can work round it. I'll help to peg out the sheets in a minute.'

'Right, thanks.'

'I'll get Jean inside first. I won't be a minute.'

'I've upset her,' Jean murmured as she waddled across the yard.

'It's not difficult at the moment, between the baby and Mam.' Mary stood behind Jean at the back door and guided her through.

'Is there any way I can help?'

'No, you've enough to think about. Get things sorted between you and Patrick. From what you said earlier he needs a good talking to. He should be looking after you at this time not being so irritable.'

'He's got a lot on his mind, at the moment between

314

worrying about me and still having trouble in work with that bloke he had that fight with before.'

'And he's not told you what that was about?'

'No, but he is one of those who opposed the strike so perhaps that's it. And Patrick does feel bad about Tom, you know, about not going to see him before.'

'I really don't know what's happening with Tom, I'm worried sick.'

'You're at it again, mithering about everybody else. Stop it. And we're fine, Patrick and me, honest.'

Mary shrugged as she helped Jean on to a chair by the table. 'Hmm, if you say so, we certainly don't need him going back to how he used to be.'

'He'll be better when the baby's here.' Jean wriggled about trying to get comfortable. 'I'll be glad when it's all over.'

'I'll be glad when a lot of things are all over,' Mary said.

There was a loud knocking on the front door. As Mary went to answer it she found herself thinking yet again, What now?

Chapter 59

She closed the door and leant against it, pressing her knuckles to her mouth. The rushing noise filled her head and she was cold. The rose pattern on the hall wallpaper spun as she stared in front of her.

'Mary? Are you coming to help me with these sheets or not?' Ellen called from the kitchen, impatience in her voice.

Mary pulled the front door open again and gulped in air, hanging on to the doorframe. An old man shambled past, staring at her with curiosity.

'Mary? What is it? Ellen touched her shoulder. She ducked under Mary's arm to look at her. 'Come on in.' She helped Mary into the hall, pushing backwards with her foot to close the door. 'Come and sit down.' In the kitchen she lowered Mary on to a chair at the table and sat opposite her. 'Is it Mam?'

'No.'

'Patrick?' Jean whispered.

'It's Tom.'

Ellen put a hand to her mouth. 'What? What's happened?'

Mary folded her arms across her waist. 'He's on hunger strike. He hasn't eaten for nearly a fortnight. He's ill,' she said. 'I knew it, I knew there was something wrong.'

'Why?' Ellen whispered.

'Who was that at the door?' Jean asked.

'A constable, he didn't say why, he just said they'd had a message at the station to come and tell us.'

They stared at each other. Jean was the first to speak. 'Is he in the prison hospital? Have they said you can see him?'

'Yes! No!' Mary swallowed, tears still threatening. 'They took him to the hospital wing yesterday. After last time, when he escaped, they won't take him to the civilian hospital. We're still not allowed to visit.' She tried to breathe slowly. 'It's like he has no rights. Just what the hell have they been doing to him?' She stared at them. 'That policeman, he was so matter of fact. He said that he'd just come to tell me that Mister Thomas Howarth, currently detained at His Majesty's pleasure in Wormwood Scrubs, is on hunger strike. Just like that. He said it just like that.' Her voice rose. 'And then he said, "Has been on hunger strike for the last fourteen days." For God's sake. As though it wasn't important.'

'Try to stay calm, love.' Jean placed her hands flat on the table and pushed herself up. 'I'll get home and tell Patrick.' She stroked Mary's hair. 'He'll know what to do.'

'We could demand to see Tom,' Ellen's voice wobbled.

'There's no point,' Mary said, 'they'd not let us in.' She'd stopped trembling. 'I'll walk back to your house with you,' she said to Jean.

'It's only two streets away.'

'I'll see Jean home, Mary,' Ellen said, blowing her nose. 'I can do that.'

'You should go in to work, Mary,' Jean said. 'Sort out that business you were talking about before.'

'I couldn't.'

'I'll finish putting the sheets out while you decide,' Ellen said. 'That still needs doing.'

'Leave the mangle.'

'It can stay where it is, it's not important.' Ellen hurried out.

'There's nothing you can do yet,' Jean said. 'Go to work.'

'Patrick?'

'I've said, I'll tell Patrick. He'll know what to do. He can tell Mam as well.'

'Mam! Oh my God, Jean, you know what she's like about Tom. This will be the final straw for her.'

'Patrick and I will see to her.' Jean said. 'You go to work.'

'I feel I should stay here … in case there's more news about Tom.' Mary was torn. 'We should be deciding what to do together. But I need to go into work as well. Find out …'

'Look, Mary, I know I've been wasting my breath about this business with Peter. I don't agree with it but I can see what you're going through. So go and sort it if you can, but for God's sake be careful. If there is any more news about Tom, I'll send Patrick up to the Granville.'

Mary stood up. 'You'll be all right?'

'I'll be fine.'

'I'll go and get my uniform on. I'm going to ask Matron what's happening about Peter. I have to know.'

Chapter 60

Mary looked up every time the doors to the ward opened but there'd been no sign of Peter Schormann. When Matron came in to check the medicine supplies with Mary, she was brusque and unapproachable. As soon as they finished she strode through the ward doors. 'Fill in your reports, Sister, and let me have them as soon as possible. I have a busy schedule before I leave this evening.'

Mary hurried after her. 'Matron, there is one thing. Doctor Schormann.'

'Is none of your business, Sister.' Matron whirled around, glaring. 'Now, those reports?'

Mary persisted. 'I only wanted to know.' Matron's eyebrows almost disappeared under her cap but Mary continued. 'I was simply concerned as I was the one who reported it.'

'Lest we forget,' Matron said sarcastically, 'it is none of our business what occurs within the prisoners' camp, Sister Howarth. However, if only to let me get on with my work, and for you to get on with yours ...' She glanced towards one of the nurses who trundled past them with a trolley full of bedpans and moved closer to Mary. 'The Commandant informed me that four prisoners were arrested and the matter will be dealt with in due course.'

She frowned as Mary said. 'It was just that I hadn't seen Doctor Schormann.'

'You are here to do your job, Sister. Not to ask impertinent questions. But since you persist. The Commandant suggested I put you on different shift to Doctor Schormann for the time being and, unless it is impossible to manage, that is what I intend doing.' She turned on her heel and left.

Mary bit her lip. There was nothing she could do except keep a lookout for Peter. All she wanted to know was that he was safe.

After her shift, Mary made herself a cup of tea in the staff room and waited by the window overlooking the compound. She'd seen the Commandant going towards his office, followed closely by a group of soldiers but nothing else. Still no Peter. Matron appeared at the door and looked pointedly at her watch and then at Mary; she'd no choice but to leave.

Before going into work she'd telephoned Wormwood Scrubs from the Post Office to request a visiting ticket and was refused. Now she called at Jean's to see if Patrick had been more successful, but the house was empty and when she got home neither Mam nor Ellen was there.

She threw her cape over the back of her mother's chair,

sat at the kitchen table and began to write. After a few minutes she heard a burst of laughter from the alleyway. Mrs Jagger was holding court as usual. Her pen hovering over the half-written letter to Tom, Mary looked out into the yard and wondered whose reputation was being destroyed tonight. She got up and banged the door shut. Back at the table she started writing again. When she finished she sat back and sighed. It was the best she could do; somehow letters were never enough. She'd learned that over these last years.

Dear Tom

The police have been to the house and told me what you're doing. You have to start eating again. They won't let me come to see you until you do. I think I know why you feel you have to punish yourself but refusing food is not the answer. Sooner or later they will force you to eat and that will be worse.

It will be another two weeks before I'm allowed to visit and only then if you've started eating again. You have been through so much and your imprisonment must, MUST, end soon. I want you home. I need you to be here. So much is going wrong and I feel so alone. If not for yourself, do this for me Tom. Please.

Yours, Mary

She put her pen down, rested her head on her arms on top of the table and wept.

Chapter 61

She woke to a touch on her cheek.

'Mary?' Ellen sat on the chair next to her. 'We've got some news.'

'Tom?' Mary sat up, twisting her neck from side to side. She rubbed her face. Her skin felt rough and dry. 'Is he all right? What's happened?'

'It's not Tom.'

Mary looked round. Patrick was standing behind her, grinning. 'Jean's had the baby, a little girl.'

'That's where we've been, at the hospital.' Mary turned to her right. Her mother was perched on the edge of her chair, a glass in her hand, her face flushed. 'Then we celebrated in The Crown.'

'So I see,' Mary said. 'I've been writing to Tom.'

Patrick shuffled from one foot to the other. 'I was going to ring the Scrubs, but then Jean started and all hell broke loose.'

'I'll bet it did.' Mary stood up and hugged him, 'Congratulations. Jean's all right?' He tensed in her arms. 'Everything is OK?'

'Yeah. Great!' He ran his palm over his face. 'Great.'

'Well, congratulations again. A little girl, eh? What are you going to call her?'

'Jacqueline.' He laughed. 'She's beautiful. And Jean says for you to be sure to go and see her tomorrow.'

'Oh, I will, try to keep me away.'

'I think I'll get to bed.' Ellen leaned over and kissed Patrick and he hugged her. 'Well done our kid,' she said. 'See you upstairs?' She smiled at Mary but her eyes were sad.

Mary stroked her arm. 'Night Ellen.'

'Mam? Night.' Ellen pushed her way through the curtain at the bottom of the stairs.

Winifred waved her glass at her. 'Night, love.' Eyes half closed she nodded her head slowly until her chin rested on her chest.

'I'd better get off.' Patrick yawned and stood up.

'Yes, see you and my niece tomorrow.' Mary smiled and gave him another hug.

'You'll be all right?' He moved away from her, nodding in their mother's direction. Winifred was softly snoring.

'Yeah, she's not been too bad lately,' Mary said. 'I think Jacqueline will buck her up no end.' She paused. 'I'm sorry, Patrick, but I will need to talk to you about our Tom as soon as possible. I'm really worried. We have to do something, though God knows what.'

'I know.' He didn't look at her.

Mary stood up, rubbing her eyes. 'You get off now. See you tomorrow?' She waited for him to answer. When he didn't she turned to her mother and hoisted her to her feet. 'Come on, Mam,' she said, 'I think you've done enough celebrating for today.'

Chapter 62

'Did you hear what they did to those four Nazis?' Staff Nurse Lewis folded the white gauze into bandage width and began rolling it up.

Mary had her back to her. She paused for a moment then added soda to the water in the sterilizer. 'No, what happened?' she said casually. She could feel Hilda Lewis watching her.

'Rumour has it they'd been threatening our Doctor Schormann.' She came and stood next to Mary.

'Oh?'

'Yes. Something to do with that newspaper the Commandant lets them have.' She snorted. 'An article the Doctor wrote.' Mary made sure the instruments were covered in the sterilizer and put the lid on, pressing it firmly into place. She moved away but the room was so small, when she turned the woman was right behind her.

'Major Taylor had them arrested in full view of all the other POWs, apparently, and put in the cells.' The nurse stared into Mary's eyes. 'Doctor Schormann was with them in his capacity as *Lagerführer*. But of course he was also the *supposed* victim.' Mary tried not to react but she saw the gleam of triumph in the woman's face. 'The Major interviewed them but they refused to speak, so then he sent the Doctor back to his barracks and the guards were told to take the Nazis out to the thirty yard range. The next thing everyone knew there were four shots and those Nazis weren't seen again.'

'They shot them?' Mary was shocked.

'That's the thing; they didn't really. They locked them in the guardroom and then, during the night, they were transferred to another camp. The Commandant did it to put the fear of God into the rest of the SS. *They* think those men were shot.'

'How do you know this, Staff?'

'Bernard Quarmby told me when I came in this afternoon.'

'Sister Watkins told me you were late for duty. Is that why? You were gossiping at the Main Gate?'

'Not at all.' The woman bristled. 'There were problems with the bus. Anyway, I've made the time up now so I'll be going.'

'After you've away put the gauze bandages, please Staff.'

The Staff Nurse did as she was told and stomped out of the room. Mary smiled but she was already well aware she had a dangerous enemy in Hilda Lewis.

Chapter 63

Peter stood at the top of the steps outside the entrance of the hospital finishing his cigarette before going in. Mary and the nurses on her shift passed him on their way out of the camp.

'Goodnight Doctor, busy in there tonight.'

'Lovely evening isn't it?'

'Glad to get some fresh air.'

Peter clicked his heels. *'Ja. Gutenacht.'*

'I'll catch you up,' Mary called to the others. 'I've forgotten something.' She ran back up the steps and into the corridor. Peeping through the ward windows, she saw the night shift staff at the far end. Matron had already left the hospital for the day. She walked quickly back to the entrance and stood in the shadows behind him. 'Peter?'

'I was asked to come over to look at a patient in Ward Two,' he said.

'We haven't spoken properly for days. Don't turn around,' she said as he made a sudden movement. 'Are you all right?' She saw him shake his head. 'Are you angry with me for telling the Commandant about those

Nazis?'

'No.'

'Then why are you avoiding me?' Mary said.

'Avoiding? No. I have been given fewer shifts.'

'Why?'

'It is not for me to ask questions, Mary. Sometimes I think you forget I am a prisoner here.'

'I wish I could forget. But even when we are on the same shifts you don't speak.'

He didn't answer.

'Peter? Tell me, what's wrong?' She waited

He blew a stream of smoke through tightly pressed lips before answering. 'Four men, Mary, they have shot four men because of me.' He kept his voice low.

'They didn't shoot them, Peter.'

'They were shot.'

'No, they pretended to shoot them, but they didn't.'

'I do not understand?'

'They were not shot. They were transferred to another camp during the night.'

'But why?'

'To teach the rest of the Nazis a lesson.'

Peter looked upwards, shaking his head.

'It's true,' Mary insisted.

'*Sind Sie sicher?* You are sure?'

'Believe me, they are not dead. I don't want you to blame yourself for something that didn't happen,' she said. 'Or me!'

'I must apologise.'

'No,' Mary said softly, 'no need.' Looking up at the nearest tower, she saw the guard was shouting down to the sentry at the gate to the compound. Neither was looking towards the hospital. Walking past Peter she locked fingers with him for a second and then walked forward to the top of the steps. She looked down, fastening the ties of her cape. 'I'm on night shift for the next week. Will I see you?'

Peter was quiet for a moment. 'They have told me that I will not be needed, only Wolfgang, but I will try to exchange with him sometime.'

'How is he?'

'Not well but he has not yet told them. He is a proud man, does not like to show weakness in front of the ...' Peter stopped. 'In front of them. But for me, he will say he does not feel well, I am sure. Then they will have to put me on duty. There is no one else.'

'Will he change shifts with you without asking why?'

'He will know why.'

'He knows about us?'

'He is a friend. He will not betray me.'

Mary ran down the steps and towards the main gate to catch up with the others. She hoped Doctor Pensch was as trustworthy as Peter said he was.

Chapter 64

August 1945

The glow from the moon framed the outline of the mill against a sky patterned with thousands of stars. A slight breeze took the edge off the heat and ruffled Mary's cap. 'It's a lovely night.'

Peter stood hidden in the shadows of the entrance,

drinking tea. '*Ja*. It is.'

Mary watched as the perimeter guard appeared and strolled past inside the fence. He waved a hand in greeting and she called out to him, 'Goodnight.' She waited a moment before saying, 'He's gone.'

They didn't speak for a few minutes. Mary felt the perspiration on her skin between her breasts. She lifted her face to the gentle wind, appreciating its coolness and willing herself to wait until he spoke but, as the silence between them stretched out, she said, 'Are you all right? You've not had any more problems with the Nazis?'

She heard him sigh. 'No.' There was a slight scrape as he put his cup on the stone windowsill. She felt him move nearer.

'There *is* something I must tell you.' He was hesitant. Mary felt the pulse in her throat quicken with apprehension. 'A few days ago, I received letters from my wife. They had taken a long time to reach me. Almost two years.' Mary turned in the direction of his voice. Forgetting about the guards, she moved towards him.

'She says she waits for my return to Germany.'

'But you say these letters; they're two years old?

'She says she loves me.'

'*I* love you.' Mary moved into the shadows to stand in front of him

'I am sorry, Mary.'

'She doesn't know you as you are now. You are not the same man you were.'

'We must be strong, *mein Geliebter.*'

'Get a divorce. We can be together.'

'*Ich liebe dich*, Mary. I love you. But it is impossible.'

'No!'

'We belong to two different nations: nations who have just fought a bitter war against each other,' he said. 'Also, I must be loyal to my wife, I have not the choice.'

'You have.' Mary reached out to him. 'You have. The war is over. We could …'

'No, you know we could not, it would be impossible. Where could we live and not be hated?'

'Here, you could stay here.'

'No.' Peter held her hands. 'I try always to be an honourable man, *Leibling*. I must do what I believe is the correct thing. I will miss you. I miss you already.' He kissed her, his lips warm and firm, then he gently unclasped her fingers and turned away. 'I must go.' He ran down the steps as the guard opened the gate of the compound. Mary backed into the shadows and watched the darkness envelop him.

Chapter 65

'I can't stay here, Mary.' Ellen tilted her head towards the sleeping figures in the chairs. 'It's like this every day. Mr Brown comes armed with bottles of his home-made wine and they polish them off between them. I can't stand it. Even when you're on nights, you're still not down here, you're asleep in bed.'

Mary stopped slicing the Spam. Not this as well! 'I'm sorry, Ellen. I thought she was getting better. It's him.' She pointed the knife at Arthur Brown. 'If we could somehow stop him coming round it'd be all right. I'll talk to her again.'

'No, it's too late.' Ellen pushed her bottom lip out.

'I shouldn't have left you on your own. It was too soon.' Her eyes were sore from crying, but Ellen hadn't noticed. Perhaps that was just as well, Mary thought. She rubbed her forehead. What could she say? The man I love, a German, has decided that he will go back to his wife?

Ellen pushed the board of cut bread across to Mary who spread the margarine thinly over it. She wiped both sides of the knife on the last piece before saying, 'I should have realised you wouldn't be able to do anything with Mam. I'll try and help more.'

Ellen shook her head, brushing aside Mary's offer. 'It'll be easier for you with Tom home.'

Mary doubted it. She hadn't shown Ellen the letter from Tom that had come in the morning's post. One stark sentence, "I am being released at the end of the month," held no hint of his feelings, nor did the rest of his short note. She was very uneasy; there was something badly wrong. It wasn't like Tom to be so short with her.

Ellen put the two plates on the table and sat down. 'I thought I would be able to manage Mam. You've done it since Dad died. I should have come home then.'

'How could you? You had enough to worry about with the … baby.' Mary sat on the chair opposite Ellen. 'Anyway you couldn't have come home, not with the way things were with Frank. You were better staying away.'

'Perhaps she wouldn't have got this bad if I'd been home.'

'It wouldn't have made any difference, love. I couldn't stop Mr Brown from coming here. I'm sure you wouldn't have been able to.'

They looked at each other, grimacing as Arthur Brown parted his knees and farted.

'Dirty bugger,' Ellen said. 'I'm sorry, Mary; I really can't carry on like this. Patrick and Jean are good to me, they've said I can go round to their house whenever I want to, but to be honest her mother doesn't make me welcome. I'm sure she thinks I'm going to taint the place or something. Even though they swear they haven't told her about the adoption.' She sat back in her chair, biting on her thumbnail. 'And then it's seeing the baby, Jacqueline. I'm not being … I can't be there so often, I can't.'

Mary went round the table to hug her. Ellen might not have noticed how miserable *she* was over the last week, but Mary had certainly heard her sister crying almost every night since she'd come home. 'Do you want to talk about it? Have you changed your mind about your baby?'

'It's too late.' Ellen wriggled under Mary's grasp. 'I'm all right. There's nothing I can do about that now. But sometimes I think about Al. Wonder how things might have turned out.'

Mary straightened up. They weren't that different, her and her sister, with their ill-fated choice of lovers, she thought. If only neither of them had met Frank Shuttleworth, how different their lives would be now. She felt such a bitter hatred it shook her and she put her hand to her throat. Peter would leave, and she knew she would never feel about any other man as she did for him. She might not have a chance at happiness, but Ellen might, if she got out while she could. 'You must do what's best for you,' she said, ignoring the twinge of envy.

Winifred snorted loudly, making the rockers of her chair move, and Mr Brown jumped, his boots coming up off the floor. But he didn't wake up.

'Just look at them,' Ellen said. 'It's disgusting.'

'I know.' Mary stared at the food. 'I don't feel like eating now.' She needed to lie down.

'I'll have some, I'm starving. I feel better now we've talked; now it's out in the open.' Ellen arranged the meat between the slices of bread. 'I know I'm leaving you with this mess and I'm sorry, Mary,' Ellen bit into the sandwich, still talking, 'but I've really tried.'

'I know.' Perhaps not hard enough, but as much as was possible for her, Mary thought, keeping the instinctive resentment out of her voice. 'Where will you go?'

'I'm going to live with Mrs Booth.'

'It's already organised?'

'I've talked to her a lot this week. She's on her own and there's room for me, now Ted's … now he won't be coming home.'

'When are you moving out?'

'I've already packed my things.' Ellen searched Mary's face for a reaction. 'I know, I know, I'm a selfish bitch but I have to get out of here.'

'Mrs Booth will wonder what's hit her,' Mary joked, hiding her dismay. 'All those clothes. Has she got room?'

Ellen smiled. 'I've left most of my dresses; they don't fit me now anyway.'

'They will soon.'

'Perhaps, but they're yours by rights. They were mostly bought with your coupons, as you once pointed out to me.'

'Aw, Ellen, I didn't mind really.'

'I know. But I can get some new things. I've managed to save some of my own coupons over the last few months.' Ellen finished chewing and stood up, brushing the palms of her hands together. 'The main thing is you're not angry with me.'

'Like I said, love, you must do what's best for you.'

'Perhaps you should do the same.'

Mary stared at Ellen's cleared plate, then at her mother and Mr Brown. She thought of the decision Peter had made. 'Perhaps.' There was a cold empty feeling in her stomach.

Chapter 66

Dear Tom

It was so good to get your news. I will be there to meet you on the platform station at Bradlow on the twenty-eighth. I will be glad to have you home. I have a lot to tell you but it can all wait. Everyone sends their love.

Yours, Mary

When she got back from posting the letter Mary leant on the back door looking around the kitchen. Like the rest of the house it was a mess; dust layered her mother's rocking chair, the sideboard and the range, and the rug needed a thorough shaking. Grey ash covered the fireplace; the remains of the fire that Mary had lit the day after Peter told her they had no future. She'd been so cold she couldn't stop shaking, even though the sun poured through the kitchen window. She'd hardly seen him since, certainly hadn't been able to get close enough to talk to him privately. Tears pricked the back of her eyes again.

She must pull herself together. Everywhere needed a good clean before Tom came home. Neither Ellen nor her mother had done any proper housework in weeks. Mary sighed. She closed and locked the back door. Carrying the mug of milk she'd forgotten to drink to the scullery, she poured it into the bottle and fitted the top back on. She stood it in the cold water in the sink. With a bit of luck the milk wouldn't have gone off in the morning. She glanced in the mirror as she dried her hands. She'd lost weight, it didn't suit her and her eyes were a mess. She needed to get some sleep; she was on earlies tomorrow.

Upstairs, in her room, Mary closed the curtains. The sky, streaked with swathes of pink, white and gold, was still quite bright and light filtered through the material although it was past ten o'clock. She dropped her dressing gown on to the chair and bent down to straighten the rag rug.

When she stood up her mother was standing in the doorway. 'God, Mam, you gave me a fright. I thought you'd gone to sleep ages ago.'

Winifred fiddled with the neck of her nightdress. She wouldn't meet Mary's eyes.

'Mam? You all right?' Mary sat on the bed. 'What is it?'

'There's something you should know.' Winifred spoke quickly. 'Arthur Brown has asked me to marry him and I've said yes. His house is rented so I've told him that, afterwards, he might as well move in here.' She held the palm of one hand to her chest, moving the fingers of her other up and down the wall as she watched her daughter. Then she turned and walked back to her room, leaving Mary staring at the empty doorway.

Chapter 67

'It was on the radio about those two atomic bombs the Americans dropped on Japan.' Mary fastened the knot of the turban tighter around her head and knelt in front of the fireplace. She dipped the scrubbing brush into the bucket next to her and swished it round before shaking off the excess water.

Jean buttoned up her blouse and held the baby to her shoulder. Jacqueline burped; a milky dribble on her chin dripped on to her mother's neck. 'Patrick says it means Japan will surrender.' Jean wiped her throat with the piece of rag she'd tucked under the baby's chin. 'But all those people, those children.' She blinked. 'Horrible.' She gently stroked her daughter's back.

'Tom knows about it, too.' Mary scrubbed the hearth tiles. Without looking at Jean she said, 'I had a letter from him.'

Jean stopped patting the baby. 'You didn't say. How does he know? I thought they weren't allowed newspapers.'

'That's what I thought but he's found out somehow and he sounds dreadfully upset; he was raving on about how the Allies' trials of war criminals should have included the Americans for those bombings.' Mary stopped scrubbing. 'There's something really wrong. I'm frightened for him.'

'Have you tried telephoning the prison?'

'Yes, they won't tell me anything. In fact the last time I rang they kept me waiting ages.' Mary dropped the scrubbing brush into the bucket and used a cloth to wipe away the oily black scum on the hearth. 'I used every penny I had and in the end they just said he was he was lucky they were letting him out at all, with the trouble he'd caused. I don't know what they meant.' She knelt back on her haunches and brushed her hair off her face with her forearm. 'But I do know he's not right. He didn't even sign his letter.'

'Well, it's only another week or so before he's home, isn't it? Try not to worry.' Jean put the baby into the navy blue pram outside the back door and tucked the blankets around her. The springs gently clicked as she moved the handle up and down. 'Have you written back?'

'No. I'd already answered his other letter; the one when he told us he'll be home on the twenty-eighth. I thought I'd better ignore this last one.'

'You're probably right.' Jean peered around the door so she could see Mary. 'I'll make a brew in a minute. Will Mam want one? Is she upstairs?'

'No, she's not in. She's gone into Bradlow with Mr Brown.'

'You'll still be calling him that when he's your stepfather.' Jean grinned.

'Patrick told you then?' Mary sidled past her in the doorway, carrying the bucket. In the yard she emptied the grimy water into the grid. 'I know what I'd like to call him.' She didn't return Jean's smile.

Turning round, she tripped on the corner of a flag and fell, dropping the bucket. It crashed on to the ground, rocking back and forth. The baby gave a whimper of protest and a dog in a yard further down the terrace began to bark. A male voice cursed loudly, doors banged and the dog was abruptly silenced.

Mary didn't get up. She lay on the dirty wet ground.

'Mary?' Jean stopped jiggling the pram and ran to help

Mary to her feet. Jacqueline immediately started wailing. 'Are you hurt?'

'See to the baby.' Tears smeared the grime on Mary's face.

'She's OK.' Jean led Mary into the house. 'Sit there, in Mam's chair. I'll make a cup of tea.' She rummaged in her handbag and pulled out a handkerchief. 'Here you are.'

'We can't have tea.' Mary sniffed. 'The range is cold. I let it go out so I could clean it. I wanted everything tidy before Tom gets home.'

'I'll get some water then.' The baby stopped crying. Jean hurried to the door, peered into the hood of the pram and rearranged the covers. 'See? She's fine.'

When she returned to the kitchen she said, 'You're wearing yourself out. Isn't Mam helping at all?' Mary shook her head, tears dripped off her chin. 'And you haven't seen much of Ellen?'

'Not since she left home. She's working in Bradlow now, in the Co-op.' Mary scrubbed at her face. 'Mrs Booth got her a job there. And at weekends she's got a spot singing at the Palais.'

'So, you've been left to do it all. As usual.' Jean perched on the arm of the rocking chair. 'Right, this is what we'll do. No arguing.' She held up both hands. 'You're going to go to bed for a couple of hours.'

'I can't, it's the only day off I'll have before Tom's home.'

'You'll be no good to him ill. So, like I said, you have a sleep.' She stood up. 'I'll take Jacqueline home and ask Mother to look after her for a while. Then I'll come back and do some cleaning in here and the scullery. And if I have time I'll do the lavvy and backyard. Then I'll nip

336

back home to feed Jacqueline and when you get up, we'll clean the bedrooms together. How does that sound?'

'It sounds like I'm having a lazy time.' Mary blew her nose and smiled slightly.

'Rubbish. And, in future, if something's wrong, I'll thank you to tell me. I've not stopped being your best friend just because I'm your sister-in-law.'

Mary gave a wobbly chuckle. 'OK, I give in.' She stood and pulled off the turban. She dropped it on the table and began to automatically rub at a stain with it.

'I should think so. Now, stop that and up those stairs.'

'I feel like the world's on my shoulders sometimes, Jean.' Mary's face began to crumple again.

'I know, love. But I'm here. I'm always ready to listen.'

But not to what I really need to talk about, Mary thought. She let the curtain fall into place.

Chapter 68

Mary hadn't been asked to sit when she was called into Matron's office and the woman's face was impassive. After a few moments she spoke, 'What I have to say, Sister, will stay between these four walls.' She clasped her hands on the desk. 'And when you have heard it, you will be exceedingly glad that is what I have decided.' She paused, frowning. 'I have been told that you have formed a very unwise attachment to Doctor Schormann.'

'No.' Mary's heart leapt.

'The Commandant has interviewed him and obviously he has also denied it. However my source is reliable and, I have to say, I have had my suspicions for a while.' Matron stressed her words by drumming her fingers on the table. 'Now, Sister Howarth, you must be aware of the penalties for fraternising with the Germans; indeed, when you came to work at the hospital it was one of the first things you were warned about. I have discussed the matter with Major Taylor. At this stage, with the war now officially over, we feel it's unnecessary to bring in any outside authorities and he agrees with me, so, for this reason and this reason only, we have decided that you will only receive an unofficial warning.'

'I've done nothing wrong, Matron.'

'In your eyes perhaps, and I have to say your attitude disappoints me, but, because in the past your behaviour has been exemplary and your work professional, I am willing to give you the benefit of the doubt. Look on this as a reprimand of the strongest order. Now, you can get back to your duties. And consider yourself a very lucky young woman.'

She picked up a pen and began to write. Mary waited a moment. She could feel the anger welling up inside her and didn't trust herself to speak. Without lifting her head Matron spoke again, 'I said you could go. There is nothing else to discuss.' She stopped writing but didn't look at Mary. 'Except perhaps you should know that as from tomorrow, we will be having two different doctors here.'

'Matron?'

'I don't have to tell you this, Sister, but I will, as it will soon be known within the camp anyway.' She opened the bottle of ink on her desk. 'The Commandant has told me the military authorities have already formulated plans to re-educate the prisoners before they are sent back to Germany.'

Now she looked up at Mary. 'Major Taylor says it will take a long time. However, there is apparently a scheme that the Government has decided will be put into operation forthwith.' She lifted the lever on the side of the pen. 'A number of German prisoners will be chosen to return home soon.' She paused to fill her fountain pen. Mary waited, the familiar rushing noise beginning.

Matron screwed the top back on the bottle. 'The Commandant has been requested to put forward names of those men who were screened as "A" ratings. Because of that, and because of his trusted position as *Lagerführer,* Doctor Schormann has been chosen as one of those doctors who will accompany the German sick and wounded back to their own country for further treatment at the earliest opportunity. It is for the best.'

Mary was trembling. She put her fingertips on the edge of Matron's desk.

'You may sit down, Sister.'

She stumbled on to the chair.

When Matron spoke again her voice had softened but she continued, 'Doctor Pensch will also be leaving us. I'm afraid he has been diagnosed with stomach cancer so, as he formerly lived in what is now the British zone of Germany, he is being allowed to go home. He is one of the patients that Doctor Schormann will be accompanying. I suggest you get back to your duties now you are fully apprised of the situation.'

Mary walked unsteadily towards the door. In the corridor she stopped. 'It is for the best Mary.' The words went round and round in her head.

'No, it's not,' she said aloud, 'it's not for the best. Not for us it's not.' She crossed her arms across her waist and turned to face the wall. Resting her forehead she whispered, 'It's not; it's not for the best.'

Chapter 69

When Mary went into work the following day Peter and some of the patients had already been taken. 'They came about two o'clock this morning,' the Night Sister said crossly, not noticing the shock on Mary's face, 'without a minute's warning. It was very disruptive to the ward. They took Eiserbeck, Becker, Jankowick and Doctor Pensch.' She pointed at each bed as she listed the names. 'It took ages for the patients to settle down after that. I'm sure they could have done it in a better way. And of course, Doctor Schormann has gone with them.' She raised her arms from her side in a gesture of exasperation. 'The only good thing is that the two new doctors are due to arrive today sometime. Except that we'll have to start all over again showing them how we run things.'

'Did you see Doctor Schormann before he left, Olive?' Mary's mouth was dry.

'What? Oh no, no I didn't. He didn't come into the ward, thank goodness. There were enough men trampling all over the place.'

'Well, how do you know he's gone?'

'It's in the notes. They went in a lorry.' She picked up a grey cardigan and shoved her arms into the sleeves. 'All that trouble we go to keeping everything sterile and they cart them away in a blasted lorry.' The sound of her voice grew faint and came back as she left the main ward to go into the staff room and returned. She was fastening her cape. 'Tell you one thing though, Mary. I'll miss Doctor Schormann. I thought he was a right arrogant so-and-so when he first got here but he was quite a gent really'. She pushed the ward doors open with her backside. 'Yes, I'll miss having him around the ward, though I suppose I shouldn't say it. After all he was the enemy, wasn't he?' Her voice faded away. 'See you tomorrow. Ta ta.'

Chapter 70

'Sister Howarth? Mary? I have something for you.'

Mary halted on the last step outside the hospital. The POW behind the fence beckoned to her. She glanced at the lookout and then towards the side gate. There was no sentry at either. Looking to her left she saw the rest of the nurses walking through the barrier to the bus stop on Shaw Road. And there was no one near the entrance of the hospital. She bent down, pretending to tie her shoelace. 'What do you want?'

'I am one of Peter's friends, Kurt Trept.'

'Peter has gone.'

'Yes. I have the note for you.'

'From Peter?'

'Yes. Here, take it.'

'The guards?'

'*Die Wachmannschaft ist sehr faul* … how you say it … lazy.'

'What?'

'Come. No guards.' Kurt jerked his head backwards a few times. 'See?'

Mary stood up and looked behind him. There was a

group of guards standing and talking by the local baker's van, which came to the camp each day. They were eating. She moved quickly. Kurt thrust the paper through the fencing.

'Thank you,' Mary said, 'thank you.' She crumpled the note in her fist and held it inside her cape. Once out of the camp, she ran along Shaw Road until she reached the turn off for Skirm Park. There she made her way to the lake.

The benches were full. Mary sat on the grass near the water's edge, away from everyone. She tucked her cape underneath her and drew up her knees. Spreading out the piece of paper she smoothed her finger along each fold. The words were scribbled on the back of the index page of a book. She read the words slowly, memorizing each syllable, the image of Peter writing them in her mind.

Mein Liebling, my Mary

I am being sent away. I have no choice. Our destiny is not ours to decide. I will love you until the day I die. I will never forget you.

I beg you - never forget me.

I love you

Ich liebe dich

Auf Wiedersehen

Always yours, Peter

Mary ran the tips of her fingers over his name. She took no notice of the tears dropping on to the paper. She put her forehead on her knees and rocked backwards and forwards. She knew he'd had no choice. But the war was over; he must believe there would be a time when all the madness was forgotten. Yet his words were so final. He knew it was over between them, he would not be coming back. He had chosen his marriage, not her.

'Nurse?' Mary felt a hand on her shoulder. 'Nurse, is there something wrong? Is there anything I can do?'

She looked up, hiding the note under her cape. The old man held his cap to his chest. 'Bad news is it? Your young man?'

Mary nodded. The wretchedness stopped any words.

'I'm sure his country is proud of him.' The man patted her again and hobbled away. 'I'll leave you with your memories, my dear.'

Mary stared after him. If only he knew. But she refused to feel ashamed. What she and Peter had was nothing to do with the war; they were just a man and a woman in love at the wrong time.

She wiped her face with her cape and stared around. Some of these people she'd lived amongst all her life. She recognised a few and one or two waved as they caught her eye, yet she felt isolated. She was strangely calm, as though part of her was locked away. It had happened, now she had to live with it. The man she loved, the only man she'd ever loved, was gone. It was over. She folded the paper exactly along the same folds and put it in her uniform pocket. Wiping her fingers over her face, she pushed herself to her feet. Keeping her head lowered so she didn't have to speak to anyone, she walked quickly along the paths and out on to Greenacre Street. She had a meal to prepare in readiness for Tom's arrival tomorrow afternoon.

Chapter 71

Tom didn't speak when he stepped off the train. The suit he'd worn going into prison was now baggy and creased: his shirtcollar, grimed and frayed, gaped tie-less, and his hair was lank. He hung on to Mary so tightly and for so long that she became conscious of the stares of the other passengers.

'Come on, love,' she said, 'let's get you home.' He held her hand, refusing to get on the bus. They stood for a while as she tried to persuade him. In the end they walked home.

Halfway there she realised he was limping. She looked down at his feet. 'Tom, these aren't your shoes, surely?' She knelt down. 'They're too small.' He looked at her, his eyes blank. 'You can't walk in these. The next bus to come along we're catching.' But he hobbled past all the stops and it took them over an hour to get to the house.

Mary had seen cases of shock when she worked at her first hospital. She was fuming; how could they have sent him home like this and why hadn't they been told he was ill? Because of what he is, she thought bitterly, because he's a Conscientious Objector. How long would he be judged by a label?

Her mother didn't help, sitting there, staring at her eldest son. Mary took the potato pie out of the range oven and put it on the tea towel on the table. It was obvious Winifred didn't know how to talk to her eldest son. At least, for once, she hadn't a drink in her hand. Not that Tom would have noticed. He sat on their father's chair, his feet in a bowl of water, his trousers rolled to his knees, gazing into the empty fireplace with his hands folded in his lap.

'I'll get a towel and dry your feet in a minute.' Mary

directed her next words at her mother. 'There must be some of Dad's socks upstairs, those wool ones? They'll stretch to fit Tom.'

Winifred went upstairs. 'I'll get some Germolene and plasters, as well'.

Cutting through the pastry of the pie, Mary glanced at Tom. 'I've got two day's leave from the hospital.'

Matron was icily distant when, at the end of her shift, Mary reminded her that she wouldn't be in work because of Tom's homecoming. 'Try to be more professional when you return, Sister,' she'd said, pulling her spectacles down the bridge of her nose and looking over the top of them at Mary. 'Your work recently has been less than satisfactory and your attitude unfortunate, despite the leeway you have been shown. I will expect a great improvement.'

Mary spooned the mix of carrots, turnips and potatoes on to three plates. 'Meat and potato pie without meat I'm afraid.' She forced a laugh. 'I thought we could have a walk to Skirm afterwards, see the old haunts?' There was no reaction from Tom. 'Well, perhaps not.' Winifred came back into the kitchen and kneeling down, took his feet out of the bowl and dried them. She made disapproving noises at the sight of the blisters.

'I'll do that, Mam.'

Winifred shook her head. She worked in silence on the lesions and then carefully pulled the socks on. When she'd finished Tom stroked her hair, his face expressionless.

She reached forward and touched his cheek, tears welling. 'Help us up, our Mary.' She held on to Mary, her knees cracking as she stood.

'Sit down, let's eat,' Mary said.

Tom sat at the table staring at his plate and the knife

and fork in his hands. He looked at Mary. Without saying anything Mary opened the table drawer for a spoon. He gave her a small smile and started to eat with it.

Encouraged she said, 'Patrick and Jean will be round later with baby Jacqueline. She's gorgeous, Tom, just wait until you see her. And Ellen, she'll be here too, sometime.'

'And Arthur.' Winifred waved her fork at Tom. 'You remember Mr Brown, don't you? Did Mary tell you me and him are getting wed?'

Tom stopped eating, his spoon halfway to his mouth.

Mary swallowed. 'I haven't Mam. I thought it better if we waited until Tom had settled in.'

At that moment the back door was flung open. 'Well, he's home then I see, this prodigal son of yours, Win.' Arthur Brown flung himself into Bill Howarth's chair. 'Mary.' He waggled his head in acknowledgment of her presence.

Tom pushed his chair back and went into the hall. His socks slipped on the lino and he trailed both hands along the wall to balance himself. Looking back at them for a second, he went into the front room and closed the door.

Glaring at Arthur Brown, Mary followed. She sat on the sofa with Tom and pulled him close to her, his head on her shoulder. 'All these changes, Tom, I know it's hard. Let's just take one day at a time,' she said. 'You're free now and no one will ever lock you up again. Things will get better, I promise.'

It was as much a promise to herself. She couldn't carry on with things as they were and neither could Tom. She had to do something. That night she lay in bed thinking. Eventually she got up and took a notepad out of a drawer in the tallboy and, resting it on her knee, began to write.

Dear Gwyneth

I am sorry we missed the memorial service for Iori at your chapel but, as I explained, Tom wasn't due to be released until today and he wouldn't have been well enough to travel anyway. He was very fond of Iori so you know he would have been there if possible. He's very withdrawn which is a great worry. It was good of you to write to him to tell him all about the service. I'll give him your letter tomorrow.

There is actually another reason I wanted to write to you ...

Chapter 72

September 1945

'This is the BBC Light Programme. And now the news on Monday the twenty-seventh of September nineteen forty-five. The defence team for William Joyce, better known as Lord Haw Haw, gave notice of appeal against his sentence today ...'

'Just get the bugger hung.' Arthur Brown waved his glass at the radio, stretching his leg out and pushing his boot against an overhanging piece of wood smouldering in the fireplace. Mary, sitting at the table with Tom, could hear the chink of fragments of unburned coal fall into the ashcan underneath the grate. She gritted her teeth. It would be her job to rake through and pick those pieces out in the morning to use again. It was the same every day: he chucked wood on as soon as the fire died down, not waiting for the coal to catch hold. Don't think about it, she told herself, it's no big deal. But it was. Arthur was wasteful and contributed nothing to the household, although she was certain he had money from various sources; she knew he dealt in the same circles as Patrick, her brother had told her. She strained to listen to the wireless through Arthur's grousing.

'Joyce's lawyers believe that the trial judge was wrong to accept the prosecution's legal arguments relating to the question of allegiance. Their dispute is that, at the time of his broadcasts, Joyce was an American citizen and, as such, had no duty of allegiance to the King; therefore he could not be found guilty of treason. Due to high treason having only one possible sentence, his appeal is only against the conviction, not the sentence itself. We await the result of the appeal. Further news ...'

'They should shoot the bugger now and have done with it,' Arthur Brown spoke loudly over the voice of the announcer on the radio.

Winifred, rocking in her chair, frowned at him. 'Shut up, Arthur.'

'Well, talking to us in his posh bloody accent about how the bloody Huns were better than us. Bastard.' Holding his glass, he pointed with one finger at Tom and Mary. 'Bloody traitor, buggered off to Germany, didn't he? Wouldn't fight for his country.'

Tom put his knife and fork down, picked up his plate and took it into the scullery.

'Actually, he's American, not British,' Mary said, following her brother.

'Don't give a monkey's arse. He's still a coward and a traitor.' He took a noisy gulp of his beer and stood up.

He waited a couple of seconds to get his balance, leaning against Bill's chair and belched loudly. 'I've gone to The Crown.' He took his watch out of his waistcoat pocket and squinted at it. 'I'll call in on my way back by eleven.'

'I'll probably have an early night,' Winifred said. 'See you tomorrow.'

'Please yourself.' Putting on his cap and jacket Arthur opened the back door. 'It's pissing down.'

He was almost knocked over by Ellen pushing past him to get into the house. 'Mary, Mam!' She held a raincoat over her head, a pool of water forming around her feet.

Mary slammed the door on Arthur and pulled her further into the kitchen. 'What is it? What's wrong?' She took Ellen's coat and slung it over the mangle in the scullery, dragged a piece of towelling off the shelf and passed it to her.

'That's just it, nothing's wrong.' Ellen rubbed at her hair, a broad smile on her face 'Not any more. It's Ted, he's alive!'

'Ted?'

Ellen nodded impatiently. 'Yes, yes. We found out today he's been a prisoner. He's not dead. Mrs Booth collapsed when the telegram came. We couldn't believe it but there was a number to telephone and the chap there said it was true. We don't know when he'll be home but isn't it wonderful?' She flung her arms around Mary and then Tom. 'I can't wait to see him.'

Winifred pushed herself up from her chair. 'That's wonderful, our Ellen. Shall I come to see his mother?'

'Yes, Mam, she'll be happy to see you.' Ellen laughed. 'Come with me when I go back.'

'You're really excited about Ted, aren't you, love?'

349

Winifred took off her apron and draped it over the back of her chair. 'Enough to give him a second chance?'

'Mam,' Mary protested, 'give over.'

'It's all right, our Mary, I think Mam's right. I've not been fair on him. Perhaps he's just what I need,' Ellen said, 'and perhaps I'm just what he needs as well. If he'll forgive me for that letter about Al …'

'I'm sure you are, love. I'll get changed,' Winfred said. 'I won't be long.'

'How is she?' Ellen said, after her mother had gone upstairs.

'Good days, bad days,' Mary said. 'I just wish Arthur Brown wasn't here so much, he doesn't help.'

'He's a swine,' Tom said.

Ellen hugged him. 'How are you feeling today, Tom.'

'I'm not bad, Ellen, I'm glad about Ted.' He looked at Mary. 'I'm going upstairs.'

'Right, love.' His footsteps were heavy on the stairs.

'He's not right, is he?' Ellen was suddenly subdued.

'Better than he was but no,' Mary said. 'This house is doing him no good either.' She nodded towards the chairs. 'Sit down a minute, while you wait for Mam, there's something I want to talk to you about.'

'So there it is.' Mary glanced up at the ceiling. The floorboards creaked as Winifred moved around in her bedroom. 'I've not said anything yet, but I've been keeping in touch with Iori's mother on and off since he died. When I saw what a state Tom was in when he got home I had the idea. And it's best he's not in Ashford anyway.'

'Why is it best? Why shouldn't he be in Ashford, it's

his home?'

'You know. The CO stuff.'

'He coped with that before.' Ellen scowled. 'There's something you're not telling me.'

'No there's not. Anyhow I think I need to get away as much as him.'

'You've not said anything about this before.'

'Be honest, Ellen, how often do you come round here for me to talk to? I'm not blaming you but you have no idea how things have changed. I thought it was bad enough when Dad was alive.'

'Mary!'

'Yes, well, it wasn't that bad for you; you were his favourite and you always did what you wanted anyway,' Mary said. 'It doesn't feel like our home here anymore: Mam's gone to pieces, Arthur Brown comes most days and Tom hates him. Arthur just goads him all the time. And like I said, the hospital's different now.' She massaged her temples. 'The POWs aren't the same. We're getting prisoners returned from Canada. They're sullen, difficult to deal with. We could at least have a laugh with the permanent ones. These are so … oh, I don't know.' She sighed and held the palms of her hands over her face. 'According to Major Taylor most of them thought they were going home when they were shipped from Canada and dumped here and some of them are really nasty. Even the patients are sullen. They don't appreciate that all we're trying to do is make them well again.' She put her hands flat on the table. 'So between work and home I've had enough and it's best for Tom we get away from here,' she said firmly. 'We're leaving.'

'When?'

'When things are sorted. I'll have to get a job first. I've asked Gwyneth to find out if there are any hospitals nearby that need staff and, of course, Tom will have to be kept busy.'

'You've got it all worked out then!'

'Don't, Ellen, don't be bitter. You sorted yourself out; give us a chance, please.'

'What about Mam?' There was a hint of panic in Ellen's eyes.

'Well, as I said, I'm hoping to persuade her to come with us.'

'And if she won't?'

There were sounds of Winifred coming downstairs.

Mary shrugged. 'I'm hoping she will, I'd hate to leave her and I think it's her only chance to get back to rights but we'll still go. We have to.'

Mary didn't tell Ellen, but she had no intention of leaving her mother to Arthur Brown's mercy. Winifred would go with them if they had to drag her all the way to Wales.

Chapter 73

'I wanted to tell you before, but I wasn't sure it would work out. But now I think it will, one way or the other. I've just told Ellen so, while Mam's gone with her to Mrs Booth's, I thought I should come round and tell you and Patrick.' Mary stood at the window watching the rain hammer down. The light from the kitchen shimmered in the puddles in Jean's back yard as the drops hit the surface.

'What am I going to do without you?' Jean was on the edge of tears. She laid one of Jacqueline's dresses on the blanket over the table and ran the iron over it.

Mary reached up and pulled the kitchen curtains together, shutting out the darkness. 'I'll miss you too. I'll miss all of you, especially my little niece. We both will. But I'll keep in touch and you can visit. You do understand, don't you?' Mary said quietly. 'I can't take any chances. I have to get Tom away from here.'

Jean bit her lip but didn't answer. She draped the dress over a tiny wooden hanger and hooked it on the back of a chair. 'Have you any idea where you'll go?' She started to press one of Patrick's shirts.

'Hopefully, Wales.'

'Wales?' Jean stopped ironing and stood the iron upright. 'Why Wales? It's miles away.'

'Exactly!' Mary ran hot water in the bowl in the sink and piled cups and plates into it. She worked quickly, scrubbing with the dishcloth. 'I've been writing to Iori's mother. You know, Iori; the chap Tom was friends with in prison? She's got a cottage I'm hoping she says we can rent.' Mary balanced the last plate against a cup. 'It's in a village called Llamroth, it's very peaceful apparently. Just what Tom needs.' She dried her hands, watching Jean ironing a shirt of Patrick's in a haphazard fashion. 'Patrick and your mother out?' she asked, picking up a tea cloth and drying a cup.

'Patrick's at the pub and Mother's next door,' Jean said, lowering the clothes rack to hang Patrick's shirt on it before hauling it back up to the ceiling. 'He shouldn't be long.' She rearranged damp nappies on the rails of the clotheshorse around the fire. Steam rose rapidly. The roaring flames sizzled every now and then as drops of rain fell down the chimney. 'How is Tom?'

'I think he'll be better when we've gone.' Mary said. 'You know why I'm worried, Jean. I've no proof it was Tom and I only wish I could persuade myself I'm wrong. And I know we've heard nothing about what happened to Frank for a while. God willing, we never will. But, all in all, I think it's better he's not in the area.'

'Has he ever said anything about it?'

'Not a word. Has Patrick?'

'No!' Jean stopped folding a pile of tiny nightdresses and cardigans and looked steadily at Mary. 'Yes.' She frowned, fiddled with the buttons on her blouse. 'I'm sorry, I should have said something before now. Patrick told me it was Tom there that day.'

The room tilted. 'Did Tom admit it?'

'I don't know the ins and outs of it, just that Patrick said that's why he went to see Tom as soon as he came out of solitary. He thought right away it might be Tom.'

'Why?'

'Well, admit it, Mary, you did too.'

'I thought it could have been either of them; either Tom … or Patrick, you know that.'

'It wasn't Patrick,' Jean blurted.

Mary raised her eyebrows.

'It wasn't. We knew you'd told Tom what Frank was doing, stalking you and all that, and we all know how protective he's always been of you. That has to be why he escaped?'

They faced one another across the table.

'But you said before he'd only got as far as Bradlow?'

'That's what Patrick said to me at the time but apparently

it wasn't true. He's told me since Tom let it slip he did get off the train here.

'But Tom's a pacifist. He wouldn't kill anyone. It goes against all his beliefs.' Mary had argued this to herself a thousand times.

Jean shook her head. 'Not so much so that he won't fight to protect those he loves. Look what he did when his, his friend … got beaten up.'

'Why did you say "friend" like that?'

'How long have I known you, Mary? I can read you like a book and I listen to what you say. I knew why you were worried about Tom and Iori.'

'Does Patrick know about them?'

'I haven't said anything.'

Mary nodded. 'Good, keep it that way.' She drummed her fingers on the table, her lower lip between her teeth. 'But you should have told me what Patrick said. I'd have got Tom away from here as soon as he came out. Is that why Patrick's hardly spoken to me for months, because he didn't want to tell me?'

The baby began to whimper. Jean went through to the hall and pulled the pram into the kitchen, gently bouncing it on its springs until the crying stopped.

'Jean? Is that why he's been odd with me?'

'No.' There was a catch in Jean's voice. She turned towards Mary. 'I … I'm sorry.'

'If it's not that …' Mary's skin tightened with a cold prickling sensation. Her stomach flipped. She knew what Jean was trying to say. 'You told Patrick, didn't you? You told him about me and Peter?'

The rain had stopped but Mary could still hear the gurgle

of water in the downspout by the back door. The fire had settled into red embers and the nappies on the clothes-horse no longer steamed. Neither woman had spoken for the last quarter of an hour, the long minutes ticked off by the clock in the hall.

Jean was the first to speak. 'I'm sorry, really I am,' she said, 'it just came out.'

Mary closed her eyes and sighed. 'When?'

'Ages ago, after I lost the first baby, I was telling Patrick how kind Peter was and it sort of came out about you and him.'

'Hmm. Well, it answers some questions. I've always thought he was still mad at me because I didn't tell him about Frank being Ellen's baby's father.'

'No. It was about Peter. He was so angry.'

'Obviously still is.' Mary couldn't stop the bitterness. 'I have to go.' She grabbed her coat and put it on.

'But he wouldn't report you, you know that. You're his sister, he loves you.' She caught hold of Mary's hand. 'And so do I. Don't be angry with me, please. Don't leave like this, let's sort it out.'

Mary fastened her headscarf. She looked from Jean to Jacqueline and softened. 'There's nothing to sort out, love. I'm not angry, not really, it's too late for that. And you're right, Patrick could have reported us and he didn't. Knowing how resentful he's been these last few years about not being able to fight and knowing his temper, I'm amazed and I'm grateful. We've you to thank for that, you've made him happier than I've ever seen him, you and Jacqueline.' She hugged Jean. 'But we've no choice now, Tom and me. We have to get away from here.' Her throat tightened. It was difficult to get her next words out. 'We have to make a new life. Peter's gone and I have to try to forget him. He's gone and that's all there is to it.'

Chapter 74

October 1945

Mary switched on the light in the front room and drew the curtains against any curious stares from people passing by on the pavement outside. Then she sat on the lumpy settee and skimmed through the letter that Winifred had propped up against the teapot on the kitchen table.

... As you know the cottage next door belonged to my parents but ever since they died it's been empty, so it's a bit damp. It would have been Iori's eventually and I couldn't bear the thought of anyone else being in it but I've made a decision. It's here if you and Tom want to rent it ...'

Mary let the piece of paper drop into her lap. It was going to happen. She could get Tom out of this place.

Iori's buried in the local churchyard, which is just down the lane from the cottages. I would really like it if Tom could help me to look after the grave?

You wanted to know if there would be any work for Tom, so I asked around. There are quite a few older people in Llamroth who told me they are always looking for odd job men to do their gardens and such.

As for the other thing you asked me to find out about. There is a hospital in the nearest town, Pont y Haven, that's looking for trained nurses. I've enclosed the details ...

357

Laughter and applause told Mary the radio had been switched on in the kitchen. There was a great burst of giggles from Arthur. The door opened. 'Can't stand that programme,' Tom said, sitting next to Mary.

'It's That Man Again, Handley.' Mary smiled. 'He's all right in small doses. Listen, there's something I want to ask you.' She paused, watching him closely. 'I've been writing to Gwyneth, Mrs Griffiths, for a while now.'

Tom now straightened up. 'Iori's mother?'

'Yes, we've come up with a plan. I think you'll like it.'

Tom twisted sideways to look at her, nervously gathering the antimacassar on the back of the settee into folds in his large hands. 'What is it?'

'Here, read her letter.' She waited, watching for his reaction. When he looked up at her again she said, 'What do you think?'

Tom dropped his chin on his chest. She could hear him struggling not to cry. When the tears came, it was a noisy outpouring of grief. Mary knelt up on the settee and held him, rocking him from side to side.

Gradually he calmed down, his breath drawn in great shuddering gasps against her shoulder. 'Sorry,' he finally said, scrubbing at his face with Mary's handkerchief. 'I didn't …'

'I know.' She let go of him. 'I didn't want to say anything until I knew I could make it happen.'

They sat quietly, each thinking their own thoughts. Out on the street footsteps hurried past, the rain drummed on the window, plopped down the chimney into the empty fireplace.

Tom sat forward. 'What about Mam?'

'I thought between us we might persuade her to come

with us?'

'Right!' He nodded. 'I've not been much use lately, have I?'

Mary smiled at him. 'Don't worry about it.'

'Everything that's happened … to you, to Dad, Mam, Ellen … and Iori, it just all built up.'

'Do you feel like talking?' When she saw the distress on his face, she leaned towards him. 'Tom? What is it?' Her first thought, please don't tell me it *was* you, was like a chant in her head. She hated the thought that he'd had to betray his beliefs to protect her.

'I can't stop thinking about Iori. It was horrible what they did to him.' He screwed his eyes shut and then opened them. Mary was horrified by the surge of relief in her. 'There were seven of them. They blocked him in the cell. I couldn't get to him, I tried I really tried, Mary.' He leaned forward, pressing his hands against his eyes.

'Yes, Tom, I'm sure you did.' She put her head on his shoulder.

'When he was on the floor they kept on kicking him, again and again and again,' he said. 'I climbed over them, I hit them, I kicked them, I was screaming for them to stop. The prisoners who stood by and watched what they did to Iori later told the Governor I went berserk.' He nodded. 'I think I did. I wanted to kill them. When I got to him he was unrecognisable. His face was all smashed in. Sometimes, when I close my eyes, that's all I can see.'

'Oh Tom.' Mary heard the clock in the kitchen strike ten and overhead sounds of her mother clattering about on her way to bed. A thought struck her. 'Did I get it wrong then?' she said. 'Be truthful, Tom, do you really think it would be a good idea going to Llamroth?' She leaned forward to look into his face. 'Would it be too painful, love? Make those memories worse?'

'Oh no, Iori loved the place.' He smiled at her. 'And when I went there, when I escaped, I loved it too.'

'You don't want time to think about it?' Mary worried. 'You're sure?'

'I don't want time to think about it,' Tom said. 'I'm sure.'

Chapter 75

The stone-fronted house looked even more neglected. A large patch of moss partly covered the enclosed area of tarmac where rain had dripped from a broken gutter. There was even less paint on the door now and a piece of swollen wood replaced one of the leaded windows.

Mary let go of the tarnished brass knocker and stepped off the smooth dip in the centre of the dirty grey step. She heard feet scuffling on the lino in the hall: Nelly Shuttleworth filled the doorway.

'I hope you don't mind my calling, Nelly,' Mary said. 'I know I haven't seen you since you came to our house, but I really wanted to talk to you.'

'No, come in. It's nice to see you, pet. The weather's driving me mad. I can't remember the last fine day.' She led the way to the kitchen. 'Brew?'

'Thanks.' Mary unbuttoned her coat, sat in one of the overstuffed armchairs and waited while Nelly made the tea.

She had her back to Mary as she asked, 'Was it something about Frank? Have you heard from the police?'

'No, it's not that,' Mary said hastily.

Nelly poured tea into two mugs, her hand unsteady. 'What is it then?' She held up a small jug. 'Milk?'

Mary nodded. 'Please. I wanted to tell you I'm moving away, I came to say goodbye. You were kind enough to come to see me after Frank's funeral.'

'I came because I thought it was something I should do.' Nelly's voice was gruff. 'He was my son and he – he hurt you.' She passed a mug to Mary. 'But he paid for it, didn't he?' She wheezed as she eased herself into the armchair opposite Mary, her skirt riding up to show her pink bloomers. 'Are you leaving because of that, because of what he did?'

'To be honest, I just need a fresh start.'

'Where will you go?'

Mary hesitated, she'd decided she wouldn't tell Nelly about Wales: if she was to protect Tom, the fewer who knew the better. 'Not sure yet.'

'You'll be leaving your family.'

'I'm hoping Mam comes with me, and Tom.'

'How is your brother?'

'He needs a change as well.'

'And your Mam?'

The image of her mother sneaking the bottle upstairs the day Nelly came to the house flashed into Mary's mind. 'She's fine, thanks.'

There was the rasp of a key in the front door lock and a shout: 'I'm back.'

'George,' Nelly said to Mary.

'I'd better go.' She hadn't forgotten the venom in his voice the day of the inquest.

George poked his head round the kitchen door, stared

361

at them and then, without speaking left. Mary heard him bounding up the stairs. 'I'll be off then,' she said.

Nelly followed her to the door. She folded her arms, the sleeves of her blouse cutting into the flab, as George came back down and slouched against the wall, his eyes narrowed. Mary ignored the snort of contempt from him as she kissed Nelly on the cheek. 'Bye then.' But she couldn't stop the shiver of fear that coursed through her body. He reminded her so much of his brother.

As soon as Nelly closed the door, the argument started. Mary stood on the path, her hand on the top of the gate and listened. The quarrel in the house became louder. She heard George shouting. 'I don't know why you let that fucking bitch in this house. She's the reason Frank's dead, you stupid cow.'

'You're talking rubbish. You don't know that.'

'Course I bloody do.'

Mary pulled the gate closed. If she wasn't already determined to leave, George Shuttleworth's words would have been enough to make up her mind. She hunched her shoulders, shoved her hands into her pockets against the sharp autumnal wind that went straight through her, and walked away.

Chapter 76

November 1945

The branches of the large sycamores opposite the camp dissected the gun-grey sky. A rush of wings disturbed the stillness of impending rain; starlings swirled noisily before settling again in the trees. Mary gathered her woollen cloak around her, glad of its warmth, and turned to look at the camp one last time. There were few prisoners still in the compound. The windows, oblongs of lights on all four floors, were crowded with the outlines of men.

Mary breathed in the lingering smell of bonfires and let the air out in a lengthy sigh, relief mixed with sadness that she'd completed her four weeks notice. She was leaving a lot of good memories behind as well as the bad. She walked down the steps of the hospital and through the barrier of the main gate on to Shaw Street without glancing back. She'd said her goodbyes.

The short interview with Matron was much as she'd expected; the woman had barely glanced up when Mary thanked her for the reference which had guaranteed her a post at the hospital in Pont y Haven. There had been an awkward silence, only broken when Mary moved to open the office door. Even then Matron hadn't looked at her. 'Try to be professional in all you do, Sister Howarth. Don't let yourself down.' Mary closed the door on the word, 'Again.'

Swollen drops of rain suddenly smacked onto the pavement. Mary dragged her hood over her hair and ran. Soon the gutters rushed with streams of water. When she passed Jean's house rainwater gushed out of the downspout and rattled on to the tin roof of the coal shed. In the alleyway, the wet cobbles were greasy and behind the blank gates on either side there was the usual night-time racket of radios, babies crying and the high-pitched fury of quarrels.

At number twenty-seven, Mary lifted the latch and pushed it open. The curtains were still pulled back at the

kitchen window and Mary saw the flickering of the fire in
the gloom of the kitchen. The rain tapped like drumbeats
on the tin bath hung on the wall.

Mrs Jagger had her back door open; the whiff of pipe
smoke floated over the wall. Even this downpour wouldn't
keep her in, Mary thought.

'Everything all right, Mary?' the old woman called out.

'Everything's all right, Mrs Jagger.'

'What a night, eh?'

'Shocking.' Something in Mrs Jagger's voice stopped
Mary. 'Are you all right, Mrs Jagger?'

'Not really, Mary. With weather like this I don't get out
much. I don't see anybody from one day to the next. Gets
a bit lonely, you know.'

'I know,' Mary said, 'I know.' She felt an unusual pang
of sympathy for the old woman. 'Goodnight, then.'

'Night, Mary.' There was another drift of pipe smoke
above the yard wall. The old woman coughed. 'Mary?'

'Yes?'

'Thanks for asking, I enjoy our little chats.'

Her mother was leaning towards the fire, a book on her
knee, her grey shawl over her head. She turned round as
Mary came in. 'I've put a shovelful of fire in the grate in
your room, love,' she said. 'It should be warm up there.'

'Thanks, Mam,' Mary couldn't keep the surprise out of
her voice. She glanced around. 'You've been cleaning?'

'Ellen came round.' Winifred pushed her shawl off
her head and tucked the book down the side of her chair.
'They've had some news. Ted will be home by weekend.
She didn't know what to do with herself, she was that
excited. She said she'd cleaned every inch of Mrs Booth's

house and she was still a bundle of nerves so she tackled this place.'

'Well, it's great.' Mary slung her cloak over the rack and hunkered down by the range. 'I'm so cold, it's miserable out there.' She put a hand on her mother's knee. 'No Arthur tonight?'

'No, not today,' was all Winifred said, but there was a note in her voice Mary hadn't heard since her father died and the hand that covered Mary's was firm.

'Tom upstairs?'

'He was tired.'

Mary's studied her mother; her hair was almost white now and the mottled skin on her cheeks was crisscrossed with tiny wrinkles. But, for once, the whites of her eyes were not shot through with red and her gaze on her daughter was steady.

'Mam?' Mary traced the raised veins that pushed against the fragile skin on the back of Winifred's hand. 'Mam, I've been meaning to tell you something.' Now the time had come, Mary didn't know what to say. She looked past her mother at the pattern of shadows thrown up by the fire's flames on the back wall. 'I've got some news,' she said, at last. 'Tom and I are going to live in Wales and we want you to come with us.'

Chapter 77

December 1945

Above the dingy canopy of the station buildings the sun was a pale vague glow in a filmy sky, the air so crisp it

365

hurt to breathe in. Mary paced the platform, stopping every now and then to make sure the plaid blanket covered her mother's legs. 'Keep covered up, Mam,' she said. 'You'll catch your death. I told you we'd be too soon.' Her words were carried on cold wisps of white breath.

Winifred tipped her head back so she could see past the brim of her hat. 'He's worse than me,' she laughed, a nervous tic moving the corner of her eye. She nodded towards Tom standing by the suitcases, self-conscious in his new blue serge suit and navy trilby. 'We'd have camped here all night if it was anything to do with him.' She pulled her gloves over the cuff of her coat to cover the expanse of thin wrist. 'Will it be long?' She leaned forward and stared down the track which curved and disappeared beyond a clutter of buildings. 'I'm that nervous, our Mary.'

'It's just the waiting,' Mary said, feeling just as bad. 'You'll be OK once we're on our way.' She glanced up at the station clock. 'Another ten minutes and it should be here.'

'I wish you'd let Ellen and Patrick and Jean come to wave us off.'

'No need to make a song and dance in public, Mam. Anyway, Ellen and Ted were moving into number twenty-seven today, they've enough on their plate without coming all the way to Bradlow on the bus and standing around here in the cold at this time in the morning.'

The stationmaster sauntered towards Tom, green and red flags clutched in his hand. Mary hurried towards them. 'Just saying to your husband, it's a funny time to be going on your holidays, Missus.'

Mary smiled and, turning slightly away from him,

pulled a face at her brother to warn him not to speak. 'Well, we'll be guaranteed a place on the beach, that's for sure.' The man laughed and went back into the ticket box.

'Nosy beggar,' Mary whispered.

Tom grinned. 'Makes me feel like I'm on the run again.'

'Don't Tom,' Mary chided but she managed a smile; it was good that he could joke about it.

'Listen,' her mother called, standing up and folding the blanket.

The faint chug and scrape of metal grew louder, there was a shriek of whistle and the train appeared round the bend in the track, white steam jetting out from underneath the engine. A broken trail of grey-black smoke belched from the funnel as, with a last blast of hot air from underneath, it squealed to a halt in front of them. The window of the nearest carriage door slid down and a hand reached through to turn the brass handle. A man in a top hat and carrying a briefcase stepped down on to the platform leaving the door to swing open. Tom carried the cases towards it.

'Don't panic, we've plenty of time.' Mary took the blanket off her mother. But in seconds the rhythmic hiss and roar increased in volume and their cases were being bundled into a carriage by a porter.

'C'mon, c'mon, up you get, Missus,' he bellowed.

Tom held Winifred's elbow to help her up the step, but she was frozen to the spot. She opened and shut her mouth. 'It'll be all right, won't it, Mary,' she shouted, her voice cracking. 'I've done the right thing? It's a long way from home?'

Mary looked beyond the station towards the chimneys

and the large anonymous buildings that dwarfed the terraced rows of houses of Bradlow and then up at the sky where the sun was almost breaking through the gauze of cloud. She thought about the way Tom had described Llamroth, the tiny Welsh village with its narrow lanes winding down the hills towards the coast and Gwyneth's cottages overlooking the Irish Sea, and she smiled at her mother. 'You've done the right thing, Mam, it'll be fine.'

They were on their way to a new life, where Peter would always be a special memory.

PART TWO

Chapter 78

Peter

March 1950

Peter stood on the platform, steam billowing around his feet as the train slowly moved along the rails and out of sight. He could see the ticket inspector watching. The long threads of rain from the canopy overhead hit the tilted brim of his trilby, ran round to the back of the hat and streamed down on to the shoulders of his grey gabardine. Unsure of which way to go, he hesitated.

'Over here, mate.' He could tell the man was getting impatient. 'That was the last train of the day and I don't want to be hanging about. I've got a home to go to.' He tapped on his counter and shoved his hand, upturned, through the gap underneath the glass. There were blue ink stains on the pads of his fingers. 'Ticket, please.' He stressed the word as though he thought Peter didn't understand.

Peter nodded but still didn't move. The man slid off his wooden stool and blew out his cheeks in exasperation. Then, with a small hook on the end of a stick he reached under the glass, grabbed the shutter and pulled it until it closed. Peter watched as he emerged on to the platform, a few feet away and held out his hand.

'Come on, sir, that's the last train tonight and I'm closing the station.' He grinned. 'Got to get home for my pie and chips or the missus will throttle me.'

Peter smiled, not quite understanding the last few words, but savouring the broad northern accent that reminded him of Mary. 'Sorry.' He handed over the ticket as the man swept his arm in a wide semicircle until his hand pointed towards the exit. Peter nodded and picked up his suitcase. He turned on his heels and walked purposefully out of the station.

Once outside the building, he faltered and stared around him. Another platform, a wooden construction, led away to the left and down to a path, now wetly overgrown.

Further on, the path widened, became ridged concrete and then turned into a road. Peter gazed towards the hills in the distance and then spun round to look the other way. The rows of allotments were tidy but empty in the late afternoon. On the opposite side of the road only two of the watch towers had survived to guard the front of the old cotton mill with its smashed windows and crumbling brickwork. The roof of one was missing and the struts that once held it pointed up towards the darkening sky. It was there that Shuttleworth had been the sentry that February in nineteen forty-five.

The ghosts of thousands of men stood outside the rusting barbed wire of the fence, a white haze of breath rising above them. He imagined he could hear the coughs, the singing of the prisoners and shouts of the guards surrounding them. The sound echoed in the stillness as they shuffled slowly forward. The frisson of fear that made him shiver was only a shadow of the terror he had felt that morning.

The image vanished as he heard uneven footsteps behind him, the sound of the man's limping gait jolting memories.

'Goodnight, then.'

Peter nodded at the ticket inspector. 'Goodnight,' then he hastily added, 'Henshaw Street? I need to know, please, how to go to Henshaw Street?'

The man nodded. 'I'm going that way myself. I'll show you.' He pulled the brim of his cap further down over his eyes and, shoulders hunched against the rain, turned right.

Peter followed.

Chapter 79

The young woman had a crying baby resting on her hip and a little girl hiding behind her skirt. 'Can I help you?' She looked harassed, brushing a strand of her blond hair away from her face with the back of her hand and jiggling the baby.

Peter looked past her into the house. 'I am looking for a family who used to live here.'

She pulled the door behind her so he couldn't see. 'We've been here for five years, before that it was my mother and father's house,' she said, suspicion in her voice. 'What name are you looking for?'

'Howarth,' Peter said, 'I'm trying to find Mary Howarth.'

Her eyes narrowed. 'Mary Howarth? Why?'

'I am a friend.'

'You're not English, are you?'

'German.' Peter waited for the usual reaction. It wasn't forthcoming. Instead the woman's eyes widened and she opened her mouth as though to speak.

'Mam,' the small girl whined, 'I'm cold.'

'Shush, go in then, find your Dad and your uncle.' The woman turned the child round by the shoulder and gave her a push. There was a draught of air as the little girl went through a door at the far end of the hall.

'Ellen, who is it?' a man shouted from somewhere inside the house.

'In a minute,' she tossed the words over her shoulder.

'Ellen, you are Ellen, Mary's sister?'

'Yes. Are you Peter,' she whispered, 'the doctor at the camp?' She held the baby close to her.

'*Ja.* Yes,' Peter corrected himself, 'Peter Schormann. I was at the Granville.'

The woman held the front door open with her foot. 'My God,' she said, 'it's true then?' She poked her head forward, glancing up and down the street before looking at him again. 'You can't ...' She stopped. 'Look, wait here a minute.' She backed into the hall and shut the door, but it bounced back off the catch and Peter watched her walk away, the baby staring at him over her shoulder. He put his case on the ground and waited.

'Who is it?' The man's voice was loud.

'Insurance, Ted.'

'Thought he came Fridays.'

'Well, this week it's Thursday, OK?'

Peter could hear drawers being opened and closed, the clattering of cupboard doors, male voices muttering.

'Keep your hair on, I'll make a brew in a minute,

Patrick.' Ellen reappeared with a small red book in her hand. When she got to the door, she flipped it open and thrust it at Peter. 'Here,' she hissed, 'take it.' There was a crumpled envelope inside. 'Now go. If them two find out who you are they'll go mental.' She smiled at him. 'Good luck, give them my love.' Then she called out, 'Bye, see you next week,' and slammed the door.

Chapter 80

'I'll 'ave another pint, Stan.' Arthur Brown pushed his cap further back on his head, scratched his scalp before he re-adjusted the peak. He swayed slowly, heel to toe: heel to toe.

The landlord moved along the bar to the beer pumps and Arthur looked around for someone else to talk to. He didn't notice the way most of the other drinkers turned their backs to him. Speaking to no one in particular, Arthur said loudly, 'Mate of mine tells me there's a bloody Kraut's been sniffing round, looking for that girl of Winifred Howarth's, bloody old cow. Fucked off and left me on my own, that one.'

No one looked at him. Someone sitting at the bench underneath the window called out, 'Shut your gob, man.'

'That'll be sixpence.' Stan Green held out his hand. 'C'mon Arthur, I've other customers to serve.'

Arthur straightened up, hiccupped, and turned to face the landlord. Fumbling in his trouser pocket, he brought out a handful of coppers and began to count them, putting the coins in a line along the bar. 'Bloody disgrace, price of a pint.' He looked around for an audience: his eyes settled on a young man who appeared at the side of him. 'Bloody government ...'

'Aye, you're right there,' the man said, 'Happen there'll be a change after the election.'

Arthur snorted. 'Change my arse. Sod all; that's what'll happen. Bloody politicians.'

Stan gathered up the money with a sweep of his hand and dropped it in the drawer of the till. 'What can I get you?' he said curtly to the man who was tapping on his glass with a coin and leaning on the bar, one foot on the brass rail that ran along the front.

'Another whiskey. Straight.'

'No trouble tonight, mind,' Stan warned.

The man ignored him. He turned, and leaning back with his elbows on the bar, gazed around the room. No one made eye contact with him.

Arthur Brown continued with his grumbling. 'I always said that girl were too pure to pee.' He tried to put the rest of his coins away, but couldn't get his hand in his trouser pocket so put them back on the counter. 'My mate, he's in charge of the station, he's the stationmaster.' He blinked. 'Actually, thinking about it, there's no one else there so he's in charge of himself, yeah?' He gave a short shout of laughter. 'Where was I?' He scratched his jaw, the white bristles moving under the dirty fingernail. 'Oh yeah, well, he said he told the Kraut how to get to their house. I said he should have told him to go to hell.' He swayed. 'Bet it was one of them buggers that were locked up at Granville, that's where the girl was, *ministering* to the sick.' He leered, licked his lips, savouring the sound of the word. 'Ministering to the bloody enemy, more like. And then what did she do? Slope off with that pansy of a brother of hers and my bloody woman, buggered off to Wales without a thought as to what would happen to me.' He saw the man next to him watching. 'Bet it weren't that long since you were fighting the buggers, eh?' He didn't get an answer.

Arthur took a huge swallow of his pint, leaving a line of foam across his top lip which he wiped off with his jacket sleeve. 'I know you, don't I?' He rocked on his heels again and held on the edge of the bar, sticky from his spilt drink.

'Should do, been coming here on and off for over five years.' The young man gave him a brief smile. 'George, George Shuttleworth.'

Arthur tilted his head to one side so it almost rested on his shoulders. He squinted. 'Aye, well, I was just telling Stan 'ere …'

The landlord, at the other side of the bar, put the glass of whiskey in front of George, took the money for it and, without speaking, moved away.

'Few years ago I could have shot a bloody Kraut and been called an 'ero. Now we're supposed to accept them wandering about all over the bloody country. Fucking country's gone to the dogs if you ask me.' He belched loudly and paused, looking puzzled. 'And it were their choice to bugger off to Wales, weren't it?'

The landlady piled some dirty glasses she'd collected onto the top of the bar. 'Watch your language, Arthur,' she said, 'and keep your voice down. Any hassle from you tonight and you're out.'

Arthur pulled a face. 'All right, all right, I'm going to sup up and then I'm off.' He banged his glass down. 'I mean, Wales, why Wales? And never an invite from them, oh no, wouldn't want the likes of me visiting. Snotty bitch!' He was getting louder.

'That's enough now Arthur. I think you'd better get off 'ome. You've had enough to drink for tonight.' Stan moved the glass.

'Miserable bugger,' Arthur muttered. He pushed himself off the bar and weaved across the room. Holding on to the large brass handle, he yanked the door open and shouted over his shoulder, 'That's what you are, Stan Green, a miserable old sod. You and that sour-faced cow of a wife.' He dropped the coins he was holding and they rolled out onto the pub's step.

'Out!'

George Shuttleworth picked up Arthur's money and followed him. 'I've had enough an all,' he said. 'Here you are.' He dropped the pennies into Arthur's jacket pocket. 'I'll walk with you; I'm going your way, as it happens.'

Chapter 81

Peter checked the address on the letter against the name on the gate. He looked up at the small cottage. The gravel path leading towards the front door was lined with heather and a privet hedge surrounded the long narrow garden, separating it from the cottages on either side.

Behind him pebbles tumbled, tugged by the waves crashing on to the beach and falling back. The sound contrasted to that of the Elbe flowing through the wooded fields near the farm he'd left behind in Saxony where the pace was ruled only by the stones and boulders it flowed over. A surge of homesickness overcame him and, not for the first time, he wondered if coming back to Britain was the right thing to do. There would be people in this country who would always resent, even hate him for what he was, what he represented.

He adjusted his suitcase in his hand. It was heavy and the old wound in his shoulder ached. Shutting his eyes, he breathed in the salty tang of the misty spray that blew over him, mustering his courage before walking up the path.

'Hello? Can I help you?' The man who appeared from the back of the house wore an old cap and jacket, his trousers and Wellington boots were caked in mud.

Peter took off his trilby and held it to his chest. 'Tom?'

The man fumbled with a pair of spectacles. He wound the wire ends over his ears and peered through the lenses. 'Yes?'

'Tom. It is Peter Schormann.'

Tom took a step forward. 'Peter,' he whispered, 'Peter Schormann?' There was a moment's pause. 'Oh dear Lord.' He grabbed Peter's hand and shook it. 'You got the letter! I never thought … I just hoped, prayed that one day you would come looking for Mary.'

'I wanted to come back so much. Each year I applied to your Government,' Peter said, 'finally the permit arrived.' A squall of rain swept in from the beach and he shivered.

'What am I thinking off? You've had a long journey. Let's get in the house.' Tom picked up the suitcase and led Peter through the garden. 'You look exhausted.'

'Travelling two days since I arrived in Britain,' Peter said. 'I had four trains, a lot of the walking and a ride in a butcher's van, finally the last walk to this village. You live a long way from Ashford.'

'And I thank the dear Lord every day for that.' They went up the steps to the back door. 'This will be a shock for Mary. She doesn't know about the letter.' Tom closed the door.

'She is well?' Peter asked, he ran his hand over his hair and wiped his damp palm on his jacket sleeve.

'Yes.' Tom washed his hands at the kitchen sink. 'I'll make a brew. Unless you fancy something stronger?'

Peter shook his head, unbuttoning his coat.

'Tea it is then.' Tom opened the cupboard door next to the cooker and fiddled with the top of a Calor gas bottle.

Peter watched him fill the kettle and put it on the cooker. 'Mary is happy?'

'She's fine.'

'She has a … friend?'

Tom took two beakers out of the wall cupboard. 'Oh yes, we've lots of friends; the people in the village made us welcome as soon as we came to live here.' He took the teapot to the back door and standing on the top step threw the used leaves over the flowerbed. When he came back into the kitchen he stopped and looked at Peter. 'Oh, you mean … no, no one like that. She always says she's too busy with her job.' He put the teapot on a stand next to the cooker. 'She's still nursing. She's a Matron now in a hospital not too far away. No, there's no one special,' he repeated.

Peter's legs shook as the relief flooded through him. 'I can sit?'

'Sorry! What am I thinking?' Tom pulled out a chair from the table. 'Sit here. My goodness, I still can't believe you're here, I didn't even know if you'd find our old house if ever you did come back.'

Peter gave Tom his hat and coat and sat down. 'I knew only the name of the street where Mary lived. She told me one time. So I ask the man at the train station.'

Tom struck a match and, turning a knob, held the flame to the gas ring. It clicked a couple of times and lit with a whoosh, then he shook the match until it went out and put it back in the box. 'Look, while it's boiling, come into the living room. It's more comfortable in there and the fire's lit. Mary will be home in about half an hour. She gets a lift from someone in the village.'

The living room was larger than Peter expected, with oak beams and paintings covering the white walls. In the corner a tall Grandfather clock ticked sonorously and the huge iron fireplace with the large rag rug on the stone floor in front of the hearth reminded him of the farmhouse he'd grown up in. Two small windows on either side of the porch door were framed by pale cotton curtains. He sat on the large dark red Chesterfield sofa and rested his head on the high back.

'She was heartbroken after you'd gone,' Tom said. 'We talked a lot about you.' He sat on a battered leather footstool by the fire and held his hands out towards the flames. 'She told me you were married?' He frowned. 'I did wonder if I was doing the right thing leaving a letter for you when I knew that ... but she was so miserable.' He shrugged. 'I'd do anything for Mary.'

'I am divorced now. When I went home my wife already had left. With an officer who was with a Unit near the farm.'

Tom's frown relaxed. 'The farm? Your home?'

'Yes, but I have sold my share of it to my brother, Werner. I can live ... find work in your country.' He rubbed his hand on the arm of the settee. 'May I ask a question?' he said abruptly.

'Of course.' Tom was cautious when he saw Peter's anxious expression. 'What is it?'

'Why here? Why did you come to live here: so far away?'

When Tom spoke there was a neutral evenness in his words. 'It was Mary's idea. We needed to get away.' He paused. 'We had our mother with us until last year. She passed away, heart attack.'

'I am sorry.' Peter bowed his head.

'It was peaceful, she died in her sleep.' Tom gazed into the fire. 'She loved it here, she was very happy for the four years she had.' He smiled.

'I still do not understand.'

'Mary thought a fresh start would be good for both of us. This village is where my ... my friend, Iori, grew up. We were in prison together. He ... he died. His mother, who lives next door, owns this cottage and she let us rent it.'

'But when I remarked you are living a long way from Ashford, you sounded relieved?'

'Too many bad memories, neither of us wanted to live there any more.' Tom spoke calmly but his hands were clenched tight. He looked at the fire again, frowning. Finally he seemed to make a decision. 'Mary trusted you. She jeopardised her whole life because of you. Can I trust you too?'

Peter nodded. '*Ja.*'

'She told me everything about Frank Shuttleworth,' Tom said.

Peter's throat tightened. 'Shuttleworth?'

'Yes, it was because of him we moved, because of what

happened to him. Not long after we got here, I realised Mary thought it was me that had attacked him, had pushed him into the canal.' Tom stuttered slightly. 'It wasn't, but I understood then why she wanted to get me away from Ashford. She was afraid that, one day, they would reopen the case.'

'Will they?' Peter's voice was hoarse. 'Open again the case?'

'Doubt it now.'

'Do you know who killed him?'

'I thought I did … once … a long time ago.' Tom lifted his head, staring steadily at Peter.

Peter took in a long ragged breath. 'Who did you think it was?' he said quietly.

'You'll say nothing?'

'I will say nothing.'

'My brother, Patrick, came to see me in prison.' Tom pressed on his eyes with the pads of his thumb and forefinger. 'It was the first time he'd visited in four years, I was so grateful. I'd been going through a bad time. It was strange; we got on really well, better than we had for years, but we had an odd conversation. He wanted to know exactly where I'd been when I escaped. I told him. It wasn't until later, when the police came to question me about Shuttleworth's death, that I thought I knew why he'd come to see me. I believed he was trying to find out if I'd killed him. I even thought he was looking for a way to protect me but then …' He paused. 'Then, after we'd moved here, Mary told me he'd said I did it. At first I was angry but I know, given the chance, I could have killed that man for what he'd done to her, so perhaps Patrick saw that in me.' He gritted his teeth. 'Our Ellen suffered

381

because of Shuttleworth as well. Oh, I had so much rage in me at that time.' He spread his fingers. 'But I didn't do it.'

His voice changed, became more decisive. 'We went over and over it. In the end Mary said the only reason Patrick lied was because he'd done it. But that would have meant he really hated me and I couldn't … don't want to believe that. In then end we agreed to stop talking about it.'

'Do you see your brother?'

'No, his wife, Jean, and Jacqueline, our niece, visit sometimes, but they always say he's busy. He has his own market stall, sells all sorts of things.' Tom leant forward and chucked a piece of driftwood on to the fire. It crackled and spat blue salt-laden flames.

'You cannot be sure that it was Patrick,' Peter said. 'Perhaps he did believe it was you but he did not report it to the police. They would arrest you. Instead he told Mary so that she could decide what to do.' Peter leaned forward. 'It could have been anyone from the camp. It is possible. The prisoners, they hated him more than any of the other guards.'

'No. No one escaped from that place.' Tom was emphatic. 'Mary told me it was impossible.'

'Yet it could be done. Many attempts were made.'

'But that's all they were, attempts.' Tom made a great show of warming his hands, holding them out to the flames and vigorously rubbing his palms together.

Tom was wrong. Peter knew he was wrong.

Wood from the bases of the bunks was fashioned into makeshift ladders and hidden under mattresses many times. In the early morning rush to the latrines a man could easily slip unnoticed out of the mill and across to a deserted part of the compound away from the guardhouse. It was possible to prop the ladder against the double fence, take a flying leap across the two coils of barbed wire at the top, roll down the banking outside the camp and wait and watch from the bushes.

'There were head counts every day,' Tom said, interrupting Peter's thoughts. 'Mary told me.'

And it was possible to get back into camp. Peter knew that too. After all, who would want to break into a prisoner of war camp? Lorries brought prisoners back to Granville every day after working on the farms. It was only a case of waiting for the one that had no guard in the back, there was always at least one, especially towards the end of the war; carelessness set in. And then a hasty run at the tailgate, a leap and plenty of hands to haul one aboard. Peter smiled at the memory of the bemused expressions that caused. The men were only counted as they filed through the doors of the mill. It was easy enough to slip away when the trucks stopped inside the compound.

Tom shook his head. 'No, it wasn't anyone from the camp.' He rested his arms on his thighs and pressed the palms of his hands together almost in supplication. 'We don't talk about it any more. It's best left in the past. Mary and I have new lives.' He smiled. 'Mary especially, now you're here. I can't wait to see her face.' He stood. 'Fine host I am. We didn't have that brew.' He pushed open the kitchen door and paused, looking back at Peter, his face expressionless. 'Just let it lie, eh?'

The sound of the key turning in the lock of the front door, followed by the cold blast of air that forced open the inner porch door, broke the tension that was suddenly between them. Both men turned towards Mary.

Mary and Peter stared at each other. She held on to the doorframe to steady herself. Before Tom could move, Peter crossed the room and caught her in his arms. Cradling her, he brushed aside the rain-drenched strands of dark hair from her face and kissed her cheek, feeling her skin cold under his lips and breathing in the familiar fragrance of lily of the valley.

He closed his eyes and the memory was immediate. Mary's screams, thin with terror, echoing through the bridge. The sounds of his boots thudding down the steps. The surface of the sullen canal rippling as a bottle sank. The fight on the muddy path, abrupt and violent. The splash of water. The snap of the branch.

The drowning man.

It was over. They were together

More from Honno to enjoy...

The War Before Mine, by Caroline Ross

A brief wartime romance leaves Rosie heartbroken
and pregnant, not knowing if Philip – on a suicide
mission designed to stop the Nazi invasion – is alive
or dead.

"a versatile and senstive chronicler of the world at war"
Sunday Telegraph

"complex and engaging" Western Mail

9781870206976
£6.99

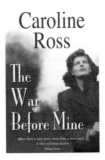

Back Home, by Bethan Darwin

Ellie is brokenhearted and so decamps home.
Tea and sympathy from grandad Trevor help, as
does the distracting and hunky Gabriel, then a
visitor from Trevor's past in wartime Wales turns
their world upside down...

*"a modern woman's romantic confession, alongside a
cleverly unfolding story of long-buried family secrets"*
Abigail Bosanko

9781906784034
£7.99

Hector's Talent for Miracles, by Kitty Harri

Hector, his mother and grandmother live quietly
in a small Spanish town but when Mair arrives on
a mission to find her lost grandfather their meeting
has explosive results, and all their lives are revealed
as fragile constructions forged in the fire of a
vicious conflict...

*"an intelligent and sympathetic exploration of the
lasting damage done to survivors of war."*
Planet Magazine

9781870206815
£6.99

All Honno titles can be ordered online at www.honno.co.uk,
or by sending a cheque to Honno
with free p&p to all UK addresses

Parachutes and Petticoats: Evocative women's stories from WWII

Edited by Leigh Verrill-Rhys, Deirdre Beddoe

Women were the backbone of the country's war effort, 'keeping calm' and 'carrying on' on the frontline and under bombardment in the UK. There were always good times alongside the bad and still love to be nurtured amidst the enmity as all these spirited voices prove in this evocative anthology.

9781906784119
£10.99

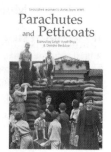

Salt Blue, by Gillian Morgan

Life is made of memories, sweet and sour: Stella's journey from seaside Wales to upstate New York, from child to woman, set in the late fifties. A first novel of tangible sensual pleasures, *Salt Blue* paints a striking picture of life in a largely forgotten era...

9781906784157
£8.99

Facing Into the West Wind, by Lara Clough

When Haz meets the rejected and lonely Jason on the streets of Bristol he decides to take him home to the family's beach house at Gower. What follows is a series of confessions and revelations which will change everything.

"a tender and perceptive tale of secrets" Guardian

"a deeply felt and accomplished first novel" Sue Gee

9781870206792
£6.99

All Honno titles can be ordered online at www.honno.co.uk, or by sending a cheque to Honno with free p&p to all UK addresses

ABOUT HONNO

Honno Welsh Women's Press was set up in 1986 by a group of women who felt strongly that women in Wales needed wider opportunities to see their writing in print and to become involved in the publishing process. Our aim is to develop the writing talents of women in Wales, give them new and exciting opportunities to see their work published and often to give them their first 'break' as a writer.

Honno is registered as a community co-operative. Any profit that Honno makes is invested in the publishing programme. Women from Wales and around the world have expressed their support for Honno by buying shares. Supporters liability is limited to the amount invested and each supporter has a vote at the Annual General Meeting.

To buy shares or to receive further information about forthcoming publications, please write to Honno at the address below, or visit our website: www.honno.co.uk.

Honno
Unit 14, Creative Units
Aberystwyth Arts Centre
Penglais Campus
Aberystwyth
Ceredigion
SY23 3GL

All Honno titles can be ordered online at
www.honno.co.uk
or by sending a cheque to Honno.
Free p&p to all UK addresses